Praise _____
THE CLOVE _____

"*The Clover House* is a gripping, tender story that spans continents and generations as it delves into the secrets of a Greek American family altered by a long-ago tragedy in World War II. Told with quiet power and authenticity, it's a reader's treat."
—Kate Alcott, *New York Times* bestselling author of
The Dressmaker

"Layered and complex, *The Clover House* is a provocative examination of family secrets and the things we inherit, a powerful search for self that feels both unique and universal. Henriette Lazaridis Power immerses the reader in a world of tradition and resilience, creating characters who linger long beyond their final pages. One of the best books I've read in a long time."
—Brunonia Barry, *New York Times* and international bestselling
author of *The Lace Reader* and *The Map of True Places*

"A rare treat: an elegantly written debut about a family mystery set during wartime, the slipperiness of memory, and the challenges of forgiveness. Plus, we get to go to Greece! What more could you want from a novel? Read it, read it!"
—Jenna Blum, *New York Times* bestselling author of
Those Who Save Us

"Sharply observed and evocative, *The Clover House* is a riveting story about desire, the cost of silence, and the power of a hidden secret from the past to change everything about the present. Henriette Lazaridis Power blends the stark, at times brutal, truths of war-torn Greece with the heady rush of Carnival into a brilliantly realized story about the consequence of an illicit love, the histories we come from, and the dreams that draw us back. This debut is a gem."
—Dawn Tripp, author of national bestseller *Game of Secrets*

"Henriette Lazaridis Power takes a collection of inherited objects and weaves an intricate story of a family's hidden past, and a Greek American daughter's key to her own tangled identity. I was thoroughly transported to WWII Greece, and could envision the ancestral farm as vividly as my own childhood backyard."
  —Nichole Bernier, author of *The Unfinished Work of Elizabeth D.*

"Readers will feel the eloquently written quandary of Henriette Lazaridis Power's vivid and troubled protagonist, a woman with one foot in Greece and the other in America; a woman who, like so many immigrants and first-generation Americans, struggles to be at home in two countries."
  —Randy Susan Meyers, author of *The Murderer's Daughters*

"*The Clover House* is a tremendously readable story of how family secrets reverberate, how war forces impossible choices, and how a very modern woman faces old longings for her mother's love and a true home. This is a smart and lovely novel."
  —Holly Lecraw, author of *The Swimming Pool*

THE CLOVER HOUSE

THE
CLOVER HOUSE

A Novel

Henriette Lazaridis Power

Ballantine Books Trade Paperbacks
New York

2013 A Ballantine Book Trade Paperback Original

Published in the United States by Ballantine Books, an imprint of The Random House Publishing Group, a division of Random House, Inc., New York.

Title page art from an original photograph by Caetano Lacerda

ISBN 978-0-345-53068-4
eBook ISBN 978-0-345-53894-9

Printed in the United States of America

www.randomhousereaderscircle.com

2 4 6 8 9 7 5 3 1

Book design by Virginia Norey

For JP

Il y a longtemps que je t'aime.

We shed as we pick up, like travellers who must carry everything in their arms, and what we let fall will be picked up by those behind. The procession is very long and life is very short. We die on the march. But there is nothing outside the march so nothing can be lost to it.

—TOM STOPPARD, *Arcadia*

THE CLOVER HOUSE

1

Callie

February 2000

On those rare occasions when she couldn't control the world around her, my mother placed the blame squarely on America, the country she had reluctantly immigrated to from Greece in 1959. My father would retort that there were flaws in Greece too, but she ignored him because he was American.

They met in 1955, when my father was based in Athens with the American mission in Greece, building roads and repairing bridges on the Marshall Plan. For four years, they lived a glamorous life of parties and dances in a city that was working hard to shed the effects of the Second World War and the civil war that followed it. Once they were married and it was time to choose a country, my father won the argument, flying ahead of my mother to purchase what would be their only home. When she joined him in the hair-sprayed suburbs of parochial Boston, knowing no one and understanding little of American life, my mother's reaction was quick and certain. To keep what she considered this unsightly world at bay, she took the brown paper from the moving boxes and covered every window of the single-story house.

She sat inside, fuming at my father and at what she knew lay on the other side of the paper. She glared at the shadows of the neighborhood children as they ran from their yards into hers and out again. They lingered before the covered windows, wondering what was hidden inside, and she watched this shadow theater, thinking of the *Karagiozis* puppet shows she had watched as a child.

After a week, my father tore the paper down. He led her to the glass and forced her to look out at the jewel-green lawn and the fat buds on the dogwood tree.

"See," he said, almost in tears. "It's beautiful."

She never agreed. In her mind, my mother never really left that papered-over room. And I spent my childhood trying to win an invitation to join her there in the Greece that she imagined and remembered.

I know this story about the papered windows because my father told it to me before he died, some ten years ago now. I don't know what made him tell me. We didn't see each other very often, so it must have been important to him that I know. Perhaps he knew that I'd be left with only my mother's stories after he was gone. Perhaps he knew they wouldn't be good for me without some sort of dilution.

For my entire childhood, until he gave up on the whole project and left, he watched me beg my mother for the stories I learned by heart—about the grand house in the city of Patras, where my mother and her sisters and brother did whatever they wanted under the benign gaze of their elegant parents; about the farm in the country, where the children climbed trees and ate fresh fruit all day. My mother was always happy to oblige my requests. She would bring out a jar of syrup-stewed oranges as she talked, spooning out the delicacy she had carried home from our summer trip to Greece into a bowl we would eat from together. I didn't like the stuff—the sweetness of the syrup barely covered the bitterness of the citrus—but I waited my turn with the spoon, happy to be sitting with my mother, nourished by her memories of a better time and place.

Sometimes I would press her to clarify a bit of history or to elaborate on a detail.

"What?" she would say, turning to me with a startled gaze. "What did you say?"

And I would pretend I hadn't noticed that she'd forgotten all about me. She wasn't really telling the stories to me; she was simply saying aloud in my presence what she was thinking about every minute of the day.

It's a Saturday afternoon in Boston in late February when the phone rings and I recognize the city code for Patras. My mother moved back there, newly widowed, and since then we go long stretches without speaking on the phone. It's better this way. Our most recent conversation several weeks ago ended with her complaining about the rudeness of her two sisters—women who have shown me nothing but love.

I let the call ring but perch on the couch and finally force myself to answer it. I'm surprised to hear the voice of my cousin, Aliki, on the other end.

"Calliope," she says.

The short *o* sound in her Greek pronunciation knocks me into a life that seems to have been just the other side of a thin wall. Legally, I'm Calliope Notaris Brown. I am the latest in a line of Muses in my mother's family, she being Clio, the daughter of Urania. But Callie Brown is my American camouflage. It makes it easier when I want to tell myself that the Greek part of me doesn't exist—that I have no connection to anyone save the people and places I choose. Now one tiny vowel sound has brought it all back. And, with Aliki's alto, the fear that she is calling to tell me my mother is dead.

"Aliki. What is it?" We haven't been in touch in a long time, but I speak to her in Greek, as I have always done.

"It's Uncle Nestor," she says, the characteristic singsong of her voice taking a melancholy lilt. "He died."

I feel relief that it's not my mother, then sadness for Nestor, then shame over my relief. I can see Nestor standing before me five years ago, the last time I saw him, his crinkly black hair streaked with white. Beethoven is playing in the background. "Listen, Calliope. The tympani," he whispers, his loose fist dotting the air in time with the music. I am sitting on his velvet-covered couch and we are drinking glasses of red wine.

"What happened?" Nestor would be around seventy now. But I'm sure only a crazy accident can have brought him down.

"It was a heart attack."

"His heart?"

"They found heart disease the year before last."

My face goes hot as I realize that I had no idea he was ill. I thought of him as the hale old bachelor who would hike Olympus in bad weather or ski across the French Alps during the holidays from his schoolteacher's job.

"He didn't want anyone to know," she says.

"But he told you."

"If you had been here, Calliope, it's you he would have told. He was so proud of you."

"Proud of me?" A little sob bubbles up.

"Paki," she says, and I smile at this old nickname. Calliope to Calliopaki—Little Calliope—to Paki.

"I'm here. When is the funeral, Aliki?"

"That's why I'm calling."

It occurs to me now to wonder why my mother isn't the one making this call. I imagine her for a second, dizzy with grief, eyes swollen, and unable to dial a number. But the thought shuts down. My mother doesn't display unsightly emotions.

"The funeral's Monday," Aliki says. "I would have called you sooner, but I thought your mother already had."

"What time?"

"In the morning."

I think about all my childhood arrivals in the blazing sun of Athens afternoons.

"Aliki, I'll check the schedules, but I don't think I can be there in time. I wouldn't be able to catch a flight until tomorrow."

"Don't worry about that. There's another thing."

"Is my mother all right?"

"She's fine." There's a tight sound in her voice that I wish I understood. "But there's the will. You kind of have to come to Patras for the will." She goes on to explain, somewhat sheepishly, that Nestor has left his squat one-story house to her and her husband, Nikos, and all its contents, including a pile of boxes and books, to me. He's also left me two million drachmas, at nearly six thousand dollars a fairly princely sum from someone who lived his life on a teacher's salary. A princely sum for me too, given the state of my bank account.

"I guess you have to come and sign the form," she says. "The Acceptance of Inheritance."

"Aliki, I'd love to come," I say, regretting the formulation. It's a death in the family, not a vacation. "But I don't think I can get away from work right now." I hold a job raising money for a private school. I speak on the phone with old-money patriarchs whose names are only slightly more WASP-ish than mine. "I'm sure I can do it here. The consulate's a five-minute walk away."

"Are you sure you can't come?" She sounds almost worried now.

"What's up, Aliki? Is there something you're not telling me?"

"I don't want to say." This isn't the Aliki I remember. Older than me by three years, she was always defiant and self-assertive. I used to watch her for lessons on how to stand up to the grown-ups and later to the men who would catcall her wherever she went.

"Tell me."

"Well, there's a reason your mother didn't call. I don't think she wanted you to make it here in time, Paki. She's acting all funny about Nestor leaving you his things."

"Funny how?"

"Like she doesn't want you to have them. Or to go through them. I think she figured if she waited long enough to tell you he had died, there'd be some legal way for her to keep his stuff for herself."

The phone crackles; a car outside on Pinckney Street spins its wheels in the snow.

"*Wow,*" I say.

"So I think you should try to come, Paki."

"Yeah," I say, and it's almost a whisper.

Nestor's living room was lined with bookshelves that held plenty of books but mostly metal cases of film and reel-to-reel tape. All of Beethoven's symphonies, recorded from the radio; Nestor's ascents of dozens of mountains, captured on his 8 mm camera. As a child, a teenager, a college student, I loved when he showed me the films or played me the music. But what I think I loved best was when he would open his wooden cases of seashells or tell me about his glass vials of sand from beaches around the world—all of it labeled by place and date of collection. He would sit me down on the velvet couch and hand me a vial, asking me to imagine the beach in North Africa or Sardinia where he had filled it at surf's edge. I promised him I would go to these places and have adventures of my own. But there I let him down, spending more time digging around in my head than in any foreign land, wearing down a path between hope and resignation. I am so sad that my last memory of him dates from as long as five years ago. I know I don't deserve Nestor's pride Aliki mentioned to console me.

"You'll have to call your mother," Aliki says.

My mother always carped on her brother's unruly home and mocked his habit of collecting odd objects from his travels. What on earth could make her want to keep these things for herself now—and prevent me from having them?

"Aliki, can I stay with you?"

A second's hesitation—she knows what my mother will say at such disrespect—and then she tells me she can't wait to see me again.

After I promise to call her as soon as I have my travel details, we say goodbye and I stand in the high-ceilinged room for a moment, listening to the hiss of the phone. Outside, the wind is blowing hard off the river, and people are walking with their heads bowed against the cold that I can feel seeping in through the windows.

Keys rattle behind me in the lock, and Jonah comes in, stomping his feet on the doormat and groaning.

"Cal, I think my nose is numb," he says. I hear him set bags of groceries on the kitchen counter that lines the other end of the room.

"You all right, Cal?"

He has hung up his jacket and hat and slipped off his boots and is standing by the door, looking at me, his brown hair falling over his eyes. Cal: my four-syllable name of Homer's Muse reduced to something that sounds like a cowboy or a baseball player. I like it.

"My cousin called," I say, tossing the phone onto the couch. "My uncle died."

"Which one?"

"I only have one. My mom's younger brother."

I met Jonah Sullivan over beer at The Sevens, and I moved in to his one-room apartment at the bottom of Beacon Hill almost two years ago. If he doesn't know the details of my family, it's my fault, not his.

"I'm sorry, Cal." He comes and hugs me, squeezing my arms against my body. His face is cold.

"It's okay." I twist free and begin to unload the groceries. "Apparently he left me some stuff. I'm supposed to go to Greece and sign a form so I can take possession of the inheritance."

"You going to?"

"I just told Aliki I would."

"Why don't you sound happy about that?"

"I'm sad about my uncle."

"Not buying it. What's the matter?"

"It's complicated. You know that."

"Cal," he says, coming closer.

"Let's not talk about it now, Jonah." I attempt lightness. "Open some wine."

"What are you afraid of?"

"Who says I'm afraid at all?"

"Cal, I know you. You have your chin sticking out, all tough-guy, but you're clearly scared of something."

He cups my chin and tugs my face toward him. I let him kiss me.

"Fine," I say. "Because I want to go. But this is exactly why I don't talk to my mother. If I go, I'll be hoping everything will be great and she's going to end up making me feel awful."

"See how this works?" he says, drawing the cork from a bottle of white. "You tell me what's on your mind and it makes you feel better. Don't you feel better?"

Jonah believes emotions are simple like that, as if you could just pour them out from giant transparent beakers. Except he forgets that the wrong combination—or the right one—can make everything explode.

"I feel better."

We make love later, fueled by the rest of the white and by an extra bottle of good champagne we never got to on my thirty-fifth birthday. I'm determined not to let thoughts of my mother drag me into a darkness that could take days to lighten. Jonah delights in my aggression. I can see it in his eyes—his pleasure and almost pride in my suggestions, my requests. It would be so easy to turn in on myself. I could lie there with my back to him, looking out over the rail of our loft at the almost-bare room below and the curtainless windows glowing from the streetlight. But I force myself to think of who I am now—my pure self, floating free of ties or heritage. And as that person, I slide my leg over him and push up against him the way he likes, knowing that the momentum of the sex will protect me.

When I climb down from the loft the next morning, Jonah is eating a bowl of cereal on the couch, his wool socks sticking up loose on his feet as if he has been padding around in them for miles. I can see a patch of pale skin where the cushions are pushing his T-shirt up.

"Nude descending a staircase," he says, smiling through a mouthful of Cheerios.

"Except I have your shirt on."

"Not from my angle you don't."

I put an extra flounce in my step and get the coffee from the freezer.

"What are you going to do about your uncle?"

"I checked for flights. I can't make the funeral."

"What about the other stuff?"

"I'm still not sure I should go."

"You already told Aliki." He says the word with heavy consonants, American sounds that come from the front of his mouth.

"She can store the stuff for me. I can look through it another time."

I run the coffee grinder.

"Maybe I should go with you."

"What?"

"You know," he says. "Go over, meet the relatives. *Impress* the relatives," he says, setting his bowl in the sink and jumping up to sit on the counter.

"I am not going to deal with a family crisis by adding another family crisis to my life."

"You saying I would be a crisis?"

"Jonah, I can't just march you in there."

"Why not?"

I give him a long look and then start spooning out the grounds. He takes my hand and runs his thumb over the three small diamonds in my ring. His grandmother's ring, which his parents let him give me.

"Cal," he says.

I glance at him. "Because I'm pretty sure you'd march right back out," I say, answering his question.

"And you don't want me to." It's a statement, but I know he's not sure of the answer.

"No, Joe. I don't want you to." He likes it when I call him that.

I knock the spoon against the counter to shake the coffee dust off and throw it into the drawer. I fill the filter, switch the maker on, and kiss him on the cheek. I go into the shower, where I run the water hot.

I stand under the shower until I can see my skin turning red in blotches. Jonah comes in to brush his teeth and grab a sweatshirt from the back of the door. I can see his silhouette through the shower curtain. I suppose he can see mine and he knows that I am just standing there, neither washing my hair nor soaping.

"You want to talk later?" he says. He reaches through the curtain and touches the back of his hand to my face. The water soaks his sleeve. The cotton will ice up when he gets outside.

"Put a dry shirt on," I tell him. "You'll be cold."

"I can skip the game if you want."

"I'm fine, Joe."

"Okay." He sticks his head in and kisses my shoulder.

After a moment, he opens the bathroom door one more time.

"Back around one. Sooner if no one else is crazy enough to show up."

"Okay."

He closes the door, and the cloud of steam in the tiny room sways in the draft.

I am glad he is gone and hope his rugby friends will defy the savage cold and the wind that will be howling across the Esplanade. I need a few hours to clear my head.

The champagne wasn't just for my birthday two weeks ago. It was for the proposal Jonah made that night sometime after the first glass. He sent me up to the loft for something, and when I turned around, he was down below with his college guitar, singing Gershwin. When he got to the part about not being the man some girls think of as handsome and how to his heart I carried the key, I couldn't keep from crying anymore.

At first I said no. I told him I liked our life together just the way it was. He pressed me and tried not to look devastated, and then he tried devastation after all, in case that would change my mind. And it did change my mind. Because I want to deserve that kind of love. I let him put the ring on me, and I've kept it on, but I'm always sliding it right to the end of my finger, just to see what it feels like. We both pretend that everything is fine, but I know Jonah wants more from me. I see it in every glance, every question about the future. Every time I pull him toward me, I have that sense that he wants to disappear into me, or wants me to disappear into him.

I've put Jonah in an impossible position. I won't tell him the full truth about my mother, and so I make it inevitable that his reaction fails to match my needs, no matter how thoughtful he tries to be. And he does try. But all he knows is that I hated the ranch house I grew up in and was relieved when, soon after my father died, my mother sold the place and went back to Greece.

Doorjambs dented by the toes of shoes; sheetrock with holes punched through; hollow doors caved in: These are the marks of a childhood I prefer not to discuss, a violence between my parents whose emotional force far outweighed even these physical manifestations. Though perhaps worst of all was the overhanging atmosphere of forgetfulness, as if I had grown up in

the land of Homer's Lotus-Eaters and no one could quite remember what was needed to take care of a daughter. They
never hit each other, and they never hit me. But they lashed out
again and again at the walls that confined them in their marriage, my family.

How could Jonah understand this when his own childhood
was so different? Two boys and two girls, Jonah the first, par-
ented by two loving and quiet parents—a Noah's Ark of stable
familial organization. In the pictures arrayed on his parents'
bookshelves, towheaded children beam into the bright Cohas-
set sun, holding pails and shovels or pulling each other in a
wagon. Once, his father caught me looking at these images and
wrapped me in a silent hug. I don't know what he knew; I
hadn't said anything to Jonah.

I step out of the shower and dry myself quickly, goose
bumps rising on my thighs and arms. I tug on jeans and Jonah's
Boston College sweatshirt, so big on me that it nearly reaches
my knees. I fold my hair up in the towel and pour myself some
coffee, a muddy brew scorched from sitting there too long. But
I drink it anyway to keep my headache from pushing forward
into my temples. I should be drinking water instead.

I slump down on the couch so the draft won't strike the
damp towel on my head, and I hold the coffee in both hands. I
remember another birthday, my sixteenth. A handful of friends
invited for a nice dinner in Boston, everyone being dropped off
at the house and drinking Cokes that my father serves while we
wait for my mother to be ready. And finally she emerges. My
friends' mothers are dressed for chores: corduroys and rubber
boots, and sweaters whose sleeves they push up, ready to help
with anything. My mother is dressed for admiration, in beige
pleated trousers and a silky white blouse with slightly padded
shoulders. Not really a tall woman, she towers in platform heels

over the other mothers. At first I am proud, but when we are ready to go, my friends vie for spots in my mother's Saab. From the passenger window in my father's car, I watch my friends leaning forward, preening, as my mother compliments them on their outfits. At the restaurant, everyone fusses over the white-chocolate cake my mother has ordered for me, and the waiters all love her. Back home, when my last friend has gone, she touches my cheek and gives me a wistful smile.

"I hope you had a good time, Calliope."

"I did, Mom," I say, suddenly anxious to reassure her. "It was the best. Really."

Even now my brain follows the old channels. Even now I almost don't remember the fight between my parents that came as I was looking over my friends' gifts. Arms grabbed, shoes thrown, a bag packed—maybe for show but maybe not—and shouting about careless gestures and deliberate betrayals.

It's a bit after one o'clock when I hear Jonah at the door. I close my eyes and slide lower on the couch. Sleep is easier to explain than brooding.

"Man—" he starts to say, and then he catches himself. I hear him slipping out of his jacket, setting his boots down on the mat, his runny nose quietly sniffling. He sits on the edge of the couch, where I am lying with my knees drawn up. When he kisses me, I start at the cold of his lips.

"Hey," he says.

There is ice in his hair. I slip off a tiny piece and hold it up for him to see.

"You're frozen."

"Make me warm."

"Hey!" I gasp as he slides his hands beneath my sweatshirt.

"Come on, you Greek goddess," he says. "Thaw this icy Celt."

Every now and then he calls me that, and I don't have the heart to tell him I hate it. The words make me think of women with heavy makeup and piled-high hair, wearing bracelets on their upper arms—sexiness that's not at all seductive.

"Here," I say, and feel under his clothes for the parts of him that are warm and slightly damp with sweat.

Monday morning I make the slow drive along the Charles River to a bend where the school campus is anchored by a new sports center I helped to raise the funds for. The buildings are grand but inviting, thanks to rows of green-tinted windows at ground level. Near the eastern corner of the hockey rink, a list of donor names is etched into the granite. Names I put there by knowing exactly how much money people have and knowing exactly how nice I need to be to them. As I pass the corner now on my way to the colonial house where my office is, I think of the time Bill Judson asked me if I was one of the Wolfeboro Browns. "No," I told him, "but see if you can get me invited." He doubled his gift. Whenever he sees me at an event, he lets me know he's still working on that invitation. He takes both my hands in his and gently tugs me over to his wife, or his racquetball partner, or his grandson who is a senior now, and he repeats my joke, which was never very funny to begin with. I'm sure he knows this, but he is too kind to stop the routine.

I'm the first one in, as usual. Lucy and Katherine come in from the suburbs, and Daniel drops his daughter off at the front gate by some arrangement that allows her to sever all ties daily before she sets foot on campus and then meet her father gladly to go home. I pull the door shut to my tiny office and sit for a minute in my coat, feeling the heat build up beneath my wool turtleneck. I think of Nestor sitting at the enormous desk he positioned just inside the doors to his garden. As a child, I would stand at his elbow, the sun warming my back, while he showed me things from his collections: a fossil, a rock, one of those vials of sand. By the time I got to Greece in the summer, he would have already darkened to a deep tan from a spring full of hiking. Where I stood, I could see the pale spots behind his ears.

Nestor never came to the beach with us. Sometimes he was away on one of his trips, and sometimes he spent the days at his desk, reading from his many history books in order to be prepared for the school year. He would laugh and say he had finally grown into his Homeric namesake, the old man advising the young. I would see him in the afternoons, when my hair was thickened with salt. My mother would leave me at the door, where brother and sister would give each other quick pecks on the cheek before parting. If they had real conversations, I never heard them. When I was old enough, I would go to Nestor's house by myself, Aliki coming with me for a time until she began to go off with her own friends. He was always the same. His kindness never varied as we moved from tinkering with small gadgets and souvenirs to listening to music or looking through his photo albums or his movies that captured my relatives in rickety motion.

I used to ask him to repeat the stories of their childhood that I knew so well from my mother's winter recitations. The one about the cow that chased his sisters Thalia and Sophia into the hayloft. Or, my favorite, the one about the time they all flooded the basement of the grand city house. I would prompt him, reminding him of how he and my mother had stood on the balcony of the house the night the war began, watching Italian tracer bullets write sparkling lines in the darkness. My grandmother Urania had grabbed them, terrified they would be shot, while they had been dazzled by the colors. He usually let me tell this story, as if it were my own to tell. Once, though, he stopped me, saying, no, the war started in daylight, with bombs dropping, not tracer bullets. He showed me a newspaper clipping from his collection. There it was, the official account, beneath a headline of block capitals, proving the accuracy of his memory.

As I become aware of the sweat rising beneath my coat, I remember what he told me during what turned out to be my last visit. I was back in Greece again, thanks to a discount flight and the good pay from my newly acquired private-school job. I had changed my mind at the last minute about the man I was supposed to be there with, so I was alone, seeking a brief respite from my errors in Nestor's familiar space. We were looking through old photographs and I asked him to identify some unknown relative for me. He gave me a name I can't remember now, then stopped himself and placed his hand on mine. "There are things you need to know, Calliope," he said. "But not now." I sit up suddenly and shake my coat off. What was it he wanted me to know, and why did I have to wait—until he died—to find it out?

There's a tap on the door and Lucy sticks her head in.

"Morning," she says, and does a double take when she sees my expression. "What's up? Did Bart Wilcox make another one of his inappropriate comments?"

I compose my face. "Nope. You just caught me cooking the books," I say with a big smile.

She shakes her head in amusement. They think I'm a card here at the office.

I wait until she's gone and let myself fall back into the chair, still thinking of what Nestor said to me that day five years ago. I left Patras suddenly that time, shot out of the city by cruel things my mother said. If Nestor had told me then what he wanted me to know, I wonder if I would have gone back to see him again. I wonder if I would have learned something that would have made it easier for me to return. But now I'm just making it someone else's responsibility. Isn't it my fault that I haven't seen my family in years? Wasn't it my decision that very same summer to walk away—not only from my mother but from Greece, and even from family members who had done nothing to hurt me?

After work, I park the car in front of our building and run upstairs to drop my stuff off before I head out to meet Jonah.

The answering machine is flashing. I stab at the button and walk away while the computer voice tells me there's one message. The only people who call our landline are Jonah's parents and my mother. Still, it catches me by surprise to hear my mother's melancholy tone on the machine. I come back into the room, red lipstick in midair, and listen. My jaw is tightening.

"Calliope. Your uncle's funeral was today." She makes it sound as if I deliberately stayed away instead of not having enough advance notice to make the trip. "Everyone was there. Everyone who is still alive, anyhow. Aliki told me she called you. But there's no need to come. I can make arrangements for Nestor's things to be given away or . . ." She trails off, her tone signaling disdain. "Call me so I can tell you what you need for the power of attorney. I don't know why Aliki called you. She should have stayed out of this. There's no need to make you come. All right?" She pauses, as if waiting for a reply. *"Geia,"* she says. To my health.

"That's nice," I mutter to the apartment.

I replay the message. It's a virtuoso performance. Guilt, sympathy, scorn, and ingratitude all rolled into twenty-six seconds. Nestor's words ring in my head: "There are things you need to know. But not now." Something new is going on with my mother, and I need to find out what. I finish my lipstick, grab my shoulder bag, and lock the door behind me, ready to tell Jonah I'm definitely going to Greece.

I step into the deep entrance of The Sevens and stomp my feet free of snow before tugging on the heavy wooden door. Even for a bar, The Sevens is dark. People don't go there to be seen; they go to shout and laugh and drink. That's what our crowd is doing when I find them in prime position beneath a television showing the Bruins game. Jonah is standing squarely on both feet, smiling, ignoring the game. Ted is telling him a rugby story, miming the action with his hands. All around Jonah, everyone is moving, gesturing, swaying, but Jonah is still. I feel a tiny gasp of recognition and relief when I see him and hope it doesn't show.

I wind carefully around the cluster of darts players, nod to Ben at the tap, and swing through the crowd to take hold of Jonah's arm.

"Hey," he shouts, turning. People have started yelling at a fight in the Bruins game. It's too noisy to say much, so I kiss him.

I look for Marcus, whose first day at his new job we are celebrating.

"Still employed?" I ask, straining over the subsiding voices.

"Yup."

"But tomorrow they'll bust him for insider trading," Jonah says.

"So soon," I say. "Such a shame."

"He's been giving out stock tips all night."

Marcus rolls his eyes, tolerant. He has a new haircut for the occasion, an extreme short-back-and-sides. I run my hand up the back of his neck, feeling the nap of his dark buzzed hair.

"Looks good," I say.

"I think he looks like a young Demi Moore," Jonah yells.

Marcus shoves him in the chest, saying, "Callie, where'd you get this guy?" He messes up Jonah's hair and tousles his shirt-front, his tie.

"We got some big news on the New Bedford case today," Jonah says.

"Yeah?"

"We won." He gives me a big smack on the lips.

"Seriously?" Marcus shouts. "You can't upstage me!"

"Jonah, that's so great," I say. I lean in and tell him, "Celebration sex tonight."

"Going for another beer," Marcus says to me. "Because it's *my* party. Want one?"

"Ben has it." The pint of lager is waiting for me on the counter.

"Jonah, I'm so proud of you," I say, and he looks sheepish for a second before his usual confidence returns. I am proud of him. I know that while he doesn't mind the contract law that occupies most of his time, he truly loves the immigration cases he works on. With Nelson, who is raising his glass a few feet away from me, Jonah handles the prosaic cases, the ones lacking any political drama save that of someone's craving for a home. The night I met Jonah, he was drinking here after a court date that hadn't gone well. It was another New Bedford case, a Cape Verdean fighting deportation. Jonah sat at the bar in a sorrow that was admirable before I even knew its source. I could have found someone else that night, but I sat down beside him, drawn to that sorrow and pulled in by the growing quiet of our conversation.

Marcus hands me my lager.

"Now you can go toast Nelson too." He's playing up the self-pity.

There are six of us here so far tonight: Jonah and me, Marcus, Ted and some woman he's dating, and Nelson. After about an hour, Brian shows up with Mollie. Since they got married last summer, they never seem to arrive anywhere on time with the rest of us. Jonah and I can't decide if it's because they're having lots of marriage sex or not enough.

Eventually, I weave over toward Mollie and clink my current glass of beer with hers.

"To our new stockbroker," I say.

"To the Broker Dude."

We drink and I think about what to ask Mollie. I settle for the generic.

"How's married life?"

"Good. Good." She nods as if I just asked her about work. I make a note to tell Jonah: not enough sex.

"Hey, that's pretty exciting about your trip," she says, brightening.

"What trip?"

"To Greece. You guys doing a pre-wedding honeymoon?"

I laugh to avoid having to answer.

"Hang on, Mollie," I say to her ear. "I'll be right back."

I reach past Brian for Jonah and grab his sleeve.

"Can I talk to you for a minute?"

He turns with a smile that drops away when he sees my face.

"Just a sec, guys."

He lets me tug him out the door onto the sidewalk.

"Mollie asked me about *our* trip to Greece."

"Yeah, I mentioned the idea."

"You did more than mention it, I think."

"Okay, I told her I was going with you. Seemed like a great way to meet the folks. What's wrong with that?"

"I didn't even know if I was going, and I told you I didn't want to bring you with me."

"*Bring you with me.* Listen to you. It's like I'm some child you'd have to drag along. I'm going to marry you, Callie. Is it so bad to want to come with you for a trip like this?"

"This trip is so I can take care of my dead uncle's stuff. It's not a honeymoon, and it's not a vacation."

"I get that. I'm not marrying you for the vacations, Cal."

I let go of his sleeve with an abrupt swinging motion.

"Would you stop that?" I say.

"What the fuck, Callie?"

"What the fuck? That's what I thought when Mollie knew all about the trip you'd planned for us."

"I didn't do a whole plan thing. I just told her I thought it would be cool. I haven't met anyone in your family, Cal, and I thought this was a good time. If you want to be mad at someone, be mad at Mollie, not me."

He steps closer so that the cloud of his breath sinks down to me.

"I don't want to be mad at anybody," I say.

"Well, you suck at it. Bad day at work?"

"Oh, shut up, Jonah."

He comes closer again and grabs my arms at the elbows. I wrestle free, yelling, "Let go," even as I register Jonah's surprise at my reaction.

A man stops on his way into the bar.

"You heard her," he says to Jonah, who glances, perplexed, from him to me. He isn't even touching me anymore.

"She's my fiancée," Jonah says finally.

The word hangs there like a burst of scalding steam. I am too mortified to say anything at all. It's as if we've been caught using the wrong language in the wrong place—Greek in America, English in Greece—and rather than clarify and risk adding to the mistake, I turn away and walk home. I hope Jonah will bring my coat when he comes back.

I don't feel the cold, but by the time I get upstairs and into the apartment, I realize that I am freezing. I stand by the kitchen counter, shivering, replaying in my mind the moment when Jonah grabbed my arms. It's not really that particular moment I see but a mood that I sense—a mood of alarm and desperation. So many times my father seized my mother's arms like that, pleading his case and eventually making some declaration or ultimatum. Jonah has never done that to me before. In three years, we have never really argued. Now this.

I gulp a glass of water down, noticing an ache knocking at the back of my head. He called me his fiancée, as if that explained why he could grab me like that, as if that established his right. He's the one caught using the wrong language, not me. I set the water glass down and rock it from side to side on the counter, synchronizing its rhythm with the beating in my head.

I don't know how long I've been standing there when I hear the apartment door click shut. Jonah has my coat over his arm and drapes it carefully over the back of the couch, setting his briefcase down beside it. He stares at the floor for a moment and then looks up at me.

"Think you might have overreacted a little?"

"You can't manhandle me, Jonah."

He sighs and goes to hang up his coat. He leaves mine on the couch.

"Look, I'm going to Greece."

"Knock yourself out."

"This isn't about you, it's about my family and me."

"No need to explain, Cal. It's always about you. I'm just a spectator to the grand mystery that is your life."

He yanks a cupboard open, then runs the tap hard into a glass. When he turns the water off, the pipes shudder. Water has splashed all over his sleeve.

"You don't let anyone in—or at least you don't let *me* in; I don't know what you do with other people you don't happen to be engaged to—and you think somehow that gives you the right to live like a solo agent."

He gulps the water down.

"*Solo agent.* What the hell is that?"

"It's you, Callie. On your own. Except when you need taking care of. Here." He thrusts the glass out toward me. "Need some water for your hangover? Can I get you something? Can I, please?"

"That's enough, Jonah. I never asked you to take care of me."

"No, you never did. Because you never talk about anything."

After a long silence, I say the thing that I know we're both thinking.

"This is what I was afraid of, Jonah. This is why I wanted us to stay the way we were."

"You can't think we're having a fight just because we're engaged."

"I don't know. Would you care as much? Would I? The stakes are too high now."

"How can the stakes be high if we love each other?"

"See, this is what I mean. You don't think it's hard to be married, so I'm not allowed to think it's hard. But I do think so. It's hard for me. Don't try to convince me I'm wrong when that's what it feels like."

"Well, then, you're lucky, because it's not too late, is it?"

"What do you mean?"

"You want to take the ring all the way off, Cal?"

"No. I'm just saying—"

"You don't really know what you're saying, do you?"

This rankles more than anything. I've never seen this kind of bitterness in Jonah, but I recognize it as the rough edge of his lawyer's charm. It's all sour now, ruined. His win, the toast, the celebration: It seems irretrievable now. I repeat what I started the argument with, as if it's my new mantra.

"I'm going to Greece. When I get back, we should talk about things."

"Fine."

I walk to the couch and reach for my coat.

"No," he says, holding up a hand. "I'm the one leaving." He grabs his coat from the closet and shrugs it on.

"Where are you going?" There's a note of panic in my voice. I only meant to hang my coat up and now he's headed out the door.

"Ted's."

He pulls the door behind him, and at the last minute, mindful of the hour, he holds it and clicks it softly shut.

* * *

The next morning, every sound I make as I get ready for work rings through the apartment. Heels on the wood floor, the toothbrush scrape, the coffee cup on the counter—all unanswered. I can't help listening for the sound of Jonah's key in the lock. I start at footsteps in the stairwell before I realize it's the neighbors heading down. No, Jonah won't come back until after I've gone for the day, and probably not until after work. They'll tease him at the office for showing up in the same clothes. And he'll have to put on a game face and make it look as if he had a big night after the win. I realize that I'm worrying about how Jonah will cope, and the disaster of our argument hits me again.

There's only one thing that can make my morning worse than it already is: I have to call my mother. I hold the phone for a good five minutes before I find the courage to dial. The double-grinding European ring makes me feel as though she and I are already fighting before the conversation even begins.

"Yes?" This is the first time I've actually spoken to her in several weeks and her voice sounds, as always, both seductive and wary.

"I'm coming tomorrow to take care of Nestor's things."

"I told you not to."

"I know, but I'm coming anyway. That all right with you?"

"Don't talk to me like that, Calliope."

"I'm sorry," I say, and I am. "It's a busy day."

"How, busy? You just woke up."

"I can't talk long, *Mamá*. Can we just talk about the trip?" I say.

"Fine."

"I'm taking the bus from Athens."

"Can't someone drive you?"

"I'd rather take the bus."

"*We* never took the bus."

"Well, I have." In the silence, I can tell she is registering this thought, startled at the reminder of my independent travels in her native country.

"Suit yourself," she says. "But you'll be in there with all the onions and the chickens."

Just before I hang up, as we are going through the formulaic salutations of a Greek conversation—regards, health, kisses that are meaningless—I break the news to her.

"I'm staying with Aliki."

Again, silence; pieces falling into place.

"She has more room," I say.

"And what will your aunts say, when they see my own child isn't planning to stay with me? You might as well put up a sign for all of Patras to see that says you don't love and respect your mother."

She manages the indignant tone she is so practiced in, but it is clear that she is imitating something she has never quite felt—not the sense of slight or diminution but the desire to nurture and welcome.

After work, Jonah returns from Ted's. We spend the evening in a quiet détente. And we are the world's most fatigued diplomats, feigning sleep whenever possible to avoid having to talk to each other until it is a plausible time to go to bed. We don't spoon, and we turn carefully beneath the covers, mindful not to hog the blanket, or to touch.

Finally, by Wednesday morning, I can't avoid him as I hurry around the apartment, getting ready for work before the evening flight to Athens. I need to put in some time on the annual campaign at school before leaving it to Daniel. I watch Jonah as he crouches over his boots, one half of an English muffin in his mouth and the other in his hand. He stands up and can't avoid my eyes. We take a long look at each other, and I see hope and pain and defiance flicker across his face. I expect he sees the same in mine.

"Do you want me to call when I land?"

"Yeah."

"It'll be first thing in the morning for you."

"Call my cell. It won't cost too much. We won't talk long."

"Jonah, we can talk, can't we?"

"I'm happy to listen, Cal, if you've got things to say."

I summon all my courage and lean toward him. We kiss once, lightly, on the lips, and that's that. I go out the door, my body almost aching with the pull back to Jonah. My stride is jagged as I pick my way over slush piles on the sidewalk.

As my plane flies from Milan to Athens over the Adriatic coast, I find myself imagining the moment of arrival in Athens, but I keep getting it wrong. I have never been to Greece in February, so I invest the place with the dry heat and white light of a summer landing. I remember emerging from the airplane as a child each June, holding my mother's hand as I stood at the top of the movable stairs, bathed in sensations that most people would have found harsh. I relished the blasting heat and even the acrid smell of the plane's exhaust, for I knew that they inaugurated three months of relative calm and that, though my mother had taken my hand, I would soon be pulled free of her into the summer's embrace of my cousin, my aunts, and Nestor.

What I can see of Croatia and Albania from the plane is gray and damp. The Adriatic should be tinged with purple, but winter has turned it into a steely blue. I will have to force my tongue into its old shapes as soon as the plane lands. I am afraid that I won't know how to do it—how to be Greek.

2

Callie

We arrive in daylight. The plane swoops low over suburban houses that are little more than cement boxes surrounded by small patches of short grass. Most are tidy, but many of the houses are only partly built, pillars of cement and rebar rising up from roofs that serve as storage areas. I see a rusty swing set on its side atop one house, a washing machine gaping on another. Here and there, I see a grove of olive trees and an old farm building painted with an advertisement for Misko pasta, in the red and gold colors I remember from my childhood. I recognize this world; I know this world.

We come in above a series of little bays to the south of Athens and then fly over apartment buildings packed in tight, their gardens still lush despite the season. When the plane banks slightly, I catch a glimpse of the city, poured like milk in the basin between the mountains, and, down below, the glass-and-marble cube of the terminal. When the new airport opens next year on the other side of Mount Hymettos, this experience will pass into history, new aerial views altering the feel of arrival. This airport already looks old and almost foolish as we descend. It seems far too small and vulnerable for its mission.

As the plane comes to a stop on the runway, several passengers applaud. The man in the seat beside me crosses himself.

"Excuse," says a woman standing next to me in the aisle.

I make way for her as she twists and reaches up to pull her bag from the compartment. I help her bring the bag down. She has spoken to me in English, and I am bothered by this, though I know I have no right to be. A second later, the woman switches on her cellphone and begins to chatter in Greek to her husband. She tells him their new grandchild is a little pinched in the face now but is sure to fill out. As we passengers begin shuffling toward the exit, she turns to me again and says, in English, "Thank you."

I emerge from the plane into the damp air of a cloudy afternoon and walk down the clanking steps of the mobile stairway. I follow the crowd as we walk across the roaring tarmac into the hubbub of the terminal. I smile, because nothing has changed in the five years since I was here last. There is no line, just a crowd massed before the window of the single passport-control officer; there is still the click and hiss of lighters as the newly freed smokers light up beneath the NO SMOKING signs, still the simmer of impatience as people jostle one another for the advantage of an elbow extended, a hip turned.

When I finally reach the window, the uniformed officer glances back and forth from me to my photograph. He must have an inkling that a petite woman named Calliope with dark, straight hair has Greek heritage. He gives me a little smile, and I return it and say my first words of Greek in Greece: *"Geia sas."* To your health. It is the polite form of *geia sou,* the message I see on bumper stickers and menus across Boston. But there it shows up as *Yasou!* and it makes me wince. It conveys no particular meaning, serving simply as a kitschy proclamation of Greekness.

I have no checked baggage, so I move quickly through the unmanned customs booth to the pay phones in a corner of the large main hall, where backpackers have rolled out their sleeping bags to rest. Stepping around the white-blond head of a young man with an Arab *kaffiyeh* wrapped around his neck, I find a working phone and make a call to Jonah's cell.

"Hey. I'm here."

"I checked online. I'm glad you called."

The line hisses.

"I wasn't sure you'd answer the phone," I say.

"I wasn't sure you'd call."

Someone bumps my shoulder and the phone slips from my ear.

"Did you say something?" I ask.

"No."

"Well, I should go. I have to catch the bus. I do love you, Jonah."

There's a pause.

"I love you too."

I let out a long breath and head for a pair of frosted glass doors that lead out of the airport. The crowd is ten deep, all jockeying for position so they can spot their loved ones the instant they emerge. I start to push through, murmuring, *"Sygnomi,"* as I go. The word releases a flood of Greek all around me.

"Pou pas, ré? Where are you going?"

"Slow down. *Siga.* They won't leave without you."

They are including me in their joking—men, mostly—but they know I can't possibly be from here. I am hurrying, refusing to be swallowed up in the happy chaos of the crowd. I belong but not quite. It's the belonging of the graduate student in the waiters' break room—harder won but never complete.

"*Geia sas,*" I say to the driver of the bright yellow Mercedes taxi by the sidewalk. I tell him I'm going to the bus station and then lean into the corner of the backseat and rest my head against the window. My head is beginning to feel heavy from lack of sleep.

I wake up when the taxi comes to a final stop. On the corner of two busy streets in a worn-out part of Athens is the station, little more than a large cement shed through which the buses pass in and out. I pay the driver from the stash of drachmas I changed in Boston and head over to a ticket booth. There is a three o'clock bus to Patras that will get me there at six, just as the siesta is ending. The station reeks of diesel fumes and oil, and there are dozens of people pushing toward the buses or the ticket booths in a mass of earth-toned coats and scarves. As in the airport, there is no line, just a crowd, so I nudge my way steadily forward.

"One for Patras," I tell the man in the booth.

"Round trip or one-way?"

"Round trip," I say, giving him the date of my return flight.

"Enjoy the *Karnavali,*" he says, as he bangs a stamp against some papers and hands me my ticket and some coins.

"I will."

But I had no idea it was Carnival in Patras. Now I realize that we must be somewhere in that four-week period before the start of Lent. The Carnival in Patras is renowned through all of Greece and Europe; if my mother is to be believed, it rivals even Mardi Gras in New Orleans. I've never experienced it, knowing about it only from my mother's stories. How as children, she, Nestor, Thalia, and Sophia threw candy and streamers from the balconies of their grand neoclassical home onto the parading crowds below. How they lit firecrackers and tossed them into the groups of festivalgoers. How their parents worked for days helping to paint and build floats representing the tennis club or the symphony. It occurs to me that Jonah would love to see it. For his Cape Verdean clients, Carnival is how they remember home. It's the one thing they fill with all their love for the place they are trying to leave behind.

I board the bus along with a group of roughly ten young men and women, smoking and joking with one another as they tussle for seats. As I take a seat toward the back, I notice that all of these people are dressed for the Carnival in some way. They wear flowing scarves, velvet, and ribbons, and the women's makeup is dark and rich. One of the men, a little bit younger than me, has a stovepipe hat of purple velvet. His longish hair is dark, with trim sideburns framing his angled face.

He tumbles into the seat in front of me, pulling a henna-haired young woman in with him. They fall together, half standing, against the back of the seat, and the woman glances toward me, saying, "Sorry," and then pressing her lips together into a tight smile. The man with the velvet hat leans over the seat, holding up a finger.

"Forgive us, for we are celebrating and we will not be silenced."

"Shut up, *ré*," the woman says. "She's a foreigner."

"Ah," he says. Then, in accented English: "Sorry."

I smile but don't respond. I want to sleep, or at least to prepare myself for the coming encounter with my mother. I slouch down and try to prop my knees against the seat in front of me, but I am too short to make this work. I tuck my legs beneath me and curl in toward the window.

I close my eyes, but I can hear the couple in front of me talking with their friends in Greek across the aisle.

"Too bad she's a foreigner," Velvet Hat says.

"I told you. I'm meeting Daphne."

"She's better-looking than Daphne."

"Fuck off," says the friend, laughing.

"He's right," says the woman. "She is."

"She's got that sexy American thing going on," says Velvet Hat. "All buttoned up, but you can tell she's got a good body."

"Probably wears a thong," says the other friend approvingly.

At this point, I have to sit up.

"A black one," I say. "Want to see?"

The four of them look at me in consternation.

"Shit!"

"You should have said something!"

"You're not American?"

"I am."

"But you speak Greek."

"Yes."

Velvet Hat is waiting, but I don't want to explain. I imagine him without the hat and realize that he is impressively good-looking, in the straight-nosed, dark way that I never see among the round-featured Greek Americans of Boston.

"Glad we have that settled," I say, and lean against the window.

"What are you doing?"

"Trying to sleep."

"You can't sleep! It's *Karnavali*."

I turn to see Velvet Hat bobbing his head. The henna-haired woman and the others across the aisle laugh as the hat waves from side to side.

"You're going, aren't you?"

"*Then xero,*" I say. I don't know. I hear the American accent in my voice.

"What are you doing here, then?" he says. "You've come a long way to not go to *Karnavali*."

Back home—and I catch myself at the thought of *back home,* as if I have been gone more than a handful of hours—Jonah and I would be laughing and joking like this group. On St. Patrick's Day, the closest thing that Boston has to Carnival, we pull on silly hats and scarves and drift from bar to bar with Marcus, Ted, and all the others. I look at Velvet Hat and think of inventing something innocuous, then decide to tell him the truth.

I say evenly, "I am here to sort through the inheritance my uncle left me when he died." I give him a little smile.

"Amán!" he exclaims, then calls over his shoulder, "Shut up, you idiots. We have a mourner here! Or," he says, looking at me again, "do you just need cheering up?"

Before I can answer, he starts to wave his head, and voices from the front rows shout and point at the hat.

"Wiggle it again, Stelios!"

"It's drooping," someone crows, and adds some new slang I can't understand that sets the rest to renewed laughter.

"Stelios! Leave her alone," says the woman. She smiles at me. "What's your name?"

"Callie," I say. "Calliope."

"Ela, come, Callie." The way she says the word, it sounds like its own Greek name: *Káli.* "You don't have to listen to this moron who stole his girlfriend's hat!" As she says this, she swipes the velvet hat from Stelios and puts it on. He grabs for her and they wrestle briefly, ending with a deep kiss. Stelios reaches under her sweater.

"Karnavali," he says to me, with an exaggerated leer.

"Stop that, you rude and crass boy," the woman laughs. "You're offending our American friend."

Knock yourselves out, I want to say, using Jonah's phrase. But I don't know the equivalent expression.

"It's all right," I say instead. *"Karnavali."*

I look out the window at the three pristine lanes of highway to the left of the bus and remember the pitted, narrow road that used to lead out of Athens when I was a child. We would drive it in a rented sedan, with my mother sailing around the turns on the edge of safety. I loved the feel of the hot sun on my arm and the wind beating my hair from my temples.

"Come on," Stelios is saying to me, and I can't understand why he won't leave me alone when he has a willing and attractive girlfriend.

"Look," he goes on, "we're sorry we were rude before. Though, actually, it's not really rude to call someone sexy."

"Stelios, shut up," the woman says, and smacks him on the chest. "Let us make it up to you," she says to me. "You hungry?"

She turns back to her seat and I can hear her opening a packet of food. She peers around the side of the seat and holds out a cellophane-wrapped sleeve of rectangular biscuits to me. I recognize them instantly: Pti Ber biscuits by Papadopoulos, a staple of car rides with my aunts. Unlike everyone else in Greece, my aunts and my mother pronounced the name with the proper French accent, *"petit beurre,"* a tribute to their years of lessons.

"Want some?"

"Oh, I love these," I say, taking the sleeve. And as I push three biscuits up with my thumb, I realize how familiar the action is to me—as familiar as the toasted-butter smell, the smooth, hard surface of the biscuits, then the moistened crumbs sticking to my palate. I smile up at her, and I can tell she thinks I am just hungry. But it's more than that. With surprise, I realize that I fit in here. No matter that I tried to cut Greece out of my life, along with my mother. The Greekness isn't gone. Stelios and his girlfriend and their friends and I—we have a common bond, a shared culture.

I take two more biscuits and hand the sleeve back to the young woman, chiding myself for having stayed away from Greece for so long. Right, I catch myself: You think a relationship with your mother is as easy as a relationship with a biscuit.

I learn that Stelios's girlfriend's name is Anna and they are spending a long weekend in Patras, maybe longer if their friends have space. It is *Tsiknopempti,* Roasting Thursday, when, they tell me, everyone eats grilled meat and dances in the street. They are both graduate students on the dole, as is the rest of the group. Stelios studies history and Anna is a mathematician. They are both nearly thirty and have been dragging out their degrees for years, and neither one of them seems bothered by the fact that they are skipping some lectures. I watch them explain this to me, glancing at each other with laughing eyes, and I admire their irresponsibility.

I tell them what I do for work and where I live. And I tell them the simple facts of my reluctant trip.

"And . . ." Anna points at my left hand.

"No," I say, blushing. "I'm not married."

"But you wear them on the left in America, right?"

I always forget that Greeks wear their wedding rings on the right, as my parents would have done had they worn their rings at all. Whenever I asked my mother why they didn't, she claimed the rings didn't fit. I stopped asking once I understood the real reason.

"It's an engagement ring," I say. "I'm engaged." My face goes immediately to full burning and I'm sure my distress is visible. But they don't seem to notice.

"So who is your *fiancé*?" Stelios asks, exaggerating the French accent.

"Jonah."

Stelios and Anna look at each other, murmuring Jonah's name and searching for the Greek equivalent.

"In the Bible," I say. "With the whale."

"Ah."

I brace myself for the next question—when is the wedding—but the bus is crossing over the Corinth Canal and, though the new highway makes it hard to see, Stelios and Anna turn to look for the channel through the window.

"Behold Peloponnesos!" Stelios announces to the whole bus. We have crossed from Attica to the square-shaped landmass near whose northwestern corner Patras sits.

The highway drops one lane, and then another. The bus moves to the right, straddling the solid white line that marks the breakdown lane. Speeding cars and motorcycles pass us, pinching in as traffic flies by on the other side. This is the main road to one of the country's largest cities, and it is an undivided two-lane highway.

The people in the front rows of the bus are singing a song about the Carnival.

"You should come with us, Callie," Anna says. "I'm the only woman with these *men*."

"Where?"

"The Carnival!"

I shake my head.

"I have work to do. My uncle was a big collector. There's lots of stuff to go through."

"You're going to want to take a break. Let me call you."

"You just met me."

"That's what Carnival's for: making new friends. What's your mobile?"

"I don't have one. Not here."

Anna groans.

"Your cousin's number?"

Aliki's number comes back to me in the musical chant I memorized as a child when the house belonged to my aunt Thalia and my uncle Demetris.

"Two, three, eleven. Forty-four, seven."

Anna enters the number into her phone.

"Done."

Dusk falls and my eyes begin to close, even though it is only nine-thirty in the morning in Boston. Jonah will be at his desk, looking for his chance to grab the morning's second coffee.

"I'm falling asleep," I tell Anna.

"Sleep now. There's no time for sleep once you get to *Karnavali*."

As I drift off, I think about the fact that, though I have been in the country for just a few hours, I have already made friends on my own, and the heaviness of my American consonants is beginning to disappear. I have the absurd thought that Nestor will be proud of me.

I wake up to find the bus at a stoplight and I realize I've been asleep for more than an hour. We are surrounded by traffic—motorcycles, cars, scooters—and the street is decorated with lights and streamers. Stelios and Anna and their friends are singing again, pushing toward the doors at the front, and the driver is telling them to get back to their seats. Outside, I can hear not just the horns and revving of the street but the hum of a crowd and of different kinds of music coming from every direction. When the bus starts up again, everyone at the front stumbles in the aisle and joins in a loud cheer. Stelios comes back down the aisle, velvet hat pushed low on his head, and falls into the seat. He calls someone on his cellphone.

"Hey, *maláka*! Where are you, you wanker? Get your sorry ass down to the bus station! We have arrived!" This last he shouts to the entire bus.

The bus stops at the station with a hiss of air brakes, and we all gather up our bags and push toward the door. Or, rather, the others push, and I let myself be nudged along. All my earlier enthusiasm is fading now as I step down into the bustle of the station, down into my mother's city.

Anna and Stelios are drawing their jackets tight around them, but to me the air feels balmy, blowing a faint salt aroma from the harbor.

"Callie," she says, "we'll call you."

"All right," I say, certain that she'll forget.

"We'll call you," Stelios repeats. "Have fun with your inheritance!"

They kiss me on the cheeks and head off. I watch the velvet hat bob through the crowd until it disappears in the dark.

I decide to walk rather than take a taxi to Aliki's house. This is foolish, I soon realize, because the streets are packed with people going to the various celebrations for Roasting Thursday, and the Carnival has rendered everything unrecognizable. Banners obscure the façades of the boxlike apartment buildings, and strings of lights throw strange shadows on the city's distinctive colonnaded sidewalks. Every doorway seems to hold a shop whose windows are covered in neon-colored cardboard letters. Motorcycles are chained to every lamppost and door grate. Cars are parked nose-in, many of them over the curb and resting just feet from a rack of clothes or a table of women's shoes set up beneath the colonnades. Where is Plateia Olgas, Olga's Square, where I used to play with Aliki in the mulberry trees? Where are the streets whose small section of Patras's grid I knew by heart: Riga Ferraiou, Kolokotronis, Maizonos?

People are blowing whistles and shaking tambourines and rattles, and samba music booms from loudspeakers on every corner. It seems that everyone throughout Patras is dancing to the same joyful rhythm. I twist through the dancers, heading in the direction I think is west. It is nearly seven o'clock, and I am sweating beneath my knapsack. My hair is frizzing in the humidity and I imagine I have begun to resemble the mop-headed little girl and teenager of my summers here. Finally, I find Kolokotronis Street and start the last few blocks to Aliki's apartment on Kanakaris. The air beneath the colonnade is thick with greasy smoke from street grills on which costumed men are turning spits of *souvlaki* and sausage. I shake my head to get the hair out of my eyes, and the scent of grease blows across my face.

I am hungry, and I think of stopping for a *souvlaki,* but I know I will be in Aliki's kitchen in a moment or two. She will take me in, feed me, and show me to a well-made bed with ample blankets.

I press the bell by the door and, after a pause, a man's voice comes over the intercom as the buzzer sounds.

"Get up here, *maláka,* we're all starving." *Maláka:* the Greek man's term of insult and endearment.

"Wait," I say. I wedge the door open with my foot and strain to shout backward into the intercom. "It's me. It's Calliope."

The intercom goes dead, so I go into the lobby and toward the two elevators at the back. It is as if I never left—never stopped riding the elevators with Aliki during the siesta, to the consternation of Mario, the superintendent; never stopped coming back from the Plateia with a comic book and standing on tiptoes by the intercom; never stopped falling into Thalia's open arms when the elevator let me out on her floor for the first time each summer. Nothing has changed except that this is Aliki's house, now that widowed Thalia lives with her never-married sister, Sophia. I swing my arm up in the perfect arc to press the call button, and I tug the heavy metal door open and step aside with exactly the right timing. My body fits this place just so, with ease and grace, the way it fits against the hard planes of Jonah's hips.

There is noise and cigarette smoke coming from an open door at the end of the hall. Through it, I can see Aliki's living room and beyond into the dining room, where a group of adults and children is standing around the carved walnut table that used to be Thalia's. The rest of the furniture that I can see is light and airy: blond-wood chairs, an ash sideboard, and a beige canvas couch. It was a good apartment decades ago, when Aliki's father bought it on the earnings from his taverna, and it's a good apartment still.

Aliki comes out of the kitchen with a platter, sees me, and gasps.

"Calliope! *Ré*, Nikos," she says, "it's Calliope."

She puts the platter down on a side table and embraces me, then holds me out in front of her to take a closer look. As she studies my face and body, she gives me a look that is both welcoming and cataloging, taking stock. I can tell Aliki sees not only the passage of time but traces of America on me. I dress in what passes as stylish for a WASP-y private school: small earrings, medium heels, and layered tops. I wear my hair long and straight with feathered bangs, and my jeans and sweater, though slim, are just a shade looser and more rugged than those of the women I have seen today.

"You must be exhausted," Aliki says, and I laugh, suddenly aware of how true this is.

A large man has come over to stand beside Aliki and I recognize Nikos, whom she married when she was only twenty-four. She takes his arm.

"How good is her Greek?" he says quietly to Aliki.

"Pretty good," I whisper, leaning forward.

Aliki tugs his arm.

"Sorry," he says, then adds to Aliki, "It's been so long, I forgot." He turns to me again. "It's good to see you, cousin."

He kisses me on the cheeks and I can feel the stubble on his face. He is dark and tall; his face is almost perfectly round, with round eyes and a double chin. Standing beside him, Aliki looks tiny. I see now that she is wearing an apron and that Nikos is wearing slippers, while she is in shoes.

"Do you know it's been almost ten years, Paki?"

"Five," I say, as if that will make it better.

"We missed you last time," Nikos says. "Weren't you supposed to stay with us?"

I look at Aliki. I shouldn't blame Nikos for not knowing the whole story.

"You know I couldn't stay in Patras."

"I know."

"Not after what she said to me."

"I know, Paki." Aliki puts her hand on my arm.

Nikos looks from me to his wife and back again, then shrugs.

"You'll tell me what I need to know when I need to know."

Aliki smiles and rubs her hand up and down my arm briskly, as if erasing the troubling past.

"Demetra," she calls, "come see your aunt Calliope."

Three girls wander over, two looking curious, the third guarded. Aliki pulls the third girl forward.

"This is Demetra. She turned nine last week."

Demetra was named after her grandfather Demetris, who was always busy at his taverna but whom I remember as a kindly figure, redolent of the kitchen. We would stop sometimes at his place for lunch on beach days, and he would bring us wedges of juicy watermelon or heaping plates of fried anchovies that we would eat whole. Demetra is tall, like her father, and I hardly have to lean down to kiss her. I wish her happy birthday and glance over at the dining room, where the other adults are talking loudly.

"You hungry?" Nikos says. "*Tsiknopempti*. We all eat meat."

I want to tell him that I know all about *Tsiknopempti*—as of this afternoon—and that he doesn't need to revert to idiot's Greek, but I am too tired.

Aliki leads me into the dining room and introduces me to the two other couples: Marina and Phillipos, Lena and Elias, and their collective children, one boy and two girls.

"Here," she says, and drags her chair to the corner, pulling a heavy armchair to the head of the table for me.

"You don't have to move," I say.

"No, no." She opens a drawer in the sideboard and pulls out a place setting. "You're the guest of honor," she says, as she slides the heavy silver into position on the tablecloth.

It's my aunt Thalia's silver; I remember it from special occasions when we were little. I smile at the others around the table and realize everyone else has knives and forks with bright red Bakelite handles.

After a brief silence while Aliki takes her new seat, we all begin passing platters of meat and bottles of red wine.

"Nikos caught this," Aliki says, as she hands me a platter of some sort of poultry.

"Caught it?"

"She means I killed it," Nikos says, "but she doesn't like to say that. Daughter of a taverna owner and she doesn't want to know where the food comes from. Who wants some Mavrodaphne?" he adds, brandishing a bottle of the local vintage.

"I'll make an exception," Elias says, and leans toward me. "Avoid the stuff if you can, Calliope. It should never be drunk unless—"

"It should never be drunk, period," I say. The wine is cloyingly sweet and has always given me a blinding headache.

"Oh, so you've been to Greece often?" asks Marina.

"Most of my life, for the summers." I glance at Aliki, though it's not her job to confirm this.

"Calliope and I were great summer playmates," Aliki says. "Every day, it was the two of us with my mother and Sophia buzzing around us. Imagine, Marina, a little swarm of women."

"Your parents sent you alone?" Marina asks.

Aliki looks at me.

"Her mother came too," she says.

"She just didn't buzz quite like the other two." I laugh, and so do Marina and the others.

"What do you do for work, cousin? I can't remember." This is Nikos. He's smiling, as if he's playing some sort of game with me.

I think of simply translating my title—Assistant Director of Development—but then explain, "I raise money for a school."

"What do you mean?" asks Phillipos.

"I identify wealthy people and ask them to contribute money to a school."

Nikos raises his eyebrows. "You mean you beg rich people for money."

"Nikos! Calliope is tired," Aliki says. She is trying to protect me, but only because she finds the idea of asking wealthy people for money a shade distasteful.

"Yes," I say. "You could put it that way."

"Like the Arsakeion, *ré*, Nikos," Aliki says, naming the old Athens girls' school founded by one family's donation.

The meal winds down and Aliki begins to clear the dishes as the children, who have been coming and going all through dinner, scramble off again toward Demetra's room. Nikos pushes his chair back from the table and lights a cigarette.

"Let me help," I say, but Aliki presses my shoulder.

"Sit. You've traveled far today, Calliope." She takes a load of plates into the kitchen.

"Besides," Nikos says, "guest of honor."

Marina follows Aliki with an empty platter in each hand.

"What do we have for dessert?" Nikos asks when they return.

"Karythopita," she says.

When Nikos finishes his cigarette, he leads me into the living room with the men, sits down on the couch, and puts his slippered feet up on the table. Elias teases him about being lazy, but neither Nikos nor the other men offer to help. I sit and watch as Aliki, Lena, and Marina bring small plates and fresh cutlery to the coffee table. These women are only a few years older than me, but they have long marriages, children, settled lives. I feel like the lone child at the adults' table.

All the same, Aliki's compliance surprises me. As a teenager, she trumpeted her critiques of sexist culture and swore to do what she pleased in life. But Greek women possess a strong streak of obedience that even independence of mind cannot

THE CLOVER HOUSE | 49

cancel out. My own mother would follow a day of fury at my father with a dinner at which she brought him everything, getting up several times during the meal to fetch him things he could have reached himself. I think of Jonah getting groceries on that frigid day when Aliki called about Nestor. Aliki and my mother would be shocked.

The *karythopita* is good, a winter dessert I have had only the few times when my mother's nostalgia spurred her to make it. I used to think her fits of baking were meant to include me, to share with me the world she valued so much. But I learned soon enough that I did not figure in my mother's nostalgic re-creations. And her version of the walnut cake was so over-drenched in syrup that its sweetness made me ill. Even my mother must have felt sick after eating it and must have realized that it bore no resemblance to the *karythopita* her mother had made for her long ago. Aliki's cake is light and nutty, and the syrup tracks over it in fragrant loops.

After dessert but before the guests start to leave, Aliki shows me my bed in the spare room and sets out towels for me.

"I'm sorry about all those questions at dinner," she says.

"It's not your fault. They weren't trying to be mean," I say.

"No, they were just being Greek. They can't stay out of other people's business. But still."

She pulls a blanket from a high cupboard and hands it to me.

"Do you want to call Clio?" she says. "Let her know you're here?"

"Not now," I say, knowing my mother will be angry that I am waiting a day. But I am tired and don't want to face her now.

"Anyone else you want to call instead?" She is fishing.

"Not right now," I say, smiling.

"What happened to the one who came here with you that time, before we moved into this place?"

"Luke." He read *Zorba the Greek* before the trip; by the end of two weeks, he was greeting people and ordering meals with a decent accent.

"I remember he changed Demetra's diaper for me." She shakes her head in amazement.

"It didn't work out."

Luke was more in love with Greece than with me.

"I'm sorry Nikos brought up the whole thing about when you left so suddenly. I've never told him what happened."

"It's all right."

After Luke there was Sam. Sam led to Pete, who seemed nicer than he was. Each of these relationships was shorter than the one before. But Sam was the one I thought might stick for a little longer. We had rented a tiny house on the island of Zakynthos, where we were going to try out being serious about each other. But days before we were to leave Boston, I broke things off. For some reason, I stopped in Patras at my mother's before heading to Zakynthos alone. I should have known that no conversation with my mother could have gone well, but I had no idea how spectacularly badly it would actually turn out. I never got to Aliki's at all and reached Zakynthos in a state of suspended fury, still shaking from the accusations and insults my mother had aimed at me so expertly. The island's earthquake-blasted landscape seemed just right for my hollowed-out state.

Fatigue must be letting my emotions show, for Aliki touches my arm.

"I'm sorry, Calliope."

"It's all right."

The guest room is a small, tidy space between Demetra's room and her parents' bedroom. The bed is narrow but fine for one, and there is a good light on the low table that serves as a nightstand. I dig through my bag for my T-shirt and bottoms and take my turn in the bathroom to brush my teeth. The layout is just as I remember it—like a galley version of a bathroom—but Thalia's chrome and porcelain fixtures are all gone. In their place are what look like sculptural artifacts. It takes me nearly a minute to figure out how to run the water. It seems out of character for both Aliki and Nikos, but I remind myself that I really don't know Nikos very well.

As I lie in the narrow bed in the dark, I can hear Aliki talking to Demetra in the next room. She is tucking her in, and her voice is soft and low. The little girl's voice slides into and out of a loud whisper as she tells her mother about her day.

I try to sleep, listening to the sounds of Aliki putting Demetra to bed, padding around and turning off lights, Nikos flushing the toilet, kicking his slippers onto the floor. But my body thinks it is late afternoon and, after what seems like hours, I give in and get out of bed. The apartment is chilly from the damp air that comes off the Gulf of Patras, so I pull on a sweater over my T-shirt and slip out into the hall. I walk around the living room and the dining room, peering at photographs in the orange glow from the balcony windows. There are photos from Aliki and Nikos's wedding, the two of them with flower crowns on their heads connected by a white ribbon. They are smiling, and in the background, out of the flashbulb's glare, you can see guests laughing as if at an inside joke. There are photos of Demetra in various school and church celebrations: her baptism, Easter, a Greek Independence Day parade in which she and her classmates all wear their blue uniforms and carry little Greek flags. Here are Demetra, Aliki, and Nikos in bathing suits on a pebble beach; here they are sitting around a Christmas tree with my aunts Thalia and Sophia. And with my mother. The sight of her there in a Christmas photograph—in someone else's Christmas—shoots a pang of jealousy through me. Alone in the dark room, I shake my head, chiding myself for this slip into sentiment.

I remind myself that tomorrow I will have to speak with her—that I will have to see her in person and, more important, that she will have to see me. She will, no doubt, find me inadequate in some way. And even at thirty-five, I am still worried by this possibility, this inevitability. Never mind that the last time we saw each other I promised myself never to care about her again. Never mind that I decided that letting her in made me vulnerable to her malice. Here I am again, back for more, hoping as always that this time will be different.

As if to remind me that I am no longer a child, the next thing I see is a folding frame with a pair of black-and-whites that depict Aliki and me. On the right, we are small children digging in the sand at the water's edge at the Bozaïtika, a beach on the outskirts of the city near Demetris's taverna. On the left, we stand side by side at ancient Olympia. I am twelve and she is fifteen, with breasts and long wavy hair and slender legs. I remember that trip to Olympia. I remember an argument between my mother and Aliki that began shortly after this picture was taken. And while I can no longer remember what the fight was about, I remember watching Aliki stand up to my mother and wishing she could teach me how to be defiant like that.

3

Callie

Friday

Aliki pours a coffee for me and slides a plate of biscuits across the kitchen table. I curl my feet up on the chair and hunch around the cup. It's a cozy kitchen, with just enough room for the round pine table and the four chairs tucked beneath it. When I lean back after taking a sip, my head riffles the pages of the wall calendar. February's photograph is the peak of nearby Panachaïko dusted with snow.

"I'll take you to Nestor's house later today," she says. "I started trying to organize it for you, but I didn't get very far."

"Is there as much as I remember?"

"Probably more. No rush, but when you're done, we're moving in."

She gets a cup and saucer from a cupboard stacked high with plates.

"It'll be nice to have more space," she says. "Nikos says he'll redo the garden, and we're probably adding another level."

"You'll change the house?"

"It needs it."

I tell myself that it's all right that Aliki feels this way. She can do this. For her, this is simply another move into another hand-me-down property. And just as she has made my aunt Thalia's house her own, so will she make her own life in Nestor's house. Just as he made his life in the house his parents moved into when he was still a young man. It's a question of making do with what you're given. And there is no reason I can't do the same, if there is something of Nestor's that I want to bring with me to Boston.

"You're doing all right, then, money-wise?"

"People need electricity, and Nikos can give it to them." Aliki shrugs, but it's more impressive than that. Aliki stays home with Demetra because Nikos earns enough for both of them, a rarity in Greece. He started his own business, running an electrical-supply store, and the fruits of his bootstrap initiative are visible in the clean lines and blond wood of the apartment. The light fixtures are bright and modern, except for a pair of old sconces by the bookshelves still there from Thalia's time.

"You can use the morning to go to your mother's," Aliki says, filling her cup from the coffeepot.

I look up at her.

"Calliope, I know it was awful last time, but you have to go see her. Her brother died."

"I know." I glance over at the refrigerator—a compact stainless-steel model in the place of Thalia's bulbous enamel one with the levered handle that I used to like to yank open. "I will. At some point," I say.

"You know you can't leave it beyond today, Paki," she says.

"And *you* know it's never that simple between me and my mother. Especially after that last time."

She wags her head in sad agreement.

I dip a biscuit into my coffee, thinking of the Pti Ber from the bus ride. Anna and Stelios are probably on a friend's couch, sleeping off hangovers and sex.

"You've never talked to her, have you?"

"I've talked to my mother."

"You know what I mean, Paki. About"—she waves a hand—"her."

"No."

"Paki, you're an adult now. You can confront her, or at least try to make her understand. Why won't you give that to yourself? Create a solution."

Aliki must see how uncomfortable I've become, because she leaves her chair suddenly to top up a cup that's already full. "I drink way too much of this stuff," she says.

Create a solution. I wish I could. But this is no *Sound of Music,* and I'm embarrassed to admit that my mother still scares me. What if I push her and she pushes me away for good?

"You know they argued."

"What?" I say.

"Your mother and Nestor."

"What about?"

She swallows a sip, shaking her head.

"He wouldn't tell me," she says. "But I showed up at the hospital one time just as she was leaving and I heard their voices raised. Which meant something, because Nestor was pretty weak by then. Your mother gave me that look she has—you know the look." I give a rueful laugh. "And Nestor was all upset."

"She would argue with a dying man." Here is proof that my mother shouldn't be confronted. "Did she say anything to you?"

"No."

I think back to the voice mail my mother left. I wonder if that argument in the hospital had anything to do with her insistence that I not come to Greece. Did he tell her something that convinced her I shouldn't be left alone with his things?

"The aunts can't wait to see you," Aliki says brightly. "I convinced them not to come over last night. It would have been a bit too much."

"The aunts," I say, happy for the change of subject.

I am eager to see them, one spinster and one widow, living together with the cozy friction of an old married couple in what used to be Sophia's apartment. Sophia is always expounding on something, and Thalia is always giving a little smile of friendly mockery. It is as if each woman's personality was determined by the meaning of her name—Sophia's by wisdom, and Thalia's by comedy.

"I don't suppose there was room for all three sisters to live in the one place," I say.

"Sophia and your mother tried that decades ago, before she met your father. It didn't go well, apparently."

Aliki's face tightens just a bit, and I feel again the vague shame I felt in childhood, for a mother who was somehow apart from her two sisters, who was treated with love but held separate for some reason I could not understand. Only Nestor tried to keep the childhood relationship alive, but she wouldn't let him. And now, with this argument right before he died, she must have ruined any chance of reconciliation. She kept coming back to Patras, bringing me with her every summer, but I know my mother sensed the way her sisters kept her at a slight distance, and during the waves of sadness that often hit her once we were back in America, she raged at me against these unexplained slights and insults.

As I did back then, I want now to defend my mother. When

she finally returned to Greece for good soon after my father's death, she'd spent more than three decades in America. Surely some of that country she insisted on disliking had rubbed off on her after all those years. It must have been hard for her to fit back into the Greek life her sisters had been living. Defiantly not American, she was no longer altogether Greek either. Still, she moved back ten years ago. In all this time, did Thalia and Sophia never ask her to join forces, even just to save a little money on rent?

We finish our breakfast and I take a quick and uncomfortable shower, struggling to shampoo with one hand while the other holds the spray nozzle. As I pull on jeans and a white turtleneck sweater, I realize that postponing the visit to my mother will only make things worse, so I tell Aliki I will stop by after all, but I need her as a buffer.

"Paki, I can't. I need to stay with Demetra. Extended school holiday for *Tsiknopempti*."

"Can't Nikos stay with her?"

Aliki raises her eyebrows at me and makes a little laugh.

"He has work, but Demetra's my job anyway."

This is new. Marriage has turned her rebellious spirit into the stuff of stereotype. She has become the typical Greek wife, subservient but husband-mocking. I can't imagine this ever happening to me.

"Don't be afraid of her, Calliope."

"I'm not afraid." But she knows I'm lying.

"All right," I say. "I'm a big girl. I'll go alone."

We kiss on the cheek as I put my jacket on.

"You know the way?"

"I remember."

I head down in the elevator and out into Kanakaris Street, where a soft rain is falling. Compared to the February weather in Boston, the air feels mild. I leave my coat unbuttoned. A woman stares at me, as if she's wondering why I have never learned to care for myself.

The smell of grease and cooked meat hangs in the colonnade over the sidewalk, and a few idle grills are pushed up against the building walls, embers still smoking. Two skinny dogs snuffle at the base of one of the grills. Streamers and popped balloons litter the street, along with bamboo skewers and cubes of bread that pigeons are squabbling over. Besides the birds and the dogs, the street is almost completely empty. The loudspeakers are quiet.

I follow the gentle slope of Kolokotronis Street downward, turning onto Maizonos where Plateia Olgas is crammed between it and Riga Ferraiou, two of Patras's major boulevards. Predictably, the square seems much smaller now than when Aliki and I climbed in the mulberry trees that line it. It is hard for me to reconcile this scruffy, tiny space with our sense of concealment and wildness. As I pass by the kiosk—the same canopied stall that occupied the corner when I was little—the kiosk man is untying a bundle of newspapers and pinning them up on a stand. I can read the headlines, but they mean nothing to me, full of names I don't know and events I have not followed. I realize now how early in the morning it is for this city that has just celebrated one of its important holidays, and it occurs to me that I should have called my mother to give her a warning. She will want to have dressed and fixed herself up.

Astiggos is a fairly unprepossessing street a few blocks northeast of Plateia Olgas and the area of the city where Sophia and Thalia and Aliki live. My mother's apartment building is the nicest on the block, but the façade is spare and somewhat antiseptic. I can feel my shoulders tensing as I find *Brown* written in Greek letters on the list of buzzers: ΜΠΡΑΟΥΝ. An odd sensation—to be apprehensive at the sight of my own name.

It takes her a while to answer, and when she does, her voice sounds faint and wary.

"It's me," I say.

"At this hour? You must be jet-lagged."

She buzzes me in.

I know I am ridiculous in the elevator, straightening my coat, tucking my hair behind my ears, swiping a finger under each eye for stray mascara. I am going on the worst date of my life: all the dread of the familiar combined with the fear of the unpredictable. The elevator settles with a clang and I push the door open, preparing my expression.

My mother is tiny. This is my overriding thought when I see her standing in her doorway, clutching her robe. She is smiling, and I am overwhelmed with pity for her. I can't imagine that this old woman is someone I have bothered to brace myself for.

"Calliope," she says, and hugs me. Her chin reaches my chest, and my arms wrap all the way around her.

"*Geia sou, Mamá.*" The word comes out so effortlessly, riding a wave of memory and instinct. "I'm sorry, *Mamá*," I say, holding her in the embrace for an extra second.

"The youngest, and he died first. Where's the logic in that?" She pulls away. "Seventy years old. Now we'll start dying, one by one."

"*Mamá*, you're all fine. None of you are dying anytime soon."

"That's what we thought about Nestor." She gives me a look that's half suspicion, half fear.

"But he'd been ill."

"Yes," she says. She nods her head and heaves a big sigh.

"You look good, *Mamá*. You look really good."

She snaps out of her mournfulness and her eyes dart up to my face. I can see her checking my ears for piercings, my hairline for any signs of gray, then my hips and waist for added pounds. She won't find any. Quickly, I twist my ring around so that the stones are on the inside. I don't want to talk about my future with her.

"Let me take that," she says, reaching for my jacket. I can't tell whether I've passed inspection.

While she is putting my jacket away, I step toward the living room, looking for the mirror that has been a part of my mother's life—and mine—for as long as I can remember. There it is, against the wall opposite a slipcovered couch: carved walnut, in the same style as Thalia's table, and almost eight feet tall, its broad glass etched here and there with tiny black spots where the leading has pitted. This is the mirror that stood in the enormous foyer of my mother's childhood house and in which, she said, her father would check his appearance before going out—even while the city was being bombed.

Given where my mother has placed the mirror, people sitting on her couch can't escape their own reflection. I step in front of it, my heart-shaped face elongated by a curve of the glass. I see my American self against a backdrop of my mother's Greek life.

I remember when she had the mirror shipped to America, over my father's protestations that it would be too expensive. I wonder now whether what really bothered him was the vanity it represented. So much effort expended on something that allowed her to see only herself. When the mirror arrived, I half-expected it to be shattered, heaping bad luck on all of us. But it was all in one piece, and the movers placed it against a blank white wall at one end of our low-ceilinged living room so that it looked like the mouth of a tunnel. Now here it is again, my mother's familiar, giving her easy passage to the better world of her youth.

"Come in here," my mother says. She pulls me away from the mirror, as if she is afraid I will take possession of it.

I sit at her kitchen table and watch her make me instant coffee. She keeps her back to me as she putters at the counter. The room is twice the size of Aliki's kitchen but has the perfect look of a space that no one cooks in. Everything is white or chrome, and there are no personal objects to be seen.

"*Mamá,* why didn't you call me?"

"Why didn't you call *me*? I haven't spoken to you in, what, two months?"

"I mean about Nestor."

"Why?"

"To tell me he was sick. You know, that maybe I should come see him." I don't want to say the last part—because he was about to die—and make her sad again.

She puts the two coffees down on the table and settles into her chair.

"I thought Aliki would have told you."

"Aliki is busy," I say. "She probably assumed you had called me."

"In which case, she thought you didn't care about your uncle, since you didn't come."

She has been doing this forever, trying to drive a wedge between Aliki and me. I let it go now. I need to stay detached. I watch her stir two teaspoons of sugar into her coffee. She's holding the spoon by the very end, making a graceful motion with her wrist, like a dancer's.

"Was the funeral nice?" It's a stupid question, but I'm trying.

"Nice?" Her spoon clatters into the saucer. "No, the funeral wasn't *nice*. The funeral was to bury a dead man's body."

"I mean after. It must have been comforting to have everybody there to talk about Nestor and remember his life."

"I don't need to talk to anybody else to show I remember my brother."

"No." I'm starting to give up. "No, you don't."

I take a long sip of hot, watery coffee, as if it could fortify me. "Well, I've been remembering all the things we used to do together," I say. "How he used to make all those little gadgets for me. Remember his turtles?"

"Tortoises."

"Right. Tortoises. I wonder if they're still there."

"They died, Calliope. Things die."

In Greek, there are two words for dying, one for people and one for animals: *pethainounai* and *psofanai*. As a child, I used to use the people word for any pet or stray that died, as a way to grant a little extra dignity to the creature. My mother uses the animal word now, and it sounds cruel.

"I don't know why he kept those things for all those years. Such a stupid pet. Like having a snake. Probably full of all sorts of diseases."

"Wait a minute," I say, sitting up so hard that my chair grinds against the floor. "Are you arguing with your brother? He's dead. And you're picking a fight with him over what pet he chose to have?"

"I can say what I want. He was my brother."

"What is going on, *Mamá*? I heard about the day in the hospital. What could you possibly want to argue about with him?"

"Aliki told you."

"Yes, she told me." I look at her for a moment. "It's embarrassing," I say, my voice low. For me, at least, my words carry the weight of all the other times my mother's actions dragged her and me beyond the safe and comfortable norm.

"Were you there? No. So I don't see how I could embarrass you when you were thousands of miles away. You don't know anything about it, Calliope."

She is furious now. Her face has darkened and her breath is wheezing slightly. She rises to make some toast and I can see her hands shaking as she holds the plate. I want to set my hand on hers to quiet the trembling; she is so small.

"I'm going to Nestor's this afternoon," I say.

"I'm coming with you."

"No. I'm doing this with Aliki."

"What does Aliki have to do with anything? I'm the man's sister and I have a right to be there when you go through his things."

"He left them to me, *Mamá.*"

"Another stupid decision. Making you come all this way to go over piles of junk when I could have taken care of all of it. I can still take care of all of it if you sign the power of attorney."

"Well, I'm here now, so I'm going to do what he wanted me to do. And it's not junk. It's photographs and tapes. I'd like to have those things."

"Your uncle took pictures of everything, just because," she mutters. "He was *recording* our lives, but what did he record? Just groups of people, faces, sometimes just things, objects."

"Those things matter to me."

"Why?" she says with scorn.

"Because I didn't get to live it."

We stare at each other and I see a faint trace of triumph in my mother's eyes: Score one point for firsthand experience. I should walk away, but I can't.

"At work the other day," I say, "I remembered the story about the tracer bullets."

She responds right away to this item from the catalog of her adventures.

"We stood there on the balcony. It's a miracle we weren't killed."

"But, see, this is why Nestor's stuff is important," I say. "He told me it didn't happen that way. You couldn't have seen the bullets. They attacked during the day."

"What are you talking about?"

"The first bombing and the tracer bullets. It was during the day."

"It was at night, and I don't care what Nestor told you. This is exactly why his collection is useless: It's wrong. And you think you can go in there and set the record straight by looking at pictures of people's shoes."

She is agitated again, and there is no point in pursuing this. It is the same old story between us: She is living in her memories, and I am just trying to find a way in.

"Well, I'm going over there this afternoon and I'll see what I find. I need the contact info for the lawyer," I say, pushing my chair away from the table.

She looks as if she's about to say something, but then she goes over to the telephone on the kitchen counter. "I'll give you the lawyer's numbers," she says. "But you won't find him."

"Why is that?"

She is stooped over a notepad, and I can see the bumps of her vertebrae through the thin satin of her robe. "Carnival."

"Doesn't anybody work at some point around here?"

"Most people take *Tsiknopempti* off until at least Tuesday, maybe Wednesday. But maybe he'll answer his cellphone and you can arrange something."

I look at her for a moment. She is holding a slip of paper in her hand, and I see her draw herself up straight into the perfect posture of her once-athletic body.

"What were you going to say before?" I ask her.

"Nothing."

"You were going to say something a minute ago. About Nestor."

"We've said all we need to say on that subject. How is Jason?" she says, pronouncing the name *Iáson,* like the hero of the Argonauts.

"It's Jonah," I say. "He's fine." I desperately hope she hasn't noticed the thin silver band. There's no telling news to my mother. She never appreciates the good news and takes the bad news as a foregone conclusion. And what I'd be forced to tell her now is mostly bad.

"Is that the number?"

She looks down at the paper in her hand.

"Yes." She holds it out to me and I take it.

"If you need me, I'll be at Aliki's."

I kiss her on the cheeks and walk out to the elevator, the taste of her cold cream on my lips.

Back on the street, I find myself turning not toward Aliki's house or even Nestor's house but farther up Astiggos Street toward my mother's childhood home on Korinthou Street. It is only two blocks away from where she has settled in her widowhood, though her current neighborhood is noticeably scruffier than the old one was in its heyday.

By the time I was born, the family house had already passed out of the family, and my grandparents had moved into the small house that became Nestor's own when they died, when I was still a little girl. But I knew every inch of the grand house inside and out from my mother's stories. It was made of stone and stucco, with high ceilings and a wide and graceful stairway rising up through its core. Its garden, behind a wrought-iron railing, was paved with chessboard squares of marble, bordered by massive planters of heavy stone. Across the street from the city's concert hall and in a neighborhood of neoclassical homes, it was a wealthy house, with a separate entrance for the servants beneath stairs leading to double oak front doors. I suppose it was the Greek version of the mansions on the upper part of Beacon Hill where Jonah and I stroll on weekends, imagining the stately lives inside.

Inside our house—as my mother still calls it—were four bedrooms, double parlors, and a library on the upper floors, each with a balconied window. On the first floor were large communal rooms: the dining room, the sitting room, and a spacious room in which were a grand piano and scattered chairs with velvet covers. A broad atrium rose up through the center of the house, topped with a skylight of gray glass. The bedroom doors gave onto a thin parapet from which you could see all the way down to the gleaming marble floor of the entrance, where the giant mirror stood guard.

Even before I reach the corner, I can hear the hum of traffic from Korinthou Street. Once a stately boulevard, it is now a busy access road into the heart of the city. I wait for a pack of trucks and cars to pass and then cross to the other side so I can look up at the house from a distance. I scan the façade, looking for some sign of the atrium's magnificent space. I imagine the four Notaris children arrayed along the parapet on a holiday morning. And the string-and-can telephones they rigged across the void, and the pulley-hung basket with which they could whisk away the reading glasses or chess pieces of their befuddled father.

But I can't make anything out; how does an inner column of

light alter the outward appearance of a house? All I see now is an anarchy symbol and the green cloverleaf of the PASOK socialists spray-painted on the crumbling stucco, and, by the double doors, a row of small white circles that glow orange in the daylight, each one with a metal nameplate beneath it. There are no Carnival streamers or balloons here. We are too far away from the center of the new Patras. Behind me, the concert hall has been turned into a cram school, complete with a large neon sign advertising instruction in numerous foreign languages.

My mother took me on summer pilgrimages to the house, posed me before the large iron gate, and took my photograph while I forced a smile of happiness and ownership. Every year, I stood there, worrying about what the truck drivers and deliverymen were thinking as they roared by on the busy road. I worried that she would step into the rushing traffic as she framed her shot, unaware that the boulevard of her youth was gone. I hoped that no one would emerge to see my mother smiling with a superior air over a house whose stucco was soot-blackened and chipped and whose gate had rusted half shut.

Now, as I look up at the façade, I see someone draw a curtain in one of the tall windows of the second story. A man in an undershirt yawns, briefly presses his head close to the glass, and disappears into the depths of the room.

I hear a tapping above me and look up to see the undershirted man gesturing at me: a twisting of the hand, fingers extended as if he were turning a large knob. He is asking me what I want and he is frowning. I don't know how to answer him. All my life I have wanted to go into the house, but that doesn't mean that now is the right moment. If I'm allowed in, all I can do is stand in the same space as the rest of them and imagine how it used to be. There will be nothing familiar for me to see.

The man throws his arms into the sleeves of a light-blue shirt and begins to button it from the bottom up, all the while looking at me through the window. I shrug and smile. When he is finished with the shirt, he waves me toward him, then disappears from view.

When the oak door opens, I see that he is skinny, with gray hair cropped close to his head.

"I'm late for work," he says. "Spit it out." And again the sharp twisting gesture of the hand, as if he wants to wrench a confession from me.

"My family used to own this house," I say, regretting a verb that might offend his possibly socialist sensibilities. "They used to live here."

"I *hope* they owned it. Be an expensive place to rent the whole thing, don't you think? I suppose you want to see it."

He scowls at me, his dark furrowed eyebrows in stark contrast to his silver hair. I nod.

"My apartment's only a one-bedroom," he says. Probably not much bigger than mine and Jonah's—assuming it'll still be mine and Jonah's when I get back.

"I don't need to see your apartment," I stammer. "I mean, it would be all right to just see the main spaces. That would be fine."

He moves aside and waves me in.

"What part of America are you from?"

"*Vostóni,*" I say—as if this pronunciation of the word can reclaim some of the Greek identity he has taken.

The first thing I notice is the smell, damp and layered with the odors of several different breakfasts: toast and eggs, coffee, and cinnamon. It is dark inside, and I look up to where the glass ceiling of the atrium should be and see a panel of white-painted wood with a light fixture hanging from it. Two of its three bulbs have burned out.

"Got a three-story ladder?" the man asks with a laugh. "The landlord won't bother until that third bulb goes."

"That used to be glass," I say.

"Used to be a lot of things, young lady."

And this is why my mother never tried to take me inside. If anyone had waved to her as we stood before the house all those summers, she would have ignored the signal, all the better to preserve in her memory what would always be the most important version of the house. I take a few steps into the foyer, toward the tall oak door that must have led to the front sitting room. Boots and umbrellas lean against the corner by the door. A peephole has been drilled through the oak and covered over with scratched plastic.

I know the man is watching me with amusement as I spin around slowly, taking in the handful of things about the house that I assume have not changed. There is a wide expanse of wall where the walnut mirror once stood—I am sure of it—and the swinging door Irini, the cook, would push through coming in from the kitchen, and the railing around the landing on the third floor, where my aunts and Nestor dangled their baskets and hooks. Yes, it is changed now, but the space is still the same, still redolent of everything I have ever imagined in it.

"When did you lose the house?" the man asks.

"We didn't lose it," I say, turning to face him. But I don't know that this is true. Perhaps we lost it in the Second World War, or in the civil war that came after it, or during the *junta*. No one has ever explained this to me.

"Well, when was the last time your family lived here?"

"Sometime after the war."

He waves his hand.

"Ages ago when it comes to houses."

"Please," I say, "could I see the basement?"

"The basement?"

I can see he thinks I am a strange American.

"Please."

"I told you I was late and now I'm even later."

I smile at him, waiting. He checks his watch.

"Fine," he sighs. "But be quick."

I know he wouldn't accommodate me if he thought I were truly Greek.

He leads me through the swinging door and down a flight of wooden steps to a narrow hallway tiled in black and white. Several doors open off the hallway, topped with transom windows and fitted with brass kickplates along the bottoms. All I can do is stand still and stare around me in wonderment.

"Seen it?" the man says, beginning to lead me away.

"Wait," I say, reaching out to stop him. He gives me an odd look, and I wish I had not touched him. "I'll meet you in the foyer in a few minutes."

"These are private storage rooms."

"I'm not going to take anything."

"Five minutes," he says, and heads upstairs.

Here again, my Americanness helps me. If I were completely Greek, he would fear I was a *gyftissa,* a gypsy or a thief.

Alone in the hallway, I give a little triumphant laugh. The basement is the exception that proves the rule, the one unchanged place that proves that all the other stories of my mother's childhood in this house must be true. This is where my mother and my aunts and Nestor flooded the hall one day so they could slide and skim across the tiles. This is where they raised silkworm cocoons before the war. This is where my mother showed a puzzling kindness to the little Italian boy, the baker's son, sneaking free cocoons up to him through the high basement windows as he crouched on the sidewalk outside.

I begin to test the doors to find the old scullery from which the children ran the hose through the transom window on the day they flooded the basement. The doors are not locked, or the locks are all broken, and I open one after another until I find the sink, a gray soapstone tub with square sides. Another gasp of satisfaction escapes me. I wish Aliki were here, or—and the thought surprises me—Jonah. I could start here, with this, my favorite story, to explain myself to him.

The story goes that, once they had the right water level in the hall and the doors were all closed to keep the water in, the girls pushed Nestor into the scullery through the transom window with the hose so he could turn off the faucet. Then they did their prewar version of a Slip'N Slide, with poor Nestor clamoring to come back out to the hall and play. When they were done, they opened the door and the water went down the drain, leaving the floor surprisingly clean and their parents none the wiser.

To me, this story epitomized the glory of my mother's childhood. Its setting was mundane—almost everyone I knew had a basement—but the mischief was extravagant. Who poured water *into* a house? Who dared to break such a fixed rule between order and chaos, domesticity and rebellion? It seemed like a heroic thing, almost, that my mother and her siblings had done. The closest I ever came to replicating this was the time I strapped the carriages of a toy train onto my feet and skated on them down the length of our ranch house. I crashed into the walnut-framed mirror, stared at my face pressed against the silvered glass, and got my first lesson that there was no re-creating someone else's past.

Now, in my mother's actual basement, I can't find the drain that should be in the scullery floor. The floor rebukes me with its smoothness, as if it lacked a navel, an *omphalos*. As if without the sign of an umbilical cord it bears no connection to anything that came before it. I stand there like a fool, embarrassed to have given even whispered voice to my mistaken enthusiasm. Embarrassed, too, to be putting such stock in so prosaic a thing as a basement. The missing drain proves nothing either way, I tell myself. Perhaps there was a renovation long ago; perhaps I have not found the right sink; perhaps I have simply misremembered the story. I close the door to the scullery and take one last look at the chessboard hallway before I head up the stairs.

"Find what you were looking for?" the man asks. He has put on a beige zippered jacket over the blue shirt, and he is holding a motorcycle helmet in one hand. I remember seeing a scooter locked to the rusted railing outside.

"Yes," I say, to be polite. "Thank you."

"I went to see the house," I tell Aliki. There is no need to tell her which one.

"It's looking pretty bad lately."

"The graffiti? How long has that been on there?"

"Awhile. If you clean it up, they'll just do it again."

"*You* don't—"

"No. The city cleans it. Sometimes."

"Aliki, I went in," I say, watching for her reaction.

She turns from the board where she is mincing garlic and leans back against the counter.

"Oh?"

"Some guy let me in. The atrium is covered. They put wood over it, with an ugly light up there."

"It was probably leaking. It happens to all these old houses."

"I really wanted to see it, the way the aunts always talked about it, with the light coming down."

I am waiting for her to share my enthusiasm with some imagined recollections of her own, but she gives me a wistful smile in which I detect a touch of pity.

"Had you never been in?" she says.

"No. Have you?"

"Almost twenty years ago now. I knew someone who lived there, actually. We used to have parties in her apartment when her parents were out."

"Aliki! You never told me this."

She shrugs. "We drank a lot at those parties. Maybe I forgot," she laughs. "The aunts are coming for lunch, by the way. Eager to see you."

"Good," I say, but I'm not interested in them now. "What was it like?" I go on. "Must have been weird for your friend."

"Oh, I never told her. *That* would have been weird." Aliki turns back to the counter and whips at a potato with a peeler.

"I went into the basement," I tell her. "Looking for the drain."

"The drain? To what?"

She doesn't turn around.

"When they flooded the basement. The drain in the scullery."

She picks up another potato.

"The story," I say. "How can you not remember?"

Aliki stops and sets her hands on the counter. She tips her head to one side but still won't turn around.

"I remember the story a little. Something about getting Nestor in trouble. Ask the aunts."

"I will," I say. "But there was more to it. Nestor probably has something about it in his stuff. Which I want to start going over as soon as possible."

"Yes, but wait until I can go with you. If the neighbors see some foreigner fiddling with the lock, it'll cause more trouble than it's worth."

I think about the way I am dressed—my jeans and my turtleneck and my beige wool peacoat. Dark hair and a straight nose don't make up for them.

"I can't believe you don't remember the basement story. I feel like I know every word."

Aliki shrugs again. "I don't know. It's not that big a deal."

"You used to think the stories were a big deal," I say. "When we were kids."

This makes her turn around.

"I'm not a kid anymore, Paki," she says, with an indulgent smile.

We are looking at each other, not speaking, and I am about to ask Aliki what's the matter when the front door opens and Demetra's singsong spills into the apartment. Aliki pushes off from the counter and returns to her potato peeling. Nikos leans into the kitchen doorway, Demetra's coat and scarf in his hands.

"What's cooking?" he says.

"Leg of lamb. Go wash your hands, Demetra."

The girl starts to whine.

"Listen to your mother," Nikos says, reaching for a garlic clove on the counter.

"I thought you had to work," I say.

"The boss called me in," he says, pointing to Aliki. "Rein-forcements."

"I needed a break," Aliki says, and I wonder whether she planned it so that I'd see my mother first alone.

Nikos is already out of the kitchen when the phone rings. I hear him answer it, sounding mistrustful, and I wonder if it is Jonah. But then I realize Nikos is speaking Greek, and I am pleased that my brain has made no distinction.

"It's for you. Someone called Anna?"

He holds the phone over to me and pops the garlic clove into his mouth.

"Yes, this is Calliope."

"Callie! *Ela!* Come with us to the parade, or do your boring relatives have a solid grip on you?"

Anna is shouting over the hum of a crowd in the back-ground. I steal a glance at Nikos, hoping he cannot hear what she is saying.

"No, but I don't know if I should."

I want to tell her that my relatives are not boring and I am happy to be in their company.

"Why not?" Anna persists. "Come with us. It'll be fun."

"You can wear my velvet hat!" Stelios shouts into the phone.

"You heard that?"

"Yes," I laugh. "Wait." I put my hand over the mouthpiece. "Some friends want me to meet them later tonight."

"But it's the parade," says Demetra.

"Are you going?" I ask Aliki.

"Yes, but go out with your friends. I don't want to keep you."

"No, I want to come with you, if that's all right."

"Sure."

This isn't quite the welcome I was looking for, but I'd rather choose family over these people I've only just met. I uncover the phone.

"Anna, thanks for the invitation, but my family's got plans."

"Come on! How much fun can they be? They're in mourning."

I don't bother to explain that though my uncle's death is new to me, my family has already begun to adjust around it.

"Sorry. But maybe another time?"

"Look, in case your plans change, we'll be near the northeast corner of Plateia Georgiou. It's an eight o'clock parade. See you there!"

Aliki is in the kitchen when I hang up the phone. I offer to help her with the cooking, but she tells me to relax.

"Who are your friends?"

"That's the thing. I just met them on the bus. I can't understand why they care this much about me."

"They're Greek, that's why. We're social creatures, Paki, always eager for the next new thing. Or you can chalk it up to the ancient code of hospitality. Or the next hot girl," she adds, giving me a leer.

"Oh, definitely the ancient code."

"It'll be nice to have you with us tonight," she says. "Demetra will be pleased to show you all the festivities." She jabs a knife into the lamb in several places and begins stuffing garlic cloves and knobs of butter into tiny slits. "I called your mother. Must have been after you left. She's coming to lunch too."

I realize that my mother's inclusion in this family group is an afterthought, and my old urge to protect her rises for a moment. I cringe at the thought of what she will say when she arrives. How could they forget about her? How could her own daughter come to her house and not invite her to join them for the meal?

"You should have had me tell her," I say.

"I know."

The regret in Aliki's voice signals that we are allies, both of us bound up now as always in my mother's indignation.

She asks about my morning visit and I give her a brief account, sparing her my mother's complaining, which she already knows about anyhow. I remember the lawyer, Constantopoulos.

"I should call him."

"Monday," Aliki says. "Don't even bother before then. You'll just make him mad and then he'll delay you on purpose."

"He would do that?" I can't imagine Jonah ever pulling a stunt like that.

"Yes, he would."

I think about how the old Yankees with the Mayflower names can hold up a gift if they think someone on our staff has been pushy. Maybe not so different.

I hear the aunts before I see them. They are outside the door to the apartment, chattering amiably about some disagreement or other. I expect a buzzer to sound, but the door opens and Aunt Thalia leaves her key in the lock to come embrace me.

"Calliope, Calliopaki!" she cries, alternately kissing me on the cheeks and hugging me close. I look over her shoulder to Aunt Sophia, who is drawing the key from the lock. Her face is utterly serious, as if nothing were going on around her except the task at hand.

The two sisters seem far younger than their years. Were it

not for her insistence on a bun and her standard outfit of skirt-and-cardigan, Sophia could pass for sixty instead of her actual seventy-four. She likes to point out that when she retired from her job at the harbor administration, everyone was shocked she was old enough. Thalia has let her dark hair go gray but keeps it in a modern cut, with short wisps that frame her face. Both of them are wearing black from head to toe, for Nestor.

"*Ela,* Sophia," Thalia says, rolling her eyes. "Leave the key."

"Mine doesn't stick," Sophia says. "Why does yours?"

Sophia hands Thalia the extracted key and holds me out in front of her. She is a tall woman even now, and she looks down at me with an appraising eye. "Calliope. We missed you," she says, and I know that this is true.

"How long are you staying, Calliopaki *mou*?"

"Just a few more days, *Theia* Thalia," I say, using the word for aunt. "I'm sorry I couldn't be here for the funeral."

"Poor boy," Thalia says, tearing up. "What are we going to do now, two old women?"

I wince at the number, wondering again what it is that keeps my mother on the other side of the dividing line.

"Have you seen your mother?" Sophia asks.

"Is she coming?" asks Thalia.

"Yes to both," I say, and for some reason they find this funny.

They agree to sit down in the living room, where Nikos arrives to serve them small glasses of wine. I hear the two women murmuring together that my Greek is very good, all the same.

Aliki is carrying the lamb to the table when the buzzer rings.

"I'll go," I say, embarrassed that my mother is the only aunt without a key of her own.

I buzz her up and wait for her in the hallway. When she

emerges from the elevator, I can tell she is disappointed to see only me.

"Am I the first?" she asks.

"Come in," I say, kissing her on the cheeks and dodging the question. She looks younger now that she is dressed, her bumps and angles smoothed out by a black sweater over dark-blue jeans.

The sisters all kiss as if they see one another every day, but I know from Aliki that they do not. I wonder if this is their way of pretending a closeness that no longer exists.

Nikos calls us to the table, where there is some tussling about where to sit. Thalia, in her former home, expects to be seated at the foot of the table, but my mother claims the spot without even saying anything. If her daughter is the guest of honor, then my mother is owed this bit of reflected tribute. Nikos settles the debate by assigning us all to specific seats. My chair faces the tall windows screened with filmy white drapes. Behind me is a sideboard of sleek ash topped with ceramic bowls in solid primary colors; from my seat, the old walnut dining table is the only thing I can see that is not crisp and simple.

The aunts want to know about my life in the States—not too much, just the demographic details of work and marriage. My ring is still twisted the wrong way around, and I keep my hands under the table until this part of my story is finished. I explain my job and brace myself for the puzzlement I saw in Marina and the others last night.

"But you sound like a *gyftissa*," Sophia says, "begging the rich for money."

"Or like a socialist," Thalia says, chuckling.

"It's not like that, *Theies*," I say, but don't clarify.

Thalia brightly turns to Demetra.

"Parade today! Are you going to march with your school?"

"She's not coming with us," Demetra says, pointing her fork at me.

"Demetra," Aliki says. "Don't say *she*. Say *Theia* Calliope."

Theia. Only in Greece can an only child be an aunt. Though I'm her mother's cousin, I am Demetra's *theia* the way Thalia and Sophia were mine.

"No, I *am* coming," I tell her. "You can be my guide to-night."

"What else were you going to do?" My mother looks up from her food.

"Some friends asked me to meet them for the parade."

"Well! It's about time you made some friends here," my mother says.

Thalia caresses my arm, as if claiming me from my mother. I can't resist.

"Yes, I met them yesterday. On the bus with the chickens," I say, looking at my mother with all innocence.

For a while we are all absorbed in our food, commenting on the tenderness of the lamb and the crispiness of the roasted potatoes. I'm relieved that Nikos is not responsible for the death of the lamb. He passes the bread around so that we can sop up the sauce in our plates.

"This is so good," I say, savoring the dense crumb of the loaf.

"Drimakopoulos bread," Thalia says. "For generations, we've been buying their bread and no other. Even when we had the taverna."

"*Theies,*" I say. "You know, I went to the house today." They all look up. "Someone let me in."

"How was it, Calliopaki *mou*?" Thalia asks. She sits back in her chair and puts her hands in her lap. My news has canceled her interest in the meal.

"Filthy, I'm sure," says Sophia. "Students and leftists living in it." She trails off, leaving us to assume the depredations caused by such people.

"It's not bad," I say. "It's apartments."

"Well, there is a nice one on the second floor," says Thalia. "It's your room," she nods to my mother, "and our room, plus the bathroom, and a little kitchen made out of part of Nestor's room, bless his soul."

"You haven't seen it, *Mamá*?" I ask.

"Your mother won't come with us," Thalia says, and I can't tell if my mother was even going to answer me. But she has an answer ready for her sister.

"Why should I come?" she says. "I can't understand why the two of you feel the need to go visiting these people who have ruined our beautiful home."

"But that's the point, isn't it, Clio," Sophia says. "It's not our beautiful home anymore. It hasn't been for decades." There's a tone in her voice that I can't quite place. I watch her for a moment, but she reveals nothing.

"Clio, we have simply gone a few times to see how the house has changed. That's all," Thalia says. "Now, Nikos, will you stop hoarding that lamb and let me get another taste of my daughter's cooking?"

Nikos obliges, visibly relieved that his mother-in-law has changed the topic. I concentrate on my food.

"Well," my mother says. "What did you do in the house, Calliope?"

"I went down to the basement."

"What on earth for?" Thalia asks.

"Come on, you remember the story. *Mamá* must have told it to me and Aliki a million times."

"What story?" Demetra asks.

"About the old house." Aliki says it in an offhand way.

"Your poor uncle got into huge trouble for that prank," Thalia says.

"I couldn't find the drain," I say, waiting.

"Drain? There was no drain," says Sophia.

I remind the aunts of the story of the basement flood the way my mother always told it to me—with the hose, and the water, and the scullery door opened, and the drain. As I recite the story, I feel my allegiance shifting from the girls to Nestor, who never got to join the game. All these years, I have been blind to the fact that the sisters' gaiety rested on the despair of their little brother.

"That's not how it happened," Sophia says. "There wasn't any drain."

"Yes, there was," says my mother. "In the scullery. Are you sure you looked properly, Calliope?"

"I checked the whole floor. Moved boxes out of the way."

"Well, you must have missed it. Because what fool wouldn't have a drain in the scullery?"

"Then our parents were fools, because I'm telling you there was no drain," Sophia says.

"Clio," says Thalia softly, "don't you remember about the rice?"

"No."

"What rice, *Theia* Thalia?"

"When Nestor opened the scullery door to come out into the hall," Thalia says gently, patting my arm again, "the water went into that room and it had already gone into the other rooms as well."

"Water seeks its own level," says Nikos.

"Nestor wasn't supposed to open the door," my mother says.

"Can we speak kindly," Thalia pleads, "of the man who just died?"

"What were we going to do, Clio?" says Sophia. "Leave the boy in there forever?"

Sophia takes the story over, speaking directly to me, as if I am the only one who needs to have her version of family history set straight.

"One of the storerooms was full of food. Bags of rice and flour. This was during the war," she says. "Imagine."

"It was not during the war," says my mother. "I was only sixteen. I know because I remember the book I brought home from school that day."

"If it wasn't during the war, it was right before the war. Anyhow," Sophia goes on, "you can imagine what happened to that food when water got to it."

"It was one giant rice pudding," Thalia says to Demetra, pinching her cheek.

"All of it ruined," says Sophia. "When we needed supplies like that."

My mother exhales loudly. "None of it was ruined, because the water went down the drain," she says.

I shake my head. "There wasn't one."

"Then someone," she says, her voice rising, "must have changed it. Things change, Calliope, you know. Because there was a drain in the scullery in the old house when we were children before the war."

"What's so important about a dumb drain?"

We all look at Demetra, who is pouting into her plate. Thalia caresses her head.

"It is dumb, Demetraki," I say, laughing. "You're absolutely right. Tell us about the parade."

Demetra brightens and describes the floats and performers she can't wait to see tonight. We listen, happy to share in the little girl's excitement as we pick at the nuts and oranges that Aliki has set out on the table. Finally, Nikos rises and leads the aunts to the living room.

In the kitchen, I scrape sauce and bits of lamb into the garbage while Aliki stacks the plates. In the hubbub of the aunts, she has forgotten that I'm supposed to be treated specially. It feels good.

"Do you, at least, remember the story?" I ask.

"I don't think anybody does, Paki. It's all so long ago, and they're old women now. They're starting to forget things."

"True, but that's not what just happened here."

"Look," she says, setting the plate down. "*Áse to*. Leave it alone. We grew up with some nice stories. Sometimes they told them one way, sometimes another. Leave it at that. Nikos reads and reads about the war and the civil war, and he's never any clearer on the details. Even the historians can't agree on what really happened."

As I dry the plates Aliki hands me, I tell myself that she's right and I should take her approach. It shouldn't matter. These are only stories, after all. But I can't deny that it does matter to me. My mother's stories were the one way I had of connecting to her—of finding some shared refuge from the cloud of her unhappiness. During the winters when I was far from Thalia's embraces and Sophia's loving vigilance, those stories gave me a glimpse of mischief and delight. I can't let them go that easily.

4

Clio

May 1940

Clio turned and watched as a low-slung Citroën drove down the dusty street. Her father still insisted on a carriage, declaring that cars were for the profligate. Whoever owned the Citroën might be profligate, but he had passed by with a white-sleeved elbow resting stylishly on the open window, gauntleted fingers drumming the top of the door frame.

The car tires had kicked up more dust than carriage wheels did. Clio could feel it sticking to her neck where she had begun to sweat a little. The leaves of the sycamores were too young to shade the sidewalks properly, and though there were weeks left to the school year, there was a summer heat in the air. She slowed her pace and let her sisters and brother pass her. After a few steps, they turned and waited.

"Speed up, Clio," Sophia said. "Come on."

"Go on without me. I don't care."

"Fine."

Sophia turned forward again and murmured something to Thalia, who took a peek over her shoulder. Nestor pressed up behind them. They walked on like that, a few paces ahead of Clio but never outpacing her. Clio knew they desperately wanted to go faster, to get home to lunch and shade, but they were incapable of breaking free. She was their eldest sister, after all, and they always followed her—even when they walked ahead.

By the time they reached the house, Thalia could bear it no longer and bounded up the front steps. She yanked one of the doors so wide open that it banged against the house, and Clio heard a cry from inside—Irini, the cook, yelling at her again. Clio arrived on the top step and stood in the doorway for a moment, exhaling and easing her shoulders back. She pulled the door shut behind her. Thalia, Sophia, and Nestor were long gone, their leather book bags in a heap in the foyer.

Clio looked up at the atrium window, noting the direction of the shaft of light that marked the black-and-white foyer floor like a sundial. It was pointing to her left, toward the study door: early afternoon. She could hear faint sounds of clanging pot lids coming from the kitchen at the back of the house. Straight ahead of her, on the other side of the atrium, the open doors to the dining room revealed the long table already set with china and silver for lunch. A newspaper rattled in the study, and her mother said something softly, to which her father murmured a reply. Nestor burst out of the back hall, crossed the atrium, and ran up the wide stairs to the landing and the inner balcony that ringed the airy space. He went into his room, where she could hear him opening and closing his dresser drawers.

Clio turned to face the large mirror that leaned against the foyer wall in a frame of dark carved wood. She set her book bag down and nudged it away with her foot as she adopted a pose: left hip cocked, weight on the left foot, right foot slid outward with the toe pointed to the side. She moved a hand to her hip and gave her reflection a hard stare, chin out like Garbo, with the same slight waves in her shoulder-length hair. She brought her face close to the glass and raised one eyebrow, letting her lips form a tiny, mocking smile. With her face this close to the mirror's surface, she could forget about her school uniform with its cobalt-blue pinafore over a crisp white shirt. She could picture herself in that Citroën, wearing stockings and heels instead of the white ankle socks that peeked out of her brown T-strap sandals. With her face this close, all she could see was the olive skin of a young girl whose high cheekbones and straight nose were about to make her beautiful.

She drew back from the mirror and saw Sophia and Thalia standing behind her, pulling faces. She wheeled around.

"Hey!" she cried, and the other two fell into smothered laughter. They staggered off, giggling and thrusting their hips from side to side. It was fine for them to tease, but at fourteen and twelve they were children still, Sophia's braids tight and long and Thalia's curls only faintly controlled with a ribbon headband. They had no idea yet what it would mean to be grown up.

Clio gave her book bag a kick and wandered over to the square of light coming down from the atrium.

She turned her closed eyes up into the sun, thinking of what to do until her parents or Irini called her for lunch. She didn't want lunch. The food would be heavy and rich, and there would be too much of it. Two main courses to choose from, then cooked vegetables like *fassolakia* or a *gratinée,* and then fruit and possibly even dessert. She wanted something else.

"No!" Irini shouted as soon as Clio pushed through the kitchen door. "No, go right back out, young lady. The food will be out when it's ready."

Clio opened a cupboard and drew out a jar full of *vanilia,* a sticky vanilla mastic.

"I'll be gone in a minute," she said, reaching for a glass and filling it with water from a pitcher she took from the refrigerator.

"You're ruining your appetite," Irini said.

"Irini, nothing could make me skip a meal that you had cooked."

She dug a spoonful of mastic out of the jar and dunked the spoon into her water glass. This is what she wanted now, something sweet: an *ypovrichio*. A submarine. She gave Irini a smile over her shoulder as she pushed back out of the kitchen.

"Now they'll all be coming in here for an *ypovrichio,*" Irini was muttering.

Clio took the stairs down to the basement, looking for someplace quiet and cool where her sisters and brother would not come and pester her to get them a treat as well. She sat down on the bottom step at one end of a long hall lined with storerooms and sucked at the *vanilia,* gazing at her image on the back of the spoon.

The sounds of cart wheels and footsteps and the occasional car motor came faintly through the basement windows. People were heading home for lunch all over Patras. In Clio's neighborhood, cooks were spooning lamb or chicken and pilaf or her father's favorite, *moussaká,* onto porcelain platters. They were sprinkling salads with oregano and olive oil and salt. By the harbor, dockworkers were eating fried anchovies from a paper cone or tugging chunks of pork *souvlaki* from bamboo skewers with their teeth. At school, some of the boys would come back to the classroom with little dabs of oil glazing their fingernails where they hadn't thought to clean. She didn't think she could like a boy with oily nails.

As Clio was readjusting her position on the step, she spilled some water onto the tiles of the basement floor. She thought nothing of it until she rose, spoon in hand, to peer up at the sidewalk through one of the windows. She slipped on the water, and, losing her balance, spilled more onto the floor. A child now, she pushed off with one foot and let her other ride the film of moisture in a short glide. She was doing this a second time when Thalia appeared on the stairs.

"What're you doing?"

"Nothing."

"Where'd you get the *vanilia*?"

"You can't have one. You'll ruin your appetite."

"What're you doing?" It was Nestor now.

Clio should have known that they would not be able to stay away. Wherever she went, they came to find her. Even when they mocked her, that was only because they found her too interesting—or too mysterious—to leave alone.

She had an idea.

"I'll show you, Nestor. Come here."

The boy came to her side and she tousled his hair. He had dark black curls that apparently came from their father, whom she couldn't imagine as anything but bald. Sophia had joined Thalia now and they both crept farther down the stairs.

"What is it?" Thalia asked.

Clio drained the water glass and set it down by the foot of the steps.

"I have an idea. Thalia, go find some boots from the equipment room, and you two close all the doors."

"Why?" Sophia had her hands on her hips.

"Because." Clio gave her the hard look she had practiced in the mirror.

Sophia withstood it for a few seconds and then joined Thalia in shutting the storeroom doors. When they were finished, Clio beckoned them into the scullery.

"We need the hose," she said.

"I'll get it." Nestor grabbed the coiled hose from a hook on the wall. Clio attached it to the faucet and unwound the loops. She fed the hose through the transom window at the top of the scullery door and ran a length of it along the hall.

"Now," she said, "watch."

She turned on the water.

"Clio!"

"What are you doing?"

"We can't do that!"

"Yes, we can." She closed the scullery door and watched as the water spread slowly across the tiles. "Everybody grab a boot," she said. "And don't make noise or they'll come down and catch us."

They took off their shoes and socks and set them on an upper step, then stuffed one foot each into a boot, hastily tucking the laces down beside their anklebones. By the time they were done, water was lapping the thresholds of the closed doors.

"Sophia, turn the water off," Clio said.

"I can't. If I open the door, I'll let the water out."

"Fine."

Clio tossed the still-running hose back in through the transom.

"Come on, Nestor. You're the only one who can fit."

Two years younger at fourteen, Sophia was already as tall as Clio. With Sophia's help, Clio lifted Nestor on her shoulders and pushed him through the transom. His one booted foot thudded against the door as he came down on the other side. She heard him yelping at the cold spray of the hose.

"Come on," she said, and launched herself the length of the

hallway, sliding on her boot on an inch of water. Spray shot up in a rooster tail behind her, hissing against the walls and drumming lightly against the oak doors. She held her pose all the way down the hall, glorying in the stately movement. Sophia and Thalia laughed and started down behind her. She waited until they reached the end and splashed back up the hall.

"Hey," Nestor called from inside the scullery. "I want a turn!"

"Nestor, if you open the door, the water will spread all over and it won't work."

"That's not fair! I'm opening the door!"

But he didn't. And Clio knew he would not dare to do anything to make her mad.

Thalia crowed and pushed off for another turn along the tiles.

"Shh," Clio said. "Irini will hear you."

Clio took a running start and threw her right foot out in front of her, gliding along with her arms outstretched. The other two started up again, mugging for each other as they passed like gliding statues. Their hems were nearly soaked, and stray locks of dampened hair stuck to their cheeks. They swept it back from their foreheads and made faces at each other.

"You look like Tyrone Power," Sophia said.

"Like Ramón Novarro," said Thalia, in a deep voice.

"Watch me," Clio said. As she pushed off, she threw her chin up and arched her back like women she had seen dancing the tango.

Clio could hear Nestor murmuring tearfully through the scullery door.

"Not much longer," she told him.

"Come on, Clio," Nestor snuffled. "Let me open the door."

The truth was that she had already lost interest in the game, and it bothered her that her sisters seemed to be enjoying it more than she was. It had been her idea, but the promise of mischief had turned out to be more exciting than the experience.

"All right, Nestor," she said, and opened the door.

Nestor ran to the base of the stairs and launched himself across the ebbing water with a look of grim desperation on his face. By the time he reached the end of the hall, the water had gone and he jerked to a halt on dry tiles.

"Now look what you've done," said Sophia. She was standing in the open doorway, watching the water flow into the scullery.

"What?" Clio said.

Nestor kicked the end wall with his booted foot.

"Over here." Sophia was pointing to a darkened corner of the room that was piled with large sacks and bundles. The water had rolled there in a broad, flat wave. "I'm getting a mop," she said.

"It's just sheets," Clio said. "They'll dry." She stooped to drag a bag out of the way of the water. But the bag was different. Instead of the soft patina of worn cotton, she felt rough cloth, like the feed bags they gave to the horses at the farm. "What is this?"

She tugged, and the contents of the bag hissed and settled. It was rice. Next to it were five more and, farther along, six bags of flour, with black stenciling that marked them as twenty kilos each. The bags were tucked into a corner—where the room sloped down toward the outer wall of the house—and almost seemed to be hidden in the darkness of the scullery.

"It's flour," Sophia said. She held the mop out to her side, where it dripped into the film of water with tiny pocking sounds.

"I can see that now," Clio said.

"What's all this flour doing down here?" Thalia said. "What are we, a bakery?"

"It's wet," said Nestor. He had gone into the very corner of the room and was nudging at one of the bags with his toe.

There were footsteps on the stairs—three impatient steps—then Irini's voice.

"Upstairs! Now!"

Clio turned to the others.

"Close the door. We'll take care of this later."

"But the water," said Nestor.

"We have to go."

Clio made the first move, grabbing her shoes from the dry step and beginning to put her socks on. She knew the other three were watching her as they smoothed their uniforms down and pulled their socks over damp feet.

"Don't say anything about this," Clio warned them. "Is that clear?"

They nodded and marched into the dining room, where their parents were already sitting at opposite ends of the long table carved of dark wood.

"What's the matter with you children?" said their mother. Urania set her sketchbook on the sideboard, watching with a bemused expression as the children took their seats.

Their father folded his newspaper and tucked it by his plate, peering across the room through round glasses whose dark rims stood out against his bald head. He was a tall man with an upright posture, but he had a habit of slouching down in his chair, perhaps to better match his wife's plumper, smaller form. "Why so solemn?" he said.

"Nothing," Clio said. But she'd never seen such a hoard of staples in their house before. Whenever they needed anything, their mother sent Irini out to buy it. The only thing Clio had ever seen in bulk that belonged to her family were the crates of raisins piled in the warehouses for export.

"We're starving," Thalia said. "That's what's the matter." She reached across Nestor's place for the basket of warm bread from Marinelli's bakery.

"Thalia," her mother said, unfolding her napkin with a flourish. "Ask."

"Can I have the bread, please, Nestor?" Thalia said, in an annoyed singsong.

"Why is your hair all wet?" asked their father.

"It's hot out. We're sweaty," Clio said.

"Well, perhaps you should clean up before you return to school."

They passed the platters of chicken in red sauce, stewed okra, and potatoes around the table while their father asked them what they had learned in school that morning.

"Nothing," said Thalia.

"Ah," their father said. "Then what happened to you at school on this singularly uneducational day? Nestor?"

"I had a fight with Kostas Dolos."

"That wasn't a fight," Sophia said. "All you did was shove each other."

"It was a fight. I fought him."

"And why, Nestor, were you fighting Kostas Dolos?" their father said. He pushed his glasses up on his nose.

"He made fun of me."

"Why?"

"Because I'm a Boy Scout."

"You *were* a Boy Scout," her mother said, with a tight smile.

"Leave it alone, Urania," her father said.

"It's true, isn't it? Or should he join the Youth Movement, Leonidas? Because that's his only option now."

"Metaxas can lead this country out of disorder."

"And into fascism."

"Urania."

"And if our own fascism won't do, we can join someone else's. I hear there's a lively movement across the Adriatic."

"Urania, that's enough now." He had raised his voice so slightly that no one but Clio and her mother seemed to notice.

"At least the Metaxas Youth have a nice uniform," Clio said. She set her glass down and cocked her head at Nestor, trying to make him smile.

Her parents both looked at her as if surprised she had heard their conversation.

"This topic is not for you, young lady," her father said. "Or for any of us at what should be a pleasant meal."

Clio took a long drink of water to hide her irritation. She was old enough to know what was going on, old enough to have seen Nestor crying when he had to turn his Scouting things over to the uniformed boys from Ioannis Metaxas's Greek Youth. Old enough to recognize the fascist graffiti that was turning up on buildings she passed on her way to school.

The Greek Youth boys had come to the house in a group of three, calling themselves a battalion of national defenders. The Boy Scouts were a foreign institution, they said, and Metaxas was showing the nation how to reclaim its legacy of honor. There was one boy Clio didn't recognize, though they all looked the same in their dark-blue uniforms and white braided bandanas. They gave her father the stiff-armed Roman salute and left with Nestor's Scouting things, their white spats flashing as they descended the front stairs.

This meal was not the first time her parents had disagreed over Metaxas and his vision for a regimented Greece, but Clio still couldn't make up her mind with whom she sided. Her mother would sometimes simply recite the names of authors whose books had been burned under Metaxas's orders, the painters whose work had been removed from museums. When those lists failed to move Leonidas, Urania would remind him that Metaxas had abolished parliament, a rhetorical move that silenced Leonidas, at least temporarily. Clio wanted to take her mother's view, but her father said Metaxas had brought order to a nation that sorely needed it. He had pushed back the dangerous forces of communism in Greece but had even so established institutions that would take care of the population. What could be bad about that?

Out in the foyer once lunch was finished, Clio checked her reflection in the walnut mirror.

"Come on," Sophia whispered, tugging at her arm. "We need to go to the basement."

"I'm coming. Give me one second."

She redid her barrette. Thalia was making faces over her shoulder.

"Where's Nestor?" Sophia asked.

"I thought he was with you."

"Well, he's not."

They found Nestor in the scullery, swinging a mop at the water that had gathered by the bags of rice and flour. He was grunting with the effort—trying, Clio thought, to be valiant, like a Scout.

"Nestor."

When he turned, she saw that he was crying.

"I'm trying to get the water away," he said.

He let the mop fall and began to tug at one of the sodden bags. His feet scrabbled at the scullery tiles and the bag wouldn't move.

"Come on, Clio. Help me."

As she joined him in the corner, she heard Irini's voice.

"What is going on here?"

Irini headed past Sophia and Thalia and straight for Clio and Nestor, who was pushing at the mop.

"What have you done, boy?"

"It's not his fault."

"Did you do this?"

"We were playing," Clio said. "I'm sorry."

"You were *playing*?"

Clio didn't answer.

"Look at this." Irini waved her arms wide and then brought them together over her mouth. "Just look at what you've done now. All this food, ruined." She wheeled around to Clio. "Do you know what this is worth? And what it will be worth in a few months or, who knows, even weeks?"

She grabbed the mop from Nestor, who was sniveling into his sleeve. Freed of his tool, he dashed over to Clio and buried his head in her stomach.

"Sometime soon, people will kill for this," Irini raged. "Only you've gone and ruined it. Spoiled children. No sense of value."

"Irini!"

Clio's mother stood in the doorway. Sophia and Thalia moved aside to let her pass, their eyes wide as they stared at Clio.

Nestor pressed his back against the bags, as if to hide them. Clio tried to think of what her parents would take away from Nestor as punishment. There was already no Scouting. And what would they take away from her? The next dance? The new gown she expected?

"There's water," Nestor said.

Her mother gave him a bright smile, but Clio could see the dismay on her face.

"So there is! Off to school with you, though. Irini can take care of this."

"But the bags," Clio said.

"The bags?" She glanced over at the bags of rice and flour piled in the corner. "They'll dry out too," she said. "No need to worry."

Clio squinted at her, but her mother made no acknowledgment of the look. She didn't even acknowledge Irini, who stood fuming with the mop in one clenched hand. Instead, she shooed all four of them up the stairs to the foyer. She smiled over them as they gathered their school bags, held a handkerchief for Nestor to blow his nose into, and waved them out the door. Clio turned to watch her. She was standing in the open door, her hand held aloft in a wave. She looked like a figure in a painting. Her green dress stood out against the house's white façade, and a large bougainvillea billowed magenta at the corner. She smiled as if there were nothing wrong at all—as if it were nothing to store hundreds of kilos of flour and rice in the basement, and nothing to find that all that food was ruined.

Once they were a block away from the house, Nestor seized Clio's arm and began to jump up and down beside her.

"She didn't yell at us!" he crowed. "She wasn't mad!"

Clio let her arm hang loose as Nestor shook her body like a whip. She thought of the muted dismay behind her mother's smile.

"No. She wasn't."

But her mother's false cheer worried her. She suspected that soon enough she would long for her mother's run-of-the-mill anger, and for a time when there was no need for emergency supplies, or for little boys to wear uniforms except for fun, or for gangs of fascists to paint slogans on the sides of stately mansions. The time was coming when they would look back even on the strangeness of this day and yearn for its comforts.

5

Callie

Friday

Aliki and I make our way to Nestor's house through streets that are now busy with people returning home from lunches at restaurants and other people's houses. Here and there we can hear bands and small orchestras practicing music for the evening's parade. Nestor's house is on a quiet block of Ellinos Stratiotou, Hellenic Soldier Street.

As we approach it, I see that, at least from the outside, the house is unchanged: a squat one-story building with a tall, thin door, the whole thing nearly covered over with greenery. There is and always was something of the castle in the atmosphere of this tiny house near the harbor; surrounded by taller, grander buildings, it still projects an air of safety and strength. I stand on the sidewalk, taking it all in, while Aliki goes to unlock the door. It groans open, and she calls to me to follow.

"You've got your work cut out for you," Aliki says. "We both do."

Everything is exactly as it was five years ago. The square foyer with its hat stand and oval mirror; Nestor's broad desk facing out from the French doors to the garden; the velvet couch dimly visible in the living room to my right. The house smells, as always, of ground coffee, roasted dark and bitter. Aliki and Nikos will change all this. They'll bring their modern furniture in, and they'll add another story, and they'll fill the airy rooms with Demetra's toys. It's a nice idea, but it still makes me a little sad that this house, too, will exist only in memory.

I follow Aliki into the living room and find cardboard boxes arranged in rows along the shelves where books are stuffed into every open space. Papers lie on top of the boxes; books lie open on chairs and on the velvet couch.

"Is this how you found it?"

"Yes. He was working on something. He was preparing for his death, I guess, since they'd told him he was sick."

I pick up a sheaf of yellowing foolscap covered with Nestor's blocky handwriting. It is a list of song titles—Greek ballads whose names I don't recognize—each one cross-referenced with the number of a cassette tape.

"Aliki, how am I supposed to manage this?"

For the first time in my life, it occurs to me that Nestor might have been a hoarder, and that this charming habit of documenting and collecting his way through life might actually hide a grim obsession. I force myself to reject the thought.

"You think there's something in here my mother wants?"

"I had that distinct impression."

Aliki switches on a floor lamp with a dark paper shade.

"Little by little, Paki. And I'll help. Once Demetra is back in school, it'll be easier."

"You said she doesn't go back to school until after Lent begins. I need to be finished before then."

"Even if you find the lawyer, he probably won't do much until after *Katharotheftéra,* Clean Monday. There's not much you can do about it."

Clean Monday is the first day of Lent, March 6 this year. That is ten days away. And my plane leaves Athens the day before Clean Monday.

We make a space in the living room and begin to group boxes in piles according to their subject. Music by the back wall, films by the front, and photographs on and beside the couch and the coffee table. I find a box of cassette tapes and another of metal reel-to-reel spools stacked on top of one another so they look like a keg of beer. There is no dust here, and I picture Nestor in slippers and a cardigan, spending what would become his last weeks poring over the objects that defined his life.

"Calliope, look!" Aliki says, holding up a little wooden box.

I go closer and see a shallow tray in which are set a series of pits and nuts—almond, peach, cherry, hazelnut—each one identified with a label pinned beside it, the way an entomologist preserves bugs.

"From the farm," she says. "There's a date: 1940. *Amán,*" she says with a shudder. It's the Turkish word Greeks use to express dismay—the same word Stelios used on the bus when he heard why I was going to Patras.

"Poor kid," I say. "No clue what was coming."

It is a year to make a person shudder—the last year of calm for Greece. Not that anytime in that first half of the century was truly calm in the Balkans, with one war leading straight to another. But just a few months after the spring of 1940, Ioannis Metaxas rejected Mussolini's ultimatum and boys nine years older than Nestor headed off to fight the Italians in Albania. Almost every boy Nestor's age was enlisted in Metaxas's fascist youth brigades. I know there is a false poignancy here, borrowed from the magnitude of later events, but I do feel sorry for the young Nestor, who put together this tidy box of remnants from the farm as the disorder of another, bigger war was bearing down on the world around him.

"At least they always had the farm to go to," I say, handing the tray back to Aliki.

"I guess."

I think of the farm the way my mother always described it—as an idyll of everything a child could want. Fresh air and liberty to wander all day long, coupled with every imaginable treat for all the senses. There were separate orchards for cherries, pears, apricots, and peaches, and rows of high bushes producing several varieties of berry. And beyond the orchards that surrounded the farmhouse were the Notaris vineyards, full of grapes to be dried into raisins and then exported throughout Europe. The children spent their days running through the vineyards and climbing into the trees, filling baskets and their mouths with glistening fruit.

When I was growing up, there were plenty of treats around but never much real food in our kitchen—to the delight of my friends, who often helped me sneak slabs of expensive chocolate or jars of sticky Greek syrups from my mother's stash. My mother couldn't make a meal, but she could give you a great dessert any time of day or treat you to some candy for breakfast. I realized at some point that she'd probably never learned to cook, since her family had people to do that for them and she didn't live on her own until she was in her mid-twenties, after that failed attempt to share with Sophia. If nourishment occurred to my mother at all, it was as if she expected me to climb a tree, the way she and her siblings had on the farm.

I go back to the trays of cassette tapes. Beethoven's

symphonies—all of them in order—recorded from the Greek National Orchestra broadcasts in the sixties; bouzouki music; Rachmaninoff concertos. I feel the pull of these boxes and trays, the temptation to touch every object they contain.

"Which came first?" I say, sighing. "Bachelorhood or hoarding?"

"I think we just saw proof he was always like this."

"True." A little boy in shorts and high socks, sticking pins in slips of paper to identify the pits of what he ate.

I look at my watch: It's four o'clock. Two and a half more hours for today.

"Are you going to get married, Paki?"

I look at her. The nickname doesn't soften the force of the question that comes out of nowhere. I force a laugh.

"You sound like the aunts. You think I'm going to end up like Nestor?"

"Just that you haven't mentioned anybody." She's giving me a tentative smile. "Is there anybody?"

I can't answer this.

"What is it, Paki?"

I turn my head down, tucking the last batch of cassettes into a larger box. I hold my hand out, palm up, so that the stones show. It feels like I'm giving her something, which in fact I am.

"It's an engagement ring. His name's Jonah. I'm engaged."

"*Ré,* Calliope." She makes the Greek gesture of exasperation: body arched backward, chin tucked in, arms extended downward. "When were you going to say something?"

She stumbles over the piles and boxes and gives me a tight hug.

"I'm not an idiot, you know," she says. "I saw the ring last night, but I wasn't sure. Then you didn't want to call anyone. And then you turned the ring around, so I started to wonder."

"We argued before I left. We might be breaking it off. I don't know."

"Why?"

I pick at the cardboard flap on the box.

"I can't, Aliki. It's too much. There's so much . . . risk."

"But you *are* a risk-taker. You were always trying everything when we were growing up."

"Because it didn't matter. With marriage, it matters. It's the kind of thing you have to get right."

"Do you think everyone gets it right?"

"You know I don't believe that."

"Do you think Nikos and I get it right? Because we don't. Not always."

"Yeah, but my parents." I can't get the rest of the words out. After a bit, I look up at her. "Back when my mother sold the house, we took the pictures off the walls. You know what was behind them? Holes. All these places where they'd punched the walls. Marriage was like a cage for them, Aliki. Like a prison."

"Yours won't be."

"How do you know that?"

I keep picking at the box, tearing a strip of cardboard from the flap.

"So his name is Jonah?"

I nod.

"You could have told me, Paki."

"Well, you and I had kind of lost touch the last few years."

"Whose fault was that?"

I look sharply up at her. This is a surprise—and then I realize it's true. I had let myself believe the comforting notion that my disconnect with Aliki was the product of a mutual falling away. In fact, after my sudden decision five years ago not to visit her, there were several phone messages, for holidays and regular days, that I just never got around to answering. The longer I went without replying, the harder it became to pick up the phone.

"Sorry, Paki," she says. "I didn't need to say that."

"It's okay," I say. "I deserve it."

I slap my hands against my thighs and let out a big sigh.

"I'm going to slit my wrists if we keep talking like this, Aliki. Let's go back to sifting through a dead man's hoard. I'm going to switch to the other room," I say, and weave through the furniture to Nestor's study.

I twist my hair into a knot and look around me. There are boxes stacked up against the wall, each one with a series of numbers on it—some cataloging system of Nestor's devising. I open them one by one and list the carefully packed contents on the box in words I can understand: clothes; books; newspapers. There are yellowed newsprint pages announcing the end of Greek civil-war hostilities in 1949; the 1967 coup and the military *junta;* the fall of the *junta* seven years later; and the 1981 election of Papandreou's socialist government. It's hard to discern Nestor's political leanings from these, but they are all important milestones in Greece's path to a false and tenuous stability. He has carefully folded a front-page article with an image of a drachma note crossed out like a one-way street. He won't be around to see the euro take the drachma's place. I linger over the 1989 clipping about the decree that declared the civil war just that—a civil war and not a communist insurgency. Nestor grew furious every time he thought of this—this law that gave pensions to former communist guerrillas and allowed them to hold the property they had taken by force from their own compatriots.

I find a box that is marked 38/4-12/ΣΠΙΤΙ. Here is my mother's refrain: *To Spiti.* The House. When I pull back the cardboard flaps, the smell of mothballs stings my nostrils. These are freshly poured, still sending fumes into the air. I look again at the marking and wonder how recent the ink is. I reach in and wrap my hand around a tin can through whose end is threaded a length of string. I pull gently, and the connected can rattles its way out of the box. I laugh.

"What?" Aliki calls.

"Nothing. I sneezed," I lie.

But I can't believe it. Inside this box are things I wish I had seen before my visit to the old house—things that would have given me the certainty that at least some of my mother's stories are true. I carefully remove a few more things from the box: toy *Karagiozis* shadow puppets tied together with a ribbon; a basket with another length of string attached to its handle.

This is the basket the children lowered through the atrium on a pulley. These cans connected with string are the telephone my mother and the rest used to send messages across the atrium's open space. I tell myself that this box is simply one among many in a lifetime of collection. But it feels as though Nestor has assembled the contents with me in mind, folding together his and my mother's pasts with my present.

I move on to a square wooden chest and lift the lid. My hand flies to my mouth and I stand there looking down at what must be a hundred vials of sand. Each one is topped by a tiny cork, and each one rests in its own small compartment, separated by a cardboard grid. I squat down and pull one vial up, turning it so that some of the grains of sand catch the light from the floor lamp. In block letters on a tiny white label, Nestor has written *October 1952 Koukounariés,* the name of a beach in Skiathos known for its golden sand. Here it is in my hand, on the other side of Greece, golden and glimmering. I imagine I can hear the sand hissing as it tumbles inside the tiny vial. I pull up another: *August 1975 Perissa Santorini*. Black sand like caviar. *1953 Gérakas Zakynthos*. From the year of the earthquake.

I once asked Nestor if he had ever thought to put the sand in hourglasses instead. I was tipping the vials from side to side, watching the grains pile up and diminish as we talked. No, he said, and asked me if I could guess why. I was just a teenager then, but I sensed that the vials were already his way of marking time. The collection itself was a story, a chronicle of his travels and his life. To put the sand in hourglasses would be redundant. I still remember how pleased he was with this answer. He had tears in his eyes that made me a little embarrassed, but I remember the deep satisfaction I think we both felt in being understood.

"I'm going to make a coffee," Aliki calls, and I can hear her coming to the study. "Do you want one? Then we can go home a bit before the parade."

I turn and look at her with what must certainly be a goofy smile.

"Are you all right, Paki?"

"Come see this."

She comes over to the box and peers in.

"The sand," she says, with a laugh.

"We used to pull this out all the time. It's like he couldn't tell a story without starting here."

"I think that was your thing, just the two of you."

"Not you?"

She shakes her head.

"You were his audience, Paki. That's why he left the stuff for you."

Aliki goes into the kitchen, but I stay there by the wooden chest for a moment longer. Of all the things of Nestor's that I have found and will find before I finish this task, I know that this archive of sand is what I want with me. It's a strange legacy, but it's mine, a chronicle written in something that never holds a trace.

I watch as Aliki gathers the coffee makings, seemingly at home in Nestor's kitchen. I, too, could have had this familiarity if I had not chosen to stay away for so long. Nestor and his loving home with its collections and recordings; the protective touch of Thalia's hand on my arm; having a *parea,* a group of Greek friends of my own: This is what I gave up when I cut myself off from my mother's world. My world.

Aliki holds the little coffeepot so that it hovers over the gas flame, raising it and lowering it as the liquid froths. She pours me a tiny cup and slides it across Nestor's marble-topped table. She rummages in a cupboard and brings out a tube of Pti Ber biscuits, and I smile at the recollection of the bus ride—only yesterday but seeming so much longer ago. She holds it toward me as she sits down, and I slip two biscuits out, pushing with my thumbnail against the cellophane.

"Petit beurre," I say, with the aunts' French accent. She laughs.

I sip the silty coffee, wondering why Nestor wanted to give all his things to me. I suppose this coffeepot, this table, are all mine now—or they will be as soon as I sign the Acceptance of Inheritance. Was he trying to weigh me down with possessions here so that I would stay? Did he understand more than I did my need to hold on to the stories of his and his sisters' childhoods?

Then I remember the money he has left me and I blush. He has left Aliki the house because she has a family and can move into it now that he is dead. He has left me the money because I don't. It is a bequest of pity. And that's what I feel for myself now, as I think of Aliki with her husband and her daughter, with her mother and her beloved *Theia* Sophia coming over to bustle around their loving home. I feel tears starting and can't believe I'm letting this get to me.

"Listen," I say. "You've given me a lot to think about just now. Would you mind if I didn't go to the parade with you?"

"Demetra will be disappointed."

This hurts, and she knows it. I want her to say that *she* will be disappointed, that they really want me with them.

"I just don't think I'd be very good company tonight."

"What's the matter?"

"I don't know." I shrug, knowing that if she keeps showing me concern, I will certainly begin to cry. "Everybody has somebody." She squints at me, cocks her head. "You all belong to someone. To each other."

"For all the good it does us."

I try to laugh.

"Paki, shhh." She brushes the hair from my forehead, and I take the deepest breath I think I've ever taken in my life. "Nikos and I are ready to kill each other half the time," she says. "Never mind the aunts. You are so lucky you live so far away."

She realizes what she has said and leans forward, covering my hand with hers.

"No, that's not what I meant," she says softly. "You belong to someone. You belong to *us*. And you can have your Jonah," she says the name like a question, "if you want him."

After a minute, I draw my hand away and wipe the tears from my face.

"I think I'll feel better if I take some time to be alone tonight," I say. "I need to think."

"Okay, Paki *mou*. Okay." She's talking to me as if I were Demetra's age. And I love it.

I take another sip of coffee, even though there is no liquid left. I end up with muddy grounds in my mouth. By the time I pull the cup away from my face, Aliki has risen from the table and is collecting the coffee things to wash them in the sink.

At the apartment, Aliki does the explaining for me, in hushed tones that tamp down Demetra's protests before they can swell into full-on complaint. Nikos pokes his head into the guest room.

"Wise woman," he says. "We'll come home deaf and hung-over, and you'll be rested and serene. Secret to a long life."

"Yeah, but who wants a long one if it's boring?"

"You can still change your mind. In fact, I'll stay here and do your man-thinking for you, and you go hold Demetra's sweaty, sticky hand for three hours. Deal?"

"Fat chance."

Aliki tugs Demetra into the room. The girl is pouting.

"Demetra, I promise I'll take you to another parade, okay? I only got here yesterday, remember. We have plenty of time, and plenty of Carnival, to spend together."

"Okay."

She kisses me on the cheeks, a child's light, sweet-smelling kiss.

"Now go get your coat," Aliki tells her. "There are leftovers in the fridge," she says to me, "and to turn on the TV just hit the big red button and that'll turn the sound system on. Take care of yourself, Paki."

We kiss on the cheeks, and she is out the door.

The apartment is silent. I stretch out on the narrow bed and look up at the ceiling, afraid of the thoughts I'm supposed to spend the evening with, half-hoping that I'll fall asleep. But I can't relax. I get up and reprise my previous night's walk around the rooms, ending up at the paired photographs of Aliki and me on that childhood beach and by Olympia's ruins. I think of what Aliki said to me at Nestor's house this afternoon, about how I belong to someone, to Jonah.

I go to the low chair in the foyer and pick up the phone. It's the old receiver, with a thin Bakelite handle connecting mouthpiece and speaker. I crank the dial around and wait for Jonah's office phone to ring.

"Jonah Sullivan."

I hear the rustling of papers. He's picked up without looking at the caller ID.

"It's me."

"Hi." His voice is soft now, hesitant. "How is it going?"

"Okay. There's a lot to do."

"Did you see your mother?"

"Yes." I feel scolded somehow.

"And?"

"She keeps calling you Jason." I laugh.

"You told her?"

"She knows about you, Jonah." I'm smiling, but I can't even convince myself that this is a lighthearted moment.

"About us. She must have seen the ring."

"She doesn't notice things."

"And you didn't point it out." He doesn't ask. He knows the answer already.

"That's not a conversation I want to have with my mother."

"Callie, you can't let her control you like that. So she's a hard-ass, or a bitch, or whatever. It doesn't matter."

"Then why should I tell her, if she doesn't matter?"

"She should know her daughter just got engaged."

"That would work for your mother, not mine."

"I can't believe that."

"See, this is what you don't get, Jonah. You can't really understand that it's possible for a mother and her kid to not have any connection at all. I don't want my mother in my life anymore. And I wouldn't be surprised if she didn't want me in hers either."

He must hear something in my voice, because his response is tender and quiet.

"You deserve better, Callie. I will give you better."

I can't say anything for a little while. What Jonah said should move me, but mostly it terrifies me. He evokes these powerful bonds and connections, but all I can think of is what will happen when the cables snap and lash like whips at the poor souls holding on to either end.

"You there?"

"Yeah," I say. "But I should go. It's Aliki's phone bill."

"You can pay her back."

"I know, but it's easier if I keep it short."

"Sure."

"We'll talk again, Joe. I promise."

We say our goodbyes and I-love-yous and hang up. I sit back in the little chair and wipe the tears with my palms. I don't know what I expected from that conversation. Some kind of transformation of myself? A wave of insight that would show me the right way forward, the right way back to Jonah? All I know is that I feel deeply alone, and all I want is to stand with my cousin and her family—my family—in a crowd of people, cheering at the floats and dancers in the parade.

I haven't undressed, so all I have to do is grab my coat from the closet. In a few seconds, I am in the elevator, descending toward the noisy Carnival streets. Momentum carries me through the lobby and as far as Ellinos Stratiotou Street, which runs almost exactly into Plateia Georgiou, George's Square. The street is crammed with traffic now as people head home from what little work they have managed to do during Carnival, and others head into the center of the city for the night's festivities. Many of these people sport some sort of Carnival decoration, like antennae on a headband, or a giant felt flower in their lapel, or a hat made of crepe and LED lights. I wonder if they have gone to their offices like this or simply whisked their Carnival accessories out just now, anxious to be festive.

Closer to Plateia Georgiou, there are mimes on street corners, *tableaux vivants* in shop windows, musicians on the sidewalk. The first installment of the citywide Treasure Hunt began today, and I can see groups of searchers darting through the steadier crowd as they scramble for clues. The crowd becomes denser as I near the square, and everyone seems to be dancing to the loudspeaker beat I can feel in my sternum. I wonder how I will ever find Aliki and Nikos and Demetra among all these people.

They might find me more easily. I stand out, I'm sure, as the only woman in Patras who isn't dressed to impress. All around me are women in tight trousers and silky button-front blouses showing plenty of cleavage, which their open coats do nothing to conceal. Aliki doesn't dress flashy, but even she was sporting heels and a clingy sweater when they left the apartment. I am still wearing my boot-cut jeans and my white turtleneck sweater from the morning. I look young for thirty-five, but I am dressed the way these other women would dress to do yard work.

For various reasons, I am thinking this whole thing was a ridiculous idea. Never mind how out of place I look; how could I possibly have expected to find two people and their little girl in a crowd of thousands, in the dark? I start to turn back when I see a purple velvet hat poking up above the crowd. I stand on tiptoes and, sure enough, it's Stelios. I realize that my route has brought me to the northeast corner of Plateia Georgiou, exactly where Anna said she and Stelios would be.

Giving in to impulse, I push through the crowd toward where I spotted the hat.

I feel two hands on my waist.

"*Geia sou, ré,*" comes a voice in my ear, and I turn to see Stelios's face peering over my shoulder. A few people in front of me, I see Anna jumping up and waving. Now she is the one wearing Stelios's hat low over her eyebrows.

"You came after all," he says.

"I came." It's too loud here for me to explain that I was looking for someone else.

"Anna!" I call, and Stelios, with his hands still on my waist, steers me toward her. This seems a little odd to me, but I figure it's part of the Carnival atmosphere.

"Callie!" she yells. "Callie, Callie."

"*Geia sou,* Callie," says a man standing beside her.

"Andreas," Anna says, by way of introduction. "*Ela.*" She tugs me by the hand across the street that rings the Plateia. Here the crowd thins among the café tables warmed by propane heaters. Anna is dressed in the same style as the other women: a silver blouse unbuttoned to there and lavender trousers beneath a long white coat with astrakhan trim. A hot-pink feather boa circles her neck.

"The hat matches your trousers," I say.

"I know!" When she laughs long at this observation, I realize she is quite drunk.

I look around at the rest of the *parea* and see that Stelios and the others appear to have had less to drink, though they are all ahead of me. We sit at one of the cafés and order several beers, and soon I have caught up. I can stand, I can see clearly, but my limbs feel loose and easy, and I slouch back into the low chair, tipping my chin up as I laugh at a joke, twisting my head languorously to follow the conversation.

Most of the talk is inside jokes and stories about previous exploits. This is a group that has been to Carnival many times together.

"Maki, here, is from Patras," Stelios says to me at one point. "Callie's family is from here," he says to the giant, round young man who is sitting on Stelios's other side.

"What's your name?"

"Notaris," I say, a name I hardly ever hear or say. In my lifetime, it belonged only to Nestor and to nobody now.

Maki shakes his head.

"Nope. I'm Makopoulos. Ring any bells?"

"No," I say, leaning over Stelios. "Maki Makopoulos, I have never ever heard of you." Then I say to Stelios, "This isn't that guy you called *maláka* on the phone yesterday?"

He laughs in a sudden enough burst that Maki wants to know what I said. Stelios looks back at me and winks and tells Maki it's nothing.

People on the edge of the square begin cheering. The crowd pushes toward the cafés and nearly knocks over the people in chairs at the outer edge. We all get up and stand on our chairs to see the parade, which is now making its way across the top of Plateia Georgiou. The music of several different bands has melded into one cacophony punctuated by the rhythmic peals of somebody's whistle. Among the musicians are groups of dancers in brightly colored costumes, some of them seeming to move in unison and others simply prancing down the street. Some dancers carry large papier-mâché heads on long poles. I hope Demetra has a good view of all this. She must be up on

Nikos's shoulders. Among the dancers are several enormous floats—homecoming-queen style—and flying banners scrawled with political jokes. This is Greece, where beauty and politics are twin obsessions.

After a few moments, there are no more floats, just large groups of identically costumed dancers. Several men and women are pushing children in strollers, their costumes miniature versions of what their parents are wearing. My *parea*'s interest shifts to the people gathered immediately around us. Maki and Stelios are standing on their chairs and trying to knock each other off, to the jolly annoyance of whoever is standing nearby and being buffeted by the arms and legs the two men wave to keep their balance. Andreas jumps down from another chair and crouches in front of Anna. She jumps onto his shoulders and holds the purple hat with one hand as Andreas rises to full height. He grasps her thighs and slides his fingers up as high as he can. She laughs and smacks his head playfully.

I look at Stelios, who is still play-fighting with Maki, unconcerned. Carnival, I guess. And then I look at Stelios again. It's a good face to look at—angular and lean, with dark hair curling slightly now in the humid night. He sees me, and I tilt my head to one side and smile. He smiles back just as Maki, sensing weakness, aims a hip check at Stelios's side and knocks him to the ground. Maki raises both fists in the air and shouts, "Winner!"

"*Skáse,* shut up, *ré maláka*!" Stelios laughs over his shoulder. He comes toward me and crouches before my chair. "Come on," he says.

I grab his shoulders and jump up. He puts his hand on the small of my back, beneath my peacoat, and presses me forward against his head as we begin moving through the people. His shoulders are warm, his shirt slightly sweaty. His hands squeeze my thighs as I sway from side to side. It feels good. I'm not drunk enough to forget about Jonah, but I am drunk enough not to care. I'm riding that expanded consciousness that lets me see my bad behavior without changing it—and fools me into thinking that awareness makes it all right.

I allow my fingers to slip under Stelios's scarf, where I can feel the stubble of a day's beard. His head moves back against me.

"Where to, Miss Notaris?"

I lean forward and speak softly, letting my lips touch his ear. "Anywhere you like, Mr. . . ."

"Pappamichaïl."

"Anywhere you like, Mr. Pappamichaïl."

The sounds of the parade grow fainter as we go toward the harbor and away from the center of the city. From my vantage point up on Stelios's shoulders, I see couples twined together behind cars and kiosks, and I wonder if one of them is Anna and Andreas.

"Put me down," I say, and he obliges, holding my legs behind him as I slide along his back. We are standing very close to each other when he turns, and I am sure that we both want the furtive grappling going on all around us.

"Let's go find Anna," he says after a moment.

"Sure," I say. "Let's find Anna." I try to ignore the fact that I'm more than a little disappointed.

He leads me back a block and then along a road parallel to the harbor. There are smatterings of Carnival festivities here—musicians, dancers, children with their parents. I see now why there are children here: On the sidewalk before a row of simple, brightly lit tavernas is a group of stalls selling balloons, masks, and various trinkets. Among them, I spot the purple hat. Stelios, without registering surprise, goes toward it.

"*Geia,*" he says, slipping his arm around Anna's waist.

"You found us," she says. "This is where I always come," Anna says to me. "It's a ritual now. We always buy something as a souvenir. Last year it was this hat and now we've come back to find something else."

We begin to look through the merchandise, most of it plastic and made in China.

"Found it," Stelios calls, and we gather around him. "Look at these. They're pretty nice, probably handmade."

"From Zakynthos," says the stall owner, a middle-aged man in a bulky down jacket. He shows us a dowel from which are hanging wooden-beaded bracelets on thin leather cords. The beads are painted deep red, like blood. Anna takes one.

"It's like an abacus," she says.

"Yes," says Stelios. "A bracelet for my sexy mathematician."

"Four, please," Anna tells the merchant, and gives him the money. She puts hers on and passes the others to Stelios. He takes my hand and slides a bracelet over my knuckles.

"For *all* the sexy women," he says.

"Me too," Andreas says, waving his wrist in front of Stelios's face. "I'm sexy too."

It is ten-thirty now, too late to catch one of the many performances going on in the city's theaters, so we continue along the street past the stalls and the tavernas to find a bar. We settle on one that makes crêpes stuffed with chocolate and honey. Now I've been with these people long enough that we have our own inside jokes from earlier in the evening. They don't seem to care that they only just met me, and neither do I. But eventually I give in to jet lag, faking interest as my eyes close, and then dozing off altogether. I wake up at one point with my head on Andreas's shoulder. He smells of cigarettes.

Sometime later, with Maki lost to the crowd, the four of us head back to the center of town, our arms clasped together out of glee and a need for support. I tell Stelios I should be getting home.

"Don't go now. They're already in bed at this point. What difference will a few more hours make?"

But that is what I am worried about. Like my mother, I have no key to Aliki's home. If Aliki and Nikos are in bed, I will have to wake them or keep roaming the streets until we all crash on someone's floor.

At the corner of Kolokotronis and Kanakaris, Anna pulls us all to a stop.

"Pact!" she says, freeing her arms from Stelios's and Andreas's grasp. "We keep these on for the entire Carnival, and when we return next year"—she swoops around exaggeratedly to me, emphasizing the words—"we will wear them as a sign of our *parea*."

"Indeed! Done!" we all say, thrusting our braceleted hands in the air.

At Aliki's building, I take a deep breath and press the buzzer. I am startled to hear it answered immediately. She has been waiting up. With one foot holding the door open, I kiss my friends good night and vaguely agree to various offers for the next day without really paying attention.

Aliki is in her bathrobe, standing in the open door to the apartment. She presses her finger against her lips silently and follows me into my room.

"What happened to you? I was worried."

"I'm so sorry, Aliki. I went looking for you."

"In a bar?"

"No, really, Aliki, I did. I wanted to be there with you. At the parade. Then I found these friends and we watched the parade. I couldn't find you."

"No," she says. "We didn't take Demetra to a bar."

She shakes her head at me and leaves, returning with a glass of water for me. I drink it and go to bed, the smell of smoke in my hair and beer on my breath.

6

Callie

Aliki is standing over me, saying something. As I open my eyes, I am conscious of the hangover I deserve: the aching head, the felted tongue, the lids clicking over dry eyes. Aliki seems to relish the discomfort she sees on my face.

"What time is it?"

"It's already eleven. I don't think I've seen you like this since that time we went to Kythira."

"Oh, God."

"Yeah," she laughs. "Remind me again, was it you who thought we should all go skinny-dipping?"

"I didn't know there wasn't a moon!" I remember how long it took us to find our clothes in the dark afterward and how we all stumbled around on the island beach, boys and girls, wet and suddenly ashamed of our nakedness. I clutch my head. "Don't make me laugh," I moan.

She watches me try to compose myself.

"Listen," she says, "I have to go with Demetra to the Children's Carnival. Nikos is coming too, and we're meeting Marina and her family. You met her the other night."

"Too much information. You'll make me barf."

"You already did," she says. Suddenly I remember rising in the night and vomiting in the toilet. I look around me, as if for traces of the mess I must have created.

"I'm so sorry, Aliki. I left last night just a few minutes after you'd gone. I thought I'd be able to find you."

"I'd say your plan failed pretty spectacularly."

"It was stupid, I know."

"I can't have you staying here if you're going to carouse like that. Demetra doesn't need to see that." Aliki tries to catch herself, but it's too late. She's right. No little girl should have to see the adults she cares about losing control or, worse, going missing.

"I get it, Aliki. Believe me, I get it."

"At least leave a note, Calliope. This isn't Kythira. It's a city. I had no idea where you were. Demetra was worried, and I made something up so she wouldn't be upset."

"I'm sorry, Aliki," I say, taking her arm. "I promise I won't do that again."

She rolls her eyes at me. "When you've gotten yourself together, there's some cake you can toast for breakfast. Butter's on the counter. Our key is on the hall table, and I'm leaving the key to Nestor's house. I'll be at the kids' Carnival all day."

"I could come with you."

"Demetra doesn't want to be late. And you won't be ready in time."

This hurts, but I understand.

"You can go on over to Nestor's by yourself."

"I look just as foreign as yesterday, Aliki."

"If anyone asks you, you can explain it to them."

"I'm sorry, Aliki," I repeat.

"It's all right," she says. "Stop apologizing."

I've made her laugh, and that makes me happy.

I lie in bed for a while, thinking of everything I did last night. At first, I'm embarrassed. I drank too much and got carried away. But that's not quite right, and the truth is that, though the alcohol made it easier, I knew what I was doing. I run my fingers over the beads of my new bracelet. Something more could have happened with Stelios. As this thought forms, another comes suddenly: Something still could. In the three years since Jonah and I got together, I haven't touched another man that way. But it feels as if his proposal has changed everything. Now that we're engaged, he seems cautious and I'm afraid. Marriage looms over me like a sword of Damocles, hardly a good image for a blushing bride.

I'm not sure what I'm most afraid of: that my marriage to Jonah will fail, or that I might actually achieve the happiness I long for. As I stare up at the guest-room ceiling, I ponder the easy way out. If I ruin the marriage before it has a chance to start, I can save myself the despair of failure. Jonah won't be a laceration of the heart that I will have to bear forever. He'll be like Luke, and Sam, and Pete, just a guy who didn't work out.

It's now five in the morning Boston time. I sit on the edge of the bed for a while, as if at sea, letting my vision settle in its gimbal. I resolve to stand up and, holding on to the walls and doorjambs, I make it to the foyer, wondering if I should call Jonah again and explain. But I don't reach for the phone. I don't trust myself. Or, more accurately, I trust my body; I just don't trust my heart. I sit there for a while longer and then gingerly make my way around the apartment, getting dressed for another session at Nestor's house.

I go slowly down Ellinos Stratiotou, breathing in the damp air off the Gulf of Patras. My head begins to clear, but I still feel as though the slightest provocation will bring a repeat of Aliki's toilet. I have not eaten anything this morning. I feel in my pocket for Nestor's key, with its fob in the shape of a thistle, the words AULD LANG SYNE embossed on the back side. A souvenir from one of his trips. There is, doubtless, a vial of coarse Scottish beach sand or a chunk of Scottish rock somewhere among all his boxes.

I hang my coat on the rack in the foyer and stand looking at the scene of all I have to sift through. It is too much. Repeating Aliki's steps from the day before, I make a passable cup of coffee and take it to Nestor's study, where I stand looking out the French doors to the back garden. During my summer visits, the garden was always an arid space, almost unbearably hot, with the sun baking off the walls and the paving stones.

Nestor ventured into it only twice a day, to fill a bowl with water for those tortoises he kept there. Not turtles, as my mother so promptly pointed out. It must have been a suitable environment for the tortoises, because I remember seeing them every summer until I grew too old to play with them. Though I knew better, I always snuck out into the searing heat of the garden during the middle of the day, when I was supposed to be resting. Nestor would doze off as he listened to music, and I would click open the glass door that led out from the cool of the study and feel the sudden pressure of the sun on my skin and clothes. Within seconds, my scalp felt hot enough to lift off my head, but I never retreated. Around me were three high walls and the tall glass doors of the house; above me was a simple square of pale-blue sky; at my feet, the ordered black and white squares of the garden tile.

I could never induce the tortoises to do anything except pull their heads into their shells. They rejected my offers of lettuce or water; they refused to be steered toward the shade of a bushy weed. When I dared to place them on the paving stones, as though they were pieces in a board game, they snapped at me and drew their heads back inside. I suppose these were odd pets for me to be playing with. But to me then, the tortoises were exotic, something I could be proud of in a way. When I daubed water on them, I brought out the rich pattern of browns on their shells. With their heads pulled in, they became perfect disks of color and design.

I wonder if this is what Nestor was thinking—that I would see the order in the chaos of his belongings. Perhaps he trusted me especially to find the design among all his collections, the rich pattern of his life as he had recorded it in apricot pits and grains of sand. A man of details, perhaps he thought I was better suited than the rest of his family to find the significance in them.

This idea puts me in an expansive mood and, as if to conduct some kind of conversation with him, I decide to begin today with Nestor's photographs. My coffee finished, I draw the curtains open and ease myself onto the couch, flipping through endless black-and-white images on stiff scalloped paper. I know I shouldn't be doing this; I will never finish if I go so slowly over every item in the house. But the photographs are compelling. Familiar faces in their prime swim up at me from scenes of tennis courts, balconies, horses, beaches.

I go through a few more boxes and set aside roughly a dozen photographs from a box labeled 1940: three shots of a family group standing by a fence; my grandparents in tennis whites, holding wooden rackets with long handles; the farmhouse taken at different times of day, with shadows inching across the porch; and a photo of all the children in a line arranged by height, with my mother at the head; they are all wearing sailor-style collars. I am in the kitchen, looking for some sort of box to put them in, when I hear the doorbell's soft ring.

I leave the photos in the small shoe box I have found and peer out to the foyer, fearing one of the protective neighbors Aliki has warned me about. I see a tiny figure silhouetted against the glass. It could be a child—a beggar selling trinkets—but I realize as I approach that it is my mother. Here, too, it seems, she has been given no right to enter without permission. Thalia and Sophia come and go as they please, but my mother appears to be welcome nowhere. Even I, the visitor with my "Auld Lang Syne" key, have more access than she does.

I consider hiding until she leaves; with my hangover, I don't want to deal with my mother. But I realize that one sure way to find out why she doesn't want me in this house is to let her in and see what happens. Anyway, she must know I'm in here, and she will wait, aloof but demanding, certain I won't be able to resist her.

She turns slowly as I swing the door open and she steps into the house. I take her camel-hair coat and hang it on the hat stand. We kiss on the cheeks.

"You're all dressed up," I say. She is wearing gray wool trousers and a belted navy sweater with a scarf tied, foulard style, around her neck.

"You expect me to go around Patras in overalls?"

She looks me up and down, taking in my jeans, boots, and turtleneck sweater.

"No," I say carefully. "Where are you going?"

"I'm going here, Calliope. I've come to see my brother's house."

She pushes past me and clucks at the sight of the boxes piled in the living room. I resolve not to take my eyes off her.

"Look at all this junk," she says. "I told you."

She glides around the room, peering into boxes with disdain. She picks up an occasional object, glances at it, and then shakes her head before setting it back down. She wipes her hand on her jacket.

"This stuff reeks of mildew."

"What do you want, *Mamá*? If there's something you want me to be on the lookout for, I'll be glad to set it aside."

"The idea that my own daughter should be in charge of my brother's things! This is ridiculous."

She is only partly right. It's not ridiculous; but it is sad. I think of all these things from her family home that my mother never got to bring with her to America. Maybe that was why they argued that day in the hospital. For Nestor to deprive her of some keepsake from the life she shared with him seems cruel, if that's what he was really doing. Surely he understood that by giving the stuff to me he would be rubbing this deprivation in his sister's face. Or was he making me the gatekeeper? Was he hoping for moments like this one, when I would see my mother's loss and would look for something to give her?

"Look, I don't know why he did this, but I told you: If there's something you want, just tell me."

"You don't know why?" She keeps roaming around the living room, lifting books by their corners and letting them fall in tiny clouds of dust. "You were always his favorite, Calliope. He loved Aliki, but he adored you. He remembered everything you ever told him. And he was always telling me about you. Me, your mother! He always knew your flight information. That's how I found out about your last two visits. From Nestor." Her eyes give away nothing, no knowledge of how my last visit to her ended. "I used to think you were the daughter he never had, but that wasn't it. You were his friend. I think he thought of you as a peer."

I feel tears brimming and I pray they don't roll.

"Just a minute."

I go to the kitchen and wipe my eyes, peeking around the doorjamb at my mother, who is now bending sideways, looking into the recesses of a bookcase. I know she was jealous—is jealous even now—of Nestor's connection to me. I can offer her something to make amends. I grab the shoe box with the photographs I have been poring over and return to the living room.

"I found some pictures you might like. Come sit."

With a sigh, she comes to sit down next to me on the couch, scooting to the edge so that her feet will reach the floor. She doesn't look comfortable.

I leaf through the box and place a photo on the coffee table.

"Here," I say. "Here's all of you in matching outfits."

She picks up the photo.

"I remember this."

She places the tip of her finger below the image of her teenage face and holds it there, as if she were summoning her younger self to return. She reaches into the box and spreads the rest of the photographs over the table. Her hands wander over the images, sliding them clear from one another as she takes them up to study them. Her glasses hang at the end of her nose, and over them her eyes are beady and dark in a face whose coloring has dimmed with time. She stops at one of the photos of the family group—the aunts, Nestor, and several adults— standing stiffly by a wooden railing.

"Those are the Agnostopoulos cousins, right?"

"Hmm?"

I point out the figures I know.

"And these must be Popi and Marianna, right? And I can't tell where it is. Their house somewhere?"

"I didn't know he had this," she says softly, then, after a pause, "Where did you find it?"

"In one of these." I gesture at the boxes around the couch, but my mother doesn't take her eyes off the photograph.

"We're at the farm," my mother says finally. "These are the refugees who came to live with us."

"What refugees who came to live with you?"

She sits back and tosses the photograph onto the table.

"A family, I think. And one or two others. After the first bombings, we moved out to the farm and these people showed up one day. My father put them to work around the farm."

"There's a little boy here."

"Well, he didn't work, did he?" She snorts at me. "But the adults, yes. It was the least they could do for being given safety. Who knows where they would have ended up if we hadn't taken them in."

"You said they just appeared."

"And rather than send them away, we let them stay. Satisfied?"

"No," I say, and she starts at my dissent. "I think it makes a big difference whether you were at the farm alone or with strangers."

"Evidently I don't, or I would have told you about them."

And yet this is a fundamental change to my notion of the farm during wartime. The farm is no longer a sort of cocoon where the family returned to safety. Now I see that the place was porous, open to the outside world with its dangers, threats, and losses.

My mother stands up and gathers the photographs together.

"May I take these?" she says, with mock courtesy.

"Yes, *Mamá*. I'm not going to keep you from having any of this stuff."

"Oh, thank you so very much."

She heads for the foyer and hands the box to me briefly

while she puts on her coat. I stand there, waiting for my vision to clear from having risen too quickly. My stomach rumbles and creaks and I remember I have eaten nothing.

"Maybe we could go get something to eat, *Mamá*. My treat."

"Not today." She barely seems to think about it. "I'd rather take the box straight home."

"I can carry it for you. We can sit at Plateia Georgiou."

"I'd rather keep this safe, not at some café table."

"We could leave it here and come back for it after. It'd be nice to sit with you," I say. "Or we could watch the street performers. The Carnival looks fun."

"It's garish now. They've ruined it, just like they've ruined everything from the old days."

"Come on, *Mamá*. Is it really that bad?"

She laughs. "Yes, Calliope. It's really that bad. May I go now?"

"I am trying, Mother, to be sociable. But, sure, don't let me keep you. Go have a great time looking at your photographs."

She whisks out the door while I am still shaking my head in resigned astonishment, if there is such a thing.

The pounding in my head grows more insistent, so I decide to go back to Aliki's, where I can eat and rest. Equipped with a key, I make my way up and find the apartment, thankfully, empty. I grab a glass and down two large drinks of water, though there is no hope of Advil. I slice some of the pound cake that Aliki has left and manage to keep it down.

"Fuck," I say, drawing the word out.

I have screwed everything up. I am estranged—that has to be the word for it—from my fiancé, I have worried my cousin with my irresponsible behavior, I have disappointed my one niece in the whole world, I have led on some strange guy I know nothing about, and now I have renewed hostilities with my mother. And she is bent on ferreting something out of the vast piles of Nestor's possessions, and I don't know what that is.

I drop down onto the couch, as focused on my aching head as if I were watching it on television.

The ring of the phone wakes me—a harsh double peal that sounds like Morse code. I remember the standard phone greeting: *Léghete,* speak. Invitation couched in the form of a command.

"*Neh?*" I say instead. Yes?

"Miss Calliope Notaris, please."

"Who is this?"

"Your friend from the alleyways."

"Stelios," I groan. "What do you want?"

"Pleased to hear from you too," he says. "How's the head?"

I grumble.

"Don't ask for me like that on the phone," I say. "My cousin already thinks I'm reckless."

"Aren't you?"

I don't answer this. "Why did you call?"

"Some of us are going to try the Treasure Hunt today. Want to come?"

Feeling the way I do, I don't understand how they can stomach the idea of walking around the city for hours.

"Absolutely not," I say.

"Lazy."

"Jet lag."

"What about later?"

"Give me your phone numbers. I'll call you."

He tells me his and Anna's mobile numbers, which I write on the pad by the phone.

"Promise?"

"No, I can't promise," I say, putting the paper in my pocket. "You'll just have to take your chances."

"Still wearing your bracelet?"

"Pact." I shake my wrist so that the beads clink together.

I am back to sitting on the couch, doing nothing, when Aliki and the others come in, returned from the Children's Carnival. Demetra and her two friends are full of excitement, but when they see me, they quiet down and move warily out of the foyer. Down the hallway to Demetra's room, they burst into laughter.

"Someone had fun last night," Nikos says, grinning at me.

Aliki smacks his hip, and I remember Anna smacking Andreas for his wandering fingers. The one gesture made in real—or false?—prudishness, the other in flirtation. This is the new Aliki, the careful wife and mother trying to shepherd her wayward man. I wonder if Anna will turn out the same way once her carefree youth is over. She will find herself no longer on equal footing with the men who surround her now.

I excuse myself and head down the hallway to Demetra's room, where the girls are passing brightly colored magazines between them.

"Demetraki," I say. All three of them look up at me, aghast at my intrusion. "I'm sorry about the parade last night."

She begins to blush.

"I actually came to meet you at the Plateia. Did your mother tell you? But I couldn't find you after all." I feel my own face heating up as I realize how pathetic I sound. "How about if we go to another parade, just you and me?"

She nods, wide-eyed.

"We'll look at the schedule and pick something just for us, okay?"

I hear muffled giggles behind me as I leave. I'd be laughing too if I were their age, snickering at the grown-up who's afraid of a little girl.

In the foyer, Marina's husband, Phillipos, grins along with Nikos as Aliki marshals them toward the kitchen. They return to the living room with glasses and baskets of chips and nuts. Nikos turns on the television and I move over to make room for the two women beside me on the couch. Nikos surfs through a talk show, a Spanish *telenovela*, an episode of *Friends,* and settles on footage of last year's Carnival, broadcast nation-wide. With the music and the shouting playing in the background, I listen as the four of them slide into conversation about people I don't know.

It feels strange to be sitting here, among family and their friends, with children playing down the hall and food laid out on the table where shoeless feet rest. I try to hide my fascina-tion as I take this all in. It is something I cannot get used to: this easy sense of being at home, this assumption—obvious in the relaxed curve of Aliki's back and the slow rubbing together of Nikos's stocking feet—that home is where the self lives. No matter what happens with us, I have made a home with Jonah, and I've propped my feet up on his parents' coffee table many times to watch a football game. But I have not yet captured that sense of self, of my self. No matter where I go, I seem to be always trailing too many worries and ideas. Like the string of tin cans so incongruously weighing down a newly married couple.

By the time dinner comes around, it's decided that the girls have had enough excitement for the day and no one feels like going out.

"Let's not cook," Nikos says, as if he would be the one slav-ing in the kitchen. "Let's have Chinese."

Lo mein, moo shu, and General Tso: The words sound comical in Greek accents, though no more comical, I'm sure, than my own pronunciation sounds to the man behind the counter at China Star. Still, I feel as if I should be an authority on this foreign food so newly arrived here, and I supervise as we put together our order. With a pang that makes me almost sob, I realize that I miss Jonah, his constant choice of shrimp dishes that congeal in an Elmer's-colored sauce, his insistence on using chopsticks. I miss the faint crease in his neck, surprising in a man so lean, the skin so soft there when I kiss it. It is the way things are with me: The foreign things always make me think of home.

At night I can't sleep, a victim of my long nap and my confused body clock. First Aliki and then Nikos go to bed while I stay in the living room, listening to the clicking of the television set as it cools down. I dig out my book and read for a while, and then my thoughts drift back to the conversation with my mother and to the photograph that seemed to unsettle her.

With my mind clear now, it occurs to me how odd it is that never, in all my listening to all the stories, did I form the impression that there were strangers at the farm. Not from my mother, or from Nestor, or from the aunts. Perhaps it doesn't matter, but then why would it not have come up in all these years? Aliki and I knew about the various people who worked for my grandparents on the farm: Yannis and his wife, Irini, who served as overseer and cook both in the city and on the farm, and various farmhands whose names I can never remember. Is it possible that we were told also about a group of refugees and that our childish brains blended this group of dispossessed people together with all the others who were in our grandparents' employ? Is it possible that, in my desire for an image of an untroubled home, I edited the refugees from my mother's stories, cutting out the elements of the tale that would have added hints of strife and loss? Could I be the one who created the impermeable cocoon?

Tomorrow, I will ask Aliki what she knows.

7

Callie

Sunday

I pad into the kitchen in sweatpants and a T-shirt to find Demetra fully dressed, sitting at a plate of eggs and toast.

"*Kaliméra,* Demetraki *mou,*" I say, wanting to join her in this family world I feel myself getting close to. I want to be an aunt for her.

"Are you coming with us?" she asks, last night's discomfort apparently gone. "Better hurry."

"Where?" I say, tearing a chunk from yesterday's bread that is sitting on the cutting board. Can the next parade be happening already?

"Church."

Aliki comes into the room as she straightens the sleeves of her sweater.

I shift over to stand behind Demetra and mouth a question to Aliki: *Church?*

She frowns at me.

"Finish," she says to Demetra, cutting a piece of egg with the girl's fork and setting it on the plate for her. I follow Aliki out of the room.

"Since when do you go to church?"

Here was one way in which my heritage kept me apart from other Greeks. The few Greek kids I knew spent their Sunday mornings at Orthros service, joined basketball leagues and dance groups, and went to church suppers, where creamy *moussaká* was served with Rice-A-Roni. They were not Greek, as my mother always insisted, but Greek American. We, she would say, were the real thing, and that was completely different. I accepted this when I was young. I did not want to spend my Sunday mornings in a pew, though the fellowship of the teams and the dance groups was seductive. But if my mother said it was not the way to be a true Greek, then I would have none of it. Besides, what I knew from my summers in Greece was that only old women and the oddly, frighteningly devout went to church every Sunday. Greeks cross themselves at the start of a journey and they light a candle in the church entrance for someone who has died, but for most people that is it, aside from holidays and the main rituals in a life: baptism, wedding, funeral.

Now here is Aliki, going to Mass on Sunday with a daughter who has clearly done this enough times to take it as routine.

"Since when," I ask her, "does anyone in our family go to church?"

"We do. This family does."

I make a noise of protest and bewilderment, and Aliki turns around to face me.

"It's Carnival. Great. But do you know why it's Carnival? Because in just over a week now, Lent will begin, a time during which we prepare ourselves for the great holy day of Easter. It's Pre-Lent now, so today, we will go to church and pray and ready ourselves to confirm our faith."

"I didn't know."

"It's not your fault, but I'd appreciate it if you wouldn't sound so aghast in front of Demetra."

"When did this happen? When did you start?"

She continues heading toward the bathroom.

"I don't know. Maybe after *Babá* died. It doesn't matter. I just did."

She stands before the mirror, brushing her hair. She has her mother's sweet face, now become a little pouchy in the cheeks, and her father's, her *babá*'s, hazel eyes, as always sharp and bright. Beautiful eyes that used to transfix the boys and men in her *parea*.

"Would you like to come?" she asks.

I would like to come, to be a part of this, but it is too strange for me. I shake my head and she raises her eyebrows at me in the mirror. At that moment, I feel a surge of delight, to be standing this way, like sisters, like mother and daughter.

"Not today," I say. "I'm not sure how I feel about organized religion. Or about the Greek Orthodox God."

She draws her head back in mock amazement.

"Just believe or don't believe. It's pretty simple."

She turns and makes pushing gestures at me, shooing me out of the bathroom. She closes the door and I hear her peeing.

"And by the way," she shouts through the door, "today's the last day we eat meat until Easter."

"You're kidding," I say, when she emerges.

"Believe it, Paki."

Aliki tells Demetra I am still not feeling well—which I find embarrassing, not only because we are lying to a child, but also because it gives her the impression I was even drunker than I was. I suspect Demetra is old enough to know the cause of my discomfort.

I have the apartment to myself again, and Nestor's key is on the counter with Aliki's, but I don't feel like going over there. I've missed my chance to ask Aliki if she knows about the refugees, but I keep thinking about the farm—a place that, like the house, had already passed out of my family's possession before my lifetime and that no one ever took me to see. Aliki once told me it had been subdivided, but then she mentioned another time that the central part of the farm was still intact, with the low stone house still surrounded by vineyards, orchards, and fields. Surprising to think that a developer would leave this, but stranger things have happened to land in Greece, where illegal buildings are common and building codes roundly disobeyed. It was possible that the property had become enmeshed in one of the many inheritance troubles so common in a country where no one seems to prepare for death. It was a miracle, we all understood, that Nestor had left a will.

I find the slip of paper with Stelios's and Anna's mobile numbers on it and pick up the phone, hesitating about which one of them to call. I choose Anna.

She answers sleepily, and I realize it is quite early in the morning. I hear a man's voice murmuring beside her, and she sighs before repeating her question.

"*Neh?*"

"Sorry to wake you up, Anna. It's me. Callie."

"*Ela.* Come."

"Should I call back later?"

"No, no. What's up?"

"Maki has a car, right?"

"Yes."

"How would you guys like to drive out into the country?"

"What for?"

I can't believe I'm asking people I don't really know to help me on this mission. I'm not one of those people who form groups of friends all at once—at least, I haven't been until this trip. My tendency is to start with one person, sidling up to him with my loneliness and comparing notes. The groups, if they come at all, come along with him. In Boston, my friends are all Jonah's friends. A thought flashes: If we end it, I will lose them too.

I take a deep breath and explain to Anna about the farm, without mentioning the issue of the refugees. I cast it as an exploration, a Treasure Hunt of our own devising. The weather seems mild enough, I venture, to bring a picnic.

"Have you been outside?"

"No."

"It's freezing," she says. "Wait."

I hear murmuring that grows distinct enough for me to identify Stelios, Andreas, and Maki. She comes back to the phone.

"Pact! Meet you at Plateia Olgas in about an hour. We'll bring food."

Kolokotronis is deserted as I walk down toward the square. I was right about the weather, and Anna was being cold-blooded. February is almost over, and the air is moist and soft. I have clipped my hair up in the back to feel the air on my neck. I am wearing a close-fitting collared blouse with long sleeves and a long placket. Tucked into my jeans, it is sleek enough to make me look almost not American.

When I reach the corner of Maizonos and Kolokotronis, I see huge Maki standing by a red Renault that barely reaches his waist.

"You are a very funny man," I call across the street.

"I try."

The other three are already in the car, complaining about the cold. Stelios sticks his head out the passenger window, looks me in the eye, and grins.

"I can't believe you're doing this," I tell him.

"A quest for a mysterious stranger from a foreign land," he intones. "At least I think that's what Anna said."

"Shortest legs!" Andreas says. "You get the middle."

When I climb into the back with Anna and Andreas, they squeeze against me, making a show of how uncomfortable they are.

"Where is this place?" Maki asks, as he pulls out.

"I don't exactly know."

But I know we need to head out of the city toward the northeast along the edge of the gulf and then probably cut in toward the foothills of Panachaïko. Maki turns the car onto a large street that I soon recognize as Korinthou. I can see the old house up ahead on the left and I lean forward, twisting sideways to watch it as we pass. I catch a glimpse of Undershirt Man's scooter locked to the front rail.

"What's that place?" Anna asks.

"That's my family's old house."

"Your family's, as in, they own it?"

"Not now. A long time ago. Before the war."

Maki whistles from the driver's seat.

"Stelios, you didn't tell us she was an heiress."

"I told you about her uncle's stuff." He turns back and gestures at me, palms up in explanation.

"Yeah, an old man's junk. But this is a big old house," Maki says.

"She comes from money," Stelios says.

"What's your family name again?" Maki asks, catching my eye in the rearview mirror.

"Notaris," Stelios answers.

Maki tilts his head, searching. He shakes it.

"Nope. Still never heard of them."

"That's because your family's so damned poor, *maláka,*" Andreas says, shoving Maki's seat forward.

The real reason he doesn't know the name is that the Notaris raisin business disappeared well before I was born, sometime around when my grandparents moved into that little house with the walled-in garden in the back.

I sit quietly as the others haggle over the best way to get clear of the ferryboat terminal and the construction for the Rio-Antirio Bridge. As we approach the area, I can see the piers striding across the gulf like platforms for a giant trapeze. When the bridge is finished in one or two years, white cables will form a web over the water.

We have reached an area that is less thickly settled when I see a familiar name on a road sign: PERIVOLI.

"There," I shout, pointing. "Perivoli. I think that's it."

Maki turns off the road onto an unlined stretch of faded asphalt.

"I really have no idea," I say.

"Doesn't matter."

This area reminds me of the outskirts of Athens, scattered with houses in various stages of completion, topped with uprights of rebar and odds and ends of furniture and appliances. Here, as there, the homes seem makeshift, provisional, as if the universal belief in these neighborhoods is that something better will come along. Either that or the money with which to build it.

"We're looking for an orchard, right?" says Stelios.

"Orchards," I say. "Plural."

"Oh, plural," Andreas singsongs, giving me a push.

"Maki, go that way," Stelios says after a while, pointing to the left.

The road turns to dirt and I begin to wonder if we haven't found the farm after all. I remember hearing about the horse-drawn carriage my family drove down dirt roads to get to the farm, as recently as wartime. Maki pulls the car over and cranks up the emergency brake.

"What?" I say, leaning forward.

"Look."

The road ends at a chicken-wire fence, behind which is the back of a large cement-block building, a warehouse of some sort. Up ahead and to the left are posts topped with metal signs that face the other way.

"But look over there," says Stelios.

He tugs me farther forward so I can look past him out his window. I see nothing except a field with tall blond grass and a group of cypresses on the uphill side. It's quite lovely, actually, but it's not my family's farm.

We all get out of the car and stand looking around us at the warehouse, the distant mountain, and the field. Now that we're here, I want to keep looking for the farm, hoping that some scrap of orchard remains like this tiny patch of tall grass.

"It's probably all gone now," Andreas says. "Redistributed from the one to the many."

I smile at him but can't tell if he is joking.

"More like sold off in tiny pieces for less and less money," I say.

He shrugs and walks to the back of the car, where he pulls a shopping bag from the trunk. Anna fishes two bottles of wine from the well where the spare tire should be.

"Let's go. Aren't you starved?"

Andreas hands me the bag and tugs a blanket from the

trunk. Now I see that they have brought bread and cheese and oranges.

"There are chocolates in there too," Anna says.

I walk behind the others, watching their dark figures stride through the grass, their red-beaded bracelets peeking out from their sleeves as their arms extend. For some reason, I want to turn back. Perhaps because the contrast of their clothes against the wheat-colored grass makes them seem sinister, or perhaps because our dealings today are robbed of either drink or the wantonness of Carnival. In the sober light of day, these are strangers to me, and there is no clear reason why I should trust them.

"I can carry that," Maki says. I had not counted him, and now he comes up behind me and smiles, taking the bag from my hand. He is so genial that my worries fade.

Anna spreads the blanket out and it floats above the ground, a blue-patterned square suspended on the stalks of grass. I sit down on it, feeling a slight descent onto the dirt. The untrodden stalks rise up around us, hiding us completely from anyone's view. I think of the houses the aunts and Nestor used to play in somewhere very near here: toy houses carved out of fields of *trifilli*—a very tall strain of clover.

"This place is perfect for Carnival," I say.

"You could screw for days and no one would see you," says Stelios.

I lie on my stomach. Beside me, Anna rolls over onto her back and Stelios wraps his hand around her waist where her shirt has risen up. I pick at a chunk of bread before me on the blanket.

"It's nice here," Anna says after a while. "What if this turns out to be where your farm was, after all," she muses, "and we're lying where the stables used to be or something."

"I hope not," Maki says, twisting away from the blanket in mock revulsion.

"Do you think it could have been here?" Stelios asks.

"I really don't know. I only know it from stories and pictures. I'm pretty sure it's a big farm. We employed a lot of people, apparently."

"How long had it been in your family before your grandfather's time?" Andreas asks, sitting up.

"I don't know."

"And how did they make the money to establish it? Where did the fortune come from?"

"Raisins, I guess. I'm not sure."

"See?" He slaps the blanket with a dull thud. "Typical rich irresponsibility. Failure even to understand the connections of their wealth to someone else's work, someone else's labor. The connection to all those people you employed."

"You're joking, right?" I look around, smiling. "He's got the Marxist thing down pat."

But Andreas is sitting up now. "Do you suppose your grandfather gave them a fair wage?"

"Andreas, knock it off," Stelios says in a voice muffled by Anna's neck.

"Why should we soften the truth for her? Just because she's not from here?"

"She's our guest," says Maki.

"She's from the most capitalist culture in the world," says Anna dreamily, as if her words are not intended as insult.

"Hey! Look," I say, pulling myself upright. "So my family had some money once. Do you see any of it around now? The farm is gone, the house is sold and falling apart, and all my relatives have left are tiny apartments. And I live in a crummy little place where the heat doesn't work very well and there are rats in the pipes." In my frustration, I say *pípes* for pipes, instead of *solínes*.

"They use rats for tobacco?" Andreas smirks.

"Shut up, Andreas," I say. "Shut the fuck up."

But I'm not as angry at him as I am at myself. That crummy little place was where I lived before Jonah. Our place now is fine.

"Those tiny apartments, Callie, are at least in decent neighborhoods," Stelios says, pulling his head up. "Kolokotronis, Kanakaris—you think those places are bad? You have no idea. You should see what the truly poor have to live in."

I glare at him for a moment, wanting to be just as angry at him as I am at the other two.

"I'm not saying my relatives are suffering. They're not poor. I never claimed that. But whatever wealth we had—"

"Which was a shitload," Andreas says.

"Whatever wealth we had, Andreas," I say sternly, "is gone. There's no treasure, there's no vault, there's no estate. It's gone, okay? My mother, her sisters, her brother, they all started their lives over with nothing. Nothing at all."

"Andreas has a point," Stelios goes on. "Families like yours—"

"What kind of family is that, Stelios?"

"Wealthy, landowning families."

I roll my eyes, disgusted now at the crude simplicity of what he has to say.

"Families like yours have screwed things up for a lot of people in Greece," he says. "For a very long time. PASOK understood that in 1980, and now look at what the rightists have done."

"The rightists are bringing Greece into the euro. Do you think there'd be a bridge across the gulf without the euro? Or new roads or the new airport? Oh, and aren't the rightists still paying for your degrees?" I look around at all of them with mock innocence.

"Absolutely," Stelios says.

"Not me," Maki says. "I'm working."

"You weren't smart enough to take the handout," Stelios says.

I hear the echo of my words in our conversation yesterday. Absolutely not, I said to his Treasure Hunt invitation. Now, deliberately or not, with this word and this tease, Stelios is trying to claim a lightness of heart that disappeared almost as soon as we sat down on the grass.

"Try not to fuck it up anymore, now that you've got your uncle's inheritance, all right?" Andreas says.

Everybody laughs, and I allow a smile. It is Carnival. I roll onto my back and pretend I'm relaxing, waiting for the right time to end this foolish outing. The air is almost warm, and the grass smells sweet around us. I try to imagine this field as part of my family's farm, my family's capitalist, wealthy farm.

On the way back to the car, Stelios walks beside me, humming softly.

"They took in refugees, you know," I say.

He turns to me, questioning.

"At the farm. My family took in refugees during the war."

"Good for them."

"Is that all you have to say?"

He takes my hand and rubs his thumb against the inside of my wrist.

"For now, yes."

I pull my hand away.

"This was a stupid idea. I don't even know you people. And you know nothing about me. So quit judging me."

Stelios holds his hands up defensively. "Whatever you say."

We drive in silence until Maki pulls the Renault up in front of Aliki's building. I clamber out and make a point to thank Maki for the ride, and I vow to myself that I will have nothing more to do with Stelios and his friends. As I step out of the elevator on Aliki's floor, I feel the relief of shedding a false life.

Aliki is in the kitchen, cooking a beef stew.

"Where did you go?"

"Didn't you see my note?"

"Yes, I saw the note, but you have no idea where to find the farm, Callie. It's impossible. Where did you end up with these people?"

"In a lovely field, actually, behind a warehouse in Perivoli."

"Behind a warehouse!"

"Was it in Perivoli?" I ask. "I thought I remembered the name."

"No," she laughs ruefully. "Pelargos. It was in Pelargos." The word for stork.

"Well, I had a lovely time," I lie, wanting to defend my morning against this new challenge from Aliki. "We can go back to Pelargos another time," I go on. "It'd be fun. We could take Demetra."

"It's all built up, Callie. Has been for years."

"That's not what you told me."

"When?"

"A while ago."

"What did I say?"

"That the farmhouse was still standing, with a plot of land around the house where the orchards were."

She is shaking her head, looking at me as if she wants to comfort me and scold me.

"I never said that. It's not even true. Everything was built on. The last time there was a farmhouse or an orchard on that property was before I was born. And our family had sold it long before that."

"This is like that drain in the old house that no one can agree on. Doesn't anybody have any story straight?"

"Maybe not. But I can tell you the farm was sold a long time ago."

"And how do you know?"

"Because I've looked. We didn't own it after '45 or '46."

"What if you got it wrong? Like the drain."

"No, Callie. Trust me. It's been gone for a while."

If Aliki is right—and I have a stubborn inability to accept this—I understand why the aunts never took us there. They couldn't. Even if they had been able to find the way among the new and incomplete houses and the warehouses, there would have been nothing for us to see except evidence of loss. While Anna could lie in the grass and imagine how it might have been once to sit in a carriage or a bedroom on the same spot, the aunts knew that what they would need to do would be harder. It is easier to create out of nothing than to cover over reality with images from the past.

"I was telling my friends about the refugees," I say, for some reason not wanting to come right out and ask Aliki what she knows.

"Yes?" She keeps stirring the stew meat.

"This isn't news to you?"

"That you told your friends?" She laughs.

"The refugees, Aliki."

She knocks the spoon on the edge of the pot and turns to me, holding the spoon over the food.

"The refugees," she says. "My mother told me."

"When?"

"Ages ago. Some working men. And a family, I think. They took them in during the war. Paki, can you hand me the parsley?"

I find the parsley on a cutting board, minced into tiny flakes. I gather up a fistful and bring it to Aliki. She gestures to me to toss it into the pot.

And that is that. Not because Aliki is trying to hide anything—I know her face well enough to see that—but because this information is of no significance to her.

8

Clio

July 1940

Clio was sitting in one of the apricot trees on the farm, her back resting against the trunk and her legs crooked over a sloping branch, as if she were riding sidesaddle. If she bent her head at the right angle, she could see through the leaves, beyond the edge of the grove, to an area of open land behind which were the rows and rows of grapevines. Yannis had a crew of men in the vineyard now. If she sat very still, she could almost hear them talking and singing as they tended the grapes.

She loosened the braids she had allowed Thalia to put in that morning and let her hair fall about her shoulders, kinked like Medusa's snakes. She closed her eyes and pictured herself at a soirée, with her dark-brown hair flowing over bare shoulders or tucked up into an elegant twist. A voice shouted close by, but she ignored it, assuming it was one of Yannis's men.

She was tugged out of her daydream by the rising peal of a whistle. It was Sophia, signaling that the coast was clear for the children to sneak away to the clover houses. This was the one point on which Clio conceded leadership to Sophia. She had no intention of whistling or shouting for the rest of them, as if she were herding animals. When she wasn't poring over history books, Sophia liked to organize—people or information, it didn't matter what, as long as she could keep it in line. She whistled again, this time with an urgency that shook Clio from her thoughts of parties and ball gowns.

"Do you have to do that?" she called down through the leaves.

"What?"

Clio could see the top of Sophia's head just below her. Her sister looked up into the branches of the tree, hands on hips.

"Do you have to make it sound so upsetting?" She began to swing herself down from the tree. Landing on the ground at Sophia's feet, she quickly gathered her hair up into a ponytail and glared at the girl. "It sounds like the siren, for goodness' sake."

"It does not. And you can't hear the siren anyway."

"Yes, you can. When the wind is right."

Though the war had not reached Greece yet, Patras had set up a system of air-raid sirens and tested them from time to time, always in the middle of the day so that people could see with their own eyes that there were no bombers on the way. Here on the farm, they were only ten kilometers from Plateia Georgiou at the heart of the city, closer still to the city's easternmost siren. When the sirens wailed, Clio tried to ignore the sound, but she could never keep herself from that initial start and shiver as the high-pitched wail filled the air.

"You can," Nestor chimed in. "I heard it yesterday."

Clio looked at him, this little boy with a head of black curls and a wide collar. She knew for a fact that there had been no siren test the day before, but she was happy to have his corroboration now. She turned back to Sophia, drawing herself up straight to remind her sister that she was the oldest. If she said she could hear the siren, then she could hear the siren. Even Nestor's allegiance was not necessary.

"Why don't you just sing part of a song or something?"

"Fine," Sophia said. "I'll sing a Guides song."

"Can it be a Scouts song instead?" Nestor asked.

"Sure." Clio gave him an indulgent smile. Though the Greek Youth had taken his Scouting things away, Nestor was one of the few boys in Patras who had not joined Metaxas's organization. Their mother had won the debate with their father. Until it was no longer a matter of choice, no child of hers would participate in a fascist movement.

"Start us off, Nestor," Clio said.

He began to sing in his high voice, bringing his knees up high on each step, clearly relishing the opportunity to follow orders.

Nestor led them to a pasture on the west side of the house, far from the vineyards and out of sight of the farmyard. Here, Yannis had made a small village of four child-sized houses out of shoulder-high forage grasses of clover and rye. It was like the mazes in the palaces of England that Clio had read about, only, instead of paths, Yannis had cut rooms and streets and a village square. Each house had a roof made of sheaves of hay placed across the tops of the walls, and each had a window and a door, where Yannis had cut the normally tall clover short. He made the clover houses for the children every year, mowing the village down in the fall along with the rest of the crop. Clio's parents never knew.

Clio followed Nestor in his high-stepping march, occasionally looking over her shoulder to exchange a glance with Sophia and Thalia. Nestor, too, turned around, to check that his sisters were still playing along. Each time he looked back, the girls sang a little louder and stepped a little more crisply.

When they arrived at the houses, Nestor begged to play grocery.

"We've been doing your thing all the way here," Thalia said.

"Please." He looked at Clio.

"Just a little bit," she said, rolling her eyes at Sophia behind his back but making sure that she and Thalia joined in the game. This meant taking turns visiting Nestor's house and pretending to buy the odds and ends of fruit that he had stored there and set inside on top of a box. He gave the girls money made of leaves so they could use it to pay for what they bought. For change, he used small pebbles dug up from the pasture.

After a bit of the game, Clio retreated to her own house to resume the daydreaming that Sophia's whistle had interrupted. There in the dappled light, she lay back and rested her head on her folded arms. She listened to the hiss and creak of the drying clover and imagined herself stepping into a ballroom silenced by her glamour. People murmured from the edges of the room and then slowly resumed dancing. Young men lined up to escort her onto the floor. As she spun around in a waltz, jewels in her hair sent tiny reflections flickering along the walls. She closed her eyes.

A shout from Nestor pierced her reverie, and someone darted past her house, setting her clover walls swaying. She sat up, crying, "Hey!" and heard Thalia and Sophia giggling somewhere nearby.

She decided then that the fragile privacy of her clover house was not enough; she needed solitude, and there was little of that at the farmhouse. She had to find a way to get to her clover house completely alone—to be away from the others, but to be away, too, from the rest of the world, which she would soon be entering as an adult. In the clover house at night—for that seemed the best time—she could imagine her future, fashioning the story of her life so she could recognize each perfect phase as it came along.

That afternoon she crept into the kitchen, hoping Irini would be in her cottage, napping.

"What do you want?"

Irini stood in the door to the storeroom where they kept sacks of flour and grain and jugs of olive oil. Ever since the children had flooded the basement in the city house, Irini seemed to be on strict watch over the food at the farm—not the fresh fruit, for there was plenty of that, but the dry goods and the staples. Clio's mother never said anything about it, but the message was clear: The supplies were to be protected. Every now and then, Irini would prepare a cake for them sweetened with syrup made from sugar beets. "It's an experiment," Urania would say, but Clio knew it was because sugar would someday be scarce.

"Just some bread," Clio attempted. While Yannis indulged the children with treats like the clover houses, Irini seemed to resent them, quietly seething whenever they dared enter her kitchen, especially here on the farm, where the space was smaller and the outdoors more appropriate for children, in her view.

Irini tucked the morning's loaf under one arm and, with the other, sawed a slice off the end with the bread knife. She speared the slice onto the knife tip.

"Here."

Clio thanked her and retreated.

Over the next two days, she managed to sneak away a few more slices of bread, which she wrapped in handkerchief bundles, like the hobos in the movies and the tramps who, in recent months, had begun to wander into Korinthou Street. She hid a flashlight in her nightstand. She filled two old Girl Guide canteens with water and hid one under her bed, another behind a barrel in the barn.

Her preparations complete, she sat through dinner and then caught a few fireflies with her sisters and brother, arranging the glowing jars on the railing of the porch before setting the insects free again. Finally, when her mother signaled the end of the day, she went to bed in the room she shared with Sophia, tingling with the excitement of the coming adventure. She waited until she heard the wheeze of Sophia's deepest sleep and then forced herself to wait even a little longer to be sure that Thalia, down the hall, had given up watch on her older sisters. Then she slid the flashlight from its drawer and snuck out in her nightgown and bare feet, stepping on the soft wood boards toe–heel, like the Indians in the novel she had read in school.

Outside, the air was cool and still. Stars shone unchallenged by the moon, and the glowing specks of the released fireflies dotted the edges of the farmyard. Clio zigzagged across the yard to collect her provisions. As she crept toward the field, she heard rustling in the darkness and hoped it was just a fox, so that she could be both afraid and brave. She imagined the glowing eyes of foxes or even wolves peering at her through the orchard and walked a little faster, swinging her flashlight high before her to ward the creatures off. The beam cast shadows that made it seem as if a group of people were dancing and jumping among the tree trunks. Suddenly fear overtook her and she ran part of the way back to the house, leaving her canteen and handkerchief behind. Breathing deeply, fighting the notion that she had seen a figure in the shadows, she returned to her things and continued on to the clover houses.

The clover whisked her cheeks as she pushed through the

barely perceptible gap that swam up before her in the flashlight beam. So many times before, she had led the way into the field, but only now did she notice the caress of the clover on her skin. The sound, too, of the matted clover underfoot: Each step seemed now as if the ground were sighing. She passed Sophia's house and then Nestor's and then stood before the darkened rectangle of her own door. She scanned the house with the flashlight and ducked inside.

Though she had brought the food and water with her, she neither ate nor drank anything. She sat on the soft floor of the house and hugged her knees, peering up at the roof and listening to the night breathing around her. She reveled in her solitude—more than that, in her singularity, as if she felt her value increasing in isolation. For though the roof of the house largely obscured the sky, she kept in her thoughts the image of the myriad stars she had seen from the farmyard. Each one was an admiring eye looking down on her.

Clio made three more trips to her clover house over the next few nights. With each trip, she grew bolder and more at ease in the darkness. And though she continued to hear rustlings in the shadows and again thought she saw a figure looming behind a tree, she never hesitated on her way. By the third night, she knew the nighttime path so well that she switched the flashlight off and made her way in the glow of the stars. But she did wonder as she went, what if something were to happen to her in the middle of the night? She would be far from the farmhouse with only a flashlight and a metal canteen for protection. If she cried out, no one would hear her. Still, even as she formed this thought, she grew excited at the idea of real danger. She felt wiser, rendered more important by this change in the quality of her imaginations.

The following day, after Thalia had dragged Nestor and Sophia home to cadge some candy from Irini, Clio was lying on her back inside her house, resting her head on her hands and looking up at the way the sunlight showed in stripes through the roof. She became aware of a faint rasping in the clover beside her. She turned her head toward the sound and stiffened at the sight of a man looking through her window. He had a small head and wore a bluish shirt with a frayed collar. A cloth cap drooped over his eyes. She held her breath, not daring to move. It seemed to her that eye contact was what he wanted, so she forced herself to look away and stare at the beaten clover on the floor. Moving only one hand, she reached down and tugged at the hem of her skirt, which had hiked up during her rest.

In her mind, Clio ran through the dangers her parents had been warning of all summer: There were tramps about, and the beggars were getting bolder. This man must be a tramp; he was not a farmhand she recognized. Again, she heard the clover hissing and felt a change in the light of the house. From the corner of her eye, she saw that the man was crouching in the doorway of the clover house now, completely blocking the rectangle sized for a child to pass through. She clenched her fists, realizing with the first real fear in her life that she had nothing to protect herself with.

Without thinking, she sprang up into a squat. "Get out!" she shouted, her neck muscles straining. For an instant, she saw a kind of scornful surprise on the man's face, and then he turned and slipped into the field.

She fell back onto the floor of the house, wiping away a sudden flow of tears. When she had collected herself, she ran back to the farmhouse, not minding the twigs and brambles that caught at her clothes. Twisting to look behind her, she saw only fields and sky, empty and unmoving. She found her sisters and brother in the kitchen, peeling strips of cooled caramel syrup from the marble counter.

"Where have you been? You're all out of breath," Sophia said.

"The cow was looking strange again. I ran from the barn."

They laughed and rolled the candy strips up into little barrels.

"It's not funny," Clio snapped.

"Yes, it is," said Thalia. She licked her fingers one by one. "It was funny when the cow chased Irini."

"Well, it's not funny now." Clio looked down at the rolls of candy, realizing she had shown too much emotion.

"What's the matter with you?" Nestor murmured.

She wheeled on him. "I heard someone in the clover field. A stranger."

The children stopped what they were doing and stared at her. She narrowed her eyes, determined not to say anything more. Still staring, Sophia began to nod.

"Me too," she said. "I heard some strange noises by the edge of the pasture a couple of days ago."

"Like twigs snapping. I heard it when I was sitting in my house today," said Thalia.

Nestor slowly peeled another strip of candy from the counter.

"Me too," he said, as he rolled it up into a cylinder. "Someone was moving around in the clover field." He held the candy up to admire it. "It didn't look like anyone we know."

"You dope." Sophia shoved him. "You didn't see anybody!"

"I did too." He put the candy down and took on a serious look. "And he looked scary. Dangerous."

Clio waited, not knowing what to say but anxious to reclaim the story she had paid for in fear. She flushed suddenly at the thought of how she had screamed at the man, crouching like an animal.

Thalia took Nestor by the arm. "I wonder if there were more than one. He probably wasn't alone."

"They could be trying to steal food," Nestor said, "or the tractor."

"Or the cow," Sophia laughed.

"I know who they are," Clio jumped in finally. She didn't raise her voice but spoke firmly enough to cut the others off. "I saw them."

Sophia squinted at her, but Clio concentrated on the widening eyes of Thalia and Nestor.

"You saw them?"

"What did they look like?"

"Who are they?"

Clio took a deep breath, feeling her lungs fill and push her rib cage out, and watched for the precise instant when the others' anticipation was almost ready to dissolve into impatience.

"They're spies," she said, exhaling as the other children drew their breath sharply in, unable to forget the disdain with which the man had looked at her.

She elaborated, explaining that she had seen enough of these people at the edges of the farm to suspect that they had formed a network and established a system of message posts throughout the property. She speculated on the meaning of certain coded flashes of light at night and convinced the others that traitors were planning an attack on the harbor later in the summer.

"If I had known you had all seen them too," she added, "I would have said something earlier."

A few days later, Clio's father suggested they gather fireflies again for an experiment.

"Come on, Nestor." Leonidas waved at the boy. "Go on and get the jars for us."

"I don't want to."

This surprised everyone, since Nestor was always first to seize whatever equipment was necessary for an exploration.

"Nestor," Urania said, "do as you're told."

Clio braced herself for what she suspected was coming.

"It's dark now. What about the spies?"

"What spies?" her father laughed, and began to head into the kitchen to get the jars himself.

"The ones by the clover houses."

The girls had been moving toward him to keep him quiet, but now they backed away quickly, as if by reversing their movement they could undo their brother's speech. Leonidas turned back into the room.

"What clover houses?"

And Nestor told him.

Clio watched her father's mouth set and the mustache become a straight bar across his lip as he listened. She saw with dismay that her spy story had given her brother exactly the ingredients with which to finish the job the intruder had started. Nestor drew himself up straighter with each answer to his father's questions, as if he fancied himself to be defending the farmhouse with his information. Her father seemed to be under no such illusion. He summoned Yannis to come with a flashlight and frog-marched Nestor through the dark pastures to the clover field. The others followed, feeling their way in the night while Yannis swept the flashlight beam in front.

They stopped in a loose circle before the invisible door of the clover village, and their father took the flashlight from Yannis, raking the clover for a hint of the way in.

"Go on. Where's the door?"

"There isn't one," Nestor sniveled, and Leonidas pushed him forward by the shoulders.

"It's not his fault," Sophia said. "It was all of us. We do it every summer."

Clio's father stopped listening and plunged through the clover. The glow of his flashlight moved like a giant firefly through the hidden houses. Nestor was sobbing now, and Sophia and Thalia wept quietly. Clio wept too, but her thoughts were stuck on the image of the strange man whose real presence had led to the undoing of their game. What if she had drawn him to the houses somehow? What if her nighttime forays had attracted him to the field in the first place? It was her need to be alone that had started everything. Had she not found satisfaction in that first discovery of a sky full of watching stars, she would never have returned for a second visit, and the man would never have gotten the sense that she would be there, available for him somehow.

Clio's father ordered Yannis to cut the clover field down. Her mother told the children this was a way to keep them safe from the prying eyes of destitute strangers. The mowing would serve as a message to any men wandering the countryside that this particular farm could offer them no harbor.

It was a large enough operation that Yannis required farmhands to help mow as well as to tie up the bales and store them in the barn for silage. He left a message at the taverna in the nearest village, and word spread among the gaunt beggars who gathered each day behind the kitchen for scraps of food. The next morning, six men, their clothes draped loosely over their frames, appeared in the farmyard. One of them held a scythe at his side. The rest would borrow tools from Yannis's supply in the barn. For three days, under Yannis's watch, these men chopped the swaying clover down to a plain of stubble, their scythes flashing in the sun. At the end of each day's work, they huddled in the farmyard so Irini could feed them chunks of bread and bowls of stewed vegetables, but then Yannis dispersed them, making sure they understood they were not to linger on the premises.

As soon as the mowing began, Nestor, Sophia, and Thalia moved on to other pastimes on the other side of the farm, but Clio couldn't stay away. She climbed her apricot tree and turned toward the pasture, watching the slow advance of the cutting line and the bales tossed in the air onto the cart. Climbing the tree seemed childish to her, in a way that had not seemed childish at all just a week ago, but she could think of no better way to see and not be seen. For she couldn't be sure that the stranger—her stranger, as she had come to think of him despite herself—was not among them. Peering through the leaves at the men moving in the distance, she chose one man whose silhouette most resembled the lanky shape of her stranger and followed him up and down the rows. She wasn't sure why, perhaps to catch him in an attempt to come looking for her. Whenever he straightened his back to gaze around him, she remembered the moment her stranger had moved into the child-sized doorway of the clover house. She remembered his frayed collar and the dark edge of his cap and imagined his grimy fingers tugging on the cap to remove it in the presence of his superiors. But most of all, she remembered that instant in which she had seen a flash of scorn cross his face, and she wondered, with some indignation, what he had seen to be scornful of.

9

Callie

Monday

Today I can call Constantopoulos, the lawyer, and make some progress on what I have actually come here to do. I get the slip of paper my mother gave me on my first day here and dial the number.

"Embros." Proceed: another commanding invitation on the telephone.

I tell him who I am and what I need. He sounds as though he has never heard of my case before.

"It's about Nestor Notaris," I say. "I am his niece from Boston."

"Ah, Notaris," he says, emphasizing the name. "Miss Notaris—"

"Brown."

"Sorry?"

"It's Brown. My father was American."

"So, Miss Brown." He pronounces it *Braoun.* "I'm happy to help you, and I can have the document drawn up by the end of the week for you to sign."

"The end of the week! I thought the document was already drawn up. My uncle died almost two weeks ago."

"On February eighteenth, actually. Ten days ago."

He is doing this to prove to me that he is efficient. While we have been on the phone, he has scrambled for my uncle's file and has just managed to read the date of death in time to quote it to me officiously.

"If it is possible," I say sweetly, remembering Aliki's warning about fickle lawyers, "it would be very useful to have the document drawn up before too long so that I don't have to change my airline ticket."

He agrees to try.

I go to an Internet café on the near end of Korinthou Street and check email for the first time since last Wednesday. There is a message from Jonah. My scalp buzzes with adrenaline, but I force myself to save his for last. I delete the spam and read through the messages from work—about prospects to pursue, upcoming events in the annual campaign, letters to check. I skim through the messages from certain friends. There is one from Marcus that includes a picture, taken just yesterday, of all the rugby guys covered in snow on the Esplanade. Jonah's rounded cheeks are bright red in the cold, and he seems to be shouting a joke at the photographer. I don't know how I expected Jonah to look, but somehow I didn't expect him to look this contented. I'm not even sure which I'd prefer—for him to be destroyed with pining for me, or for him to be the happy, relaxed man I might be coming back to.

I click on Jonah's message. It's brief and, to my embarrassment, makes tears form in my eyes. *I love you,* he writes, *even though I don't think you always know what that means—to me or to you. There's no need to respond.* He sent the email days ago, before our phone call, knowing I might not read it for a while.

But then, there is nothing time-sensitive about what he has said. And that is, I suppose, part of the point: He's telling me there is no expiration date on his emotions. I can't deny that the idea terrifies and excites me, both. In the end, this is what I write to him. *I just got your email today. I love you too. But I don't know yet whether that's enough for either of us.*

The rest of the morning I spend alone in Nestor's house, working through the boxes and listening to a soft rain tapping on the black and white tiles of the back garden. It's afternoon when I open the door and let the smell of moist dirt seep into the house. All during my childhood, the aroma of rain-dampened dirt could send the aunts into speechless rapture. Even for me, who grew up with plenty of rain and damp; even I have always drunk in the smell. As if the aroma sent me, like them, back to summer afternoons on the farm, when the rain would soak the dirt beneath the almond trees.

I pull Nestor's chair out from the desk and turn it so that it faces the garden. I try to do nothing but notice—notice the furniture, the garden, the room, the papers, the homemade gadgets on the desk. This place will change completely in a few short weeks, and I want to remember it as it is now, as it used to be, almost my whole life. After a while, I rise to close the garden door against the chill.

Beyond the yellow lamplight falling on the desk, I am surrounded by darkness in which I can make out the towerlike shapes of Nestor's boxes and books, like crenellations on a fortification. I switch on the half-domed light on the ceiling and wander back to Nestor's things, not quite ready to plunge into another box but not wanting to leave just yet either.

I think about the simple fact of refugees on the farm. I know why my mother never told me about them: because to acknowledge the presence of someone else in that idyll would diminish or destroy the childish pleasure she could take, even now, in her memories of the place. Admitting a stranger would be like admitting an adult into a children's game.

My mother began with so much. Her father a raisin exporter with warehouses by the docks. Her mother a socialite, accomplished in the arts and in the practice of philanthropy. Enough beauty to go around the family, parents and children, so that when the aunts walked out in the evenings during their teenage years, they gathered boys and young men in a growing wake. And property that sustained and demonstrated their wealth and that could have been passed down through the generations to preserve it. We didn't lack for comfort when I was growing up either. Two cars in the garage, overseas airfare, college tuition. The ingredients were all there, provided by my father's engineering salary. But by then there was such poverty in my mother's spirit that her life sucked the joy out of my father's spirit too. Long before he finally left for good, he had vowed never to return to Greece.

I think of Andreas's politics from yesterday, his accusation that families like mine had inflicted harm on others. What exactly is a family like mine? We never became one of the little dynasties that rule Greek life. We were no Gounaris, or Niarchos, or Karamanlis or Papandreou. The Notaris name means nothing in Patras now. When my family had wealth, they did what they could; they were generous. My grandparents offered the refugees on the farm shelter and food. Yes, in exchange for work, according to my mother's new story. But Andreas turned what could have been a fair and simple exchange into exploitation.

Andreas would have me believe that the wealthy families choke off the routes to success for the rest of Greece. The truth is that there is plenty of grabbing and snatching to go around today among rich and poor alike. And the government is just as eager to buy patronage from the shopkeeper as it is from the yacht owner. When Nestor used to sigh over preferments given to his politically aligned fellow teachers, or when Nikos fumed years ago about his competitor's attempts to block his new business, I was listening. Wealthy families are not the problem in Greece. The problem is a lack of generosity, a poverty of spirit like my mother's.

Outside I hear the hiss of tires on wet asphalt. It is six o'clock, and people are heading out after their long siesta. Soon phones will start to ring again, voices will be raised, television sets turned up. With the "Auld Lang Syne" key in my hand, I lock up and head home.

"It's just us tonight," Aliki announces when I greet her in the kitchen. "Nikos is at a dinner for work, and Demetra is spending the night at a friend's house to work on their kites for Clean Monday."

"They make them themselves?"

"People sell them on the Sunday, but we make them. Tradition."

I pull out a chair from the small round table, grunting a little at the stiffness in my neck and shoulders.

"Tired?"

"Yes," I groan.

"You must be drowning in Nestor's life."

Aliki pours us each a glass of wine and dribbles some olive oil into a skillet that she sets on the stove. Moving with habits learned from her father, she beats eggs for an omelet while the sweet, rich smell of the heated oil sails up from the pan. I am caught in a rapid succession of memories, all centered on that earthy fragrance: french fries eaten at Demetris's taverna, eggs scrambled with tomatoes that Thalia would make when we were tired, the bread we dredged through the juices at the bottom of the salad bowl. Aliki's thoughts are elsewhere.

I gather tomatoes, cucumber, feta, and a cutting board. I reach around her for the oil and vinegar and grab the mustard from the refrigerator door to make a dressing.

"Do you know what I was thinking of today, while you were at Nestor's? The silkworms." She makes a sheepish grimace at me.

"Oh, no."

"See, these are the dangers of bugging me with family history." She spills the beaten eggs into the skillet and points the spoon at me. "I remember a story we'd both rather forget."

"No," I say, "your conscience is clean. The silkworms are my own personal embarrassment."

One summer, my enthusiasm for the aunts' stories reached a peak and I convinced Aliki that we should try to raise silkworms as they had done during the war. For our mothers and their siblings, the raising of silkworm cocoons had been an exotic project of tremendous success: They ran a thriving business selling succeeding generations of cocoons through the basement windows to children who handed their coins down through the grate. Everything about this story was perfect—all that a child could dream of. There was the allure of the cocoons themselves, the mystery of the faraway land the silkworms came from, the game of keeping a store, and the transformation of the mundane basement into a magic room where worms turned into hollow balls of thread. And on top of all that, I had visions of the silkworms funding a steady stream of comic books and candy from the neighborhood kiosk. Aliki and I would be set for the summer.

We set up our operation in the cluttered basement of Thalia's apartment building, the same one Aliki lives in now. Mario, the superintendent, indulged us by moving a box or two out of the way. We found an old window, its casement cracked, and lined it with cloth and newspaper. Laying it flat, we spread it with mulberry leaves from the trees around Plateia Olgas and nestled thirty or forty silkworms among the leaves. At first, the project captivated both of us. But after a few days, I had to beg Aliki to keep me company. She would much rather stroll around Plateia Olgas and flirt with the boys.

I ended up spending most of the time alone, holding on to the idea that my version of my mother's game could measure up. I sat among the broken chairs, old toasters, and disused toys and watched the worms devour the leaves. Later, I stared as they spun the silk around and around themselves, wanting, by then, to abandon the whole thing but too burdened by shame, self-pity, and even responsibility to give myself a break.

"What a miserable summer," I say.

"Don't be embarrassed," Aliki says. "You were little."

She tips half of the cooked omelet onto my plate and sets a basket of bread on the table. I toss the salad with the dressing. We both smile at the ease with which we occupy each other's space.

"I can't even remember who gave us the worms," I say, "whom I should thank for my spectacular failure."

"Nestor did. You asked him."

"Huh."

I have no recollection of this at all, but it fits. He was giving me or getting for me little objects like those he had collected as a boy.

Aliki refills her wineglass and breaks off a piece of bread, which she uses like a knife to push the food onto her fork. After a bite of omelet, she pops the bread into her mouth.

"This is that Drimopoulos bread, isn't it?" I ask.

"Drimakopoulos," Aliki corrects me. "Try buying anything else if you are part of the Notaris family. The aunts are convinced they can tell."

"*Mamá* always talked about an Italian bakery they went to when they were kids—Marinelli's. She gave the free cocoons to the little boy. He was the son of the baker."

Aliki pushes her lower lip out in uninterested doubt.

"All I know is that Drimakopoulos's bakery has been there since forever, and, if the aunts are coming, that's where I go to buy bread."

Aliki mops the egg and oil from her plate with one last swipe of bread.

"Let's go sit," she says, bringing her glass and the wine bottle to the living room. She curls up on the couch, tucking her feet under her. I ease into the cushions at the other end.

"When's Nikos getting home?"

Aliki shrugs. "These things go late during Carnival." After a moment, she asks, "Do you know about the Bourbouli dances?"

I shake my head and she proceeds to explain a series of three dances, the first of which takes place tomorrow night. The Bourbouli dances are the heart of Carnival, she says, with all the rules inverted in the true Carnival spirit. The men wear as close as they can to black tie, but the women are disguised with masks and black *dominos,* robes that hide them from head to toe. They are the ones who troll for dance partners, never revealing their identity. Many affairs have been conducted in public at the Bourboulis, and many marriages have been broken up because of flirtations discovered once Carnival has concluded.

"Sounds great," I say. "A good night for divorce lawyers."

"It's a lark." She waves a hand dismissively.

"Are you going?"

"No. Someone has to stay home with Demetra." The old Aliki would be bright-eyed at the opportunity to make some mischief.

"Wait. Is Nikos going?"

She nods.

"Without you?"

"At the Bourbouli dances, you don't really go *with* someone. That's the point. Lose someone, find someone."

"And you're okay with that?"

"Don't judge me, Paki."

"I'm not. I honestly want to know."

She twists toward me on the couch.

"I used to be okay with it. We'd both go and"—she waves a hand—"participate. Now I kind of let Nikos do his thing as long as he stops once Carnival's over. But it's starting to get to me." She gives a breezy laugh. "It's no fun unless you're getting your fair share."

"Really?"

Her thoughts have drifted.

"Is it still fun if you're both cheating?"

"Listen to you, all moral."

"No, I'm really asking, Aliki. I want to know."

She looks at me for a long time, and I remember that look from countless conversations over summer after summer, Aliki's hazel eyes never flinching, always clear.

"Yes, it is," she says, knowing she's surprised me. But then she adds, "As long as you know each of you is doing exactly the same thing and feels exactly the same way about it." She laughs.

"Ah."

"That's not what you wanted to hear, is it?"

"I'm not sure."

"Paki, don't let me complicate it for you. You should go. The Bourboulis are the heart of Carnival."

"I'll think about it."

What I'm thinking is that I can keep an eye on Nikos.

When we pour out the last of the wine, he's still not back from his dinner.

"Paki, go to bed. You're half asleep."

"You sure?"

I've been trying to conceal my yawns, wanting to keep her company.

"I'm fine," she says. "I'm used to it."

I don't know what to tell her, but she smiles ruefully and shoos me away. I leave her in the living room nursing her half-empty glass and head off to bed, remembering all those hours I sat alone in that musty basement, waiting for cocoons.

10

Clio

October 1940

By parental decree, Clio, Sophia, Thalia, and Nestor walked to school together. With Clio in the lead, they were to stay in a group and take the same route each day for safety. Talk of the coming war was everywhere now. Two months before, on August 15, Mussolini had sunk a cruiser full of pilgrims headed for the church of Agia Maria on the island of Tinos. The government had done nothing, but everybody—every adult—knew it was just a matter of time before they did. Clio suspected that those sacks of food in her family's basement were replicated in basements all over the city.

She was supposed to keep this suspicion from her younger siblings, so she led them every day down Korinthou and then Maizonos, past a row of shops that sold, in order, meat, milk and eggs, bread, pastries, and wine. In the afternoon, the shops were open and full of customers, and the pastry shop was crowded with the children's schoolmates. But the Notaris children stopped at Marinelli's bakery instead. Every Monday, Wednesday, and Friday, they bought a *karveli,* a round loaf of steaming hot bread, which Clio tore into chunks, keeping the moist core for herself. Nestor always scraped his crust clean, mashing the bread into a doughy ball that he sucked and chewed on all the way home.

Marinelli was an Italian, whose Greek rose and fell, rather than shooting out straight like the speech of a native. When he cooed at his little boy, who helped him after school, and even when he argued with his mother, his voice sounded gentle and kind. The old woman sat on a low stool at the end of the counter, from which she could see all the customers. She was always looking for a thief and muttering things in Italian to her son. Even with everyone talking of war, Clio could not understand why anyone would bother to steal bread.

Until Marinelli spoke, no one would have known he was not Greek. As the shared expression went among Greeks and Italians: *Una fatsa, una ratsa,* the Italian *faccia* and *razza* spoken with a Greek accent to say their similar faces made them one *ratsa,* one race. Marinelli certainly had the *fatsa* of a Greek man: dark eyes and skin and hair; long, straight nose; long earlobes.

"*Kalispéra,* Clio *mou,*" he said to her. "Good afternoon."

"*Kalispéra.*"

"Here they are," he said, reaching into the glass case below the counter. "Your special raisin rolls."

It was Friday, so, in addition to their usual *karveli,* the children bought four of Marinelli's sweet rolls with egg and raisins as their regular treat for the end of the week. The raisins came from their own family farm, considered the best for generations. The large, squat Notaris warehouses by the docks were piled high with boxes of golden and black fruit, much of which was shipped to Brindisi across the Adriatic and from there into

all of Europe. No other merchant in Patras could match Notaris volume and quality.

Marinelli slid the rolls into four small paper bags and handed
them to Clio.

"*Marco,*" he called to the room behind him, "*vieni qui.*"

Marco came trotting into the shop, a skinny little boy just
two years younger than Nestor, with dark curly hair very much
like his. Clio went around to the end of the counter, not the
old woman's end, and called for Marco to come and take her
money. She tousled his curls and handed him twelve drachmas.

"Thank you, Miss Clio," he said in Greek like hers. "Come
see my drawing."

He motioned Clio over to his grandmother's spot and took
from the old woman a notebook whose pages she had been
turning in her lap.

"*Buon giorno,*" Clio said to the old woman. She never spoke
to Clio, seemingly unable to use the girl's language and unwilling to share her own.

Marco had drawn a harbor with two ships, one blue, one
orange, at the dock. They both flew the Greek flag from their
mast.

"Nice job," Clio said. "*É molto bello.*"

"See you tomorrow?"

"*È possibile, Marco.*"

She liked the fact that each of them spoke in the other one's
language. Her parents were making all of them take Italian lessons along with their French, on the logic that Greek children
of a certain class should speak the fine languages of Europe.
Clio agreed, wanting to be taken for a native someday in Paris,
Rome, even Vienna. But what if war came? Were they supposed to sweet-talk the foreign invaders in their own tongue?

She led her brother and sisters outside and stopped on the sidewalk, doling out the rolls. Nestor took his roll apart, pulling the spiral like a long snake out of the bag and into his mouth as they all walked home.

Clio was the last one in the door of the house. After a quick glance in the walnut-framed mirror, she joined the others, crowding around their father in the hall at the bottom of the atrium. She wondered if he had gotten news about the war. She wouldn't ask aloud, so as not to alarm the younger ones.

"Look," said Thalia, using the hushed voice she adopted for the things she held to be the most wonderful, like a rainbow, or a butterfly, or a slice of honey-drizzled walnut cake.

Nestor held a small box in his open palm. It was a velvet cuff-link box from their father's dresser, and the lid was up, revealing three white objects, oblong in shape, with short fibers sticking up from them. They shimmered slightly, almost blue, in the broadcast light from above.

"They look like grubs with hair," Sophia said.

"They are not grubs!" Nestor cried.

"They're cocoons," said Thalia, in the voice. "For silkworms."

"Aren't those Chinese?" Clio asked.

"Europe has them too," her father said. "These came from Italy. I had them brought over with the wine shipment."

Una fatsa, una ratsa, her father agreed with everybody else, but he liked his raisins Greek and his wine Italian.

"What do we do with them?" Nestor asked.

Their father explained that he had a box of silkworms in the basement for them. The children could raise the worms so they could see the process of metamorphosis from start to finish. Clio wondered how you determined the end to a cycle that was never done.

The children set the silkworms up in four shallow trays packed with mulberry leaves and spent hours in the basement, waiting for the worms to stop chomping on the leaves and begin winding their silk thread around themselves. Clio suspected this was her father's way to offer Nestor something in place of the hikes and camping he did with the Scouts. But she went along with it, and on the day the worms finally did enclose themselves in their fuzzy white cases, she couldn't resist picking one up and holding it in her palm. She was surprised at how light it was. She expected something more substantial from these creatures, heavy with all their stages of development at once.

At Marinelli's that Monday, Clio greeted the man and called to Marco, who was sitting on his grandmother's low stool, holding a thick slice of bread. He blew at the steam and then held his palm flat over the bread to test the heat.

"*Vieni qui,*" she said. She reached into the book bag she had slung off her shoulders and gently unwrapped a small cloth bundle from the bag.

"I have something for you," she said, speaking in a hush.

"What is it?" He whispered so softly that she could hardly hear him. He was practically holding his breath.

"There."

"Ohhh," he sighed, and Clio checked his face.

"Do you know what it is?"

He shook his head.

"It's a silkworm cocoon."

He still didn't seem to understand, so she explained it all to him.

"I'm going outside," Sophia said, her hip cocked, the back of her hand propped against it. She turned on her heel, with Thalia following her out the door.

"Look, *Papà*," Marco cried, and ran behind the counter to show Marinelli.

"Marco, say thank you to Clio," said Marinelli.

"Thank you," came the boy's voice from behind the glass case. He darted around to the front again, holding a special raisin roll out on a piece of wax paper. "Here, Clio. For you."

She smiled. "You don't have to do that."

"It's all right, Miss Clio," said Marinelli. "One gift for another."

"Grazie," she said, and gave Marco a hug.

Nestor was tugging her jacket.

"What about us?"

Clio knew she couldn't ask for something for him and the girls. If she did, Marinelli would feel obliged to treat all of them and would probably give a raisin roll to each child. One roll as a trade would be fine, but four was too much for a simple silk moth cocoon that cost the children nothing. She shook Nestor off.

"Mr. Marinelli, could we have our usual *karveli,* please?"

Nestor was frowning, but Clio smiled at Marinelli as she said goodbye and nudged her brother outside.

"What'd you do that for?" cried Nestor. "He would have given us some for free."

"That's the point. Keep walking."

Out on the sidewalk, Sophia wanted to know what Clio had. Clio showed her and then had to show the others as well.

"It's from Marco."

"We get some," said Nestor.

"Don't whine, Nestor," she said, tearing off a piece and handing it to him.

"Besides," he said with a mouthful of roll, "they're Notaris raisins in there anyhow."

Clio didn't bother to remind him that Marinelli had paid for the raisins so they were his now.

After dinner, Clio followed her mother into her parents' bedroom.

"Can I sit while you get ready?"

"Of course."

Clio perched on the edge of the bed and watched her mother come and go from her wardrobe to the walnut vanity. Urania draped a dark-green silk gown over the dress stand in the corner and sat at the little cushioned stool before the tri-fold mirrors. Green was her mother's color, to go with the auburn of her hair. Urania dusted her cheeks with powder and cocked her head to the left and right as she sprayed perfume from a square-cut bottle. She held the bottle in one hand and squeezed the bulb of the cord-covered atomizer with the other as a faint rose scent drifted into the air.

"Why do you leave the dress for last?"

"Oh, I don't know."

Urania stepped into the dress, pulled it up, and asked Clio to button the back for her. Then she held her topaz choker to her neck and motioned for Clio to clip it fast.

"There."

Looking at her mother's reflected image, Clio thought she knew why Urania saved the dress for last. Without the dress, her mother could test how *she* looked. The dress would never be more than a complement; it would never be the source of her beauty. If Clio watched her mother enough, she might gain that kind of confidence.

Once her parents had gone out for the evening, her father in his tailcoat and her mother in that dark-green dress, Clio went up the back stairs to the flat roof of the house. She often went there to think and to find some of the solitude she had looked for in the clover houses. At times, she imagined herself as an adult—as an actress, or a dancer. The picture was never quite clear. But she always drew confidence from her high-up view of the city streets, reminded of her place in a world she loved, a world that was stable and fully known to her.

Whenever her father caught her coming down from the narrow stairway at the back of the third floor, he said, in a voice that was mostly bewildered but partly annoyed, "What were you doing up there? Going to Hollywood?" He pronounced this incorrectly, Clio was certain, making this very American word sound as though it were part of his native language. *Choleywooud*. With a guttural *H,* a tight *o,* and a *w* that sounded like three letters put together.

Now she opened the door of the little hut on the rooftop and felt a tiny breeze pushing past her into the house. Her hair blew back from her face for a second before she stepped out into the night air. From the northern edge of the roof, she could see the streetlights in rows running down to the giant blackness of the sea. Just at the edge, there were zigzags of light from the tavernas by the docks. And then nothing. There was nothing on the other side of the Gulf of Patras—at least nothing visible tonight—but that way were mountains and more mountains until you reached Albania. And to the northwest was the other blackness of the Adriatic and then Italy, that giant boot tossed onto the water, ready to kick.

She crossed to the southern railing, where she could see men and women in fine clothes getting out of carriages at the concert hall across the street. Looking down at the elegance of the men and women, it was hard to believe that war could touch them. There were a few cars among the carriages—long, sloping, shiny things, like exotic animals. Everything about the scene below her was sleek: the men's hair, the women's gowns.

She saw her parents walk up the front steps of the hall. Her father was tall and lean, in his tailcoat and high-collared shirt, and her mother wore a fur stole over her shoulders and white gloves past her elbows.

Her mother raised her arm to greet someone, and her topaz bracelet slid along the glove, like a stream of honey on a table-cloth. Sophia would be given that bracelet when she turned sixteen, and Thalia would get the choker Clio could see now at the nape of her mother's neck. Already sixteen, Clio had the ring. But she had given it to her mother for this evening, eager that an emblem of her be included with the other two. She imagined she could trace its outline beneath the white silk of her mother's glove. As she watched her mother swing past her father through the door, she shivered. As long as the war didn't come, it would be just months until the first parties where she, too, could wear a woman's gown.

As the days passed, Clio tired of the cocoons. At first she had joined the other children in their vigil, watching for that sign of change that would herald the emergence of a new crea-ture. But when nothing happened day after day, she lost inter-est. It was Marco who made the cocoons exciting, after all. She felt a jolt of anticipation every time she neared the bakery. She would take Marco aside and hand him one more cocoon to tuck away into a little box beneath the counter. He would check to be sure his grandmother wasn't looking, and then he would slip a raisin roll into Clio's hand and wink at her. He looked like an adult, like the men who winked at her when she walked by a taverna, clearly delighted to be doing something mysterious.

But then one day Marinelli was standing behind the coun-ter and Marco was nowhere to be seen. Clio was certain she had noticed him running down the street ahead of them a few blocks earlier. Marinelli was smiling, but there was something different about him. She glanced over to see if maybe the old woman was sick, but she was there, on her stool, tucked in by the far end of the counter.

"*Ciao,* Mr. Marinelli," Clio began.

"Miss Clio."

"Where's Marco? I have another cocoon for him." She felt the need to offer something to Marinelli, just to make him become the friendly baker he always was.

"Marco is at home. I can give him the cocoon if you want."

Clio was not sure what to say. Marco liked their secret trading. But Marinelli was still looking at her that way.

"All right," she said.

Marinelli smiled at her with tight lips, and then he placed both hands flat on the counter.

"Miss Clio, I can't let Marco keep trading raisin rolls for these cocoons. I'm sure you understand that our raisin rolls are our specialty and that we use only the best ingredients available. We simply can't afford to give them away."

What he meant was that if he didn't take in four drachmas for each roll, he would lose money, because Notaris raisins were expensive. He was looking at her in a way that told Clio he knew she understood him.

She kept her eyes on him and nodded.

"Can we please have a *karveli,* Mr. Marinelli?" She chose Greek, since it was a matter of business now.

"Of course." He turned to tug one from a bin on the wall. "Five drachmas."

She placed the coin in the bronze plate and ushered the others out the door before turning to go back.

"Please do give this to Marco." She looked Marinelli in the

eyes and her face was on fire. "It's a gift from us." She left the cocoon on the counter.

Two days later, Clio tried once more, going into the bakery with a small bag full of cocoons. There were plenty more at the house, and not even Nestor would notice how many she had taken.

"*Geia,* Marco." The grandmother was at her stool and the boy sat cross-legged on the floor with paper and a colored pencil.

"*Geia.*" He gave her a timid smile and came over to see what she was holding.

"For you," she said, and placed the bag in his hands.

Just then Marinelli came in from the back of the store. Marco slipped away, tucking the bag under his arm.

"One *karveli,* please, Mr. Marinelli," she said, and set her coin in the bronze dish.

When she took the *karveli* from him, she simply nodded.

"*Arrivederci,*" she said this time. She shot out each syllable crisply.

Friday morning, Clio heard low voices, men's voices, coming from somewhere at the bottom of the house. She leaned over the parapet and peered down, but couldn't see anything except the chairs and tall plants and the delicate hall table in the pale-blue light of early morning. The other children followed her down the stairs into the sitting room, where they found their parents standing by the radio. Their father told them that, sometime after midnight, Mussolini had sent Metaxas an ultimatum: Let us through, or we'll force you to let us through. Metaxas had answered in French, which, to Clio, seemed to confirm the utter strangeness of the situation. "*Alors, c'est la guerre,*" he had said. So, it's war. Already the newspapers and radio had reduced this debonair statement into one force-ful word: *Ochi!*

"*Ochi!*" her father repeated, slamming his fist into his palm. "*No!* Our soldiers are in Albania even now, pushing those Italians back where they came from."

"I thought you liked the fascists, *Babá*," Nestor said.

"I like Metaxas, Nestor. Not that clown Mussolini."

Clio didn't say anything, but she thought of Marinelli and his grim mother.

"So, we get to stay home today?" Nestor asked.

"Nonsense. Everything's fine. We're not going to run around screaming. Go have your breakfast."

Clio did not know what to make of this. Nestor and Thalia chattered away while they ate, but Clio held her biscuit in her sweet coffee too long and it fell in. How could the others eat? All summer and all fall, everyone had been waiting and waiting for this war, and now that it had come, they were all behaving as if everything were normal.

Clio led her siblings down Kolokotronis to school, proud to be walking down a street dedicated to a leader of the War of Independence, this day of all days. She saw Marinelli's up ahead, and for the first time in her life she wished she didn't have to pass it. It was more than the confusion of the new war; she was suddenly overcome with shame for the way she had focused her eyes on Marinelli two days before and the way she had spoken to him. She could not believe she had dared to behave that way. And that word, *arrivederci,* which rang so oddly now that Italy was their enemy. It was no different from *au revoir,* but that wasn't what she had meant when she had said it.

Clio turned her head as if she were intensely interested in the groups of people on the other side of the street discussing the ultimatum. But as she approached the school, she couldn't help noticing Marco standing by a doorway. He didn't move until she reached him, and then the little boy sidled away from the building and fell in beside her.

He seemed about to cry.

"What's the matter, Marco?" she asked. "Are you worried about the war?"

"No," he said, shaking his head vigorously. "It's the cocoons. My father says they're charity and I need to pay you today or I can't have them."

Suddenly she was glad she had stood up to Marinelli. He had turned this into something serious, when she had only been trying to play a game with his little boy.

"Sorry." Marco kicked at the sidewalk.

"It's not your fault, Marco." She crouched down to him. "Don't worry. We'll figure something out, and I'm sure your father will let you have the cocoons."

Clio could see that he was not convinced, but she tousled his hair and sent him off to the right, where the lower school was. She sent Nestor along behind him.

The teacher began French class by leading the students in the national anthem. Everyone made swooping gestures to accompany each reference to a sword. Clio was waiting for something else—a discussion of the war, an announcement of safety plans—but, once the singing was finished, the teacher insisted they return to their seats and proceed with the lesson. Still, it was clear that even the teacher was distracted, constantly looking out the windows. Clio was certain she chose the text from Racine with Mussolini in mind: *Ses yeux indifférents ont déjà la constance/ D'un tyran dans le crime endurci dès l'enfance.* Indifferent eyes, a tyrant hardened in crime since childhood.

It was math class in the middle of the morning when Clio

noticed a few children by the window, looking up from their textbooks. She followed their gaze but couldn't see anything besides the tops of the buildings across the street. Then there was a drone and a whine and a roaring crash and the room shook. Glass blew in from the windows and children began to shout and cry. They all began to run.

There was nobody in charge. Out in front of the school, children grabbed hands and ran off. Clio was looking for Sophia and Thalia and Nestor. There was a plane in the sky, drifting over the city, and she stopped in her tracks to watch actual bombs drop from it, simply falling out of its belly and sailing down like giant loaves of bread. It was a fascinating image, something she had never seen before. In one instant, she lost sight of the bombs and heard and felt them explode. There was smoke and fire and the sounds of tumbling stones. Shocked out of her daze, she screamed for her sisters and her brother, and she saw Sophia, who had Thalia by the hand. Together, the three girls ran to the lower school and found Nestor crying and darting from one gate to the other. Clio grabbed him to her and then thrust him away, yelling at all three of them to run.

She led them down Maizonos, as she was supposed to do. Sophia and Thalia insisted on holding hands, and Nestor would not let go of Clio's, so she dragged him along.

"My arm, Clio!" he cried, as he dangled awkwardly from her grasp.

"I'm sorry, Nestor. Come on. Over this way. Sophia! Thalia!" she shouted. "Hurry up!"

Another plane roared into view and the girls screamed, pressing themselves into a doorway. Clio ran back to them, Nestor by her side, and pulled them back out.

"It's gone. We need to run!" she yelled.

Ahead of them, a hole was ripped out of the street. Two

houses were torn in half, a bureau hanging over the edge of a shattered floor. Men and women were bleeding and screaming, holding their heads. An old woman in black was clutching her head and crying, crouched beside a dark form on the ground. Clio dragged her siblings to the right, but soon there was another bomb site in front of them, with smoke still rising from the rubble. They went left. Now they heard the drone of yet another plane coming over the city. They ducked into a doorway. A bomb crashed farther up the street, showering them with dirt and hard pellets of concrete or plaster. Clio tasted salt on her lip and spat out grit and blood. She retched at the thought that the blood might not be her own. She dragged the others to their feet; they began to run again. They were all crying and yelling now, covering their heads, moving vaguely northeast until a crater would force them to turn.

It went on like this until, up ahead, Clio could see the portico of the concert hall and she knew that they were near their home.

"Almost there," she yelled. "We're close."

She heard a man's voice calling her name and, through dust and smoke, made out her parents running down the middle of the street. The sleeve of her mother's dress was torn and there was dirt on her father's face.

"It's all right," Urania said, hugging the children around her. "It's all right. We're all safe." But Clio knew that they were not safe at all anymore.

When they made it home, they saw smoke coming from the house two doors away from theirs. It was missing its top left corner, which lay in pieces in the street and in the walled garden of the house. The neighbors were standing in the street, crying. Clio's mother tugged all of them up the stairs and pushed them inside, where Clio was almost disappointed to see that nothing appeared to be altered at all. The house was quiet. Everything was as they had left it that morning and every other morning. The sun had risen to fill the atrium window, casting stark shadows down into the hall.

"Come," her mother said softly. She took them to the kitchen and washed their faces gently with a warm cloth. When it was Clio's turn, she held her elbow tight. "Sophia," she said, over Clio's shoulder, "take your brother and Thalia upstairs and find your father. You'll be fine there."

Clio looked in her mother's eyes as she dabbed at the dirt on her cheek.

"You kept them safe," Urania said. "I'm proud of you."

"What happens now, *Mamá*?"

"I don't know."

No one spoke very much for the rest of the day. Clio's father tried the radio, but all he got was patriotic music with the national anthem thrown in from time to time. She wondered if they would have to go to school now. And where would they go to take shelter from the bombs? Her parents, Irini, the neighbors—they were all shaking their heads, stunned, caught off guard, as if they had never believed the war could come to Patras.

That afternoon, she went up to Hollywood, bracing for the sight of an enemy plane. The sun had turned the buildings golden and the sea a dark purple. Across the Gulf of Patras, a broad mountain rose up almost from the water. And to the west, the island of Ithaki stood out clearly in the calm October air. She wanted the landscape to reveal a sign of the change she knew was finally, actually, upon them. In books and movies, it always rained when the heroes were sad. But that day the landscape did not cooperate. It was indifferent to their situation.

When Clio woke the next morning, she remembered the bureau hanging in midair, the crouched woman crying in the street, and the missing corner of the neighbors' house. And then she remembered the first bomb that had blocked their way on Maizonos Street, and she wondered if Marco was all right. She thought of the bag of cocoons his father would not let him accept. She had been planning to see him again, but that had been before the war had started. She begged her parents to let her go out, and eventually they allowed all the children out to see what they could do to help. Clio waited until no one was watching and headed for the bakery.

The streets were full of people clearing rubble, walking from house to house with food or water, standing in the street and talking. On Astiggos there was a ruined house with a black mourning cloth draped across the door. Along Maizonos some of the shops were open and people were buying tins and sacks of food. Someone passed Clio, pushing a cart loaded with a piece of beef and a large paper bag full of loaves of bread. In front of Marinelli's, Clio saw a woman carrying a *karveli*. The bakery was open. Marco was all right.

But the woman was going into the bakery, not out of it. She came out again empty-handed and frowning. Then another man came out through the door and, seeing the owner of the cart, called out to him, "Hey, where'd you get the bread?"

"Drimakopoulos." The cart owner nodded up to the sign over the door and laughed. "Today I'd rather buy from a Greek."

"Marinelli's flour is bad anyhow," said the other man. "Full of bugs." He walked off toward Drimakopoulos's bakery.

In no more than a minute, as Clio stood there beside the door, *full of bugs* was tossed from one person to another until no one went into Marinelli's at all. People glanced up and shook their heads at the name on the sign and then continued down the sidewalk.

Clio went to the door and peered through the glass, but it was dark inside and she could make out only the counter that ran across the front. She pushed the door open. Marco came to her side. The old woman was sitting in her regular place at the end of the counter. But Marinelli had his back to Clio. He was reaching up into the bins where he kept the bread—loaves he must have baked only hours after the bombs fell—and he was doing something with his hands. Then Clio saw the moths. There were dozens of them, crawling over the bread and falling into the spaces between the loaves and then pulling themselves up again.

She made a noise and he turned around. He had a small bandage on the side of his neck and he looked tired. He was not smiling. *Ses yeux indifférents,* was all Clio could think of.

"Marco, vieni ad aiutarmi," he said to the boy.

"Sì, Papà."

When Marco twisted back to look at her, she gave him an uncertain smile. But he didn't seem to register whatever it was she was trying to say.

Clio left the bakery, knowing people would think she, too, had refused to do business with an Italian man. Two women on the sidewalk nodded approvingly at her, encouraging what they thought was her decision. She walked home and saw Nestor's face in the basement window.

"Clio!" he called. "The cocoons are hatching. Come see."

She went in through the main doors, past the walnut mirror, and started up the stairs. She was glad that Nestor was happy. But she couldn't bring herself to see why.

11

Callie

Aliki has told me where you get a *domino* if you're going to the Bourbouli, so Tuesday morning, before starting a day's work at Nestor's house, I follow Kanakaris to Ermou Street, where a temporary shop has been set up near the harbor to sell Carnival supplies. There are sacks of papier-mâché makings, piles of masks adorned with feathers and sparkles, and, on the wall, a row of black *dominos* in various fabrics. The proprietor uses a long pole to lift one off a hook and bring it down to me.

"Try it on," he says. "You're short. You can't have it trailing behind you."

He motions to the back of the store, where a handful of women are gathered around a trio of mirrors, laughing and talking. I wait in line among them, as one by one they step on the small platform and check their black reflections in the mirror. I am surprised to see that some of the *dominos* are not shapeless but are instead tailored to come in at the waist. Some versions hug the hips, making the wearer look like a kind of sinister mermaid. As they turn to face their friends, the women give me polite smiles, as if I am intruding on a private party.

Eventually it's my turn. I pull the *domino* over my head and arrange the hood so that the opening falls symmetrically over my face. At the top, there is a brim, like a short beak. The whole effect is to make me look not so much like a mermaid but like a little bird of the kind that pecks insistently at the ground. I can't be bothered to find another, but one of the women watching hands me a *domino* from a pile of their discards.

"Try this one," she says. She is roughly my size.

As soon as I have this one on, I see the power of the Bourbouli. Looking at myself in the three-way mirror, I feel sophisticated and seductive. The *domino* tucks in just right at the waist and skims my hips before falling perfectly to the ground. It is made of a light jersey, and though the seams pull a little over the top of the head, where the brim comes to a tiny peak, it is well made.

"That's the one," says the woman.

"You can do whatever you want in that one," says another, giving all of us a knowing smile.

I buy it, along with a glittering red mask that ties behind the head with a black ribbon.

As I walk along Riga Ferraiou Street with my shopping in a plastic bag, I feel as though everyone must assume that I am simply another local—or a Greek out-of-towner—getting ready for Carnival. I smile to myself, proud to have errands to do, like everyone else.

It's a long walk across the city to Nestor's house, but the air, once again, is mild and moist. In Boston, it will be dry enough now to make the insides of my nostrils crackle with each breath. As I walk, I remember running errands with the aunts when I was younger—the shopwindows decorated with soap paint announcing the summer sales, the vendors on nearly every corner selling grilled corn on the cob, the hundreds of motorcycles buzzing through the traffic so that an aunt always had to whip her arm out in front of me to keep me from stepping into one. Then my aunts' lives descend like a scrim over my own, and I begin to imagine what the city was like when the three young women strolled long-legged down these same streets—my mother and her two sisters, known throughout Patras for their beauty.

Today the streets are only at half strength, and even the vendors' stalls are closed. It's a lull in the Carnival, perhaps because everyone is preparing for the purported chaos of the Bourbouli. I wonder how bad it can be. These are modern times. You can misbehave all you want every day; you don't need the cover of a *domino* for permission.

I haven't spoken to Stelios and Anna since Sunday's drive out to the country, and I plan to keep it that way. If Aliki asked me, I would tell her I'd rather spend my free time with her. And though this is true, the reality is that I am embarrassed about the politics of that conversation in the field. Stelios's charm notwithstanding, he made it clear he sides with Andreas, both of them criticizing me for things I cannot help. I'm so much closer to them than to any landed gentry.

And still I feel guilty—because of the safe farmhouse my family could retreat to once those bombs began to fall; because of the servants they employed; because of my mother, who gave cocoons for free to a little Italian boy. But all of these, even my mother's adolescent *noblesse oblige,* involve a measure of kindness. By the time I reach Nestor's house, I have worked myself up into irritation at Stelios and Anna for coming along with me only to set me apart.

In this mood, I stand in the foyer and scowl out at the room, resenting the obligation that has brought me to Patras in the first place. When I got back from that trip to Zakynthos, I finally had it all worked out—my thoroughly American life in Boston free from these European tragedies of property and class. I would pretend I had no mother, no history. Now I have history, with all its blessings—and its responsibilities. I like to think it was all much easier the other way.

I sit on the couch in Nestor's living room, wondering why I can't seem to leave the notion of Stelios and Anna alone. The world is full of couples like them, people who connect without obligation and who come and go without consequences. But there's something about these two that fascinates me, and I don't think it's just Stelios's good looks. I think that Jonah and I used to see ourselves that way, loosely tied, connected to each other only by proximity, our relationship tenuous and shifting. But the truth is that we couldn't manage it. It wasn't long before we understood ourselves to be more firmly tied, in love. We still held on to that looser image, though. It was the counterweight to the committed truth of our relationship. When Jonah proved the frivolity to be fake, I didn't know what to do. I still don't.

I stand up too fast, and the room goes cloudy dark and then brightens again. Through lingering dizziness, I look out at the boxes. At this rate, I will never finish in time. I will have to either take all of Nestor's things home or rent someplace in Patras to store them. Perhaps this was his way to keep me coming back to his city, to his life. This from the man who traveled all over Europe but always returned, going into and out of this little house with the foreign phrase on his key ring as the password. "Auld Lang Syne," to days long since—days accumulated in a life passed shuttling back and forth between home and away.

I fetch the Pti Ber package from the kitchen and look over today's collection of boxes, pushing biscuits up with my thumb and eating them rapidly as I go. I start hauling boxes down from their stacks. A new set of rules emerges. I pull a sheet of foolscap from a pile in the center drawer of Nestor's desk and write three columns. *Keep: tapes, film, photographs; important-looking papers; war years.* This last I underline twice. *Give away: clothes. Throw away: receipts and paid bills; anything plastic.* Most of the furniture will be for Aliki and Nikos, if they want it. After I've been working for a while, my throat is dry from the dust and my eyes sting. But I feel better. I am doing something productive to make up for my earlier delinquency. I have four more days to finish this work and get Constantopoulos to produce the document for me to sign. And—the thought nags at me—to find out what I can about the refugees at the farm.

I'm startled by a knock on the door.

"Who is it?" I say.

There is no answer. It has to be my mother again, refusing to shout through the door like a peasant, as she would say. I go to the door and find that I was right.

"What is it, *Mamá*?" I say, after we kiss on the cheeks.

"Do I need a reason to come see you?"

I want to ask her right away to tell me more about the refugees, but I hold back. Besides, I suspect it's not me she wants to see. If I return to my work, I'll find out soon enough what she really wants.

I go back to sifting through a box of papers, scanning each sheet for significant words and then flicking the document into one of two ragged piles.

"How long are you planning to stay here?" my mother says.

"I'm leaving on Sunday."

"I mean here." She waves her arm in mock grandeur. "Aren't you going to the Bourbouli?"

I'm surprised that she knows about my plans, but, then again, she must have assumed that I would go to this key event of Carnival.

"Maybe not," I lie. "Aliki's not going."

"So?"

"So I don't feel like going alone."

"If you want, I can stay here and do some of this for you."

Clever woman.

"It's okay, *Mamá*."

I make a show of continuing to work, but my concentration is on her. She roams around the room, making disdainful noises. She lifts a stack of books from the coffee table.

"Those are sorted," I say. "Can you please put them the way they were?"

"Sorted into what? You're not keeping these, are you?"

I ignore the question. She finds the box of fruit pits that Aliki and I discovered on the first day. I brace myself for her reaction, half-fearing she will tip the contents out onto the floor. This keepsake at least slows her down. She lets out a long breath and gently replaces the cover on the box.

"From the farm," I say stupidly.

Now it's her turn to ignore me.

She resumes her gliding motion around the room and comes to the papers I have been sorting. Nestor's correspondence with the head of an Austrian hiking club is on top of the keeper pile. My mother picks up one of the letters, glances at it, and flicks it toward the floor.

"Calliope! Throw this junk away. Why on earth are you keeping this?"

"Maybe I'm not."

"Oh, come on. I can tell. This pile is lovingly arranged. The way you used to do with all your little things."

My little things. These were my treasures—more often than not, souvenirs from summers in Greece, which were meaningless to anyone but me: a matchbox with a pretty cover, a bean-shaped pebble from Bozaïtika Beach, a ring purchased from the kiosk at Plateia Olgas. I used to keep them in talismanic arrangements on my nightstand.

"Can you just leave the stuff alone?" I say, feeling the familiar tightening in my neck. "I'm trying to get something done here."

She has moved on. From the top of a bookshelf, she picks up a wooden carving of a bear standing on hind legs. Around the base are Gothic-print letters in German next to an image of the Swiss flag. She peers into the bookcase as she puts the bear back.

"What on earth was your uncle thinking? Such ugly things."

"Is that fair?"

"Yes, it's fair. Nestor isn't above criticism just because he is dead."

"Maybe he should be," I say. "What do you care if Nestor wanted to keep that bear? Is it bothering you? Is it affecting your life?"

"He was my brother. Of course he affected my life."

"I don't see how he possibly could. You are clearly so far superior to him. Surely his poor taste can't taint you."

"That's enough rudeness, Calliope. I came here to offer you some help."

"Oh, come on! Who are you kidding? What is it that you want to find?"

She doesn't say anything for a long moment, and when she does speak, it's in a suppressed seethe.

"I don't know why you think you can speak to me like this. You learned this in America, where *everything goes*." She says this last in English.

"No, *Mamá*. I learned it from you and Dad. Should I remind you?"

As I say this, I feel my heart banging in my chest. It's exhilarating, but I'm also terrified—terrified that this tiny woman will find a way to make me regret my outburst. I take a breath and go on.

"Nestor did us all a huge service. He tried to make a record of the past. Maybe he wasn't so good at editing the record." I reach behind me for the first box I can grab. It is small, cardboard, with the bottom nesting in its lid. "So maybe we don't need to have a box full of feathers from the farm. But at least he left something—for me—that was meaningful."

My mother looks at the box in my hand. Inside it are four long black feathers.

"Where did you get that?" she says.

"Right here." I wave behind me, caught up in my anger. "In a pile of Nestor's crap. Why? Does it mean anything?"

"You said it yourself. Just Nestor's crap."

We glare at each other, saying nothing. I think of Aliki that time she was fifteen, staring my mother down in that argument at Olympia. Here is the defiance I always admired in her and saw again in that photograph. It's in me now—uneasily but unmistakably here. But my mother, too, is defiant, even reckless, going so far as to use a word she considers vulgar.

"You always do that," I say. "You always assume that if you

don't value something, it *has* no value. You're like that with everything." I pause. "With everyone."

"Who don't I value?" She draws closer.

"Who?" My throat tightens. "Are you kidding? You don't value me."

"When did I say that?"

"I'm not going to talk about it," I say, turning away.

"Calliope." She grabs my arm and pulls me back around with surprising force. "When did I tell you I didn't value you?"

"You don't remember. Five years ago. I came to you before I went to Zakynthos. Like an idiot, I was hoping . . . I don't know, that you might have something nice to say about my being alone."

"There's nothing wrong with being alone."

"No?" I tug my arm free. "Then why did you tell me I would always be alone, that no man would stay with me, that no man could love me?" I stop for breath, and the last part comes out in a hoarse sob. "That *you* sometimes couldn't love me."

I stare at her, feeling the tears spill from my lids. I can see her thinking.

"I did say that," she says finally. "That is true." I spin away. "Come back, Calliope. Sit down."

She points at Nestor's velvet couch. Partly from weariness, partly from habit, I obey her.

"You are not always easy to love. People in love want to be close to each other. Not their bodies. Their thoughts."

"I can't listen to this."

"You wanted me to explain," she snaps. "I'm explaining." She begins again, softly this time, but she won't come nearer, staying instead in the middle of the room. "You don't let people close. This *Iáson*, it's a miracle he's still with you. Or you're pretending and he hasn't noticed. But he will notice. I promise

202 | *Henriette Lazaridis Power*

you. Because when you don't let people in, they eventually go away."

All the energy suddenly drains out of me and I feel like a deadweight on the couch.

"Why do you think I don't let people in, *Mamá*? Why do you think I don't trust love? Over and over I tried to reach you, and did you ever let me in? No."

My voice barely rises above a whisper, but I can see in her eyes that she heard me.

For a while we stay still, me on the couch, she a tiny figure ringed by Nestor's boxes. The light changes in the room and I realize that the sun has dipped down below the back wall of the garden. Perhaps it's been only a few minutes, or it could have been hours, the two of us frozen like Medusa's victims.

I put my palms on my thighs.

"You know what?" I say. "I think I'm done for the day." I press the lid onto the small box that has ended up beside me on the couch and set it on the table. My mother stays there while I go to the back doors and check that they are locked, stow the biscuits in a tin on the kitchen counter, and begin to switch off the lights. I pass her on my way to the foyer. She's standing by the table where I set the box down.

"I'm locking the door," I say.

"Very gracious, Calliope. I'm coming."

She catches up with me as I button my coat and pick up my bag with its *domino* inside. The silky black fabric seems useless now. I am too drained to be seductive and mischievous.

When we reach the sidewalk, something makes me ask my mother the question I know she will say no to, so I ask it with a clipped voice, negation built in.

"You coming to Aliki's with me?"

"I can't. I have things to do."

We kiss tensely on the cheeks, and I watch her start the short walk to her apartment. In the dark that has fallen, she looks vulnerable and frail.

"*Mamá!*"

She turns.

"Just come with me, all right?"

She considers for a moment, though I can't really see her face.

"Fine. But don't walk too fast. I have no intention of sweating my way there."

I stand back from Nestor's door, letting the glow from the streetlight fall on the lock. Arms extended, leaning back, I turn the key and hear the now-familiar chunk of the deadbolt being thrown across. I wait as my mother comes back, and we head off together at a graceful, loping pace. It's clear we will not speak about what happened this afternoon.

On Maizonos, the cars are jammed, three lanes created where only two should fit. Motorcycles weave slowly through the cars, their rear tires swinging from side to side while the woman in the back—there is always a woman in the back—lurches against the driver.

"Is there some important event going on?" I ask my mother while we wait at an intersection.

"This is *rush hour*." She says it with a disdain that's aimed either at the English words or the thing itself, or both. "Patras never used to be like this."

I buzz Aliki, hoping she'll stay on the intercom so I can at least warn her that I've brought my mother with me. But no such luck. As soon as I speak, the buzzer sounds and I need to dash for the door before the lock closes again.

204 | *Henriette Lazaridis Power*

I hold the door for my mother, who glides up the steps as if into a ballroom. The elevator drops an inch or two when we step in and then jolts upward, metal rattling.

"One of these days, it'll just snap and go crashing to the basement."

It's a rather stark statement for my mother. But what sticks in my mind more is the question of how often she visits here. She doesn't have a key of her own, but maybe she visits more often than I imagine.

Nikos is the one who meets us at the door.

"Clio," he says, beaming. "A pleasant surprise. Come in." He raises his eyebrows at me once she's passed him.

"I didn't think she'd say yes," I whisper.

He turns quickly and takes my mother's coat, hanging it carefully in the closet. He escorts her to the living room and calls for Aliki. I notice that my mother has still not said more than two words to him.

"Aliki, can you bring your aunt Clio a glass of water, please?"

"My aunt Clio?" Aliki steps out from the bathroom, her hand holding a brush that's embedded deep in Demetra's hair.

"Ow!"

"Shh! Aunt Clio is here. Finish this yourself."

"But, *Mamá*—"

"I'll do it," I say, and Aliki mouths *Clio?* at me as she heads for the living room.

"*Theia* Clio," I hear her say, her voice muffled as she's kissing my mother on the cheeks. And then I grab hold of the brush that's sticking straight out of the side of Demetra's head.

"What are you, a horse?" I say, as I hold her head still and pull the brush through.

"That's what my father calls me."

"Does he brush your hair?"

"Sometimes."

Aliki comes back to the bathroom.

"Your turn," she says.

I wave to my mother and then stoop to pick up the shopping bag I set down at the edge of the foyer when we came in. It's my plan to get it out of the way, happy that she hasn't asked about it yet. But my timing is off, and my mother sees the bag, in which the *domino*'s black fabric is now visible.

"Did you buy a *domino*?" I can't tell if she's impressed or shocked.

"Who bought a *domino*?" Nikos comes out of nowhere and takes the bag from me.

"Hey!"

"What'd you get?" He pulls out the mask and holds it up to his face, mugging for Demetra, who has come into the room, her hair sleek. "What do you think?" he asks her. "Did *Theia* Calliope make a good choice?"

Demetra takes the mask from him and holds it up to me, testing the red with my coloring.

"It's nice," she says, handing it back to me.

"Nikos," my mother says coolly, "doesn't the child know to greet her elders?"

"Demetra," he says, tipping his head toward my mother.

"Hello, *Theia* Clio," she recites, and goes to kiss my mother lightly on the cheeks. I think my mother gives her air kisses, but I'm not sure.

"Let me see," my mother says, taking the mask from Demetra.

"What do you think, Clio?" Nikos asks her.

She holds it up in front of her and squints at me like a painter.

"Not bad."

"I don't really feel like going, though."

"You have to go," Nikos says. "Tell her," he calls to the kitchen. "Aliki, tell her she should go."

Aliki calls back, "You should go."

I take the mask from my mother and go see Aliki. She is pulling a pan of stuffed tomatoes from the oven. The air in the room smells clean and crisp, like summer.

"Aliki," I say quietly, "I'm not going to go to the Bourbouli."

"Why not?"

"It's been a rough afternoon. The last thing I feel like doing right now is dancing."

Nikos comes in and takes me by the arm.

"Listen, cousin," he says. "The three Bourbouli dances are the three best nights in Patras."

Aliki presses her lips together at this.

"Except Easter," she says.

"Except Easter, when we all try to blow each other up with firecrackers, yes. But besides that fantastic and wholly pagan celebration, the Bourboulis are it. You *will* go," he says. "I insist."

"This isn't a good night for me to be alone in a crowd of revelers."

If my mother was right about me, though, I should get used to solitude.

"You won't be alone," he says. "You'll be with me and therefore with my friends. You'd be with Aliki too," he says, "if she'd only decide to leave Demetra with her mother and go."

"You could leave her with *my* mother," I say.

"Poor child."

"Come on, Calliope," Nikos says. "I'll make sure you stay out of trouble." He winks at me.

I look at Aliki, whose face has tightened into a rigid smile.

"All right," I tell him, but now I am thinking of Aliki and this martyr's mood that she seems to have embraced. I will go for her; I will be on the alert.

We sit at the table, my mother joining us in the seat that Thalia usually occupies. It's strange to have this one of the three sisters here without the other two. I find myself hoping that she'll surprise us all. I imagine a story in which, away from her sisters' alliance, she reveals herself to be warm and relaxed. Despite everything, I feel badly for her. She doesn't seem to want to talk to Nikos, and she doesn't seem to know how to talk to Demetra. After a few salvos, she grazes through the meal in silence. It occurs to me that perhaps she is upset, too, by what I said to her at Nestor's, and I find myself almost moved at the thought of her potential weakness.

Nikos gets the bathroom first after dinner. I offer to help Aliki in the kitchen, but she is having none of it.

"Are you kidding? You brought her here. You talk to her."

I sit with my mother in the living room. "You used to go to these, didn't you?"

"We were too young. And during the war there was no Carnival."

"What about after?"

"After . . ." She trails off. "We were too busy getting through the civil war. It wasn't a time for parties."

"There were no Carnivals?"

"Yes, eventually there were Carnivals."

"So did you go? You were still living in Patras, right?"

"What is this, an interrogation? I don't remember, Callie."

"I just was curious to know. About your experiences, *Mamá*."

"Well, go to the Bourbouli tonight and have an experience of your own."

I look at her, wondering if this is a dig inspired by this afternoon.

Nikos makes an admiring whoop from the foyer, and Aliki whaps him on the arm.

"Experience, cousin!"

Aliki holds him by the shoulders and steers him away. I can hear their voices hissing in the kitchen.

"Bathroom's yours, cousin," he says, returning.

"Go," says my mother. "I'll wait."

Nikos disappears into the bedroom to put in collar stays, shirt studs, and cuff links, leaving behind a fug of alcohol and cologne in the bathroom. I rummage through Aliki's makeup to find some thick mascara and some liner and shadow darker than anything I have brought from Boston. Even though I'll be wearing a mask, I go for a smoky eye, which seems right for the occasion. I draw the liner out a bit past the outer corner of my eye, Cleopatra style. Aliki brings me a wineglass and a skirt of hers to wear with a pair of black boots I have brought with me. I pull on my white shirt with the long placket and then pull the *domino* over my head.

Taking a drink, I see Nikos in the mirror, his heaviness slimmed by the jet black of his tuxedo. He stands a few feet behind me and looks at my reflection with an appraising eye.

"See, I told you you should go," he says. "Wouldn't want to waste this. Aliki," he calls over his shoulder. "You didn't tell me our cousin was a woman of mystery."

"That's me, all right. Woman of mystery." I think of what Stelios called me: the mysterious stranger from a foreign land.

I finish the wine before squeezing past him into the hall. The mask makes it easier to face my mother.

"What do you think?" I ask her.

"Appropriate," she says.

Nikos gathers up his wallet and keys from the small table in the foyer and, without saying anything, hands me the spare key to the apartment. When I frown at him, he murmurs, "Just in case." I hike up the *domino* to slip the key into the pocket of the skirt just as Aliki and Demetra come into the foyer to see us in our Bourbouli finery.

"What are you doing, *Theia* Calliope?"

"Adjusting, Demetraki *mou*." I smooth the fabric back down over the skirt.

"I'm leaving now too," my mother says.

Aliki makes the customary sounds of regret, but no one is fooled, so the three of us go down in the clanky elevator, with Nikos and me in our Bourbouli getups and my mother in her tailored coat and foulard scarf. We kiss on the cheeks, my mother being careful not to smudge my makeup, and go our separate ways.

I wasn't planning to pull up the hood of the *domino* until I reached the Bourbouli itself. No reason to walk about the streets covered from head to toe, like some woman in a *burka*, while the man struts beside me in his best suit. But when I catch sight of a group of *domino*'ed women across the street, all of them with hoods and masks, I am reminded that this garment is more about revealing than concealing. Carnival: everything turned upside down. The women opposite me move with lithe steps down the slope of the street, their gloved arms making elegant gestures to punctuate their laughter. Nikos must feel like an aged uncle, having to walk with me while he would rather be getting a head start on his seductions.

"So, Nikos," I say, pulling my hood up against the chilly air. "Why won't my mother talk to you?"

"Don't you know? It's because I come from nothing. I have no name."

"But your business . . ."

"I know," he says breezily. "I started out stripping wires for outlets and now I've got four lighting stores, with plans to build a fifth. But it's *new* money. And I have no education." He shakes his head in mock despair.

"Oh, brother."

"Don't even ask about him!"

I look over, but Nikos just smiles.

"I thought there was a chance that having your mother there would drive Aliki out of the house. Maybe she'd have come with us."

"What's going on with you and her?"

"What kind of a question is that?" he laughs. "So American!"

"No, this is a serious question. Why is she so docile all of a sudden? Why is she letting you get away with all this?"

I expect him to be flustered, to deny, to feign ignorance. Instead, he smiles down on me and wags his head sagely from side to side.

"Why not?" he says.

"Oh! So we're talking about the same thing?"

"If you mean my life as a normal, flesh-and-blood Greek man, then yes."

I stop and turn to face him. A group of people in street clothes parts around us and then re-forms.

"That is such shit, Nikos. Are you really going to claim that as a defense?"

"I don't need a defense, dear Calliope, because I'm not doing anything wrong. Maybe in America where you're all so prudish. But not here."

"I don't think Aliki agrees with you on that, Nikos."

He resumes walking.

"Well, then Aliki needs to be reminded of a few events from her past."

"Yeah. She told me."

"Oh, you discussed it?"

"I was worried about her. Just because she played around before doesn't mean she's okay with it now. We all do stupid things when we're young. You're an adult now, Nikos. Time to grow up."

"Look who's talking. You're the one who's in a state of perpetual childhood."

"What's that supposed to mean?"

"How old are you, Calliope? Thirty? Thirty-two? No kids, no husband. Now you've come here to take care of this inheritance, but instead you're cavorting around with these young guys you hardly know. And your excuse is that you can't get anything done because it's Carnival."

I am clenching my jaw, trying to keep my fiercest, most unassailable expression on my face. Nikos leans toward me, placing a hand on my arm. I fight the urge to shake it off.

"I've noticed the drinking, cousin."

"Oh, come on! You all drink wine with every meal. You're complaining about me?"

"We drink when we're happy." He takes his hand away and shrugs. "It's just something I noticed. So maybe you're not the only one on the lookout. Don't get me wrong. The women in this family have it pretty tough. You and Aliki have my sympathy."

"Oh, we do?" It is all I can trust myself to say, a clichéd irony.

"You do." He is so earnest and well meaning all of a sudden. I want him to be the slimy Greek man he was just a few moments ago. "It can't be easy to be their daughters."

He slips his hand under my arm and leads me down Korinthou Street toward Plateia Georgiou, where the lights from the square are glowing orange. He is laughing now.

"Don't let Sophia and Thalia fool you: They bicker all the time."

"Not that I can see."

"You're not here that much, are you, cousin?"

The question smarts. I don't like thinking of my aunts in conflict.

"Nestor was the only smart one, poor man," Nikos goes on. "He traveled. He got away. A lot like your mother. Both outsiders, both of them wanting to see more of the world."

I think of my mother covering the windows of the ranch house with brown paper.

"I don't know why Nestor and Clio argued so much," he says. "Not like Sophia and Thalia. Real arguments."

"They hardly spoke to each other," I say, remembering all of a sudden the sarcastic questions and curt replies that made up their conversation.

"Right. They should have been allies."

Against what? I wonder.

We reach the edge of the square. The Apollon Theatre is to our right, a grand neoclassical building lining the entire block, with a colonnade at street level echoed by a colonnaded balcony above. Giant floodlights in the square are aimed at the building's façade. Shadows flit over the pale-yellow stucco as people dart across the front of the enormous bulbs. Most of the people here are in *dominos* and tuxes. The *dominos* move with purpose toward the entrance, while the tuxes wander among them, already maneuvering to be chosen or to choose.

Nikos stops at the edge of the crowd and turns to me.

"Look, Calliope, about Aliki. I don't have a problem with

what she did, and she really doesn't have a problem with what I do now. If she does, though, we will talk about it. She and I. So, you see, there's no one you need to defend. No one you need to watch over."

"I'm not so sure of that."

"Besides," he says. "You're not here to watch over me. You're here to be seen. Admit it."

"In this thing?"

He puts a hand under my chin—not altogether comfortably.

"No woman paints her eyes like that when she wants to blend into the crowd."

I am conscious that people have noticed us. I am enough shorter than Nikos that it's possible people think I am his daughter, a wayward girl caught by her father on the way to a secret dance. I don't say anything—because I sense Nikos is right.

"Let's go," Nikos says, and pulls me into the wave of people heading toward the doors. As soon as we are into the colonnade, he lets go and blows a kiss at me over his shoulder. I call after him, losing him immediately, as the force of the crowd pushes me into the dance.

The room is much bigger than I had imagined, and it is packed with people. Techno music thumps loudly; people are dancing beneath a web of streamers hung from the carved ceiling. I see now that not every man is wearing a tux and that some have opted for business suits, while others are wearing jeans and button-front shirts. The disparity between the openness of the men and the concealment of us women is startling. As I stand by the wall, I have the odd feeling of having wandered naked into a room full of the dressed. There are many more men here than women. I spot the women in the crowd from the shininess of their fabric—a fabric whose slinkiness and thinness makes them, and me, look vulnerable. But there is nothing vulnerable about what is going on a few feet away from me. A woman with a parrot-blue feathered mask is drawing one gloved arm around the neck of a handsome young man while, with the other, she tugs his hip toward her. His face bears a look of exhilaration tinged with fear. Perhaps this is his first Bourbouli.

I think of how Jonah would be in this gathering. No tux for him: He would be wearing his button-flies with a good white shirt; he would have chosen his skinny dark-green Pumas to signal he was dressing up. Would he stay with me, or would he go and find someone else, I wonder? Or would I?

To my left, an older man is drinking from a plastic cup, looking out a bit dazedly at the dancers. I don't want to be standing here, like him, with nothing to do—and I wouldn't mind some wine, regardless of what Nikos said. So I make my way around the edge of the room, eventually finding a long table where waiters are handing out plastic tumblers of red wine. I take a few sips, wincing at the sweetness, and stand back to scour the crowd. I have no hope of finding Nikos, and I wonder if I will run into Anna, for I am sure that she is here, wearing a domino like mine. I remind myself that Anna and I will remain a mystery to each other tonight—as will all the women in the room. It is Stelios I will look for.

My thoughts go back to the day in the field: two days ago, long enough for it to be over. Whatever *it* is. A friendship? When I hardly know him. A relationship? When he has a girlfriend. An acquaintance? More than that, if I consider all the flirting. I don't like to be manipulated, and I know I have been.

I feel a hand on my waist. It's the young man from the parrot-blue woman.

"I followed you," he says.

I tilt my head to the side. "It's not supposed to work that way. You're supposed to wait until I choose you."

"Why didn't you?"

"I wasn't interested," I say, enjoying the ease with which I am falling into this role.

"Choose me now," he says.

In answer, I lead him into the center of the room, among the dancers, and for a while we make the small shuffling dance steps that serve as an excuse to rub your body against someone else's.

"Want some wine?" he shouts over the music.

"Sure."

But after he hands me another plastic cup, I manage to wander away from him to another part of the room. It is darker here, shadowed by the mezzanine that overhangs the space. Here, people are freer—holding on to each other, wrapping themselves around each other. I cast a look about for Nikos but don't see him and am relieved. But I do see Stelios. He is walking through the edge of the dancers, scanning the shadows for someone. When he moves out of the dance-floor lighting, I step toward him.

Keeping my mask in place, I slide my arms up around his neck and remember the stubble I felt there when he carried me from the square on the night of the parade. He runs his hands up into the sleeves of the *domino,* along my arms and over the smooth fabric of my blouse. I step closer, pushing against him, giving him the signal that there can be more. Now I feel the exhilaration I saw on the young man's face before, with the parrot-blue woman. And now I understand the power of the *domino.* It is the power of being no one, with no identity and no ties, no origins and no home. I have spent so much time lately looking for this kind of freedom, and here it is, behind a mask and beneath a tailored shroud of black cloth.

Stelios has pulled his hands out from my sleeves and is moving them along my sides. He lets his thumbs glide over my breasts. So this is what he does when Anna is not around. I dismiss the scolding thought of Jonah. I am enjoying this and it seems important. I pull his face down to me and begin to kiss him, a deep, dirty kiss.

"I'm glad you're wearing this," he says afterward.

Me too, I say to myself, thinking of my *domino*. I notice he is holding my hand, playing with the red beads of the bracelet Anna bought for us all.

"*Shit!*" I hiss, biting back the word before it is out.

"What did you say?"

Before I can answer, he pushes my mask onto my forehead and kisses me, hard. His tongue flicks along the edges of my teeth, as if inviting me to give up. Of course he has known me all the time, and I have been ridiculous. I thought I was playing him, but he was playing me. I bite down on his tongue, not too much, but enough to let him know I've understood his game.

He makes a noise of surprise and pulls back.

"Did that hurt?" I ask, mocking.

"No. Does this?" He pinches my nipple, beyond the point of pleasure.

"No," I lie.

"Good."

He pinches it again, only this time just enough to make me want him. I rub my hand across his crotch and feel him getting hard.

All this time, we have been moving backward, toward the darkest section of the room. Now we come up against a wall and he pulls me around so that my back faces outward. I suddenly realize that the *domino* that gave me such a sense of power is actually getting in my way. Everything I think of doing with Stelios is foiled by the damned thing. I have a sudden urge to punish him—for playing me, and for playing around while Anna does whatever she is doing elsewhere in the room. I want to leave him aching with desire, his pants tented over his straining cock, and I want to bring Anna to find him.

"Hey!" he protests, and I ease my grip on him. He is trying to reach up between my legs, but the *domino* is too tight. I already hitched the thing up once today, to put the spare key in my pocket so Nikos could stay out all night; I don't need to hitch it up again.

I pull away, slowly, and slide my mask back over my face.

"Callie," he says, grabbing my hand. "Don't say anything to Anna."

"I won't," I say, smiling. "It's Carnival." I hold my hand up in the air and shake the red beads. "Pact!"

I wander out into the Plateia, dizzy from desire and wine, and start walking toward Aliki's, not because I want to see her—or anyone—but because it is the only route I can follow without having to think. If I think, I will remember, and if I remember, I will have to think about what just happened. I walk a block before realizing my mask and hood are on. I would leave them on, an armor to disappear in, if I didn't think I looked strange to the others on the street. It is too early for any self-respecting reveler to be walking away from the Bourbouli.

I push the hood back and draw my hair out so that it spreads over my shoulders; the back of my neck is sweaty. A man coming toward me on the sidewalk gives me an approving look. Farther down Korinthou, a group of men and women are standing outside the door of an apartment building. The women are wearing cocktail-length gowns beneath coats draped over their shoulders. The men are in suits. As I pass, the buzzer sounds and they file slowly in through the door one of the men holds open. When I reach the corner of Korinthou and Agiou Nikolaou, I have to make a choice: continue toward Aliki's apartment or keep walking. I head home.

Grateful to Nikos for the key, I let myself in and take the elevator upstairs. I close the apartment door as quietly as I can but turn to find Aliki sitting in one of the living room chairs.

"Hi," I say, drawing up from my crouched tiptoeing.

"Calliope, what's the matter?"

It suddenly occurs to me that my makeup must be smudged. I must look like a mess.

"Nothing. I was just tired." I smile.

"And Nikos stayed."

"He said he'd be coming soon," I lie.

She tilts her head at me. I wince.

"We got separated."

She laughs a single snort.

"I'm sorry," I say.

Aliki stretches and rises from the chair, her finger in her book.

"It's all right, Paki. It's not your job to keep my husband on the straight and narrow. Come on." She motions me to the kitchen.

She moves a stool out of the way to close the door that is always propped open. I see now from the oven clock that it is just past eleven. To me, it feels as if it is the middle of the night—the kind of night you awaken from unsettled and upset without knowing why. Aliki pours us each a glass of Coke

Light. I take a long drink of the stuff, slightly sweeter than its American version.

"You were thirsty."

"I guess."

"So. Nikos. I bet he left you at the door."

"Pretty much. I didn't see him at all once I got inside." As soon as I say this, I wish I could take it back.

"He finds a way of disappearing. Or so I've heard."

"Aliki, he's not a bad guy," I say, and she laughs again, more openly this time.

"Did you think he was?"

I make an equivocal gesture.

"No," she says. "He's not a bad guy. Sometimes he does bad things, but he's a good man."

"You should go to the Bourbouli with him."

"There's no point in going unless I want to have a Carnival fling of my own. *Been there; done that,*" she says in English.

I wonder briefly if it might be all right to tell her about Stelios.

"I told you," she says, refilling my glass. "He's not the only one. It's just—" She pauses, restarts. "It's time to stop."

I look at her for a moment before asking a question I would never dare ask in broad daylight.

"Do you love him?"

She takes a sip.

"Yes." She speaks slowly, choosing her words carefully. "And I like our marriage and our responsibility for Demetra. We owe it to her to be good together. It's a good thing, marriage, Paki. It can be."

"I know," I say.

As I clean the makeup off my face in the bathroom, I think

about what Aliki has said about Demetra. She must have known I would be glad to hear it—the parents taking responsibility for their child, turning their marriage into a safe space for a little girl to grow up in. Except that now it seems clear that Aliki has chosen to trade her own independence, her force of character, for her child's happiness. Was that what my mother was trying not to give up, her force of character? Did the war make her need it more, value it more? Maybe I was the burden she couldn't bear without losing some of herself.

"You need more than a cotton ball, girl," Aliki says, handing me a cleansing wipe she draws from a blue packet. "What happened to your face? Or do I not want to ask?"

Now is not the right time. I don't even know what I would say.

"Just tell me," she goes on. "Was it a bad thing or a good thing?"

I know she is worried about me.

"It was a good thing," I say, but I'm not sure that it's the truth.

12

Callie

Nikos has gone to work when I get up the next day, and I am glad not to have to face him. Demetra is in her room when I walk by, standing by a dollhouse in her pajama bottoms and a red long-sleeved T-shirt. I take a good look and realize it's the large wooden dollhouse that my grandfather built especially for my mother. There is an artist's studio on the top floor, where a tiny doll made to look like my mother stands among the props of her imagined futures: a tiny easel, a ballet barre, a little stage. None of those futures ever came, and neither did the dollhouse. During my childhood, the house was one of the many things my mother pined for but was told—by my father and others—that she could not bring to America because of the expense or the trouble.

A blue sweater is draped over the roof of the house.

"Do you not play with that anymore?"

"Not really. I'm too old."

She pulls the sweater on over her head. Bits of woolen fuzz cling to the tiny shingles on the roof.

"Maybe *Theia* Clio would want it back," I say, trying to sound offhand.

"She's the one who gave it to me," the girl says brightly.

I take this in. I suppose here is the surprise I was looking for yesterday. My mother showing generosity to a little girl she doesn't seem capable of communicating with.

"There's another parade today," Demetra says, following me to the kitchen.

"You going?"

"Want to go with me?"

"Demetra, go put some pants on," Aliki says. The girl turns around and heads back to her room, grunting in dramatic irritation.

"So," Demetra says when she returns. "Come to the parade with us. It's a musicians' parade."

"What time?"

"Eleven."

I look at Aliki.

"I was hoping to talk to the lawyer today. Is there even a point in trying?"

"Go now," she says, "and maybe you'll catch him."

"Then I'll go with you, Demetraki, to the parade. I promise."

"Can this be our thing? You know, our thing that we do together, just you and me?"

"Your aunt Calliope will be coming from the lawyer's, Demetra. So I have to bring you," Aliki says.

"Well, then, you can leave when she gets there."

"I'll stay." Aliki tries to make it sound offhand. But I know what's going on in her head. She's not sure she can trust me to show up. And once I'm there, she's not sure she can trust me to take care of her daughter. I don't blame her. This is what a mother should do—stand guard over her kid to make sure she doesn't follow bad examples like me.

Aliki and I make plans to meet near here, on the corner of Korinthou and Agiou Nikolaou, at eleven o'clock. By the time I'm ready, I have to rush several blocks down Korinthou Street without getting anything to eat—which I soon regret, as I feel my dry mouth and my churning stomach.

I find Constantopoulos's name among the labels by the door of a ten-story building. Someone buzzes me in, and I ride a whirring elevator to the top floor and find a shiny wooden door at the end of the hall. It clicks open as I push, and I enter a reception room lined with blond wood and thick white carpet. I worry that a practice this successful won't have time for my small concern.

I announce myself to the woman behind the blond-wood counter; she acknowledges me only with a slight lift of her head. She returns to whatever she is doing for a moment, then calls into a phone for Constantopoulos.

"Miss *Braoun,*" she says. "The American."

Constantopoulos sweeps into reception and takes my hand. He is around fifty years old, very tall and very thin, and he is wearing an elegant suit with cuff links made of a deep-blue stone.

"I'm so sorry, Miss Brown," he says. "It is too early still. We won't have the document until tomorrow, I'm afraid."

"But once I sign it, everything is done? I can dispose of the property as I wish?"

"Oh, no," he says, as if this is not an enormous problem. "It needs to be assessed by the tax authorities, and then you need to pay taxes on whatever is of value."

"But it's nothing. Nothing of value," I say, feeling a slight pang for all of Nestor's treasures.

"Nevertheless, we still must follow protocol."

More like you hope I'll pay you off for not declaring the full value, is what I'm thinking, which is not going to happen.

"Well, great. How long will that take?"

"It's difficult to say." He pauses a second, as if to dispose of that issue. "I have the package for you now."

"What package?"

"As we explained to your mother, Mr. Notaris left an envelope, to be opened only by you."

"My mother."

"Yes."

"Was that protocol, Mr. Constantopoulos, to tell my mother?"

He spreads his manicured hands wide.

"She indicated that she had your authority."

This explains a lot. She figured she had to act fast, before I saw whatever was in that package.

"I'd like this envelope now, please."

"Of course, we need to ascertain that there is nothing taxable within it."

I would kill Jonah if he took this tone with clients.

Constantopoulos ushers me to his office and begs me to sit while he pulls a file from a credenza made of the blond wood that is everywhere. He lays the file open on his desk and turns a few pages of a document that looks puzzlingly familiar. It's the paper. It's the same foolscap that Nestor used for his list of song titles and that I used the day before to write up my rules. Suddenly I want to cry, picturing my uncle Nestor at his desk, drawing sheets of thin paper from the top drawer to write his last wishes. It hits me that I am failing him, the way I'm failing everybody else in my life. How can I possibly discharge his wishes, and how can I possibly sort through his things and sort

out everything I have thought and seen and found and done in
the last few days?

"Here," Constantopoulos says, handing me an envelope and
a letter opener.

I slice through the crinkling paper.

Constantopoulos peers over. I hold the envelope open so
that he can see, as I do now, that there is only what looks like
one small sheet of paper, not the usual foolscap, inside.

I open the white sheet and look down at loops of Nestor's
blue ink, but I can't make out the handwriting. It seems mess-
ier than the writing I have seen on Nestor's boxes and books,
and I wonder, with tears welling, if it is because he was ill.

"May I?" Constantopoulos says, seeing my difficulty.

I nod.

"Dearest Calliope,

*There is much more to say than I am able. And there are
some things that are not mine to tell. But now as you look over
what remains of our lives, know that it is all there for you to
understand. Remember that silence is not always the enemy
and that what seems important now was once insignificant
and will become so again.*

*Your loving uncle,
Nestor."*

Constantopoulos clears his throat and I realize that I have
been sitting there for a few moments.

"Can I keep this?"

"Now that it has been read, of course."

"Can I ask why you didn't mention this two days ago?"

"We are a large firm, Miss Brown. I apologize that it slipped
my mind."

I restrain myself from a rant that won't do any good. He puts the folder containing Nestor's will away and aims a solicitous look at me.

"We will have the Acceptance of Inheritance for you to sign tomorrow. If you return at ten in the morning."

He escorts me out, as if I were an unruly drinker at a nice restaurant. I make my way to the Internet café near Aliki's to eat something. I could use a drink, but it's too early, so I gulp down a coffee and a croissant. It all makes sense now. My mother knew there was an envelope for me; she didn't tell anyone else about it in case they let me know; that's why she kept snooping around Nestor's house. She's convinced he's hidden something in there for me and whatever was in the envelope would tell me where and what it is. And that is absolutely what they were arguing about that day in the hospital.

I rush across town and find Aliki and Demetra waiting for me on the corner of Korinthou and Agiou Nikolaou, as we have planned. Aliki is on her cellphone but closes it as she sees me coming. The air has turned balmy since I left this morning. Aliki is wearing a pale-blue gabardine coat over a blue-and-white-striped shirt. It is the brightest clothing I have seen her wear since I arrived.

"I have lots to tell you," I say.

"Come on, *Theia* Calliope," Demetra says, and takes my hand.

"I'm coming!" I say, feigning exasperation. I make my arm go limp and let Demetra tug me along. I slow down every now and then to give her something to do.

We can hear the parade as we dash down Agiou Nikolaou to where it crosses Maizonos. And then we see it: a long string of loosely formed bands wearing regional or national costumes. There are musicians from Crete, with black-fringed scarves tied around the men's heads; from Epirus, with rich embroidered vests and skirts; and a German oompah band, whose men bravely wear *lederhosen* and feathered hats. When these pass before us—their songs distinct, then blending into cacophony—there is an enormous group of bongo drummers followed by a band of teenagers playing "Mamma Mia" on kazoos. Over all of this noise is the constant pulsing of the music from the city loudspeakers.

"Nestor left me a message," I say to Aliki, shouting over the music. As I explain it to her, it all sounds like something out of a Victorian novel. I keep remembering the way my mother peered into everything and the way she focused on that little box with the feathers on the top. There's something in there that she wants to see.

Demetra spots some friends from school on the opposite sidewalk and convinces us to dart across the parade route in between bands so that she can talk to them. A cheer goes up as we negotiate the brief opening between a salsa band and a troupe of Morris dancers in their startling white. It is much cooler here on the shady side of the street, and I turn my collar up for warmth and my mind goes back to Nestor's words. *What seems important now was once insignificant and will become so again.* True enough, I suppose. Very Zen, even. Or maybe it was an ashes-to-ashes thing. We all think we're important, but we were babies once and we'll be worthless again once we're dead. But that last part doesn't ring true. Nestor, more than anyone, believed that treasured objects held their value simply because someone had valued them once and because they were the repositories of our stories. The more I puzzle over his note, the more confusing it becomes.

"I'm freezing," I say to Aliki. I need to do something before I make myself crazy.

"I'm cold too," she says. "It's nearly lunchtime, anyhow, Demetraki. Daddy's eating at home today."

I wonder whose idea this was: Nikos's atonement for whatever he did at the Bourbouli, or Aliki's punishment for it?

We leave the parade behind and head up to the apartment. Demetra collapses melodramatically on the couch before Aliki rouses her to put her coat away. She and I move quietly around the kitchen, getting together the lunch of chicken and stewed vegetables.

"Calliope," Nikos says, as we are putting the food on the table. "Come help me choose the wine."

I give him a wry smirk and follow him into the kitchen.

"Do it fast," Aliki calls. "The chicken's getting cold."

"Very funny," I say to him when we are out of earshot.

He rests his hands on the counter behind him and looks at me for a moment. I can't read the expression on his face. I have a flash of worry that he is about to tell me bad news—about my mother? Jonah? Has Jonah called here?

"I saw you, cousin, at the Bourbouli."

His measured tone tells me exactly where and how. My face suddenly burns astoundingly hot.

"It wasn't me," I say, fooling no one.

He smiles sadly.

"Look," he says, "I told you before. I don't have a problem with infidelities of a certain sort. Especially during Carnival. But I don't know if you are made of the same stuff, Calliope."

"You don't know me that well, Nikos."

"Better than you think."

He turns and fishes a bottle of white wine from the refrigerator, holding it up for me to see and then beginning to uncork it.

"He's a handsome man, I'd say," Nikos continues.

"Nikos, stop."

He sets the corkscrew down. "What I really want to tell you is to watch yourself. These little infidelities aren't as easy as they seem. Trust me."

"What makes you think I have to be faithful to anyone?"

He gives me an almost sad look, and I realize that of course Aliki has confided in him.

I sit through lunch in a state of nearly unbearable tension. It is unusual for Nikos to return home for the meal, so Aliki is drawing it out, taking time between the chicken and the salad and the vegetables. Nikos sips his wine slowly, appraisingly, and I wonder if he, too, is slowing the meal down—to torture me. When Aliki sighs and pushes her chair back, I jump up to help clear the table and load the dishwasher.

"Listen," I say to Aliki as I wipe my hands with the dish towel, "I really need to get some stuff done at Nestor's. If I don't speed up, I'm going to have to change my flight."

"Want me to come and help?"

"No. It's better if I just slog ahead. No distractions."

I hate lying to her, but I am desperate to be alone.

"If you say so."

"I'll call you from there when I'm done. I'm going to stop by my mother's. I have some questions for her."

"There's another dance tonight," Nikos says. I look at him. "But it's not a Bourbouli."

I nod thoughtfully, feigning regret.

"See you later," I say, grabbing Nestor's key and my jacket and heading out the door.

My uncle was a saver, a hoarder, and an archivist, even a tinkerer. But he was never a puzzler. Now here I am, back at his house, hanging everything on some scrap of paper or a receipt or a button. I go to the desk and pull out the drawers one by one. Bills, phone books, stacks of stationery, and, in the center drawer, the foolscap Nestor wrote his will on. I riffle through those papers in case I've missed something, but all I see is my own English writing, recording lists of boxes. Nothing here. I let out a long, frustrated groan.

I begin to flip through photographs, sorting out any image in which I can't recognize the all-ages versions of the people. It's almost six o'clock when I come across a picture of a young man carrying a basket of what look like apples—the same young man I saw in the photographs my mother seemed so eager to have. He is tall and lean, and his hair is dark and straight, cut in that short-back-and-sides style of the war years that gives men a look of rugged grace. It's like Marcus's haircut that night we toasted his new job—a night that seems like years ago now.

The young man's eyes are mischievous. He seems to be at the farm, or *a* farm. I wonder who took the photograph. Who is he smiling at with such a lazy joy? I think about my mother's reaction to the pictures I gave her, and I convince myself that this young man's eyes hold the answer to that question. I prop the photo up on a bookcase and keep on sifting through the collection, every now and then glancing over at that smiling face.

There is a rap on the front door and I see right away that it is my mother for the third time, coming like a troll in some fairy story. Her small, erect shape is a blurred shadow on the frosted glass.

I swing the heavy door open and stand on the sill.

"You're persistent."

"Good afternoon, Calliope," she says.

"What are you doing here, *Mamá*? Didn't we say enough yesterday?"

"Calliope," she whispers loudly, glancing over her shoulder. "Let me in, for God's sake."

I let her in and stand back while she walks through the foyer like someone who has never been to the house before—slowly, as if not wanting to disturb the air.

"Let me guess," I say. "Constantopoulos called you."

"Who?"

"The lawyer, *Mamá*."

"Yes, I understand you've opened your uncle's letter."

"I have. Why didn't you just tell me it was there? We could have gone together. I might have even let you read it first."

She snorts.

"Why don't you trust me, Mother? I have no reason to keep you from your brother's memory. But what I don't understand is why you seem to feel I shouldn't be here. It's what he wanted. Don't be mad at me, be mad at him."

"Oh, I am mad at him, Calliope. I am furious at him."

We stare at each other for a moment. Her face reddens uncharacteristically.

"I'm sorry it's all like this, *Mamá*. Maybe you can help me."

She gives me a wary look. I sigh, exasperated.

"Fine," she says.

To start things off easy, I bring her the photograph of the young man.

"Who is this?"

She gives the photo a quick glance.

"I don't know."

She moves toward a stack of papers on a low table.

"Are you sure?" I ask, bringing the photo closer. She peers at the image, then sighs dismissively.

"One of the refugees. At the farm."

"Like in those other pictures I gave you?"

"Yes." She shrugs and turns back to the papers, riffling through them casually.

"How long were they there?"

"A few months. I don't know."

"That's a long time. Who were they?"

"What do you mean?"

"Where were they from, what did they do? Who were they?"

She walks over to the other side of the room, where I have set the war-years pile.

"They came from Patras, Calliope, because their houses were destroyed during the bombings."

As she talks, her hands continue their restless movement over the boxes, nudging them aside to read Nestor's labels on the tops, lifting the lids. I think about that box from yesterday, with the feathers in it. That's what she's looking for. But I can play this game, pretending neither of us knows what's going on. And, besides, it's the refugees I want to hear about now.

"When did they come?" I ask.

"When? After the first day of the war. The planes came over from Italy, started dropping bombs, and the teachers sent us all home while the bombs were falling into the streets."

"They didn't send you to a shelter?"

"Nobody had a shelter. Nobody thought about shelter."

"So these people just showed up one day because they were bombed out. What were they like?"

"Again with this question," she mutters.

"Well, I want to know. And maybe it will help. What was his name?"

She bangs her hands on the lid of a box.

"It won't help anything. Why do you care so much about these refugees? They showed up one day, we took them in, and they left. They were poor people with no homes and we helped them. Isn't that enough?"

Her face is trembling and her jaw is set. If I didn't know her any better, I would think she was about to cry.

"I think," I say slowly, "you were in love with him."

My mother bursts out laughing. "In love with him? With the *refugee*?"

Her emphasis on the last word makes it clear that my suggestion of a class-crossing romance is preposterous. She is offended, but I can also see that she is relieved at my mistake. I decide to push, using her laughter and my own smile as cover for a harder question.

"You must have been in love with *someone* then, *Mamá*."

Instantly, her mood changes; whatever opening I had closes shut.

"You're in here all day, finding things you don't know the meaning of and that you will never understand, and you are getting everything wrong." She slaps the box and picks up her coat from the chair where she has draped it. "You've gotten everything wrong."

"I've already asked you: Help me."

She turns around. The guarded look is back, without the smile.

The phone rings, and my first thought is that it could be Constantopoulos with another message from Nestor.

"Help you do what?" my mother asks.

"Help me get the story right."

"No," she says. "It's not your story. It's not anyone's *story*. It's my life."

She catches herself, and I know she has admitted too much.

I signal her to wait and I go to the study to pick up the phone.

"*Neh?*"

"Callie." The voice is hushed, almost somber, and it takes me a second to recognize Stelios. My breath catches.

"Stelios, how did you get this number?" I cup my hand over the mouthpiece.

"Your cousin." He pauses. "Callie, I need to see you."

"Why?"

"Where are you?"

"In my uncle's house, Stelios, and you can't come here."

"Callie, I can look it up. Nestor Notaris. He'll be in the book."

"Stelios, don't."

"Calliope!" my mother calls.

"Wait," I tell her.

"Who is that?" Stelios asks.

"My mother is here," I whisper into the phone.

"Get rid of her," he says, and his voice sounds like sex.

"I can't."

"You can't tell me that was all you wanted last night."

It wasn't. The thought of letting Stelios in now and clearing space among the boxes makes every inch of my skin flush with warmth.

"It was," I say. "I'm sorry. What would my *fiancé* say?"

"What would *you* say?"

"And what would Anna say? Are you forgetting her?"

"What would *you* say?"

Nothing, for a while. My mother clears her throat. I can hear Stelios breathing. I curl myself around the phone, and into this space that seems to hold his breath and body and lips, I answer slowly.

"What do you want me to say?"

"The name of the street where your uncle lives."

"Ellinos Stratiotou," I tell him. "Number forty-two."

The line clicks off and I place the black handset down in the cradle of the phone as if it were made of glass. When I turn around, conscious that my cheeks are burning, my mother is still holding her coat in her hand. I have a moment's fear that she has just removed it and is planning to stay.

"Meeting someone?" she asks.

I think of lies I could tell her, like a teenager whose mother is actually paying attention.

"Yes," I say.

"Remember what I told you yesterday," she says.

"It's too late for advice, *Mamá*."

I take her coat and hold it out for her. She looks at me for a moment before stretching her arm into the sleeve. As soon as I have closed the door behind her, I go to the kitchen to open the bottle of wine I have spotted in one of the cupboards. I pour a large glass and drink it quickly, then walk around the house, alternately knowing I should never have told Stelios the address and waiting to see his silhouette against the streetlit glass of the door. When I do finally see a shadow in the glass, I open the door and draw him in, already loosening his belt while he shrugs off his jacket and undoes the buttons of my shirt.

We don't wait for the clothes to come off. We stop long enough for me to put the condom on him and then keep going. Our skin squeaks and chafes and our bones press into the floor, against the furniture, into the walls. The sex is hard, nearly violent, and it is fun. When he makes me come, I tug so hard at his hair that he cries out, brings his head up, and bites a fold of skin by my navel.

Afterward, we don't say much as we straighten the dining room chairs and stand the coatrack back up. We each take an end of the hall rug and set it back into place.

"Must have been a burglary in here," he says, trying to make me laugh.

"We can't leave any sign, Stelios. If we do, they'll know."

"In this mess?" He gestures at the boxes.

He dusts his hands off on his pants while he stoops to dig his shirt out of a corner of the living room. I am putting on mine but he starts to do the job for me, kissing once between my breasts for each button.

"When do we get to do this again?"

I laugh. "No, Stelios. This is over now. There's no again."

"Come on, Callie. What's the harm?"

"Anna. There's the harm."

"You don't get it." He laughs. "We're not that way, Anna and I. It's just not that serious."

"I'd rather hear that from Anna, if you don't mind—which isn't going to happen, because no one is going to find out about what we did."

"In which case," he says, talking over me, "the only one who matters is Jonah, and you haven't said a word about him the whole time I've been here."

"We weren't exactly having a conversation, Stelios."

Of course he's right. And when I finally get him to go, I sit on the chair in the hall and think about what he and I did and what that means for me and Jonah. I have to tell him. And when I tell him, we'll both realize that it was over as soon as he proposed to me, and he will write me an email telling me good-bye. My mother will have been right. When I return to Boston, my things will be in boxes, just like Nestor's things, stacked in a corner of the room so that I hardly need to set my foot in the apartment to get the hell out of his life.

I stay in Nestor's house until the hunger in my stomach becomes too painful to ignore. The kitchen clock says it is ten thirty-five. I toss back the last of the wine, rinse the glass, switch off the lights, and leave.

13

Clio

November 1940

Clio and Sophia were in the kitchen of the farm, boiling sugar beets in a giant pot to make a thick syrup. The smell from the pot was bitter and sharp, and Clio hated to think that they were reduced to putting this mess into their coffee and cakes as a substitute for sugar. Never mind that she and her sister now had to help in the kitchen, since there were so many more chores to do. She gave the pole-handled spoon to Sophia and went to chop some more beets for the next batch before Irini could come in and scold her for being lazy.

She heard a man clearing his throat and turned to see a tall figure in the doorway. From the shape of his shadow against the sunny farmyard, she could see that he was wearing a suit and that he held a fedora by his side.

Clio gripped the chopping knife tightly. This time, at least, she would be able to do more than scream and run away, as she had last summer.

"Please," he said, taking one step into the kitchen. "I've come from the city. I'm looking for somewhere to stay."

That was why the Notaris family was at the farm. The Italians might be losing the war up north in Epirus and Albania, but down here they could terrorize the Greeks from the air. Patras's harbor was easy pickings for them, so close to Brindisi just across the sea, so they continued to pound it with bombing raids that hit the rest of the city as well. Though only ten kilometers away from the harbor, the farm was beyond the zone that the Italians aimed for. Their bombers seemed almost too lazy to bother with the countryside, though they must have known that many had escaped there.

Clio saw that this stranger was a young man, no more than twenty, with dark straight hair and a cleft chin.

"You'd better talk to our father."

"And that I will," he said. "Where would I find him?"

"In the main part of the house. By the porch."

The young man tipped his hat before putting it back on and heading out into the yard. Clio rushed to the door to watch him go, but Sophia pulled her inside.

"Don't gawk," she said. "You don't know who he is."

"He's wearing a waistcoat and a watch chain. He's not a tramp."

"He probably stole the watch. And the waistcoat."

But Clio had already been drawn in, attracted by the way the young man had waved the hat above his head, nodding downward as he did so but peering up at her with a grin. She waited until he was up the stairs and through the house door and then followed him across the farmyard, stopping on the porch so that she could peer into the house through a window.

He was with her parents in the sitting room, telling them who he was and how he had arrived at the farm. Her father eased himself into an armchair and motioned to the young man to do the same. Her mother left the room after the young man had been speaking for some time and reappeared with a pitcher of water.

His name was Lambros Skourtis, and he was from a hard-working family in Aigio, he said. His parents had sent him the thirty-five kilometers west along the coast to Patras to train as a tailor. He had recently begun working as an assistant to an elderly tailor in the city, a man who had sewn a few of Clio's father's suits. Skourtis rented a room in a hotel near the harbor, and the place had been struck by an Italian bomb. He had salvaged a few things that he had brought with him in a suitcase; he waved toward the farmyard, where it appeared he had left the bag. Though he wanted to return to Patras, he was hoping to wait until the bombing was done. He leaned forward eagerly to say he guessed it would be only a matter of days before Greece pounded the Italians on the Albanian front and shut them up for good.

"Let them go fight in Africa," he said. "They can't handle us Greeks."

Clio wondered why he hadn't become part of the *us* himself, why he wasn't fighting in the Albanian snow like every other young man.

"Are there others like you?" her father asked him.

"How could there be?" Clio murmured. "He's gorgeous."

"The roads are crowded," Skourtis said. "Some carriages and cars, but mostly people on foot. I don't think I'll be the only one to ask you for a favor."

Clio could see what her parents were thinking. In the glances they exchanged while Skourtis turned his hat in his hands, she saw the calculation they were making. Theirs was a simple equation concerning refugees, beds, and social standing. No matter how high his social standing, a lawyer, for instance,

THE CLOVER HOUSE | 241

would be of little use now. But a tailor who could mend socks and trouser seats could be very useful indeed.

"We can make up a bed for you in the overseer's rooms," her father said, and Skourtis leapt to his feet and shook his hand in both of his.

Clio pulled away from the window as Skourtis and her father came through the door. She leaned over the porch railing, staring out at the pasture, where the family's small herd of cows was grazing.

"Clio," her father said, "tell Irini that Mr. Skourtis is going to be moving in to one of their rooms for a short time. Irini will show you where to go," he said to Skourtis, and went back inside.

"We haven't been introduced," Clio said.

"You're Clio," he said.

"Miss Clio Notaris." She extended her hand.

"Lambros Skourtis," he said, taking her hand as if to shake it and then, after a quick glance to the house door, kissing it lightly.

"Wait here," Clio said, turning bright red as she snatched her hand away.

In the city, Yannis and Irini had their own home somewhere. But on the farm, their home was a collection of small rooms in a long and low outbuilding, almost all of which opened directly onto the farmyard. Skourtis was installed in a room at the corner of the building, giving Irini and Yannis some privacy but taking away the one space where they had sunlight from two windows.

A few days after Skourtis arrived, a grizzled older man with broad shoulders and only a loose jacket over his shirt limped up the steps to the porch. Seeing him through the window, Clio at first thought he might be the stranger who had tried to attack her in the clover houses. She ran to bring her father to the door.

"What do you want?" he said, holding the door in his hand, ready to shut it.

"A place to sleep."

"I'm sorry. I have no room."

"I'm hungry and I'm willing to work."

Something in the way the man stood made Clio's father look down at his legs.

"You're hurt."

"It's a bruise," the man said, and turned to go.

"Let me see that." The man was dragging his right leg. "Lift your cuff." He did so and revealed a wide gash of spreading flesh. Leonidas pulled his head back sharply and turned to her.

"Clio, tell Irini to bring some first-aid supplies. This man is wounded."

Clio brought Irini from the kitchen to the porch, trailing Sophia and the other two children behind her. Skourtis stood watching from the farmyard as Irini rolled the cuff up, swabbed at the hairy grime on the man's leg, and wrapped the wound with cloth bandages. Irini didn't say anything to the man as she worked. When she was finished, she looked at Notaris and nodded.

The wounded man rose to his feet and straightened his cuff around the new bandage. Her father asked him his name.

"Manolis Vlachos," he said. "I work at the docks. I got hit during a raid. I'm old, but I'm still hauling cargo. I would go fight Italians if they'd take me." He aimed a glance at Skourtis. "But they only want young men. Like that one there."

Irini left, then returned with a bedroll and a pillow and led him over to the cottage, where he would share Skourtis's room.

Clio watched Skourtis's face for a sign of irritation, but he simply smiled vaguely as Irini led Vlachos away.

Skourtis and Vlachos fell into a rhythm of work on the farm. Skourtis carried bags of grain to the barn so that Vlachos, whose wound still made it difficult for him to walk, could heave them up and dispense the grain slowly between the millstones for grinding. Skourtis went out to the woods to cut firewood, and Vlachos stacked it up into neat cords. Clio would watch the two of them sometimes, wondering what charming Skourtis made of this glowering and silent old man.

She fell into step with Skourtis as he emerged from the kitchen one afternoon, dusting flour from his trousers.

"Miss Notaris," he said, with a flourish of the hand.

"Mr. Skourtis." She gave a little curtsy. "Where are you off to?"

"More wood for the stove. Irini's orders."

"Is she working you too hard?" She made a face of mock concern.

"No," he said brightly. "Just earning my keep. What are you doing to earn yours?"

"Mr. Skourtis! I am shocked at your impudence!"

"My most sincere apologies, Miss Notaris."

He stopped and made a deep bow.

"Apology accepted."

They reached the woodpile along the side of the barn, and Skourtis began to stack skinny logs of cedar and ash into a small wooden cart.

"Shouldn't Vlachos be doing this?"

Skourtis shrugged. "He's around somewhere."

She watched Skourtis work, noticing that he lacked Vlachos's compact efficiency. Skourtis carried one log at a time, compared to the bundles of four or five that she had seen Vlachos loading. But while Vlachos worked like a piston, up and down from the knees, Skourtis made graceful sweeping movements with his arms, swinging his body as if in a dance.

"Here," she said, taking a log from him. "I have nothing else to do."

They worked together. Skourtis lifted the logs from the woodpile, swung them over to Clio, and she set them down into the cart.

"You've got enough wood here to last the whole war," he said. "You'll be all right here."

"You don't know how long the war will last."

"How long can it take?" he said. "We'll get them. You'll see."

She thought for a moment.

"Mr. Skourtis."

"Lambros."

"Lambros," she said, blushing. "Why aren't you fighting?" She remembered what Vlachos had said when he first arrived. Skourtis's youth alone was enough to raise the question.

He laughed. "Someone has to repair the uniforms," he said. "Might as well be me."

"There aren't uniforms here."

"Well, the clothes, then. Someone's got to repair the clothes you all wear."

He stepped past her and added the log to the pile. But she watched him, not sure what she was looking for. Perhaps guilt or shame draped over his shoulders.

The next morning, Urania sent the children to gather apples, handing each of them a small basket and chiding them ahead of time not to eat everything they picked.

"I expect to see those baskets full of apples, not cores."

Clio led the way through the farmyard, beyond the almond grove, where the apple trees stood in six short rows. The day was cold for November, and the sky was a dark gray as if it might snow.

"What if we were fighting here?" said Nestor in an awed voice.

"The front is a whole country away," said Sophia.

"No, I mean what if it's like this, and you have to hide behind the trees so the Italians won't get you." He began to stalk along beneath the branches.

"I don't think the trees would be much protection," Sophia said.

"Why would you say that?" Clio snapped. "Are you trying to scare him?"

"I'm just saying what's a fact. They could bomb the farm just as easily as they bombed the city. I don't know why we came here."

"And I don't know how you can take everything so literally." Sophia made a face.

"I know how to hide in trees, Sophia," Nestor was saying. "We learned camouflage with the Scouts. And I bet I know how to cover my tracks better than you do."

"Nestor," Thalia called. "Take my picture."

The boy had been given a camera for his tenth birthday a few weeks ago and had used it mostly to photograph battle arrays among his tin soldiers. He would set up miniature ranks of the Italian Julia Division where they could be easily shot down by the Greek soldiers he arranged behind rocks and on the edges of ravines. In Nestor's war, as in reality, the Greeks were winning.

Thalia threw her arms around a tree trunk and kicked one

heel up. In the sunlight, her hair showed hints of the auburn in her mother's hair. Nestor pulled the camera out of his jacket and held it at his chest, fiddling with a switch on the side.

"Hurry up!" Thalia switched her pose.

"Stay still."

"Well, hurry."

"I'm doing it."

The camera's viewfinder snapped open and Nestor stared down at it, shuffling from side to side as he tried to frame the image.

"Come on, Nestor!"

"Wait!" He pressed the shutter. "There."

"Can we go now?" Clio asked.

Nestor folded the flaps of the viewfinder back into place and jammed the camera inside his jacket.

"Wait," Clio said. "Chin up." She took hold of Nestor's collar and gently tugged his zipper all the way to the top. "You can take my picture later, all right?"

"All right," he said, pouting.

The apples were too cold to eat, so within a short time they had almost filled their baskets with green and red fruit. Clio heard a crackling nearby and spun around, ready to bolt for the safety of the farmhouse.

"Stop eating!" Skourtis emerged from behind a tree, holding a large empty basket. "I've been sent by your mother to make sure you're not eating everything in sight."

"Look," Nestor said, showing him the apples he had collected. "See?"

"Well done, young man. What's the matter?" he said conspiratorially to the boy. "Aren't they any good?"

"I don't know."

"Let's see." Skourtis held an apple up with suspicion. "No

worms. No poison—that I know of." He took a large bite. "Very tasty," he said, with his mouth full.

Nestor snatched an apple from his basket and did the same, so that both of them were talking to each other through mouths full of apple.

"Nestor Notaris!" Sophia snapped. "That's enough. Where are your manners?"

"Come on, Sophia," said Thalia. "It's funny." She grabbed an apple and took an enormous bite.

"They're behaving like slobs. Like animals."

"Sophia," said Clio, glancing at Skourtis.

"Why should I care what he thinks?"

"Sophia!"

"All right, you two," Skourtis said, pretending not to have heard Sophia's insinuations. "Let's clean ourselves up."

Sophia sidled up to Clio.

"I don't care if you like him," she whispered. "He's low class, and he's teaching Nestor to be an animal like him."

"He is not an animal. There's something refined about him."

Sophia rolled her eyes. "Is that why he's not fighting?"

"I don't know why," Clio said. "Maybe he's ill. Maybe he couldn't pass the test. But I like him."

"Can I take your picture, Mr. Skourtis?" Nestor said.

Sophia began to say something.

"Let him," Clio said.

"Of course you can, if you call me Lambros. Here," he said. "Make it look like I'm being useful." He poured some apples into the large basket and held it up on his waist.

"Hold still, Lambros," Nestor said, and this time he found the controls with confidence. As he cranked the film, he gave his sisters a look of vindication.

The children went back to work, refilling their baskets that had been emptied into the larger one. Skourtis started near Nestor, picking from the high branches and setting the fruit in the boy's basket. But as the children spread out across the trees, he ended up at Clio's side, where he stayed as the others could be heard later agreeing to head back.

"I'm coming," Clio called, but she made no move toward the house.

"You're not cold?" Skourtis said.

"A little."

"I don't need this." He tugged his scarf off and wrapped it loosely around her neck, pulling her hair out from under it. He grazed her skin with his fingers.

"My hands are still cold."

He took them in his and blew.

"Let me see," she said. His fingers were long and delicate, not at all the rough hands of the lower class. "Lambros, you cut yourself," she said. There was a fresh scrape across the top of one knuckle.

"Must have been a branch."

"Here." She pulled a handkerchief from her pocket and dabbed at the cut.

"That's better."

She turned her face up to his, and they stood for a moment with their lips a tiny distance apart, like two opposing magnets. And then something flipped and their lips were pressing together and then pressing open. Clio had kissed Takis and Thanassis, before his awkward mustache had sprouted, but never like this. Skourtis was three years older than she; he was a man. The feel of his mouth confirmed for her her own maturity and, because she was enjoying it, the rightness of what they were doing.

They sat down at the base of an apple tree, with Skourtis's arms around her.

"I wish you didn't have to do all this work around the farm."

"I'm not a guest, Clio. I need to earn my keep."

"But you're not a laborer."

"I work with my hands."

"You're an artist." She caressed his fingers, noting his carefully trimmed nails. "I'm going to be an artist," she said, blushing at the admission. "Or a dancer. Or an actress."

"Oh?"

"When the war's over, I'm going to the School of the Arts, and then I'll make my way to Athens."

He laughed.

"I'm serious."

"Your parents know about this?"

"Of course."

The truth was more complicated, though. Even before the war, she had begun to feel as though her dreams for her future were fantasies she had outgrown. All her notions of performing or being the center of attention were starting to reveal themselves as something different. It wasn't the dream of the crowd itself that she wanted; it was the solitude and the isolation that allowed the dream. That was what she was drawn to, like the hours she spent alone in Hollywood, watching and unseen. How could she say this now to Lambros? He would think she was a fool. And maybe she was, since she didn't even know what it was that she wanted.

She stood up and held the ends of the scarf with outstretched arms and made a few graceful passes on pointed toes.

"Let me make something for you," he said.

"A gown?" He could make her one just like her mother's.

"A gown for you to take the stage in," he said, standing and coming toward her. "I'll tailor it just for you. To match your figure."

He ran his hand up her side beneath her jacket.

Over the next few days, Clio watched Skourtis around the farm, looking for hints of frailty or delicacy in him—something to justify his civilian state. This was the story she had decided on: that Skourtis possessed some inner weakness—of body, not of character—and that he suppressed a noble frustration at not being able to fight for his country. Despite this frailty, and because of it, he worked so hard and so companionably alongside Vlachos, a man who would make most people uneasy.

But Clio couldn't deny that the truth was otherwise. Skourtis, in fact, did not work particularly hard. She saw him one day sitting on the woodpile, rolling a cigarette in those long fingers of his. As soon as Vlachos appeared at the edge of the farmyard, Skourtis popped up and began to haul logs into his arms. Clio saw Vlachos squint at him and mutter something before he crouched down, took up four thick logs in a burly embrace, and placed them in the cart. Turning her gaze back to Skourtis, she noticed how unbalanced his load was, even after days of experience, and how he himself still tottered beneath a far lighter weight than what Vlachos had just lifted. Once the cart was full, Vlachos stepped into the yoke and began to tug it across the farmyard toward the kitchen. As soon as he was out of sight, Skourtis sat back down on the pile to smoke.

She drew her cardigan closed around her neck and stepped outside. Skourtis stood when he saw her coming.

"Miss Notaris."

"Why won't you pretend for me?"

"What?"

"You pretended for Vlachos. I saw you. Why won't you pretend for me?"

"Ah." He stubbed out his cigarette. "Because I'm a little afraid of Mr. Vlachos, truth be told."

"You're not afraid of me?"

He pulled her to him, looking around to see that no one was watching. She stepped back.

"If I could see you, Lambros, what makes you think no one else can?"

"Fine. Come into the barn, then."

He drew himself up, stretching his arms above his head as if to ease some strain, and strolled around the corner. Clio followed him but remained at the edge of the barn's dim space, one foot on each side of the shadow line.

"Why don't you work?" she said.

"I have an ailment," he said. "Weak lungs. Otherwise"—he shook his head ruefully—"I would be in Albania shooting Italians with the best of them. I didn't want you to know."

She cocked her head.

"It's true," he said. He reached his arms out toward her. "Listen."

He beckoned for her. She hesitated but then stepped into the barn's shadow.

"Here." He pulled his jacket open and undid one of the buttons of his shirt. He placed his long fingers on her cheeks, turned her head sideways, and pressed her ear to his bare chest. She drew a deep breath.

"Shh," he said, and pressed her head closer. "Do you hear it?"

She had no idea what to listen for. The beating of his heart was all she heard, that and her own intake of breath, as if she were breathing through her ear. His heartbeat seemed so inconsequential, nothing more than a bird's wing fluttering against a window, his body so slight for all its sudden immediacy. This was the body she would consign to frigid air, to snow, to bayonets and guns.

"Did you hear it?"

"Yes," she said.

He held her head there for a moment longer and then tilted her away. With an apologetic look, he buttoned his shirt again and pulled his jacket tight. He shivered a little.

"Don't tell your father, will you? I don't want him to think I'm weak."

"I won't."

Clio wondered what she had heard. A weak heart? Weak lungs? A heart—his or hers—fluttering with the excitement of nearness? She couldn't be sure. But she couldn't stop thinking about that moment. The shadow on one side of the barn door, the light on the other, and Skourtis with his arms outstretched, his shirt open to reveal his vulnerable chest. Nothing like that had ever happened to her. The more she thought of it, the more she was certain nothing like that ever would again.

When Skourtis asked her a few days later whether she would accept his tailoring of a gown, she said yes. The next day, she took the mirror down from the wall in the bedroom she shared with Sophia.

"Where are you going with that?"

"Never mind."

She couldn't tell Sophia or anyone about the gown. She felt that to explain it she would have to describe that moment by the barn. Even if she were capable of conveying the moment, no one else could possibly understand.

She met Skourtis in a small room at the back of the house,

bringing first Sophia's mirror down and then another one from Nestor's room. She waited until after lunch, when everyone was supposed to be resting, and changed into one of her mother's dresses, a sleeveless silk in a deep blue that Urania had long ago told Clio could be hers. Together, she and Skourtis set the mirrors up at an angle to each other and placed a small crate before them. Skourtis reached out his hand, and Clio saw again the image of him at the edge of the barn's shadow, reaching his arms out toward her. She took his hand and stepped up onto the crate.

"Plenty of extra," he said, pinching the fabric in at the sides and looking her up and down.

She turned as he instructed while he sketched lines with chalk along her sides, her neck, and her hem. He made the neckline dip down, the back dip even more but not too much, and turned the shoulders of the dress into three-inch-wide straps. As he worked, first with the chalk and then with pins, his hands skimmed over her hips, her thighs, her breasts.

"That tickles," she whispered.

"Sorry."

He crouched to pin the hem and she touched his hair. She wanted to place her hands on either side of his head, as he had done to her. If he stood up close to her, she would kiss him.

He moved behind her.

"The zipper will go here."

She felt his finger drawing down along her spine, slowly, over each bone. She arched her back as the press of his finger reached down almost to her bottom.

"Isn't that a little low?"

"It's the latest fashion, I assure you."

He spun her around so she was facing the mirrors.

"You're beautiful," he said.

He reached down into his tailor's box and pulled up a length of gold braid.

"This," he said, holding it up to the neckline, "will make the gown almost as beautiful."

"Where did you get that?"

"I don't know. Around."

"Around where?"

Skourtis shrugged and ran the braid through his hands, flicking his fingers as if water were trickling over them.

"Lambros, this is my brother's. You can't have it."

"Don't you want it for your gown?"

"Not at his expense. It's from his Scout uniform."

"He doesn't need it, does he? Anyway, he should be wearing Metaxas blue."

She reached for the braid, managing to pull it from his hand. He grabbed at her and then made a sort of gasping groan. She let go.

He laughed and held the gold braid above his head.

"I thought you were in pain."

"No."

"But your lungs."

"It's just for fun, Clio."

"I don't know what's going on, but you had no right to take that."

"I was only making you look glamorous."

"It's my brother's."

"I confiscated it to give to you."

She slapped him. From her position on the crate, she swung across and slightly downward in a blow of some force. Skourtis staggered back, one hand still holding the braid aloft, and the other clasped to his cheek.

"Now how do your lungs feel?" she asked. "Or was it your heart? I can't quite remember."

He dropped the braid on the floor.

"You're a coward and a thief. Get out of our house," she said quietly. "Or I will find someone to haul you away so you can die in Albania where you belong."

Skourtis didn't move for a moment, and Clio had a flash of fear that he would hurt her. It was clear to her now that he was not frail at all but lazy and scared. Finally, he swept his hair back over his forehead, pulled his sleeves down, and gathered up his things. He closed the door softly behind him. Clio picked up her brother's gold braid, sat on the crate, and listened to her heart pounding.

14

Callie

Thursday

Now, the morning after my fling with Stelios, which is what I have decided to call it, my head is pounding and I have bruises on my hips, my knees, and my left elbow. Sitting in the chair at Nestor's desk, I can see straight ahead to the hall and to the doorway to the dining room. At some point last night, Stelios made a comment about the dining room table and chairs, whose claw feet were right by his head. "More wealth for my heiress," he said, running a hand along the carvings. I grabbed his wrist and pinned it to the floor.

"I'm not your heiress," I said. "You don't own me."

"No, but, seriously," he said later as we were getting dressed. "Do you own this place too?"

"I told you. I don't own anything. We lost it all after the war."

But now that I have been to Constantopoulos's office again this morning, that is no longer true. I have signed Calliope Notaris Brown to the Acceptance of Inheritance form, and I have agreed to take possession of everything inside this house.

The claw-foot table, the claw-foot chairs, the rug Stelios and I rumpled beneath us, and the vase I held on to so it wouldn't be shaken to the floor: All these are mine. They are all markers now—of the end of Nestor's life and the end of something in my own.

I toy with Nestor's pen, flipping it around on the sheet of blank foolscap I have set out on the desk. If I don't do something, I will start to cry—the kind of crying that, like vomiting, shocks you with your inability to control it, disgusts you with your body's betrayal. It's not the sex I mind. In fact, what bothers me is the likelihood that the sex is irrelevant to my relationship with Jonah. If we're over, it's because of bigger issues than a one-night stand.

I push the chair from the desk and head into the living room. I need to do something to keep my mind from thinking about all this. There is something here in this house, I am sure of it. I start on one side of the room, looking impatiently through boxes whose contents have now become familiar. After a few moments, I see a small box upside down by my foot. I remember Stelios laughing, reaching behind him for support, and then the feeling of something ticklish, like paper, brushing against my hip. I grab the box to set it right and see beneath it the black feathers from the other day. Crouching, I gather up the rest of the box's contents that have spilled onto the floor: a piece of dirty white silk, a woman's ring, a brass-colored bullet, and the four black feathers, which I now see are roughly six inches long.

So this is the box that my mother has been looking for. But it could easily pass for a box of garbage. While all of Nestor's boxes contain objects of the same category, this one has no apparent meaning, no system determining what it holds. And yet this one has held my mother's attention ever since she first glimpsed it. She seems in fact to have *recognized* it. There is a story here that I have not yet understood.

I sit down on the floor and concentrate on the contents. Each item leaves me more confused than the last. The feathers lead me to think of the farm, and the silk turns my mind to the city. Again, the silk is dirty, with what look like rust stains on it, and this leads me to question how it could ever connect to a ring with a rectangular topaz stone set into a thin gold band. Then there is the bullet, which seems to cancel every possible attempt at connection. I can think of no way to put these things together.

If my mother did indeed fall in love with a refugee—with the handsome young man in the photograph—what could these objects have to do with that? Did he give her this ring? Was she wearing that dress? And how did it get so dirty? I picture a teenage Clio rolling in the dirt with a young refugee and shake my head. The image doesn't fit.

The phone rings and my ears tingle, as if the sound were a solid object pushing into my head. I go to pick it up, irritated already at the thought that my mother is hounding me.

"Ti?" I say—What?—before I notice the click and hiss of a transatlantic phone call.

"Cal?"

"Jonah." I exhale a long breath.

"Your cousin gave me this number."

"I'm at my uncle's."

"I know."

"What is it?"

"Well, Cal, I got your email."

"Okay."

"About what you said, about how maybe it's not enough—"

"Jonah—"

"Just wait. If we stay together, I'll be happy to listen to anything you want to tell me. I said that when you left and it's still true. But right now, I have to talk." He pauses and I force myself to wait. "I don't like your silences," he goes on. "They're not good for you and they're not good for us. But I love your stillness. Without you here, I feel like I'm making stupid, meaningless noise all the time. You are always so still, so centered. I love you, Callie. And I don't want to play around anymore."

I don't know what to say. Jonah's words are so beautiful, so peaceful. That's the overriding sensation I have, listening to him: peace. But it feels as if that beauty and quiet exist in a glass room I'm not allowed into. Or, actually, a glass room that I've shattered with what I did the night before. Jonah's idea that I'm still and centered seems so wrong to me. So utterly wrong that I wonder how he could love me and not see the truth of who and how I am.

"Aren't you going to say something?"

I know what I should say, but I'm too afraid to say it. All I want right now is to postpone the moment when it all comes apart.

"I don't know, Jonah. It's beautiful. Thank you."

"But?"

"I don't think we can talk about this over the phone. You've had time to go over all this. But I feel like I'm drowning in other people's lives. There's so much family stuff to understand here. I don't know what I'm doing half the time, with my mother, and Nestor, and everything. Can we talk about it Tuesday?"

"I thought you were coming back on Sunday."

"I need to stay longer."

"Were you planning to tell me, or was I supposed to find out when you didn't get off the plane?"

"I was going to call."

"Callie, you've been gone since last Wednesday and all I've gotten since you landed is one phone call and one email. I know we weren't talking a lot before you left, but I didn't think we'd gone into radio silence."

"It's busy here. And there's the time difference."

"I know all about the time difference, Callie." I wince. "I know how that one works. Why do you need the extra days anyhow? What the hell have you been doing all this time?"

"Don't swear at me, Jonah."

"Look, I'm sorry. But you know, Cal, I'm trying to make a life. With you."

"And isn't that what we said we needed to think about? I told you I want to wait until I get back. We can't be talking like this on the phone."

We are both silent for a long time, listening to each other's breath and to the crackle of the line.

"Jonah, you can't be all understanding about my coming here and taking some time and then get mad if you get to the answer before I do."

"Who said I was all understanding?" His voice is weary. "What was I going to do? Stop you?"

"Jonah."

"Yeah?"

I squeeze my eyes shut.

"We should probably hang up."

"All right, Cal," he says, and his voice croaks with tension.

"You want my new flight info?"

"Sure."

I tell him the number and the arrival time, and we say good-bye.

I feel sick to my stomach. I sit there by the phone for what seems like hours, moving only to hug my knees and press my forehead against them. If I could stay like this, it would be all right. If I could never have to make a decision, never have to take a chance like this on another person—or let that person take a chance on me—it would be all right. When I finally do get up, I am trembling as if Jonah and I have had a shouting match. I look at the clock and see that it is almost twelve-fifteen, which means that Jonah called just after five in the morning. At the thought of him sitting in the dark apartment, just risen from a bad night's sleep, I feel my stomach churn. I go to the bathroom and wait to vomit, but nothing comes. I deserve this.

I need to get out. Out of Nestor's house, out of the city. I am startled to find the air warm outside. I walk fast to Aliki's house, feeling sweat roll slowly down the back of my neck.

When she hears my voice over the intercom, she buzzes me in, but I wait and ring again.

"Aliki!"

"What's the matter?"

"Come down and let's go for a drive!"

"Now? Are you all right?"

"Come on. It's warm out. Let's just go. I need to get out," I say. "I'm going crazy."

"Wait."

The intercom clicks off and then back on.

"Callie?"

"Yes."

"Okay. We'll leave Demetra at my mother's and we'll go. But not for too long."

"Fine."

We walk the few blocks over to Thalia and Sophia's apartment, holding hands with Demetra, who swings between us on each rapid step. I try to let the girl's lightheartedness rub off on me. Aliki lets us into a lobby strewn with flyers and leads the way up two flights of stairs that wind around an old-fashioned elevator shaft. The cage-style elevator drifts down past us with an old man inside.

"*Geia sas,* Mr. Stoukidis."

"*Geia sou,* Miss Aliki."

Aliki knocks and, hearing Sophia call through the door, unlocks it and steps aside for Demetra to push through. The girl is swept up by her grandmother and great-aunt, who take her into their kitchen for something to eat.

"Did you sign it?" Thalia asks me.

"This morning. Nestor left me a note, *Theies.*"

"What did he say?"

"That silence is not always the enemy, and some other things."

"Silence is almost always the enemy," Sophia says.

"Here."

I pull the note from my bag and show it to the two old women. Sophia holds it while Thalia reads over her shoulder. Thalia wells up with tears and has to excuse herself for a tissue.

"I can remember him as a little boy," she says.

Sophia smooths the note out on her knee, then folds it carefully into halves and then quarters. I wish she wouldn't, but something about the deliberate nature of her movements keeps me from interrupting.

I wait a little before asking both of them my question.

"Do *you* know what he meant?"

"There are some things Calliope should know, now that she's accepted the inheritance," Sophia says, handing me the folded note.

"Time for that later, Sophia," Thalia says. Sophia starts to say something else, but Thalia cuts her off. "So where are you off to?"

Aliki blurts out, "Nafpaktos."

I look at her. Nafpaktos is a ferry ride away, east of the narrows that divide the Gulf of Patras from the Gulf of Corinth.

"There's going to be a bridge, *Theia* Calliope," Demetra chirps.

"Yes," Thalia says. "Calliope should see where they're building the new bridge. Big progress for our little nation, Calliope."

"Too much too fast," Sophia says, her grim mood seeming to spill over all her thinking. "Who's going to pay for this? The government will cook the books, and we'll end up paying. You'll see."

"Go," Thalia says, steering us out of the kitchen with a roll of her eyes. "It's too nice a day for such gloomy politics. Go and have a good time. Why not?" She turns to Demetra. "Say good night to your mother and aunt."

"Good night?" I ask.

"Nikos and I are going to a party later. She'll stay here overnight."

"I could have stayed with her."

"It's all right," Aliki says.

"We don't see her as often as you'd think," says Thalia. "Or you either," she says, squeezing my arms.

Aliki kisses Demetra and sweeps me from Thalia's hold.

"Let's go for that drive!" she says.

We call goodbye from the hall on our way down the stairs.

Her Fiat is trapped behind a double-parked delivery van on Kolokotronis, so I stand beside the little white car while she honks the horn in jaunty triplets. I am itching more than ever to get out, to go somewhere. Finally, the driver appears and gets in the van, moving off without acknowledging us.

"Nafpaktos?" I say. "Where did that come from?"

"I don't know," Aliki says. "I've just always liked it and I never go."

We crank down the windows as we poke along in midday traffic, but after a few moments we are on the road leading along the shore to the ferry landing. With a warm wind blowing our hair around, we drive beneath eucalyptus and sycamore trees, past a row of low whitewashed buildings and an abandoned swimming complex, before we reach the ruins of the medieval fort at Rio. We join a line of trucks and cars jockeying for position by the lowered gate of the ferry. We roll up our windows to keep out the pungent waves of diesel exhaust. A man at the head of the line is banging on the car hoods to tell the drivers where to go. This is not what I had in mind. I wanted to drive, fast, on an open road—to shake myself free from the mistakes I've made and that seem to be clinging to me like barnacles. Instead, I am stuck here, unable to move or to get out, and my errors and thoughts have had plenty of time to catch up.

We park. The other cars are so close to us that it's a tight squeeze to get out through the Fiat doors. The air is baking hot from the engines and the sun beating down on all that metal.

"This way," Aliki says, and leads the way up a staircase to the skinny deck that rims the car area. Here the breeze is blowing off the gulf, fresh and cool and salty. I lean over the side and watch the water churning turquoise as the engines back us out of the slip.

"So, you want to tell me what's going on?" Aliki gives me a little shove as she rests her elbows on the rail beside me.

"Everything," I say, buying time.

Seagulls are making a ruckus above us, trying to catch the bits of bread a woman is throwing into the air. In the distance, I can see the mouth of the Gulf of Patras where it opens into the Ionian Sea. To the southwest is Zakynthos, hidden now by the mass of Peloponnesos; I think of my solitary week there so many years ago. This is better, to be among family, to be loved. Maybe Aliki was right: I do belong to them.

"I did something stupid, Aliki," I say. "God, I was so stupid."

She doesn't say anything, but I feel relaxation in her shoulder and arm and take encouragement from that.

"That guy I told you about?"

"Stelios."

"I slept with him." I will not tell her where. I can't bring myself to admit that I had sex with a near stranger in my dead uncle's house.

"Ah. And Jonah knows this?"

"He knows something's wrong."

"He sounded fine enough when he called the house."

"No, he was pretty upset. He wants us to stay together."

"Is that good?"

"It can't be good now, when I've gone and slept with Stelios. You know something's not right if I went and did that."

"Were you drunk?"

I look at her, wondering if she and Nikos have been talking.

"Not when I made the decision."

I've chosen my words carefully. It was a decision to sleep with Stelios, not an impulse, and she needs to know that. I need to know that.

"Well, then! I can see why you needed to get away."

After a minute, she turns to face me. "Which is worse?" she asks. "That you slept with this Stelios or that you might tell Jonah?"

"I have to tell him."

"Why?"

"Because it's the truth. What did Sophia say? Silence is always the enemy."

"Not according to Nestor. And you'd take relationship advice from an old woman who's never been married?"

"Maybe it's better than relationship advice from an old *man* who never married."

"Point taken," Aliki says. "But, if you don't tell Jonah, you have a chance to fix things. If you do tell him, I'm guessing that will be it for the engagement."

"I can't lie to him, Aliki."

"That depends."

"On what?"

"On whether you want to go ahead with the marriage."

When Aliki says this, she knows she has hit on the only important issue here. It's not about Stelios, or about sex, or about secrets. It's about whether I want to stay with Jonah or not, whether I even can. Am I made for marriage? Am I good enough? How can I make that kind of commitment to someone else when I'm not sure I deserve it? Right now I feel I'd have to go farther away from Jonah than Greece to find the answer.

We have reached the middle of the narrow gulf, near the third of four piers for the new bridge. From here I can see barges butted up against the piers and a handful of men at work on the concrete. In a few moments we will be on the other side and driving east along the coast to the tiny harbor of Nafpaktos.

"What's the party you're going to? Isn't there another Bourbouli?"

"Friends from Nikos's work. You're more than welcome to come with us."

She must have assumed I would be going out with Stelios and Anna, but she is kind enough not to say so now.

"And Nikos isn't going to the Bourbouli alone," I say. "How'd you manage that?"

She gives me a wry smile.

"It's pre-Lent, remember? This is the week of the Prodigal. Nikos is Contrite, and I am Forgiving." She stresses the words as if they were titles.

She gazes out to the last of the four piers, just behind us now as we near the mainland.

"It won't be long before these ferries are gone," she says, "and we're all speeding across the gulf in our cars."

"That's kind of sad."

"Not at all." She shakes her head. "It's progress, Paki. They'll keep a ferry or two for those who don't want to pay the toll, but the country's moving on. Nikos and I plan to be on that bridge the very first day it opens."

My eyes sting as I hear her say this—the image of the two of them, Forgiving and Contrite, moving on into a shared future. I can't say anything to her for a while, and she seems to sense this. We watch the boat's wake curling a blinding white out of the dark-blue water.

Nafpaktos is just a few minutes' drive down a winding two-lane road along the coast. We arrive after the lunchtime rush and park on a side street running off the embankment road. We walk back to the almost circular harbor ringed by several tavernas. Their tables look out at the thick stone walls that reach out like protective arms from the jetties on either side. We find a spot by the seawall and order fish and fried potatoes and a salad.

"Should we get wine?" I ask Aliki.

"If you want."

I order a carafe of white, pretending that this hasn't become an issue.

We sit looking out at the calm water within the harbor and the white-dotted deep blue of the waves beyond. The Battle of Lepanto was fought here, I know, but I can't remember against whom. I don't bother to ask Aliki; I have had too much history for one day. It is a little too cool to be sitting outside, but we wrap our jackets tight around us and make do as the waiter brings us two plates of filleted whole fish and a salad bowl of artichoke hearts in oil and vinegar. The fries smell of olive oil and salt and crunch in our teeth.

"This is nice, Paki," Aliki says, reaching for her wine. "I wish you were staying longer."

"I didn't tell you. I've changed my flight after all. I leave on Tuesday."

"Good! You'll be here for Clean Monday."

"That's not why. I have too much to do on Nestor's stuff."

"And," she says, pointing a fry at me with her fork, "you can put off going home to Jonah."

I concentrate on my fish, searching for bones. I take a drink of wine.

"Aliki, did you notice anything funny about Sophia today?"

"No, but I was doing stuff with Demetra."

"She kept getting all serious and saying things must be said."
I intone this last part.

"What else is new."

"I found this box in Nestor's house. I think my mother
wants it, but she won't talk about it."

"What's in it?"

I tell her about gathering the spilled contents of the upturned box and about my theory that somehow it and Nestor's
will and the photograph of the young man are all connected to
my mother's past. She shakes her head.

"I don't think it works that way, Paki. People's lives aren't
that straightforward."

"This isn't straightforward. I wish it were."

"Not straightforward, then. Clear. You're assuming that
these objects have an exact correlation to some event or some
message from the past. But think of it. Most of us don't even
have clear lives in the present. How much more confused do
our stories get when a few years go by? Or when we hand the
stories down? Our mothers' stories. They've been told so many
times it's a wonder they can still hold together. You use something that much, it's bound to wear thin."

"You don't believe our mothers' stories?"

"Sure I do. Just not as pure fact. They stopped being that a
long time ago. Now they're just good stories. Which is fine."

"Don't you want to know?"

"If I thought I really could know, maybe. But I don't think
I can. So what's the point? I'd rather talk with my mother about
what Demetra did today, or about the parade yesterday, or
about the liturgy for Forgiveness Sunday."

"You need to understand, Aliki, that it's different for me. I
don't have a present with my mother. You know that. All I

have—all I ever had—was her past. My whole life I've felt like I was listening for the rules of the game, waiting for her to give me the password to take me back to her childhood. Because that was the only place she ever wanted to be. But I could never hear what I was hoping for. It was as if she was standing at the mouth of a cave, telling her stories from there but keeping me from getting inside. Now there's this box and she seems to care about it and it seems to mean something important. Maybe if I can figure out what it means, it will make a difference."

I drink more wine and stare out at the harbor, where a brightly painted fishing boat is making its way in through the arms of the jetties. Aliki sets her fork down and puts her hand on mine.

"I'm sorry, Paki," she says. "You should do what you think makes sense. Tell me if you need my help."

I shrug, self-pitying now. "It's all right. You just have a different point of view."

I think about the missing drain in the basement of the old house, where this whole trip to Patras seems to have started. Shouldn't that have been lesson enough that stories aren't reliable, that memories shift like sand?

I sit in the living room, pretending to read, while Nikos and Aliki are getting ready for their party. They exchange very few words and fewer glances as they come and go from the bathroom to the bedroom to the hallway mirror. Still, they don't seem tense. It is instead as if they have returned to a familiar orbit, Nikos revolving around his wife with just enough separation from her to avoid being sucked in.

"You're staying in?" Aliki asks, but it is a reminder, not a question.

"I'm not going anywhere." I give her a tired smile. I almost tell her how much I'm enjoying watching the two of them get ready, basking in their quiet contentment.

Nikos is in his tux again, and Aliki has put on a cocktail dress of green satin with an empire waist that makes her look taller. Around her neck is a choker with a large topaz at its center. She sees me looking at it.

"My mother's," she says, touching it briefly, as if to make sure it is still there.

"Aliki, the ring I told you about. It's topaz."

She raises her eyebrows.

"Sophia has a bracelet," she says. "Topaz. *Yiayiá* gave one to each daughter." She is animated now. "Of course: *Mamá* had the necklace, Sophia had the bracelet, and Clio had the ring. That's your mother's ring, Paki. I bet that's what she wants and she thinks it will sound greedy to ask for it."

"So what's it doing in Nestor's box?"

"Find out. There's your assignment."

I think of all the other things that have ended up in houses other than my mother's. Has this ring, like those objects, been taken away? Or has it been given?

"See you later, if you're up," Aliki says, throwing a garnet wrap around her shoulders.

"You look gorgeous, you know."

She smiles back at me.

I read for a while once they are gone and then switch to television, surfing through old Carnival footage to a rerun of *Law & Order* dubbed into Greek. But the emotions of the day have exhausted me, and even my thoughts of the three topaz stones scattered among the sisters can't keep my eyes from closing. I am on my way to bed when the phone rings and I answer it.

"Callie!"

I freeze at the sound of Anna's voice.

"Where've you been all this time?" she says. "Come out with us." I wait for sarcasm in her tone, but she is cheerful and sincere.

"Where are you?"

I hear music and shouting in the background.

"The Bourbouli. Come meet us in the square. You shouldn't miss the Bourbouli. The Bourbouli is the best part of Carnival."

She is drunk. For a moment I envy her, imagining the sweet release of intoxication.

"I can't," I tell her. "I'm exhausted."

"Stelios wants you to come. And Maki and Andreas. We want to show our American friend what Carnival is all about. Here, wait."

The phone rustles and then Stelios's voice comes on the line.

"Did you hear that?" he says. "She wants you to come."

"She has no idea about last night, does she?"

"I told you. It's all right. She wants you to come." He lowers his voice. "*I* want you to come."

"Forget it, Stelios."

"I'll make you get off," he goes on, "right there at the Bourbouli."

"Fuck you."

"We could do that too."

"No," I say. "Fuck you and don't call me again."

I hang up and stand by the phone, bracing myself for another ring. After several minutes, there is still no call, so I go to bed. They will all have gone into the Apollon Theatre now and paired off with people they do not know and whose faces they cannot see.

I'm drifting into sleep when I hear noises coming from the

foyer. Sitting up, I realize that the sound is coming from outside the apartment, and it's a man's voice speaking softly while he seems to fumble with the lock.

"Hold on," I grumble. Nikos must have lost the key, and I'll be able to get back at him tomorrow about how much he had to drink.

Hoping to stay half asleep, I don't switch the light on but just open the door and head back to bed. Someone yanks my arm back. I turn, ready to yell at Nikos, but it's Stelios who is holding me by the upper arm, twisting my skin.

"Stelios, what the fuck?" My voice comes out like a stage whisper.

"Is that a nice way to greet me?"

"What are you doing here?"

"I'm here to see you, Calliope. I couldn't stay away."

He's still holding on to my arm and now grabs my other one, pushing me farther into the apartment. In the light from the street, I can see that he's moving with the looseness of alcohol, though his gaze is focused, intense.

"So here's another Notaris property. Let's have a tour."

"Stelios, you need to leave."

He looks around quickly. "You're alone, aren't you? Family left you behind?" He pulls me close, pushes my hair off my face. "That's all right. More room for us."

"I told you we were done, Stelios."

"So prudish. This is Carnival, Calliope. Once is never enough."

He presses his mouth onto mine and reaches under my T-shirt. I don't have the angle to kick him in the balls, and I know that if I do I'll have only a minute before he's up again. I need to get him to the door, where maybe I can thump his nuts and shove him out while he's groaning on the ground.

I let him feel my body relax and I kiss him back. He pauses, surprised, and renews his efforts. His mouth tastes sour and his stubble scrapes my face. I shuffle us toward the foyer. Let him think I'm headed for a bed. He tugs on my T-shirt. I see an opportunity. I join in, step away from him, and pull the shirt over my head. He comes toward me again, and as he kisses my breasts, I spin around slowly so that his back is toward the door.

"Now you," I say, and make as if I'm reaching for his belt. And then I swing my knee into his balls. He crumples, whining through clenched teeth. I open the door and start to shove him into the hallway.

"Callie, what on earth are you doing?"

It's Aliki, and behind her is Nikos, just coming out of the elevator. I am standing topless in the hallway over a drunken man who is clutching his groin. This does not look good.

"Who is this asshole?" Nikos says, grabbing Stelios and heaving him to his feet. "Is this the guy, cousin?"

I nod.

"So you're the guy." He throws Stelios up against the wall.

"Easy, man," Stelios manages.

"Nikos, quiet," Aliki says. She comes over to me and folds her garnet wrap around me.

"Oh, no, Aliki. There's no need to be quiet. This—what's his name?"

"Stelios," I say. "Stelios Pappamichaïl."

"This Stelios Pappamichaïl deserves for everyone to know what kind of scum asshole fucker he is."

Nikos jams Stelios's head back and sticks his nose into Stelios's face, Nikos's round features right up against Stelios's sharp ones.

"Listen, you fucker. You come near my family again and I

know ten guys who will have a great time beating the crap out of you while the police look the other way. You understand?" He shoves him again. "You understand?"

Stelios nods. Nikos walks away, making a show that Stelios is no longer dangerous, and calls the elevator from its return to the lobby. We wait for what seems like an eternity—an odd-looking group for the neighbor who I'm sure is peeking through the peephole at us. Aliki in her lovely gown, me in her wrap and a thong, Stelios rumpled and sweating, and Nikos hulking but impeccable in his tuxedo. Finally the elevator clanks into place, and I hold the door open while Nikos shoves Stelios in. He leans over and presses the ground-floor button.

"You even try to come back and I will make it so your mother won't recognize you."

We watch the elevator descend, then go back into the apartment. Aliki turns on the light and starts to move me toward my room. Nikos picks up my T-shirt from the floor and hands it to me.

"In case you change your mind about the topless thing," he says, putting on a wistful face.

Aliki asks me if I'm all right and if I want to explain anything. I haven't taken it all in yet.

"*Make it so your mother won't recognize you*? Where did he pull that one from?"

"He watches a lot of movies," Aliki says. We try to laugh.

"I'm so sorry, Aliki."

"Why are *you* sorry?"

I shake my head. "If Demetra had been here—"

She puts her hand on my arm to silence me. But I can see it in her face. She is thinking the same thing.

"I'm really sorry," I say again. "I brought this to your home. I made this happen."

"Calliope, if a man does something to deserve a kick in the balls, it's not your fault. You had him all taken care of, anyway. You didn't need Nikos's help."

I suppose she's right. I had already managed to get myself safe before Nikos and Aliki showed up. All I had to do was close and lock the door and maybe call the police to finish the job.

"Will you be all right to sleep?"

"I'll be fine."

I lie awake for a very long time, well after the sounds of the apartment settle into stillness. Aliki was wrong. It is my fault. I was just lucky I could keep things from getting worse. I listen to the refrigerator humming, to Nikos snoring, and I wait for my heartbeat to slow down.

15

Callie

Friday

In the morning, Aliki, Nikos, and I step gingerly around one another as we get something to eat. I can tell they want to talk about what happened, but they're waiting to take their cue from me. As I butter my toast I consider various approaches and then settle on light.

"So, you really know ten guys who beat people up?"

Nikos considers this. "Seven. It seemed a good time to exaggerate."

"I'm impressed. I think."

We chew.

"Paki, what was he doing here?" Aliki asks this with a release of pent-up energy that tells me this has been her main concern.

"He just showed up."

"You didn't invite him?"

"Aliki, no! You thought I'd invited him here? While you were gone?"

"You'd have had the place to yourselves."

"That's not what happened. He just showed up. I thought it was you. I thought you'd forgotten your keys. Next thing I knew, he was in the house and I was trying to figure out a way to get him out of here."

"And you did a great job, cousin," Nikos says.

"Aliki, when I said I brought this trouble to your home, I didn't mean it literally. But he came here looking for me. I'm really sorry. I picked the wrong guy and you got dragged into my mistake."

"No, I'm sorry, Paki. Sorry I misunderstood."

But I can tell she's still worrying about it.

"I'm going to get ready," I say, gulping down my coffee and nearly scorching my mouth. "I want to talk to my mother some more about that box. How about you two?"

"We have stuff around the house before we get Demetra back."

They're nesting, making their home safe again for their child.

I have Nestor's box tucked in my bag and I am standing at the door to my mother's building with my hand on the buzzer. There's a chance she'll be out at the market, but a phone call would only have given her time to prepare. I want to see my mother as she is, without her defenses up. Maybe I can reach her then.

She buzzes me in and greets me at the door with a guarded smile before leading me to the kitchen. She has been eating breakfast and is still in her bathrobe. The sharp odor of slightly burned toast lingers in the air. Dark crumbs litter her plate and cling to the edge of her knife. It suddenly occurs to me that she is not just old but elderly—and that the bad timing that led her to burn her toast this morning could soon turn into general forgetfulness and worse. The war and the civil war delayed her life, so she was over forty when I was born. Now I feel a moment's panic at the thought of me living in Boston while my mother is so many miles away.

"Want me to make you some?" she says, with her hand on a loaf of bread.

"Sure," I say, though I'm no longer hungry. "That'd be great."

She pops the bread out of the toaster golden brown and brings it to the table on a plate for me.

"Drimakopoulos's bread?" I ask as I take a bite.

She shakes her head. "From the supermarket in Rio."

"How do you get all the way out there?"

"Taxi," she says. "I refuse to take a bus."

We sit together in her small kitchen, eating our toast and sipping coffee. I watch my mother eat.

"I changed my flight," I say. "To Tuesday."

"Good. You'll be here for Clean Monday." Aliki's words.

"What is so special about Clean Monday?"

"It's the day Lent begins. A big family holiday."

"What do you do for it?"

"People picnic and fly kites."

"No, *you*. What do *you* do for it?"

"I go where I'm invited. If I'm invited."

"*Mamá,* of course you'll be invited."

She shrugs, and I guess I know a little bit about how she feels, though it's not anyone's fault but my own.

I'm conscious of Nestor's box sitting in my bag in the foyer.

"*Mamá,* you were looking for something the other day."

"When?" She picks up her knife and smears more butter onto her cold toast.

"At Nestor's." I go to my bag, catching sight of the large walnut mirror casting reflected light on the opposite wall. I bring back the box, holding it flat on my palm like a tray. "You were looking for this, weren't you?"

"I've never seen that box before in my life."

My mother is holding her toast midway to her mouth, unmoving, her eyes on the box. I tug the lid off and watch my mother's expression change instantly, from feigned indifference to what I can only describe as sorrow. She sets her knife down very carefully and wipes her hands on her robe. Without saying anything, she lifts the feathers out and sets them carefully down on the table. She plucks out the topaz ring and holds it by the bottom of the band, staring at it for a long minute. She holds the bullet between thumb and middle finger, frowns, and sets it down. Then she removes the scrap of silk and drapes it across her fingers. She reaches back into the box and picks at the edge where the side meets the bottom.

"There's nothing else," I say. I had planned to be forceful, but I can't bear to push at her when it is so clear that simply the sight of these things has shaken her. For an instant, I wonder if she is putting this on, hoping I won't pry if she manages to look frail and sad. But she has set the ring down beside the feathers, the bullet, and the silk, and is just sitting there with her shoulders hunched. Even my mother cannot fake so authentic a posture of dejection.

I rest my hand on her arm.

"This is your ring, isn't it, *Mamá*? Why did Nestor have it?"

She waits a minute before she answers.

"I gave it to him. When I left for America."

She goes back to her coffee, but her eyes peer over the rim of her cup at the feathers, four of them, thin and long, with a blue-black sheen. They seem utterly exotic in my mother's kitchen with its slick surfaces of white and glass.

"And he was supposed to keep it?"

"I forgot about it."

I'm not sure I believe her. "Even when Aliki wears her matching choker? Doesn't that remind you of your ring?"

"Can't we talk about something else?"

"Well, why did he have that bullet, then?"

"How should I know?" She glances at it. "It probably belonged to Yannis. For hunting."

"What about these feathers? And the silk?"

"They're just old things, Calliope, from the past."

"Why? Why would Nestor bother to save them?"

She bangs her cup down, spilling coffee into the saucer.

"Why can't you leave all this alone? You come here for the first time in years and have the nerve to hound me about my life?"

"I'm asking because there are things I need to know."

"No, you just want to know them. Don't confuse your desires with what's necessary."

"Nestor wants me to understand. He told me in that note. And you're trying to hide something, *Mamá*. Or you're hoping you can find it before I do."

"Don't be ridiculous," she says. "You're like a child. A complete child. That was *Iáson* you were talking to the other day, wasn't it?" she says, getting Jonah's name wrong again.

I remember Stelios's voice on the phone.

"You're having trouble with this one too," she says, nodding at me.

"Don't start that." I slide my hands from the table and draw myself up. "These are my things, now, *Mamá,* whether you like it or not. Tell me what they are, or I'll ask Thalia and Sophia. I bet they know."

My mother's face is trembling, and her jaw is set with that forward thrust that sucks her cheeks in. She takes a large breath and exhales loudly, resting back against her chair as she does so. She picks up her coffee again, not noticing the spilled liquid dripping from the bottom of the cup. She sets the cup down, looking at me with an expression of unconcern that she knows appears completely false. She is playing this game to win.

"I will tell you, Calliope, since you feel compelled to know. That man you admired so much, in the photograph?"

I nod.

"His name was Skourtis, and he was a refugee. He came to the farm in late November, not long after we ourselves had left the city because of the bombing raids. He worked for us on the farm to earn his keep. He milked the cows, he helped harvest whatever had to be collected, he picked fruit. That's what he has in that basket in the photograph—which Nestor must have taken with the camera they gave him for his birthday. His tenth birthday," she adds, as if she is clarifying the record for a reporter. "The Germans attacked Greece in the spring, and they let Mussolini tag along after we'd beaten him in Albania. They gave him Patras, but the British tried to win it back. You could see the dogfights and hear the whistling of the planes. We watched them from the hill beyond the farm."

I want to ask her about the bombs, about a shelter, but I don't dare move until she has stopped.

"One of the Italian planes fell in the woods near the farm. We could see the smoke, but after a few days we forgot about it. Then Skourtis showed up one day with a parachute. He had it bundled in his arms, with the strings dragging behind him in the dirt. In the movies, they look white, but this one was gray, dirty."

I look down at the piece of silk on the table. It is a dirty gray.

"Yes, Calliope," she says with disdain. "That is from the parachute that Skourtis brought us. See?"

She picks it up and waves it close to my face.

"See those brown spots? They're blood," she says, tossing the scrap down by the basket of sliced bread. I want to tug it away, to keep the dirt and the blood from the bread she will want me to eat.

"Why is there blood? Do you want to know? Of course you do, because you want to know everything about everything. Skourtis found the soldier hanging from his parachute in a tree. Skourtis cut him down, took the parachute, and killed him. Probably not in that order."

She bites into her toast.

My eyes widen.

"You're shocked. You can imagine we were too. This man we had taken in, whom we had accepted into the farm against our better judgment. This man we knew nothing about—his family, his schooling, if he had any. And he repaid us with this act of violence."

"Or self-defense," I say. "The Italian was an enemy. Maybe—"

"Maybe the soldier attacked him? The man was in a tree, probably hanging there for days. No," she snaps. "Skourtis showed himself to be a thug, an uneducated laborer. All he knew was violence."

"What happened to him?"

"We turned him in, of course."

"To the police?"

"There was no police then. We gave him to the Italians. As soon as the occupation started, a week or so later, they came looking for who had killed their soldier."

"And you told them?"

"Skourtis was a thug. Why should we have risked our safety to protect him?"

I am shaking my head.

"I can't believe *Papóu* would have turned a Greek over to the enemies."

"This isn't a movie, Calliope. This was the war, and it was painful and violent and sad. What you believe or don't believe is completely unimportant."

This last comment snaps me back to my own life. I puff out a laugh, reminded that this is my mother I am talking to. The unimportance of what I believe was established long ago.

I start to pack up the silk, the bullet, and the feathers.

"What are you doing?" she asks.

"Going."

"Where?"

"I don't know. Back to finish, maybe."

I see her looking at the ring.

"You should have that." I leave the ring on the table, press the cover down on the little box, and prepare to leave.

I go straight to the aunts' apartment. Demetra lets me in and I can't believe it's still only Friday morning, the day after Stelios came looking for me.

"Demetraki," I say, giving her a hug and a kiss. "Were you good for my aunts?"

"She's always good for your aunts," Thalia says, coming into the hall.

"Thalia," I say, so eager to start that I forget to kiss her hello.

She leans toward me and kisses me on each cheek, so I am forced to wait. Thalia draws back, her hands still on my upper arms, and frowns at me.

"What's the matter?"

"I need to ask you," I say, sitting down on the edge of the living room couch and placing the box on the coffee table. I lift the lid, and Thalia makes a sighing noise from a sharp intake of breath.

"Look at that," she says.

"What?" Demetra leans against the coffee table and pulls a feather out.

"Put that down, Demetra!" Thalia says.

I look up at her. I have never seen her look so serious. Neither has Demetra, it seems. The girl is looking at her grandmother with wide and liquid eyes; her hand is held out stiff, the feather a sinister curl across her palm. Thalia gently takes the feather from her and sets it back in the box. She is smiling when she tells Demetra to go to the kitchen and ask Sophia to make me some cinnamon toast.

"But I already ate."

"It's all right," Thalia says. "You can have some more." This will be my third breakfast.

Once Demetra is gone, Thalia sits beside me on the couch.

"What are these, *Theia* Thalia?"

Thalia looks over her shoulder toward the kitchen.

"I don't think I should tell you."

"But you saw Nestor's note to me. There's a story he wants me to find."

Thalia sits silently for a while and then lifts all the feathers out, sees the silk and the bullet, places the feathers back in the box, and sighs. I wait for her to say something, to do something. Finally, she puts a hand on my knee.

"All I can tell you is this: Those feathers come from the hat of a Bersagliere."

"A what?"

"An Italian soldier. The boys used to sneak up behind the soldiers and light the feathers with a match."

"Was this the soldier Skourtis killed?"

Thalia looks at me, confused. "All of the Bersaglieri had them. What exactly did Clio tell you?"

I repeat what my mother has told me about Skourtis and the parachute and killing the soldier. Thalia's face is hard to read. Finally, she presses her hands together in her lap.

"Calliope, you need to leave."

"Why?" My eyes sting with ready tears.

"Don't make me explain, but it's for your own good. Please. Please leave before Sophia finishes making that toast."

"Thalia, this is about my mother."

She stands up and gently, very gently, places her hands on my back and pushes.

"Please, Calliope. Trust me."

She looks so sad, the way I've never seen her. She looks as if her heart will break if I stay—or as if she's afraid mine will. I turn and kiss her on the cheeks. I think she's a bit surprised at my compliance.

"Okay, *Theia* Thalia," I say softly. "I'll go."

I stand on the sidewalk outside their apartment building. With a motorcycle parked by the next door, and a dumpster farther along, and some discarded boxes in the other direction, there's not much room, and people jostle me as they pass. I wait for a break in the foot traffic, then I turn toward Ellinos Stratiotou. I don't have to force Thalia to tell me, but that doesn't mean I can't try to find out by myself.

When I reach the busy intersection with Maizonos, I see that Plateia Georgiou is full of Carnival floats: huge confections of papier-mâché in vivid purples, pinks, and greens. Some have political messages—which I can read, but which mean little to me—and some represent the standard characters of Carnival, the smiling harlequins, the grinning clowns. Men in blue jeans and leather jackets lean on the floats, smoking in groups or dancing to the disco samba that's back on the loud-speakers. I won't be watching this parade. I can't; I have to keep following the thread of this story—this story that Thalia won't tell.

I keep going, pulling Nestor's key from my bag before I even reach his block. With the "Auld Lang Syne" key ring in my hand, I could be returning to my own home from a morning of errands. I've spent so much time at Nestor's that I can almost imagine the place as my own. My desk, where I have made my lists; my kitchen, where I can make coffee with Nestor's grounds; my garden, whose smells of earth and damp remind me of the tortoises he kept. I try to stop this train of thought here, to leave it at these new-made memories that connect me to the past. But my mind goes to other things: my floor, where I pushed Stelios down beneath me; my sideboard, where I sat, legs spread, as he kissed me. Memories I would like to forget.

I unlock the door and go in, heading straight for the living room, where I drop the bag and begin looking—for what, I'm not sure. I start with the part of the room where I found the box, riffling first through a pile of papers and then forcing my-self to take the sheets from the pile one by one, look at them, and set them in a new pile. These are letters and receipts, bills and notices, that might put together a narrative that would be interesting to somebody. But not to me. I want documents about soldiers, about the war, the refugees.

I almost don't recognize it when I see it: a page of light-blue paper, not much larger than a postcard, on which dark-blue ink runs in upward-sloping lines across the width. I rotate the page and see that this is the last page of a letter, and there is my mother's name at the bottom: *Clio.* Above it: *I see you for what you are: a crude and weak man with a base nature.*

I keep reading backward, moving up the page, sentence by sentence, and then I start at the top and take it all in.

> *myself now, to think that I could fall in love with someone from so disgusting a country as yours, full of lust and baseness. I thought fascists were better than that. If you were a true fascist, you would know that man has to be noble. Man is noble. You are precisely the kind of danger that fascism is going to uproot. I thought you were unique, a soldier who was sensitive, a pacifist who would defend his country, a man whose confidence allowed him to relinquish aggression and embrace sensitivity. I even admired how you enjoyed my strength in certain things. But now I see that you are weak. So weak that you would humiliate a little boy who admired you. So weak that my own father, thirty years older than you, could send you running from the rooftop with a bleeding nose and swollen eyes. You should be ashamed of yourself, not me. But I am ashamed. Ashamed that I joined in as you mocked my brother and drove him to undo all our plans. Ashamed that I was so foolish as to bring you up to Hollywood—laugh now at the word, I don't care anymore—where I thought we could talk about our dreams, our thoughts on art and love and life. Ashamed that the baseness in my own nature made me let you do to me what you did.*
>
> *For months, you have fooled me into thinking you were gentle and refined, that you appreciated me and understood me. Now I see you for what you are: a crude and weak man with a base nature.*
>
> *Clio*

I breathe in sharply when I'm done and flip the page over, even though I know the other side is blank. I tear through the remaining papers in the pile, looking for the other page, but I find nothing. I grab the phone and call Aliki.

"I'm at Nestor's and I'm going to be here awhile," I say.

"Should you be there alone?"

"I've locked the door. And I won't open it for strangers."

"You sound funny," Aliki says.

"I found something."

As the rooms darken, I search through every single pile of paper in Nestor's house. My eyes sting, and tiny sparks of light dart across my vision. I force myself to get a drink of water from the kitchen and chug it down all at once so that my throat hurts from the cold. I check under the rug, the furniture. I dig through the garbage, where I find Stelios's condom but no sixty-year-old letter from my mother to some man. Pressing my hands against the small of my back, I straighten and take the garbage bag to the bin by the front door. I turn and look back into the house: cones of light breaking up the shadows, everything sorted through and piled neatly, Nestor's life arranged in orderly collections whose one bit of error contains all that is most meaningful to me now.

I get a piece of foolscap from the desk and write down what I know.

> Skourtis kills soldier
> Skourtis turned in
> Nestor gets feathers
> Italian with Clio
> father catches them
> beats up Italian

letter
ring
silk
bullet

And then, over all of this, the one last important piece I don't write down but commit to memory: *Nestor undoes their plans.*

Skourtis the refugee killed an Italian soldier and took the parachute. My family turned him in to the Italians. Nestor saved the feathers from some other soldier's hat. My mother was in love with an Italian who seems to have wanted more than just to talk about their dreams. The Italian made fun of Nestor, who did something to screw things up for my mother and her Italian. My grandfather beat the man up on the roof of the city house. There was a gun to match this bullet. But who was holding it, and who was it aimed at? And who really gave Nestor my mother's ring? The man she was in love with: Was he a soldier? Just how many men are there in this story?

I sit on the floor and lean my back against the wall, holding my list. I have no idea.

16

Clio

April 1941

Clio was sitting on the ground at the base of an almond tree. She looked up through the branches, through the white blossoms that dusted the bare wood, and sniffed the thin almond fragrance, so sweet it was like breathing in a macaroon. The air was warm, almost summerlike. The sky had been quiet for several days, but the radio was full of dire news of German progress through Bulgaria and other places just north of the Greek border.

They were calling the fortifications there the Metaxas Line, but everyone was worried that the line wouldn't hold. Clio pictured the Germans pushing through with their stubby helmets that made them look like human bullets. If Patras was occupied, they would have Italian soldiers, Bersaglieri. She had seen pictures of them, with their wide-brimmed hats cocked at a jaunty angle, flamboyantly decorated with festoons of long black feathers. It hardly seemed possible to be an enemy if you were dressed like that.

She had turned the almond grove into her new Hollywood, even better than the apricot tree she had climbed last summer.

She came here nearly every day to be alone and think, going through the sad calculus that she had taken up just before Christmas: what she was doing now measured against what she would be doing if there were no war. Today, she was going to finish darning a basketful of socks; but if there had been no war, she would have been going for a stroll in the Psilalónia section of the city, flirting with the boys in the square there and spooning a syrupy dessert from a bowl.

She heard a high-pitched grinding sound and, before she realized what it was, the hairs on her neck stood on end. She jumped up and began to run to the house, answering the wail of the homemade air-raid siren, cranked by her father on the front porch.

By the time she reached the house, she had seen what her father had seen. A group of five Italian planes was swooping over Patras. Little spots marked the sky like punctuation on a piece of paper.

"Get in!" her father said. He never shouted but spoke clearly and firmly, the way one would to a dog or a horse.

"But they're not here."

"I said get in, all of you."

Sophia, Thalia, and Nestor had come running from the barn, where they had been swinging into the hay. Clio saw bits of it stuck in their hair.

Their father led them down the stairs to a small basement area they had turned into a shelter. When they were all in, along with their mother, Vlachos, Irini, and Yannis, he pulled a sheet of corrugated metal over the stairwell and then closed the door.

"Where do the workers go, *Babá*?" Nestor asked.

Ever since Yannis had taken him to deliver Christmas wine

to the vineyard workers, Nestor had not stopped asking about their well-being.

"I told you. They have their own place," their father said.

They all sat, waiting for silence. Clio almost wished they were in Patras, to hear the all-clear sounding from the municipal sirens. Here they had to listen for a change in the cadence of the bombing before their father could emerge from the shelter and turn the siren crank to signal their own relief.

She looked at the bench across from her, where Yannis and Vlachos sat, with her mother at the head of the row beside Irini. The two women and Yannis gazed up at nothing, listening to the rumble of the bombs. Vlachos always looked down, as if he were waiting for a bus. She hated that he seemed so calm. It was almost insolent not to share the concerns of the people who had sheltered him all these months.

Vlachos suddenly stared right into her eyes, and seconds later she heard what had made him look up: the sound of one engine, separate from the collective din of the bombing.

"It's coming this way," Nestor said.

"Shh, no."

But it *was* coming toward the farm. The sound grew closer and Clio was sure she felt the air grow denser. The plane seemed to pass right over the house, heading for the foothills where the cypresses grew.

"As long as it dodges the vineyards, we'll be all right," said Clio's father.

Nestor stammered in consternation, worrying about the workers.

As soon as Clio's father slid the metal sheet out of the way, Nestor was up the stairs into the house. Clio ran after him into the farmyard, where she saw the plane disappearing, a tiny speck sweeping around to the east, toward Corinth. It veered again, to the northwest this time. Heading home.

"Crazy Italians," Yannis said, and trudged down the porch steps to return to work.

The next day, Clio was bringing eggs back from the chicken coop when she saw Vlachos driving the horse cart out of the almond grove. The cart was stacked with freshly cut wood, but a large bundle of light-gray cloth billowed over the pile and dragged in the dirt.

"What is that, Vlachos?" she asked.

"A parachute. Italian."

He climbed down from the cart and, with surprising delicacy, gathered the fabric up in his arms.

Clio's father met him on the porch.

"What's this?"

"Parachute. Italian. There must have been a second plane yesterday and—" He made a cutting motion with his hand.

"Did you see the wreck?"

"No. It's probably up in the mountains. Pilot ditched too soon."

"What are you doing with it?"

"I don't want it," he said. "It's for you. For the children."

"Leave it in the barn, then. They'll find some use for it."

Clio went to get the others and brought them into the barn to see this new treasure. Sophia pulled the cord for the light-bulb. Vlachos set the parachute down on the dirt floor, where it subsided with a soft exhalation, as if it were alive. In the glare of the bulb, it glowed a soft gray, with its radiating seams picked out in white.

"A parachute," Thalia said, in her awed voice.

"You can have it," Vlachos said. He stood over the parachute—as if he had killed it, Clio thought.

That night, the children gathered in Sophia's and Clio's room to discuss Vlachos's gift, if indeed they could see as a gift something whose origins were so mysterious. Their first concern was with the whereabouts of the Italian soldier who should have been attached to the parachute.

"We saw the plane fly away," Sophia said. "If there was another one that crashed, we would have seen something."

"What if the plane dropped a spy into the forest and that's whose parachute it is?" Nestor's eyes were wide with the thought.

Clio wondered if her lie from last summer and the clover houses could have somehow come true and there really would be spies lurking in the pastures now.

"What if he's sneaking into the farmyard now?" Thalia said, shaking Nestor by the shoulders and using an ominous voice. "What if he's creeping up on you," then she shouted, "right now!"

"Thalia, cut it out!" Nestor said, smacking her arm.

"What I want to know," Clio said, putting a calming hand on Nestor, "is how Vlachos got the parachute in the first place."

"He told us," Sophia said. "The soldier was gone. Probably dead."

"Maybe he chased him away," Nestor suggested.

But Clio had darker thoughts. Either the man was dangling from a tree somewhere, wounded horribly and crying out where no one could hear him, or he had died in the fall. Or he survived but Vlachos had killed him. Clio imagined Vlachos stooped over a fallen cypress, chopping its trunk into logs and suddenly seeing the paratrooper limping toward him, with blood perhaps smearing his face. A swift blow of the ax would have been enough to kill the wounded man. Then Vlachos would have followed the bloody trail back to where the parachute hung draped in the trees.

Thalia's voice brought her back.

"What if the soldier's lying there dead and we're going to find him someday when we're out playing?" As Thalia spoke the words, Clio saw her realize that she had described an actual, and terrifying, possibility.

"I'm sure he's just gone, Thalia," she said.

The idea of an Italian soldier loose in the neighboring forest was far less worrisome than the idea that Vlachos might have used violence against an acknowledged enemy. The soldier was exotic, connected in her imagination to the cloud of airy silk he must have descended with. Vlachos was the squat, stubbled man she had first seen bloody and dirty in the farmyard.

She made a point to watch Vlachos carefully, and when she encountered him in the kitchen the next afternoon, she braced herself, waiting for him to seize a knife and reveal the violent man he had been all along. He simply greeted her in his usual gruff way and took a basket of scraps out to the horse trough.

At dinner, Clio's mother announced her plan for the parachute. The time for Carnival had come and gone, but there had been no official Carnival in Patras that year. So they would hold a Carnival of their own on the farm, and they would use the parachute silk to make costumes.

"I thought wings would be nice," her mother said. "Butter-fly wings."

Clio remembered the dusty brown wings of the silk moths and wondered if the dingy gray parachute could turn into something better.

Work started the next day. None of the rooms of the house were large enough to spread the parachute out into an un-creased circle, so they all carried the fabric to the pasture. Each child held an edge of the silk and tossed it up so that it crackled smooth. Then they backed away from one another, pulling the fabric taut, snapping it flat before laying it back down on the new grass. With a fat pastel crayon, Clio's mother traced the outlines for the wings onto the silk and then cut them out with shears. She gathered the silk toward her little by little, the shears grinding with each cut.

Vlachos passed by the pasture once or twice with the cart while they helped with the cutting, but he only scanned the scene for an instant before moving on. Clio suspected he did not like to be reminded of the violent deed that had put the parachute in his hands. He was anxious, she thought, to have the thing cut up and turned into something else, something unrecognizable as an Italian soldier's potential lifesaver.

But so was she. The longer the parachute remained intact, the more her imagination would continue to play out violent scenarios. Whenever they shook the cloth out into the air, a faint odor of oil and metal wafted up from it, and she could almost feel the gritty slide of engine grease on her fingers. She could not imagine wanting to place this cloth next to her skin or across her back, and the idea she had had of asking her mother to make the extra fabric into a gown for her now seemed abhorrent. Then there was something else. When she had picked up the parachute to lift it for the very first time, she had seen that there were thick canvas cords sewn onto the outer edge of the cloth in several places but that these cords had been roughly cut. Now the image in her mind was of Vlachos swinging at the Italian's harness with his ax and then watching the man slam down to the ground. Clio might have been reluctant to join the others in their silken wings, but she could not wait until the parachute and all its reminders of death and danger had been cut into pieces.

Once the pattern pieces were cut out, Irini helped Clio's mother clean them in the galvanized washing tub with water boiled on the stove. When the washing was done, the children carried the wings out to the clotheslines behind the kitchen and pinned them up to dry. In the afternoon sun, the pieces of silk glowed white and gray and blue where their shadows over-lapped. As Clio walked among the growing number of wings hung up on the lines, her shadow passed across the silk as if on a set of screens.

"Sophia, stand over there," she said, directing her sister to the other side of a piece of cloth.

Clio struck a series of poses—arms extended, toes pointed in an arabesque, back arched. She flipped up the collar of her jacket and thrust her hands into her pockets. She stuck her chin up and out.

"Who's that?" asked Sophia.

Clio snapped out of the pose. "It's Hepburn," she said, hands on hips now, her shadow arms making sharp points at her sides. "Can't you tell?"

Thalia laughed, catching Sophia's eye.

"I thought you were a man."

"No," Clio said. "If I were a man, I'd look like this." And she turned sideways, slouched, and pulled her jacket out to make a fatter stomach. It was the shape they all knew from watching Vlachos, unmistakably his squat and almost sullen posture.

The next morning, they gathered the wings from the clotheslines and spread them out across the floor of the porch. Their mother had assembled her paints and her brushes and had pulled on the wide smock she always kept in her easel. She asked the girls to hold the silk taut and began to paint the fabric with bold strokes of magenta and orange and a fine tracery of black lines to connect the patterns. Clio stared down at the oil paint, waiting for the moment when the lines and colors would resolve themselves into the whorls and circles of a butterfly's coloring.

"Clio, let it lie smooth," her mother said, and she saw that she had been rubbing the silk between her finger and thumb the way a baby worries a blanket. She put her hands in her lap and sat back from the cloth.

By early afternoon, the porch was scattered with painted silk, and the children stood around as if dazed, sighing in admiration of their mother's work. Urania, too, sighed happily at what she had made and brushed her auburn hair out of her face with a paint-dotted hand. The wings were beautiful, Clio knew, and she forced herself to concentrate on that beauty. But when she lifted a wing from the porch, she felt the tiny stitches of the seams like scars running across the fabric. Staring down at the painted silk as she walked toward the clothesline, she lost the pattern. All she could see were patches of color striated with the lines of the brush and dotted here and there with bits of grit that had blown onto the porch. Only when she reached the clothesline and pinned her wing back up in the sun did she manage to replace the image of the stranded Italian with the fact of the light shining through the painted fabric. She stood back and saw the silk transformed finally into a butterfly wing, brilliant in its coloring and complex in its design.

For the rest of the day, Clio found reasons to wander over to the little yard behind the kitchen and watch the wings swing in the breeze, their brilliant colors catching the sun. She half-expected the summer's butterflies to come early, swarming over the silken wings, drawn to the farm by the fragrance of the oil paint and by these grand images of themselves. Nestor wandered around the corner of the house and suddenly stopped, mesmerized by the light sway of the painted fabric.

"Oh," he sighed.

Even the adults were tempted by the wings and stood in the kitchen doorway or by the side of the house simply to enjoy these splendid decorations. When Vlachos saw them, he smiled, but Clio remembered the cut cords she had noticed around the edges of the cloth and shivered at the image of Vlachos cutting down some handsome, dark-haired young man.

17

Callie

Saturday

I wake up very early, with only a dim gray light coming through the edge of the curtain. I lie in bed, relishing the duvet's cloud of encompassing warmth, eager to swap my heavy wool and flannel for one of these as soon as I get home. I miss home. I miss Jonah. Fingering his grandmother's ring, I roll onto my right side, the side that faces Jonah in our loft bed, and try to imagine myself without him. Not just without him in the bed, or sitting on the couch, or by my elbow at The Sevens—but without him in my life. I have done this before: sent a man away, or made it inevitable that he would send me packing. And, every time, the separation has felt not only inevitable but intrinsic to who I am. I am a person apart.

Of course I recognize the fallacy in this. A truly solitary person wouldn't mourn a lover's loss. A truly solitary person would find him, love him, and then kick him out. I suppose in her strange way, my mother was trying to warn me not to be this kind of person. As I lie here, I realize I don't want to run through this same sad process with Jonah. And what is it about Jonah that has made it so? I have no idea.

Through the wall, I notice a faint thudding, and I realize this is what must have woken me up. A woman's voice lets out a stifled cry. I smile and roll the other way, and I pull the duvet up around my ears to give Aliki and Nikos their privacy.

With Jonah, I always thought it started with sex. But it really began with that evening of quiet sadness by the bar and went quickly from there to a different need: my need for some other person from whom I could hide, someone who got so close that the act of holding back would be a source of solace. Jonah is, or was, that person.

I wait for the noises to stop in the next room and then I get up and get dressed. I tuck a red button-down shirt into my jeans and fasten a wide black leather belt that goes with my boots. I brush my hair silk-straight.

I find Aliki in the kitchen in her nightgown. Nikos is in his pajamas, watching soccer on the television. The apartment has the feel of Christmas, with the adults relaxing so visibly and Demetra in a state of high excitement. She comes sliding into the kitchen on stocking feet outstretched as if on a skateboard and crashes into the table.

"It's the parade, it's the parade, it's the parade!" she crows, and Aliki presses her hand gently across the girl's mouth, steering her back out of the kitchen. As soon as Aliki releases her, Demetra resumes crowing until Nikos shushes her and turns up the soccer volume. Aliki wipes her hand on her apron.

"She licked my hand!" she says, in amused disgust. "You're getting out just in time," she says, seeing me dressed and ready. This is the day of the biggest parade, when every club and team marches with its own float.

"I'm going over to the aunts'," I say.

"More questions?"

"Aren't you dying to know?"

She shrugs. "Dying, no. But tell me what they say."

Nikos shouts at the television and smacks his leg in exasperation. It occurs to me that I have been treating him as tangential in all of this, even though he seems to understand how our family works better than the rest of us.

"Hey, Nikos," I say. "Take a look at something for me."

I bring the box over to him and wait for him to turn his attention from the game. He looks into the box and reaches for the bullet, picks it up, and rolls it in his fingers.

"Where'd you get this?"

"That's the thing. Nestor had it. It's a bullet, right?"

"A cartridge. Spent."

"My mother says it could have belonged to Yannis. For hunting on the farm."

He examines it closely.

"She's wrong," he says. "It's from a Breda."

"What's a Breda?"

"An Italian heavy machine gun. Nestor," he adds softly, "you surprise me."

"Why?"

Nikos is looking admiringly at the cartridge. "The Italians used Bredas with tanks, or they set them in fortified positions. They weren't the kind of guns soldiers just carried around with them."

"Nikos, why does Nestor surprise you?"

"Well, the only way Nestor got this was from the Italians themselves. The Breda didn't leave brass around." I give him a confused look. "Which means the spent cartridges went back into the clip after you fired them. Someone had to have pulled this from the strip for Nestor to get it."

I look at Nikos, who sets the cartridge back in the box. His information seems important, and I can't understand why he isn't acknowledging that.

"You're a history nerd," I say finally. "You know that, right?"

"Don't tell," he says, putting a finger to his lips.

As I gather up my things, Aliki tells me about the plan for tomorrow: lunch at a taverna in Psilalónia, the hilly district of the city, followed by family attendance at Agios Andreas for Forgiveness Sunday after the very last parade, which takes place in the afternoon. I keep myself from commenting on this new observance. Then again, I have never been here for Carnival before; perhaps this has been a part of my family's life all along.

"But first there's Nestor's memorial service later today."

"We're doing one?"

"It's part of Pre-Lent, for all the dead. We did one when *Babá* died and it meant a lot. It kind of converted me." She shrugs, smiling. "You and the aunts can come meet us here together," she says. "And I called your mother. She's meeting us there."

I'm glad Aliki was the one to call her. So full of questions for her these past few days, I find myself now hesitant to speak to my mother until I know the entire story. And I do know that I will have to get it from someone else.

Thalia leads me to the kitchen with a worried look on her face. Sophia is there, washing dishes. When she sees me, she unties her apron and folds it in front of her. I show her the piece of Nestor's foolscap on which I have written my list.

"This is what I know, *Theia* Sophia. You have to tell me the rest."

"*Letter,*" she reads. "What's this letter you list here?"

"From my mother. To a man."

Thalia jerks her head to the side, making no attempt to hide the fact that I have flustered her.

"*Theia* Sophia, there are three men here: the Italian, the soldier with the feathers, and Skourtis. I know they were connected, but I can't tell how. Please tell me."

"Paki," Thalia says, "why do you care? This all happened ages ago."

I don't quite know how to articulate my reason. I know that this story has taken hold of me in a way that none of my mother's and the aunts' stories ever has. The other stories were all complete, little gems of adventure or grace. This one is rough and messy; it has more of real life about it, and that is what I want to understand: my mother's real life.

"Nestor wanted me to know," I say. "I'm sure of it."

"I've said all along that she needed to know," Sophia says to Thalia, who is looking sad again. Sophia stands almost a head taller than her sister and surely knows how imposing she appears now.

"But, Sophia, we were never certain."

"Well, then, I'll just tell her the facts." She buttons her cardigan and smooths it down over her skirt. She turns to me and speaks as if she were reading from a piece of foolscap of her own. "The letter was for an Italian soldier, a Bersagliere named Giorgio. The feathers in your box belong to him. He gave them to Nestor."

"Why?"

"For carrying messages between him and your mother."

I take this in but don't want to lose momentum with the aunts. Thalia is sitting down now, hugging herself as if she's suddenly cold.

"And that piece of silk?"

"It's from a parachute. From an Italian soldier."

"From Giorgio? Did he give Nestor that cartridge?"

Sophia waves my question away. "This happened at the farm. There's a lot you should know about the farm."

"Sophia, don't," Thalia says.

"I'll tell her what I want to tell her."

"This is not your story to tell," Thalia insists.

"Of course it is. It affected my life, didn't it? It affected all of us."

"Sophia, we don't even know the truth."

"The girl should know what we know."

"She told me about all that," I say. I can't understand why the aunts are bogged down on this minor story. "Skourtis killed the Italian and your father sent him away."

"Is that what your mother told you?" Sophia shakes her head. "Poor Skourtis was too much of a coward to do anything like that. She just had to make him a villain. It was Vlachos, an old man from the docks. He killed the soldier and *Babá* turned him in."

"Was *Papóu* a collaborator?" I hate to even ask the question.

"It was the occupation, Calliope," Thalia says. She takes my hand and pats it a few times. "Things were complicated."

"But why did Nestor save these things?" I ask. "Why are they all in one box? That letter says Nestor did something. That he ruined their plans."

Sophia starts to say something, but Thalia jumps up and takes her sister by the elbow. I am stunned. I have never seen Thalia so anxious. She tugs Sophia's arm back, trying to lead her out of the kitchen.

"Stop that, Thalia," Sophia says, leaning against her sister's pull. She lets out a laugh, but there's no humor in it.

"*Theia* Thalia," I say, stepping toward them.

"Just come here, Sophia." Thalia ignores me. "Come out here," she says. "Please."

"No! Right here. Here where the girl is, so she can understand what her mother's done."

"What are you saying?" I push my hands through my hair. I feel tears coming.

"Sophia, don't you see that this is bad for the child? You stand on principle all the time. Everything has to be so precise."

"I believe in accuracy, Thalia. In truth."

"And that's admirable, but there are times when human beings don't need truth. They need a little solace. The child needs a little comforting."

"From what?" I say, but they're not listening.

"I've said all along that there would be a time when she would need to know," Sophia says. "And *that* would be a comfort to her."

"To carry a burden? What world is that where guilt is a comfort? Sophia, you're taking this too far." Thalia lowers her voice, as if I won't be able to hear. "You always do this, Sophia. You put abstract principles ahead of people. People you love."

"Don't you dare," Sophia says.

"I haven't said anything about this for years. For decades. But you'd be married to Michalis now if you hadn't objected to his politics."

"That's enough, Thalia."

"No, it's not. You made yourself unhappy because you couldn't love a socialist. Why make Calliope unhappy now simply because you want to tell the truth? What's so wonderful about the truth?"

This is the first time I've heard of a man in connection with Sophia's past. She was the one sister who never married and who always seemed satisfied with her life. I barely have time to contemplate this before Sophia grabs Thalia's arm and succeeds in dragging her all the way into the living room. I stay where I am, listening to the sounds of their argument, the crackle and hiss of their voices. I could go closer and hear what they are saying. Isn't that what I want? To learn whatever it is they're hiding about my mother's past and their own? But I can't. I'm a child again—the child they've been talking about—and their voices are sucking me back to my parents' anger and my mother's despair.

I finally force myself to step into the room.

"*Theies,* please," I cry, and there must be something pained in my voice, because they both stop to look at me. Sophia's bun is awry and Thalia looks as if she's been crying. She steps toward me and forces a smile, brushing my hair from my face.

"Paki *mou,* don't cry."

"You have to tell me what she did. My whole life, you've treated her different. We were here every summer, but the three of you were never really *together.* Now Sophia is making all kinds of accusations. Are you holding some grudge for something she did when she was just a kid?"

"No, Calliope, no," Thalia says. "It's not that."

"Then, what? Why?"

Neither one of them makes a sound for a long time, and I'm about to leave when Sophia speaks.

"She didn't treat you right. We never could abide a mother not taking good care of her child."

The world jolts, and it feels as if we just had one of Patras's frequent earthquakes. Then my balance settles. I'm still standing in my aunts' living room. They are still two old ladies looking at me with sad eyes. And everything else is utterly changed.

* * *

I start walking, letting the slight downhill of the street carry me toward the water. When I was little, the harbor was bordered by a narrow strip of cement on the other side of the main coast road. On the near side were snack bars and tavernas where you could buy souvlaki on a skinny stick topped with a slice of bread. You could get right down to the water and walk along the old jetty where my mother and the aunts used to swim. Now Patras is a giant port, where cruise ships and ferries loom over a wide apron of pavement edged with bollards the size of a large dog. There are traffic lanes to steer you to Brindisi, or Ancona, or the nearby islands dotting the Ionian. It was like this already when I took my trip to Zakynthos, but my childhood memories are stronger than that more recent one. As I reach the sidewalk opposite the central gate, I feel as though I am in a new city, unsure of where to go.

Already on the northeastern edge of Patras, I turn so that the water is on my left and walk out of the city. As I leave the port behind me, the paved path draws nearer to the water and I can feel the spray on my face. When I wipe my hand across my cheek, it comes up wet, my tears mingled with the sea. The gulf is teeming with *provatákia,* little sheep, waves herded along with me by the stiff wind.

I am trying to think my mother's story through, to piece together the scraps and fragments into a whole I can keep in my head. Images begin to form in my mind—of this Vlachos, whoever he was, with his hands tied behind his back; Giorgio the soldier snipping feathers from his hat; and my mother embracing a Bersagliere during the war.

But it's not just my mother's story I need to piece through now. It's my own. The story of a little girl whose aunts tried to protect her from her own mother.

18

Clio

April 1941–February 1942

Clio rushed to the window to see the source of the strange crunching sound outside. She caught a glimpse of a black car, and then her father was pushing her away from the window.

"In the back room. All of you."

"Come on, girls. Nestor," her mother said, ushering them into the small room where Skourtis had set up his sewing months before.

"What is it?" Nestor asked.

"I saw a car," Clio said.

"Italians!" Nestor scrambled to the door, but his mother pulled him back.

"Sit down and wait for your father."

A moment later, Leonidas came to the door.

"Where's Vlachos?"

"Fetching wood," Clio's mother said.

"Tell Yannis to go find him. It's all right," he said to the children. "You can come out."

They edged out of the room and crept slowly to the windows that gave onto the porch. Outside were two Italian officers.

"Lieutenants!" Nestor gasped.

They stood in black uniforms with their backs to the house, hands clasped behind them, swords glinting in the sun. A few paces away was their car, a dusty black vehicle, long and low like an insect.

What happened next seemed to Clio to be part of a movie. She could hardly hear what was being said, but the gestures and actions were clear enough. Yannis met Vlachos and the wood cart at the edge of the farmyard, grabbing the bridle with one hand. Vlachos saw the Italians, started, and made as if to jump from the cart. Yannis stopped him, said something to him, and led the cart the rest of the way, stopping the horse beside the sleek black car. The horse nickered and pawed the dusty ground.

Vlachos swung himself down from the cart and listened as the lieutenants spoke. They were close enough now for Clio to hear that they were talking about a plane and a pilot, about a stolen parachute. One of the officers pointed to the foothills. Both officers turned to Clio's father, and he nodded, seeming to confirm their tale. Vlachos reached out as if to ask for help, but Clio's father ignored him. He nodded again and watched as the officers each took one of Vlachos's arms.

They tied his hands behind his back and frog-marched him to the car. Clio rushed to the porch, waiting to see Vlachos struggle or protest or even spin around and shout condemnation up at the house of his betrayers. But he walked along with the Italians until he reached the car. And then he faced the house and spat. One of the Italians slapped him across the face.

"Oh, my," her mother said softly.

Clio didn't know what surprised her most: Vlachos's insult, the officer's violence, or her mother's sympathy for the rough old man.

By early fall, once the bombings were finished and the Italian occupiers had made it clear that order had returned to Patras, the family returned to the city. Greece was fully occupied now, divided up by the Bulgarians to the east, the Germans to the west of them and in Athens and Crete, and the Italians everywhere else. In Athens, where the Germans had raised the Nazi flag over the Acropolis, things were very bad, with famine spreading and reports of people dying where they stood. Patras was luckier. The Italians had turned the concert hall across the street from the family house into their officers' club, and they seemed at least as interested in enjoying themselves as they were in keeping control of their new subjects. In the evenings, Clio went up to the roof and watched as the Bersaglieri came and went, their feathered hats giving them a carefree and dashing air. They hardly looked like soldiers at all to her.

One day in late November, she was standing on the sidewalk in front of the house, waiting for Nestor to catch up to her, when one of the Bersaglieri sauntered across the street.

"Good afternoon, Miss Notaris," he said, doffing his feathered hat.

"Good afternoon."

The soldiers never spoke to her, but this one, a lean young man with curly black hair and a slightly crooked nose, had made a habit of nodding at her from his post whenever he saw her emerge from the house. She liked the looks of him, and it pleased her that he knew her family name. Still, she was not certain she should be engaging in conversation with the occupying army.

No matter how much the people of Patras had believed in *una fatsa, una ratsa,* they now worried constantly about collaborators. If they thought you were in league with the occupiers and that you were profiting from that association, they might do more than boycott your store, as they had done with Marinelli; they might kill you. Still, Clio wondered how you were supposed to obey an occupying army without being friendly. How nice was she allowed to be to this Bersagliere, who now stood there in his blue wool uniform, his tidy gaiters, and his dashing feathered hat?

She turned to look back up at the house. She would have shouted for Nestor to hurry, but she didn't want the Bersagliere to think she was vulgar.

"Are you waiting for someone?" His Greek was accented, like Marinelli's.

"My brother."

"I can command him to come out."

"Please don't," she said, before realizing he was joking.

Clio walked back to the house and pushed the door open, her back tingling from the awareness that he was watching her.

"Nestor!" she hissed.

"He's getting a bag to put the bread in," her mother said, calling from the sitting room.

Clio sighed and turned to face the walnut-framed mirror while she waited. She undid the clip that held her hair—bobbed now—in a wave over her ear and clipped it up again. She tilted her head this way and that, confirming that the shorter cut of her hair emphasized the planes of her cheekbones and the length of her neck. Her green dress was shorter than she would have liked, but there had not been enough fabric to adjust it to her new height. At least her coat fit her properly, and her shoes were up to the current occupation-determined fashion: platforms on a thick rubber wedge.

Nestor came from the kitchen with a canvas sack.

"There you are. Button this," she said, tugging at the folds of his peacoat. Nestor smiled up at her, letting his body shake freely as she fastened the buttons. "We're going," she called, and led Nestor out of the house.

The Bersagliere was still there. He saluted them crisply as they passed before him. Nestor giggled.

"Do you need an escort?" the soldier said.

"No. No, thank you."

They were only going to Drimakopoulos's for some bread. A week after that first bombing that began the war, Clio had found Marinelli's place boarded up, with no sign of Marco or the old woman, and *Mussolini = Marinelli* scrawled in red across one plank. He would have been all right now, Clio guessed, and maybe the Bersaglieri would have craved his raisin rolls. But soon after the war had begun, Marinelli, Marco, and the old woman had disappeared. No one had seen them since.

At least Drimakopoulos made good bread. Every other bakery in Patras had been reduced to baking heavy loaves of cracked grain and whole wheat, but Drimakopoulos lightened their loaves with white flour. Nobody knew where they got the flour, and nobody wanted to ask. It seemed collaborators could be tolerated if they gave people what they desired.

"Young man," the Bersagliere said to Nestor, "tell your sister that I am available to make sure none of these *sciocchi* bother her." He waved a black-gloved hand toward the two Bersaglieri guarding the officers' club. The men had wandered closer and now posed in mock affront.

Nestor stopped short, glancing between the soldier and Clio. Clio put her arm around him and kept walking.

"We can take care of ourselves," she said.

"Oh, I'm sure you can."

At this, she turned, scowling. He tipped his hat again, smiling with no apparent malice. The long black feathers bobbed behind him as he set the hat back on his head.

"I'm going to get matches from *Babá* and set his hat on fire," Nestor whispered.

"You are not, Nestor."

"Kostas Dolos did."

"Kostas Dolos is older. Besides, this one doesn't seem so bad."

The next day, when she went out to meet some friends, the Bersagliere approached her again, this time walking a short way with her. His name was Giorgio, information she wasn't sure he should have told her. She told him her name was Clio.

"The Muse of History," he said.

"You know the Muses?"

"Of course." And he reeled them off, his lilting Italian accent making a song of Melpomene, Terpsichore, Calliope, and the rest. *"Una fatsa, una ratsa,"* he said, and she thought of how the phrase had lost its meaning. Giorgio went on. "Our countries are too much alike to really fight each other."

"We beat you in Albania."

"If you beat us, then why am I here wearing a uniform?"

He answered his own question, placing one finger across his upper lip like a mustache.

"Jawohl," he said.

She laughed and found herself still smiling when she reached the Plateia.

"What's going on?" her friend Marianna said.

"What?"

"Why're you smiling?"

The other girls clustered near her, sensing intrigue. The boys stood awkwardly around the edges, not really caring but not wanting to be too far from the girls. Clio glanced at them over her friends' shoulders. Ares with his mouth slightly open; Takis with one ear higher than the other; Thanassis with that faint shadow of hair on his upper lip. She tipped her head down as Marianna and the others drew closer.

"I was talking to a man," she said.

"Who?" Marianna frowned.

"One of the Bersaglieri."

"You can't do that," Ares said.

The girls stared at him and he stepped away, as if now shocked to realize he had spoken.

"He's right, though," Marianna went on. "You can't do that."

"Come on. I can't even say hello? Besides, I wasn't very nice to him," she said, even though she knew that wasn't true.

The rest of the afternoon, the boys hovered around her as if she had become newly fascinating. But all they accomplished, in Clio's mind, was to prove that they were no match for a Bersagliere. So what if he was part of the occupying army? He was a grown-up, and they were children who never even knew what to say to her.

That same evening, Nestor knocked on the door to her room. He handed her a piece of paper folded into quarters.

"What's this?"

"Open it." He sounded like Thalia with that breathless voice of hers.

She unfolded the paper, noticing a watermark of the Italian *fasces* printed on the stiff sheet.

"Nestor, go away." Her face grew hot, and she wasn't sure if it was because of the sight of the occupiers' *fasces* or of the name at the bottom of the note.

Clio turned her back to Nestor and read the message again.

Dearest Miss Clio Notaris, Muse of Korinthou Street,
*   Do me the honor of meeting me to discuss further the*
similarities between our two oppressed nations. Around the
corner from the officers' club, at 9:00.
*   Giorgio Tartini*

"Where did you get this?"

"From the Bersagliere."

She passed her hand behind the paper, noticing how its shadow showed through where the watermark was. Then she folded the paper back up and pulled out her dresser drawer to tuck it inside.

"No, you're supposed to write something," Nestor said. "Then I can give it back to him."

"I thought you didn't like the fascists."

"He gave me two million drachmas to buy chocolate with." Nestor held out two small banknotes, newly printed for the occupation. She didn't have the heart to tell him that, even if he could find any chocolate in a shop, even two million drachmas wouldn't buy it now. "And he said he'd give me some old feathers from his hat if I brought you the message."

"That must be better than burning them. Kostas Dolos will be jealous."

She took a pen from her nightstand and began to respond below Giorgio's signature. Then she smiled and wrote in Italian: *Va bene.*

During dinner, she told herself it was folly to go, to sneak out of the house to meet a man, never mind an Italian soldier. Nestor said he had delivered her message, but what if there had been some error? What if he had given it to the wrong soldier or if Giorgio had changed his mind? Worse, what if it was all a trick to make a young Greek woman look foolish?

But the war had made everything so dull. The occupation had been going on for more than six months, and even though the Germans were in Greece too now, they seemed so far away, in Athens and Crete and other places she had never been to. In Patras, it seemed that there had been no real change since the bombings and dogfights had stopped and the Italians had won. Clio had to have something to do. And Giorgio was handsome. She guessed he was close to her age, yet he was so different from the boys in her circle. The uniform and that wonderful feathered hat made him dashing, like a character out of *Captain Blood*. By the time her mother signaled that they could leave the table, Clio had convinced herself to meet him. She went down to the basement and from there crept out the servants' door to the black-and-white-tiled patio and then out onto the street.

She had forgotten to get a coat and hugged herself against the cold. Turning the corner, she saw a figure she thought was Giorgio, the red bead of his cigarette moving in the air like a firefly. He stepped out of the shadow and, seeing her, removed his jacket.

"Allow me." He swung it around her shoulders. The wool was heavy and scratched where it touched her neck.

They didn't kiss until several meetings later, and Clio took it as a sign that he was not like the soldiers she had heard about, who only toyed with the young women they seduced. Besides, he had not seduced her at all. The messages they sent, with Nestor's help, went both ways. *Psilalónia at 7:00,* she wrote, or

Behind the house at 3:00. And from him: *I need to see you. Meet me at 8:00 in Plateia Georgiou, in the colonnade.* It was a mutual arrangement. It was love.

Two days before Christmas, Clio left the dining room table after lunch and went to her room. She pulled the top drawer of her dresser open, rooted through the socks, underpants, and bras, past the box where she had long ago put their very first silkworm cocoon. The cocoon's empty shell was still inside the box, but she couldn't bring herself to either look at it or throw it away. She reached for the makeup she hid in the very back of the drawer. Quickly, she applied some rouge and lipstick and was combing the mascara wand over her eyelashes when Sophia and Thalia came through the door.

"I was right," Sophia said.

"Go away."

"Where are you off to this time?" Thalia sang. She drew a scarf from the top of the dresser and waved it in the air so that Clio could see it snaking behind her in the mirror.

"Never mind."

Thalia wrapped the scarf around her head, a mass of curls peeping out like bangs. She batted her eyelashes at Clio.

"Thalia, stop it," Sophia said, pulling the scarf away. "We're not joking, Clio. People will see you."

"No, they won't. I know how to get out."

"But people on the street will see you."

Sophia twisted the hair at the end of her braid, as if she were trying to squeeze the water from a paintbrush.

"It won't be the first time."

"Even more reason for you not to go."

"Sophia says people are talking about it," said Thalia, plopping down onto Clio's bed.

"Who?"

"People."

Clio looked inquiringly at Sophia.

"Eleni and Alexandra saw you last week. They were calling you a collaborator."

Clio jumped up from the chair she had drawn before the mirror.

"Oh, thank you so much, Sophia, oh, wise one." She swatted at Sophia's braid. "I think you've butted into my life enough. A collaborator! He's my boyfriend." She saw the other two startle at her use of the word. "I'm older than you, anyway. I'm already eighteen, for Christ's sake." This was more forceful language than they usually used, and Thalia registered it with admiration.

"But he's *Italian*." Sophia said it, as she had said it countless times, slowly and loudly. "I heard there was a woman in Aigio who got beaten up because they saw her just walking with a Bersagliere. They almost killed her."

Clio didn't answer right away, but then she picked up her mascara wand again and waved it in the air.

"That's Aigio," she said. "We're not in the provinces, Sophia."

"If *Mamá* finds out, *she'll* kill you," Thalia said.

"And she'll be mad at us for not stopping you," Sophia added.

"Then why don't you tell her?"

Sophia glared at her.

"Go ahead," Clio said. "Tell *Mamá*."

Clio knew Sophia wouldn't call her bluff. The children's allegiance was to one another first, then to the rules laid down by their parents.

Finally, Sophia answered. "I'm not going to be a tattletale. It's your secret. Your responsibility to tell."

"Well, I'm not going to tell. And, by the way, maybe you've

noticed that *Mamá* and *Babá* don't seem to care whether I go out or not."

"They just haven't seen you do it."

"If they wanted to, they'd have seen me."

She knew her parents were worried by the occupation, but it stung a bit that while they had been so concerned about Nestor's loss of the Scouts, they seemed unaware of all the ways in which the war had changed their daughters' lives. She busied herself with her eyelashes until Thalia broke the silence.

"Sophia didn't want me to say, but *I* think he's handsome."

Clio left her sisters and crept through the napping house and down to the basement, where she followed her usual route out. She didn't look at the officers' club but kept going north toward the outskirts of the city, where the tall neoclassical houses gave way to mews and stables. She tried not to think about Aigio and the woman who had been nearly killed there. Aigio: where Skourtis was from. Surely they *were* uncivilized there, and surely something like that couldn't happen in Patras. Things were different between Giorgio and her, anyway. He pretended he was rough, but Clio knew that he had been afraid to fight, joining the elite troops of the Bersaglieri only because his father and grandfather had forced him to. Not because he was a coward. That was Skourtis. Giorgio was a pacifist at heart. It couldn't be wrong for her to be with an enemy soldier if he was a pacifist. He was practically on her side.

By the third stable down on the right on Kilkis Street, she stopped and waited. Then she saw Giorgio strolling toward her, his black-belted uniform pressed crisp, his sword at his side, and the black rooster feathers that marked him as a Bersagliere bobbing proudly from his hat. As he neared her, he slowed and lit a cigarette. After they kissed, he held it out to her and let her have a puff. She pretended to like it.

322 | *Henriette Lazaridis Power*

"I have something for you," she said.

"Oh?"

"I want you to have it, as a memento of me."

"I don't need a memento. I have you."

He pulled her into an alley and kissed her again. It made her feel truly adult to hear him say these things, to be kissed like that and to kiss him back. She traced a finger over the surfaces of his uniform, the smooth leather of the belt, the sword swinging against her leg, the scratchy wool of his back.

"I want you to have this."

She reached into her coat pocket and held out the topaz ring that her mother had given her for her sixteenth birthday.

"You want me to wear this?"

"No, Giorgio. Keep it somewhere safe, so when you see it, you can think of me."

She had a notion that lovers did this sort of thing. It would have been better if this were a ring she wore all the time, so he could know that it bore some traces of her. Better still if he were giving her something instead. But this was the best she could do. He was laughing now and placing the ring on the tip of his little finger. When he saw her face, he stopped, pulled the ring off, and held it to his heart.

"I will keep this close to me, Clio. I promise."

He tucked it inside his uniform and took her in his arms again.

Carnival began, but there were no parades and no celebrations in 1942. The occupation drove the festivities into private homes, where people stayed overnight to beat the curfew. Guests played cards and roulette until the wee hours, when roomfuls of men and women changed out of evening clothes into pajamas and spread out on the bedding that had been laid on the floor. For the Bourbouli dances, there were larger parties. Women made *dominos* out of blackout curtains they no longer needed, or, craving something finer in a time of limitation, they fashioned costumes out of scraps and outgrown clothes; they made masks from papier-mâché, painting over ripped headlines that announced battles won and lost. The Notaris family party was scheduled for the night of the final Bourbouli, and all the best families in Patras would be there.

The day of the Bourbouli, Clio took Nestor with her as a ruse to get out of the house. He wanted to play ball, she said, and she would grudgingly take him to Plateia Olgas to meet his friends. Once they reached the sidewalk, Clio steered them instead toward Kilkis and its shadowed doorways. Nestor tugged on her arm.

"It's this way."

"We're not going to the Plateia, Nestor."

"But I have my ball."

"Not today."

"Why can't we?"

"We're meeting Giorgio. You like Giorgio."

"But I already sent a message for you today. And I'd rather play with my friends."

"You can do that tomorrow."

She tugged him along, cajoling him when he dragged his feet or dropped his ball and had to go fetch it.

"Come on, Nestor. We don't have forever."

"You shouldn't bring him to the house, you know."

"Does it look like I'm bringing him to the house, Nestor?"

"Not now. Tonight. He's a foe." Nestor said the word grandly.

"A foe." Clio laughed. "Is that from the Scouts?"

"Yes."

"You like him, don't you?"

Nestor nodded.

"Well, then, he can't be a foe."

Eventually Nestor's resistance dissipated.

"Do you think he'll have the bullets I asked him for?"

"Why would he give you bullets? To shoot Italians with?"

"You told me yourself: He's a pacifist. Anyway, he said he would give me spent ones. I've never seen a real bullet," Nestor said.

"Yes, you have."

"Up close."

"Why do you want one, anyway?"

"To add to my other war stuff." He shrugged. "I already have his old feathers and some old buttons."

"Well, maybe he'll bring a bullet for you, then." Clio didn't want to remind Nestor that he'd seen worse than bullets. He'd seen bombs, and people with their heads split open.

Giorgio was standing in the arched doorway to a stable. When he saw them, he dropped his cigarette and twisted it beneath his boot heel.

"How's my boy?" he asked Nestor, tousling his hair. With his other hand, he pulled Clio into a kiss.

"Do you have my bullet?"

"What?"

"He said you were going to give him a bullet. I told him that was a stupid idea and that a soldier would never give his bullets away."

"You didn't say that," Nestor said. He was tugging at her sleeve, but she turned further into Giorgio's embrace.

"Nestor, pal, I have one right here, but I need you to do me

a favor first. Go to the officers' club and fetch me more cigarettes."

"But that's a long way."

"He'll do it," Clio said. "Won't you, Nestor?" To Giorgio,
she said, "I swear he's the one who's in love with you. Not me."

"I am not."

"Come on, lover boy. Cigarettes, please," Giorgio said. He
pressed a hand on the small of Clio's back and kissed her again.
She pulled away for a second. Nestor was standing at her shoulder, looking at her with an expression of pure dismay.

"Go, Nestor!" Then she took his ball from under his arm
and held it out for Giorgio to take. He stepped away from Clio
and, in one motion, drop-kicked it down the street. Nestor ran
after it, beginning to cry.

"That's what I'm talking about," Giorgio laughed. He
brought his face toward her. "What's the matter?"

"Nothing," she said.

The household was too busy with preparations to notice that
Nestor had returned from his outing without his sister. And
when Clio returned from Kilkis Street much later, again, no
one paid particular attention. She went straight upstairs to arrange her costume, forgetting to seek her brother out. That
night, for the party, Clio chose to wear the butterfly wings her
mother had painted vivid magenta, pink, and orange on the
farm almost a year before. Whatever blood had stained the silk
was painted over now and blotted out in her mind by memories of far worse.

She was eighteen and could opt for a *domino,* but the wings
were better, adorning one of her mother's old blue satin dresses.

She wanted to be more like a princess than like a sultry, mysterious figure. Her message to Giorgio that morning had told him to come through the back stairs and up to the roof at eleven o'clock. With a mask and a dark suit, no one would know who he was.

She went up to the roof, to her Hollywood, and waited for him, looking out over the city. The streets were dark. Only the officers' club was well lit, with the iron sconces of the concert hall now shining on the boots of the soldiers who stood guard by its doors. A small number of houses, most of them in this, the best neighborhood of Patras, had lights on, visible around the edges of drawn curtains. From below she could hear the music and the voices in her own house, wafting up through the open door of the stairwell. She was not sure what she wanted, but she sensed that this evening was unique. She had already forgotten that business about Nestor in the alley.

Giorgio was there, wearing a black mask and his blue wool uniform. He had removed the belt and sword, making Clio wonder if this was a violation of some military rule. But before she could ask him, he held her hands out from her sides, smiling at the unfolded wings.

"They're beautiful," he said. "You're beautiful."

"And you're handsome. But I can't see you in that mask."

He raised his mask and began to kiss her, but she turned him away. They were in Hollywood, not the dirty alleyway. Here they could be romantic.

"Wait, Giorgio. Look at the stars."

"I don't care about the stars, Clio. Listen."

The sound of a slow American song was drifting up to the roof. He took her in his arms and began to dance with her on the rooftop, and she thought how lucky she was to have this romance in her life. When the music stopped, his hands began to roam.

Now it was clear to her why this night had felt unique. On any other night, she would have stopped him, but now she let him run his hands along her sides, over her breasts, over her bottom. Her own hands moved too, and soon he was steering her to the back side of the little tower through which the stair came up and taking off his jacket to spread it below them. The wings came off, and he undid the long zipper down the back of her dress. She was cold, but he rolled on top of her. He held himself up and she could breathe better. With one hand, he was fumbling at his belt, and then he took her hand and pressed it against the leather, showing her what to do.

She had both hands on his buckle, hurrying to finish this mechanical task before it broke the mood, when suddenly the noise from the party grew louder. She heard Nestor's high voice somewhere nearby and pulled Giorgio down tight against her. They froze. But it was too late. She heard Nestor cry, "There!" and scrambled to pull the top of her dress up, tugging the satin against Giorgio's wool.

Giorgio was working at his belt when Clio's father lunged for him, one large hand grabbing at Giorgio's shoulder and heaving him off her.

"Get up, you bastard. Get up!"

He tugged Giorgio to his feet and shoved him up against the little tower.

"*Babá*, stop! Giorgio and I are in love."

Her father punched him twice in the face, and, when Giorgio brought his hands to his nose, he punched him again, in the stomach.

"Bastard," her father said, breathing hard.

Giorgio dropped his arms to his sides, his nose and lip bleeding.

"Giorgio, tell him!"

"Clio, go to your room," her father said.

"What are you going to do to him?"

"I said, go to your room." He turned to say this, looking at her for the first time. "Get dressed." She had never heard his voice like that, low and choked.

She reached behind her for her zipper, but the teeth kept catching.

"Let me," Giorgio said.

Her father's punch dropped Giorgio to his knees.

"Nestor, what did you do?" She went for him, and he seized his father's arm, beginning to cry. "What did you do, you stupid little boy?"

"Don't you speak to your brother like that. He did the right thing."

"Telling secrets," Giorgio mumbled through swollen lips. "Did you at least get money for it, Nestor?"

Nestor let out a sound that was half shout, half sob.

Clio was crying now too. She took a few steps toward the edge of the roof.

"Get back here."

"I'm getting my wings."

Her father grabbed her arm and tugged her back toward the stairs. His fingers were twisting her skin so that it burned.

"Go now and don't say a word."

She stumbled down the stairs and ran along the parapet toward her room, hugging the wall so she wouldn't be seen by the guests in the foyer below. She could hear Nestor sniveling behind her and didn't care.

She slammed the door to her room and rushed to the window, through which she saw her father emerge from the house, holding Giorgio by the arm. Giorgio had put his jacket back on, but half of the collar was turned up. Her father walked over to the officers' club, where the two guards broke their pose and descended the stairs toward their bloodied comrade. He said something to one of the guards, who disappeared into the club and reappeared with a man she recognized as the lieutenant. She pushed the sash up and tried to hear. Her father spoke to the lieutenant for a moment, smiling and shaking his head in a bemused way. She heard something about a fight and drunkenness and then he wished the officer good night. As soon as her father's back was to the officers' club, the fury returned to his face.

Clio kept watching as the lieutenant lit a cigarette and gave it to Giorgio. The two men stood on the steps for a minute, talking softly, then the lieutenant clapped Giorgio on the back, laughing, and sent him inside.

She sat at her desk to write one last message to Giorgio, scratching her pen across the paper and nearly tearing the envelope as she stuffed the two sheets into it. She waited until the next morning and called Nestor into her room.

"Please don't be mad at me," he said.

"It's too late for that, Nestor. But if you don't take this last message for me, I'll tell *Babá* that you were lying all this time about where you were going."

"You were lying too."

"He already knows that, Nestor, doesn't he?"

Nestor found Giorgio in the alley behind the officers' club, pumping air into the tires of one of the staff cars. He was too afraid to speak to him, but eventually Giorgio looked up from his work.

"What the hell do you want?"

"I have a message," Nestor said.

"No more messages, lover boy. And your father's going to wish he'd never lifted a hand against me."

Before Nestor could fish the paper from his pocket, Giorgio took his hand, opened the palm, and pressed into it a small ring with a honey-colored stone.

"Give this ring back to your cock-teaser of a sister."

Nestor had never heard the word before, but he understood. He walked away, looking back over his shoulder to be sure Giorgio wouldn't come after him. But when he caught the soldier's face, there was only a look of scorn.

A day later, Clio was in a downstairs room of the house when she saw the lieutenant and another officer coming up the front steps. She heard them ask for her father and listened as Irini took them into her father's study. She crept from the room and stood outside the door, but she could not hear anything. After the two officers had gone, her father sat in the study alone for a while.

"What did they say, *Babá*?" she asked.

"They're taking the raisin business and the farm." He said it as if it was unimportant.

"Why?"

"It's a trade, Clio. I get to punch an Italian soldier, they get our livelihood."

"Why would they do that?" She pictured it for a moment as if her father had sought out a chance to strike an Italian.

"There are limits to what a Greek man can do under Italian occupation, even when he's trying to defend his daughter's honor."

"You can change their minds. We could talk to them."

"Talking to them is what got us into this mess."

"Nestor shouldn't have told you."

He snapped his head up and glared at her, color rising on his bald head.

"Well, he did. And none of this would have happened if you had simply kept away from the enemy. Kept away from a Bersagliere." He almost shouted the word. "Did you think this was all a game, like your cocoons and your parachutes? Did you not realize that this is a war? And to let that man—" He caught himself.

Clio bit her lip, letting the tears run down her cheeks. She made herself stand there and listen.

"Nestor told the truth," her father said, falling back in his chair. "Who's to say that was the right thing to do? I don't have the answer, Clio. Do you?"

He looked at her for a long time, as if he really wanted to know, and then she couldn't bear his gaze anymore and turned away.

19

Callie

I have walked all the way to Bozaïtika Beach, a stretch of gray and white pebbles with a steep drop-off into water that used to be over my head. Behind the beach, a taverna nestles in a grove of eucalyptus trees with their trunks whitewashed to keep the bugs from climbing. I walk a little farther to the next taverna along the shore, which I recognize as Demetris's old place. Thalia sold it when he died, and it is closed now anyway. The trees, usually crowded with tables and chairs, now stand alone like columns in a ruin. But I remember clambering into straw-seated chairs beneath those same trees, with the salt crusting on my suntanned skin, reaching for all the good things Demetris would bring us. I sit on the beach now and stir the pebbles with my hand, occasionally tossing one into the sea. The sun is warm on my face, though the wind is still brisk. As it gusts, I feel my face going hot and cold and hot again.

I sit for a while. I am not much of a smoker anymore, but I wish now that I had the comfort of a cigarette. I imagine the arguments my mother and her sisters must have had as she prepared to see her Bersagliere. Thalia might have tried to keep

Nestor out of it, and my mother—what would my mother have done? Nestor was her ally, but somewhere along the way she blamed him for what went wrong. I can't piece together what he did, and I don't even know what it was that went wrong. A little boy of ten or twelve back then—what could he possibly have done to be deemed complicit?

I walk inland down the little roads until I find a taverna that is open this time of year. I eat a beef *kefte* and some fries smelling of olive oil; I drink some wine. A young waiter is standing by the kitchen door, smoking, and I smile and bum a cigarette, my first in weeks. I drink two coffees while I smoke, sitting and thinking about all that I have learned and imagined.

The truth is that what Sophia said isn't news to me. I have known it my entire life, but, like those secret shames we don't admit, I could never acknowledge even to myself the fact that my mother didn't take care of me. Besides, as a child, how could I understand neglect when it came in the form of liberties and extravagances? It was only later, when adolescence made me an expert on the ego, that I could see my mother's gestures as what they were: gifts for herself. I thought her permissiveness was a blessing, when in fact it was inattention dressed up as a treat. That time in Kythira when Aliki and I were drunk and skinny-dipping, it was Thalia who scolded us about the risks of what we'd done, while my mother got herself ready for her day at the beach.

What sticks in my mind the most from all of this is the image of two old women snapped out of a rare argument to confess that they couldn't stand my mother because of how she treated me. What surprises me even more than that revelation is the feeling it calls up in me. Not just gratitude, not guilt either, but sadness. It's not my fault that my mother's sisters distanced themselves from her, but it's because of me. And I'm saddened to think that I have inadvertently caused my mother pain. I could say that she deserved it, but that suggests a universe in which events are tidily paired: crime and punishment, and—less often, it seems—kindness and reward. But that's not how it is at all, I'm convinced. Just from what I've read and heard and guessed at during these past ten days, I know that there are few perfect matches, or pairs, in our lives. Only connections and compromises that bind some of us together but pull some of us apart.

It's nearly eight o'clock when I finally make it back to Aliki's apartment building, physically exhausted and emotionally spent. As soon as she hears my voice through the intercom, she buzzes me in, and the long buzz has a peremptory, strident quality I haven't noticed before. I step out of the elevator to find Aliki, Thalia, and Sophia crowding around the frosted glass door.

"Where were you?" Aliki says.

"I went walking."

They bundle me into the house and close the door behind me quickly, as if I'm some form of contraband. I look around at them. Three worried faces, and Nikos behind them with his head tilted, half scolding and half bemused.

"I'm sorry, everyone. I didn't mean to make you worry."

Thalia barges through the others and grips me in a tight hug.

"We knew how upset you were," she says.

"And when you didn't come to the memorial . . . ," Sophia adds.

"Oh, *ghamóto*," I say—fuck—and catch the frisson of shock, irritation, and amusement that sweeps across their faces. "Oh, no." I fall heavily into the low chair beside the telephone table. Aliki stoops over me.

"I was worried about the asshole from the other night," she says. "I was afraid he'd done something."

"I should have called."

"You should have come to the memorial is what you should have done," she snaps.

"*Theies,* I'm sorry I wasn't at the church. It's not that I didn't want to go—"

"Where were you, Paki *mou*?" Thalia asks. I have never seen her like this. While the others have calmed down now that they can see I am safe and sound, Thalia is still racked with worry. Her face is creased, her shoulders are squeezed near her ears, and she's wringing her hands, actually wringing them.

"I went to the Bozaïtika."

"All the way there!"

"It's not that far. I found the taverna," I add brightly.

"We said too much," Thalia says, refusing to be drawn into other thoughts. "We shouldn't have let you hear any of it."

"Now someone has to tell me what is actually going on," Aliki says.

"We told you, Aliki *mou*," Thalia says. "Your aunt and I had an argument, and Calliope became upset."

I sit up.

"I was upset because you wouldn't tell me what I need to know." As I say it, I realize I'm hiding what upset me most.

"This again?" Aliki goes into the kitchen and starts emptying the dishwasher, banging the pots and dishes into the cupboards.

"Yes, Aliki. This again." I go after her. "There's something they're not telling me. About the farm and my mother and some Italian. Something they're not telling us."

Aliki wheels around and smacks her dish towel onto the counter.

"Don't lump me in with you, because I don't really care, Calliope. Today was about something that happened now, not sixty years ago. Your uncle's memorial service. We prayed for a sweet man who just died, and you weren't there to be a part of it. You were too busy digging through things that don't matter anymore."

"But they do matter, Aliki. They've mattered all our lives."

"I'm not going to listen to this anymore."

She brushes past me but I stay with her.

"Why do you keep pushing this away? Are you afraid of what you'll find?"

"Don't do that. Don't paint me as the coward, Paki. Ask yourself which is the braver thing: to live your life every day or to lug some mysterious past around with you as an excuse not to."

I stop still, and Aliki realizes what she has said. There is a moment here when she could offer an apology. We both know it. And we both wait for it—she, as if it's not her decision to make. One fact runs through my head, and I sense that Aliki knows what it is, the counterargument that confirms the cruelty of her words: My mother isn't here. Why wasn't she worried about me, like the rest of them? I don't say it, because that's part of the burden she doesn't want me to lug around. But Aliki doesn't say her apology either.

We stare at each other for a few seconds more, and then I snap out of it. It's too late for me to change course now. I go back into the living room and find Nikos stooped over the aunts. He is holding each woman by the hand, and their heads are bowed—in prayer or in contrition, I can't tell.

"How many more arguments do we need to have before you'll tell me?" I ask. "Just tell me."

I don't know if it's the weariness in my voice or something Nikos said that makes the aunts sit down on the couch, side by side, and look at each other. Sophia begins.

"It was almost exactly sixty years ago. In '42. The night of the last Bourbouli. The Italians didn't allow Carnival celebrations during the occupation, but the prominent families held parties in their homes. It was all right as long as people stayed overnight and no one defied the curfew. Your mother's Bersagliere, Giorgio, showed up at our party. Something happened. He caused a disturbance and our father took him over to the officers' club so his own people could deal with him. The next day, the Italians came to the house to talk to *Babá*. They knew about the farm because we had helped them when Vlachos was arrested back in the spring. And of course the Notaris raisin business was well known anyway. So they commandeered them. The farm and the business."

Sophia pauses, giving me time to absorb this.

"You have no idea what it was like for us because of that. Didn't you ever wonder why we didn't have the farm anymore, or why Nestor became a schoolteacher instead of following his father into the business, or why we lost the nice house on Korinthou? It was because of this, what your mother did. Our father was forced to work as a simple employee under an Italian who knew nothing about the business. Every day, he dragged himself to the warehouse and had to answer to this Italian fool. Until the Germans took over and he had to work for them, earning even less than the Italians had paid him. But do you know what might have been the worst?" Thalia takes her sister's hand, and Sophia seems emboldened by her grasp. "The worst was that he had to watch his own countrymen betray him." Now Sophia is glaring at me, and her voice is shaking. Thalia caresses her hand but makes no move to silence her. "When the Germans left, the business should have been restored to us. But instead of thinking about restoration, we Greeks were at one another's throats. For five years we killed one another and stole from one another. How's that for national unity after a war?"

"I know, Sophia," I say. "I know the civil war was a terrible time. But you can't blame my mother for the fact that PASOK didn't give the business back."

"I'm doing no such thing. And it wasn't a civil war," Sophia scoffs. "It was a *guerrilla* war, because communists were attacking the government of Greece."

"We're supposed to call it the civil war now, Sophia," Thalia says.

"Just because Papandreou decreed it twenty years ago? No, thank you. You can't change history just by calling it something else."

I remember this Michalis that Thalia said Sophia loved and wouldn't marry. Is this why her hatred of the left runs so strong?

"So, yes, it was a terrible time, Calliope. Ask the parents whose children were taken away to Bulgaria and Romania to be turned into baby communists. Ask the people whose husbands and boyfriends had their throats slit with the lids of tin cans."

"Sophia."

Sophia pulls her hand from Thalia's and smooths her hair into its bun. "I'm fine."

"But *Papóu* wasn't hurt," I say.

"Not like that," Thalia says gently. "But in 1949, the communists gave the business to someone on their side, and we never got it back. Your grandfather never recovered."

Sophia starts to say something and catches herself before beginning again in a steady monotone.

"From 1940 to 1949, we had war and famine and death. During all that time, our family could have had some security and wealth. But instead we had nothing. Your mother couldn't go to the School of the Arts. Nestor became a schoolteacher, always at the whim of the local government. Your grandfather went from owning an international business to working as a warehouse clerk. We lost a business and a farm that would have protected all of us for years. Your mother is my sister and I will always love her, but she was the one who brought this pain into our lives."

Sophia is finished. In the brief silence, I can see that she is utterly drained.

"Sophia, I understand all this now, but you can't blame my mother, can you?"

"She angered the enemy. During a war."

"We told her not to see him," Thalia says.

"*Theies,* read the letter she wrote to him. She wasn't the only one involved. It was Nestor too. That's what he wanted me to understand."

"What letter?" Aliki says. She has come into the room and is leaning against the wall, hugging herself.

I pull the page from my mother's letter out of my pocket and hand it to her. The aunts follow the paper with their eyes, and I can see that its presence in the room has rattled them.

"Nestor did something," I go on. "He made it so your father found them out."

"Calliope, you don't have to defend your mother," Sophia starts.

"I'm not trying to defend her. I'm trying to tell you what happened."

Sophia laughs. "Sixty years ago and you're telling *us* what happened?"

"We kept telling her to stop," Thalia says, "and she wouldn't."

I don't know what to say. It's as if they can't even hear me. This all seems ridiculous—a chain of events linked now by the memories of wounded and perhaps resentful old women.

"She was a teenager, for Christ's sake. She was in love."

"A very expensive love, it turned out," says Sophia.

I know she's right, but I can't listen anymore.

"I need to go," I say, pushing myself to my feet.

"Cousin," Nikos says. He pulls me into the dining room. "You just got here. Give the old ladies some peace of mind. Stick around."

"Do you hear what they're saying, Nikos? God knows I know my mother is trouble, but this is ridiculous."

"If you're going, then go talk to your mother."

"Why?" I know I sound petulant, but I don't care.

"Ask her about that machine-gun cartridge. I think she knows more than she's telling."

"Nikos, I don't want more mysteries. I want solutions."

"Just try. Ask her. It might help."

I look at Nikos's round face and his round eyes. I laugh, once again surprised by his patience and kindness.

"Sometimes he has good ideas, Paki," Aliki says. "Why not try?"

"Fine," I say. "I'll go. Can I have the letter, Aliki?"

She places the letter into my outstretched hand. She holds my hand for a second in both of hers and looks at me.

"Are you okay?"

I nod.

I turn to the aunts and tell them that there's no need to worry.

"Thank you for telling me what happened," I say. "Thank you."

I start walking to my mother's apartment. As I walk, I picture myself stepping through her door, handing her my coat, sitting in front of the giant walnut mirror. But I can't think of how to begin. Should I ask her why she didn't join the others in wondering where I'd gone tonight? Or why she never told me the truth about the loss of the family's wealth? Or do I really start with a question about that cartridge, which seems so irrelevant now to what I've learned?

She buzzes me in and stands silently in the apartment door when I step out of the elevator. She's still dressed in what she must have worn to the memorial service—a wool skirt and a trim sweater—but she has slippers on her stockinged feet. She watches as I take off my coat and toss it on a little chair. On any other day, she would pick it up to hang it or would scold me for being so careless with my clothes.

"You don't seem surprised to see me," I say. "Or worried," I add, in spite of myself.

"Calliope." She sighs. "Do you want me to make a fuss over you? You're thirty-five years old, for goodness' sake. What you do with your private life is no concern of mine."

"What? You think I've been with some guy, don't you?"

"No. I asked Thalia to let me know when you turned up. She just called."

"Make up your mind. You *are* concerned or you're not?"

"Calliope, stop it. I'm your mother. Of course I'm concerned."

I realize that she assumed I would come to her sisters and not to her when I was back from wherever I'd gone. I wonder how that feels, to be your daughter's second choice. But then I remind myself that I know how it feels to be your mother's.

"Thalia said Sophia told you a long story tonight," she says.

"Yes."

She goes into the kitchen and fills a glass of water from the tap. She drinks almost all of it down and turns to face me, leaning against the sink. She seems younger, in a strange way, as if the knowledge that the truth is out has restored her energy. Or maybe she is simply mustering her strength to deny whatever it is I'm going to say.

"Well." She is waiting.

My face heats up and I can feel my pulse beat faster. I am afraid. Afraid to ask a question that might heap more unpleasant truths onto what I have already learned, afraid to arouse my mother's wrath or to summon the kind of anguish that can overwhelm her and me both. I look at her and see that her face is relaxing. She thinks I'm going to back down.

"Okay, *Mamá*. Tell me about that cartridge."

"What cartridge?" She says the word as though she doesn't really know what it means.

"The bullet thing. In the box. You said it must be from Yannis and his hunting, but Nikos says it's from an Italian gun."

"So maybe Yannis had an Italian gun."

"An Italian machine gun. A Breda, I think. From the war. Nikos says the only way to get the cartridge from a Breda is to pull it from the ammunition clip. Who had this cartridge, *Mamá*? And who gave it to Nestor?"

She turns back to the sink and drinks more of the water. She runs the tap and fills the glass again, drinks again.

"*Mamá!* Are you trying to drown yourself or something?"

There's a long silence and she remains with her back to me. I realize that I am holding my breath. When I take in air again, I do it quietly, like sipping something that will burn my lips.

Finally my mother turns around, and I see that any youth I spotted in her moments ago is gone.

"That is what your uncle and I argued about in the hospital."

"The cartridge?" I can't help but sound surprised. I picture the two of them arguing over possession of it, but surely that can't be the case.

"In a way, yes."

My mother sits down at the kitchen table, her hands in her lap.

"Your uncle Nestor and I share a great shame. He wanted to tell you his part in it, but I didn't. Not because I wanted to preserve my own honor. But because I wanted to preserve his. You don't believe me, Calliope, but it's true."

She must see the doubt in my face, but she goes on.

"War has a funny way of making people behave the opposite of what you think, Calliope. It confuses things."

"You couldn't have done anything shameful. You had no power."

"Why on earth would you think powerlessness exempts you from shame? Even the occupied can behave in shameful ways, Calliope. That's one of the things an occupation does to you: turns an honorable person into a cheat, turns an innocent into a guilty soul."

I sit down now, barely pulling the chair out so that the edge of the table presses against my ribs.

"Nestor got that cartridge," my mother goes on, "from the partisans. Greeks who had gotten weapons from the Italians when they surrendered to the Germans." She must notice the confusion on my face, because she breathes an irritated sigh. "It was complicated, Calliope. The Italians occupied. Then the

Germans occupied. And the Italians who didn't get caught hid in the hills and ended up helping the partisans." She waits a moment, but I don't say anything. "One day, after the Germans had taken over, we went to the camp where the Germans kept their Italian prisoners, and one of them called to us from behind the fence. I should have walked away right then. Everything would have been different if I had walked away and taken Nestor with me."

She stops, fighting against a decades-old frustration. I can see her twitching slightly in her chair, as if she could pull her teenage body away from what became so obviously the wrong course. I reach across the table and touch her shoulder.

"*Mamá,* do you mean you wouldn't have lost the farm?"

I don't see how this is possible. But maybe I can offer some source of solace she has overlooked in all these years.

"No. Why would you say that?" She looks at me, and I can see her trying to piece together what exactly her sisters have told me. "This is worse than that. All these years, Nestor and I have had a much bigger worry than money and wealth. We had a darker sin on our conscience."

I lean back against the chair, my mind scrambling to think of what she could possibly mean.

"We knew this soldier. Giorgio. He had befriended Nestor at the start of the war. Nestor went to talk to him. I gave in and I let him. Nestor gave him something to eat. The Germans were starving them. They were starving us all. In Athens, but even in Patras, people were dying on the streets." She looks up at me sharply. "Do you understand that, Calliope? Can you imagine such a thing?"

I nod. I know she's not telling me the whole story about Giorgio but I don't want to disrupt her momentum. After a moment she starts up again.

"Nestor must have gone to the camp again without me, and Giorgio told him where the Italians were hiding with their weapons in the hills, and Nestor told Yannis and must have brought him there for the guns. Yannis had left us when we couldn't pay him anymore, and we suspected he had joined the partisans. Probably on the communist side, but who cared as long as he was fighting the Germans. One day Nestor and I were the only ones home. Your aunts were out in the *plateia* and my father was at work. I don't know where my mother was that day. Maybe none of this would have happened if she had been there. Two German soldiers came after Nestor, and they said they would kill him if he didn't tell where Yannis was. They said Yannis had led a partisan group that had killed two Nazi soldiers the day before."

"But how did they know about Nestor?"

"Maybe he boasted to someone, or maybe they saw him talking to someone. But they were right. He had been to the partisan camp. And they came after him to get to Yannis." She takes a breath. "So I protected him."

She stops and closes her eyes. I wait for a while, but she doesn't move. I'm afraid that she will begin to cry.

"You protected Yannis?"

"No. I protected Nestor. I *betrayed* Yannis. That's all, Calliope."

"What do you mean? How did you betray him?"

My mother opens her eyes and looks at me with a sadness I have never seen.

"I'm only going to say this one last thing," she says. "Yannis was found the next day hanging from a tree."

We sit like that for a long time, and I discover a rhythm to the whir of the refrigerator. I pick at a tiny scratch in my chair, rubbing a fingertip over the spot where the scratch cuts across the edge of the seat. At some point, it occurs to me that my mother has forgotten I am in the room, even though I am just across the small white tabletop from her. I can't imagine what she is thinking, but I know that I am struggling to see through a kaleidoscope of muddy shards of glass.

I picture her and Nestor in that high-ceilinged house. I picture soldiers in movie-version helmets and boots. I picture a body spinning slowly from a rope in a tree. And a young woman, my mother, standing somewhere, doing something. That is the part I can see the least clearly of all.

As I think about all this, what emerges for me is a sense of some perverted equilibrium, a distorted balance in which the life of a young boy and the life of a man must be weighed and judged. My mother protected Nestor, she says, and for that, or because of that act, Yannis was hanged. She gave the Germans what they wanted—or she convinced Nestor to—and she earned her own and her brother's survival in return. She gave a greater value to the life of her brother. How can she blame herself for making that choice? *That's all,* my mother said to me. Meaning that was all she did that day during the war? Or that is all she's going to tell me now? Surely the act of protecting one's brother from being killed can't be dismissed with *that's all.* It's a heroic act. It's the right thing to do. It is far from trivial. Am I being callous to absolve her and Nestor both?

But there is another balance too, between my mother and Nestor, the two of them sharing a sin that burdened them all their lives and that led them to argue even as Nestor was close to death. Besides my mother, only Nestor and those Germans knew what happened in the house on Korinthou Street. It's not hard to imagine that my mother must have done something to distract the Germans from their vengeful course. My mind can't even hold the thought that they enacted their vengeance

on her all the same. Now that Nestor is dead, whatever happened to my mother that day is a burden she is carrying alone.
She won't even share it with me.

I draw my hand out from under the table and place it on my
mother's. She starts, sees me again, and draws her hand away.
Another time, another day, she would have pulled it away more
quickly. Another day, I would never have put mine on hers.

"Why did he want you to tell me?" I ask the question without even realizing.

She looks right at me.

"I don't know."

I see something hardening in my mother's face and I decide
I need to leave right away, so that I can preserve the slightly
softer image of her in my mind. I ask her if I'll see her at the
church for Forgiveness Sunday or for Clean Monday lunch,
and I'm pleased that she says yes for both.

"Demetra's been working hard on her kite," I say.

I shrug my jacket on and give my mother a kiss on each
cheek before heading out into the hall. She closes the door
softly behind me while I wait for the elevator.

Out in the street, I can hear the insistent thumping of the
bass from the loudspeakers that ring Plateia Georgiou. It's the
final Carnival parade, and it feels as if it belongs to another
world. I have no desire to seek out the revelry, and I don't trust
myself to go back to Aliki's yet, lest I say something to reveal
what my mother has just told me. And this is one thing I am
certain of: This last piece of information from my mother's
past I will not pass on to anyone else.

Something makes me decide to try my luck again with the
old family house. It seems the right thing to do, to fold the

reality of my days here in Patras into the new history of my mother's life. The closer I get to the center of the city, the more clearly I can hear the parade music, a cacophony of amplified samba, whistles, and an echoing voice booming from a microphone. I reach the house on Korinthou and stand there, gazing at the double entrance door at the top of that short flight of steps. There are lights on now, blazing out from bare windows. I imagine the house on the last night of the Bourbouli in 1942, with light filtering through thick curtains and people arriving in splendid gowns slightly out of current fashion. I walk up the steps and press a buzzer. A woman's voice answers after a moment.

"I'm wondering if I could ask you a favor," I begin, but the intercom clicks off.

I try three more with similar results. One woman thinks I am a gypsy begging for cash. Finally I hear a voice I think I recognize.

"Remember me?" I say. "You let me in last week to look around. My family used to live here."

"The American?"

"Yes."

The buzzer sounds and I push the heavy door open. I am in the foyer again, and the bulb is still burned out. Except for the street light coming through the windows on either side of the door, the space is in deep shadow. It would be easy to go down to the basement now, as I did that other day, which seems like a lifetime ago. The door to the stairs is just there, across the foyer. But on that earlier visit, I was looking for the site of an innocent childhood game. Instead, I learned that even a shared experience can splinter into conflicting memories.

I hear footsteps on the stairs and make out Undershirt Man, now wearing blue jeans and a sweater the same bright red as my shirt. A large yellow and orange flower is pinned to his chest like a clown's brooch.

"All right," he says, not unkindly. "What do you want now?"

I suspect he will think I am crazy, but it is Carnival, and he is dressed for it, so perhaps it will be all right.

"Could you let me go up on the roof?"

"What?"

"I'd really like to see the roof. That's all."

"You planning to jump? Because I want no part in your suicide."

I assure him that is not my plan. "It's a family thing. Something I need to see."

"You Greek Americans and your heritage," he mutters. "The door's over there. Just watch the laundry up there. You mess it up, you'll have to wash it."

He leads me as far as the door but stays behind as I walk up the stairs. I emerge from the little hut as if from the conning tower of a submarine, and I do feel as if I have surfaced from a deep immersion—in my mother's guilt and sadness, in my own age-old mistakes. I feel the breeze on my face, diminished to a soft caress, and look up at the sky. There is too much glow from the city now, but I imagine that the night my mother stood waiting for Giorgio, the sky must have been dripping with gems of light. I walk to the edge, where there is a low wall, and I look down at the street. Across from me is the building of the old concert hall, now lit up with a long vertical sign announcing classes in English and German. Two young women are sitting on the steps smoking, and through the propped-open door I can see a brightly lit patch of linoleum.

It seems reasonable now for a young woman of my mother's disposition and with my mother's dreams to come to this roof and feel she had the world at her feet. And it seems reasonable for her to keep from me the truth of what happened on that roof—an event that could have been simply an embarrassment within the family, even a humiliation, but that the war and its way of playing with consequences turned into a tragic loss. Most of all, I see now that her sense of a shared shame over what took place when the Germans found her and her brother alone must have colored everything she did with Nestor from that day onward. It doesn't matter that I don't quite understand her shame. What matters is that I understand, a little bit, that she felt it. Her departure with my father in 1959 now seems less like a reluctant acquiescence and more like a necessary escape. His Americanness must have been a balm to a woman whose life had taken a bad turn just when the idea of being Greek was at its most fraught. How much worse it must have been, too, when the marriage began to fracture.

I see now why Nestor wanted me to know all this, why he wanted my mother to tell me. He couldn't reveal the truth outright without betraying the sister he was bound to in an allegiance of guilt. But he could set the conditions so that that sister might relent and tell her daughter that she had suffered. By stripping away her masks and fabrications, Nestor gave me a way to understand my mother's story, to understand her.

I think again of what my mother said about the occupation, how it turns innocents into guilty souls and makes the honest cheat. But she left something out. The war gave my mother reasons to feel ashamed, but it gave her honor too. Honor in loving her brother, honor in keeping to herself a secret that might have won her a measure of sympathetic peace. I wish she had told me sooner. And I wish I had wanted to ask.

From a distance, I can hear a marching band's music separating itself from the general din and getting louder. Just as it was during my mother's childhood, the house is on the parade route, except that now this is the end of the route, far from the more lively commercial section of the city. Back then my mother would have stood on the balconies with Nestor and the aunts, tossing candy down onto the passing floats. Now, as the parade approaches, I hear doors opening below and, when I lean out, I see people coming out onto their steps, cheering and blowing on whistles and horns.

The parade appears, led by dancers in white harlequin leotards with jester's hats of multicolored velvet. The first float is of the Carnival figure himself, a smiling clown face with big ears and a turned-up nose. The spectators jump into the parade, dancing along with it and then running back to their starting points to jump in again. They carry on this way for nearly half an hour as the parade goes by, letting the revelry sweep them along for a bit and then going back to start over. I like this idea. I like the idea of starting over—the way these people do it again and again and again, celebrating the dance and the renewal.

I take a last look around and head down the stairs. I meet Undershirt Man at the door, where he and a group of others are watching the last float disappear down the street. I thank him and start the walk home.

20

Clio

October 1943

Clio leaned against the kitchen's marble sink, watching her mother cut thin slices from a flat loaf of brown bread. Urania was wearing one of Irini's aprons, the strings coming all the way around and tying in the front. The apron was one of many Irini had left behind when they had let her go the previous summer. Over the year since then, Clio had marked the effects of the occupation on her mother's once plump torso, as the apron strings wrapped farther and farther around her mother's frame.

Clio took the slice of bread Urania handed her and spread it with just a little margarine. She ate standing up, chewing small bites so as not to gag on the dry bread.

"Where's mine?" Nestor said, coming into the room.

Urania handed him a slice, saying nothing. He held it up for Clio, but she slid the knife and the jar of margarine over to him.

"Go easy," she said.

He coated the bread thickly, folded it in half, and wrapped it in his handkerchief.

"Nestor," Urania said. "Eat."

"I'm not hungry right now," he said, stuffing the piece into his pocket.

How could he not be hungry? Clio was always hungry, always aware of a tingling in her stomach, aware of a strange freshness in her mouth that came, she supposed, from all that wasted saliva. They had enough food. But only enough. And it was tasteless and boring and sat in your stomach for hours after you ate it, as if to tease you with a false satiety. Sugar made of beets; bread without yeast; and every now and then a stringy piece of chicken from some bird that had spent the war running from the Italians. Just weeks ago, the Italians had surrendered and the Germans had taken over. And the Germans made sure their officers' club was stocked with all the wine, vegetables, and fluffy white bread that Patras had to offer, while the Greeks starved.

"Where's your father?" Urania asked Nestor.

"On his way out."

"Wait," she said. "Clio, take this to him."

Clio grabbed the hunk of bread her mother ripped from the loaf and ran out to the foyer, where her father was just draping a scarf around his neck. She was about to speak to him but paused, watching as he gazed briefly at himself in the walnut mirror. His mustache had grayed, and his once-confident posture had become a stoop, as if he were always ducking beneath a beam. She watched now as he drew his shoulders back and raised his chin, his neck tendons stretching. He turned from the mirror, buttoning his coat.

"Babá," she called. "Here." She placed the bread in his hand and held it there. He looked at her for a moment and then kissed her on the forehead.

He picked up his briefcase and stepped out the front door,

closing it crisply behind him. But Clio knew that once he descended the stairs and reached the street, his shoulders would resume their stoop. She wondered when he would eat the bread her mother had given him. He would be ashamed to eat it on the street, with the risk of passing beggars who had had nothing to eat for days. And he would be too proud to eat at work, preferring hunger over the disclosure of his family's now-modest means. Clio pictured her father stuffing the bread furtively into his mouth as he returned home, famished, in the evening darkness.

After the Italians had commandeered the farm and the Notaris raisin business, they had installed one of their own as manager of the warehouse: Marinelli, the beneficiary of the war's almost farcical way of overturning fates. But they had soon realized that Marinelli was just a baker and knew nothing about managing a warehouse. They brought Notaris in to serve as Marinelli's employee. Every day, Notaris went to the warehouse he had once operated from a walnut desk in a secluded office and paced the aisles of crates, ensuring that Notaris raisins were loaded efficiently onto ships bound for Brindisi and trains stocking the *Wehrmacht*'s supply stores in Athens. At home, he never spoke about his work, but once, months ago, he had come into the kitchen and set a small canvas sack onto the pine table in the center. They had all stared at it. ΝΟΤΑΡΗΣ was stamped on the side, and it bore the sweet grassy smell of raisins.

"A gift from Marinelli," her father had said.

Clio's mother had put the sack on a high shelf. Nestor would occasionally remember it and beg for some raisins, but no one ever brought the sack down.

Clio heard Thalia's and Sophia's laughter above her. The girls emerged from their room and started down the stairs, only to hush suddenly when they saw their older sister in the foyer. They wore their hair in identical bobs now, Sophia's sleek and Thalia's still crazed with curls.

"What?" Clio said.

"Nothing." They said it together, and Thalia began to giggle again. Sophia elbowed her.

"Fine," Clio said. "Where are you off to?" There was no school, no Girl Guides. There were no parties. A trip out of the house could only involve choosing a particular square in which to stand around where the Germans wouldn't harass you.

"Psilalónia," Thalia said, naming the square on the heights above the center of the city. After a pause, she added, "Do you want to come?"

But Clio could sense that her sister had asked only out of obligation. Thalia and Sophia ran with a different crowd now. Or, rather, they ran with a crowd, and Clio spent much of her time alone, thinking. Often she drew, sketching memories of the farm or drawing portraits of Irini and Yannis, smiling at their faces as they drifted up from the paper. She was good at this, and she found comfort in the way her body curled around the paper, sealing it and herself off from the world outside.

"I'm staying here," she said.

Thalia and Sophia headed for the door.

"We told *Mamá*," Thalia said.

Clio shrugged. It wasn't her job to monitor her sisters' travels. She returned to the kitchen, putting off the moment when she would have to decide how to spend the day.

Nestor was eating a slice of bread. Clio could see the package he'd wrapped before still stuffed into his pocket. He grinned at her, then opened his mouth wide.

"That's disgusting, Nestor. Shut your mouth."

He chewed vigorously, smacking his lips.

In another second, he would be hoisting himself up onto the counter beside the sink, only to have Urania swat him down. Urania barely seemed to look at him anymore, simply flinging out a hand at him in silent reprimand while she bent over a pot of cracked wheat, or plucked a chicken, or hand-lettered one of the many signs the Germans brought to her for painting. *Müller, Stettner, Lanz.* Clio's mother's delicate hand painted the serifs and umlauts on each one.

If Urania had looked, she would have seen Nestor's features sharpened by time and war. Though only thirteen, he had adopted the swagger and the smirk that had become typical of the city's boys. Clio knew he sometimes went out with his friends to pour sugar into the gas tanks of the German staff cars. The Germans could kill a boy for a stunt like that. He pretended to listen to Clio when she told him to quit, but she knew he snuck into the kitchen at night to scoop some of their precious brown sugar into that handkerchief of his.

"Clio," her mother said, "take Nestor out of here, please. He's constantly in my way."

"No need, *Mamá*," he said. "I'm leaving."

"Take your sister with you."

"I can go out by myself."

Urania was washing her hands and reaching for a jar of paintbrushes. She would take them down to the basement, where she kept the German signs.

"Come on," Clio said to Nestor. "I'll take you."

He scowled, but she signaled to him to go along with her. Their mother's jaw was set, and she had the abstracted look Clio had come to know.

Out on the street, Nestor tugged his arm from Clio's grasp.

"I don't need babysitting."

"You know she doesn't like us to see her when she's painting."

"She would have been in the basement. You could have stayed upstairs."

"She doesn't want us in the house, Nestor. Just let her have that."

One day, Clio had heard her parents' voices raised in the basement and had crept down the stairs to see what the trouble was.

Her mother was bending over a pale-green sign with black Gothic letters marching across its surface.

"I can't let you do this anymore," her father was saying. "Urania, stop."

"I'm not stopping, Leonidas. This has to get done."

He pulled at her hand that held the paintbrush, but Urania snatched it back.

"Damn it!" She grabbed a white rag from the table and dabbed furiously at the black paint that had spattered onto the sign. "That's all I needed."

"Who cares if their sign gets damaged?"

"Just stay away," Urania said. She rubbed her free hand over her eyes. "Go upstairs and have one of the girls get you something to eat." As Clio crept upstairs, she heard her mother say, "You're tired, Leonidas. Go and rest."

"The girls need the food more than I do."

Her father had been right. Thalia and Sophia had been losing weight, and though they had initially greeted this development with glee and had posed for each other in the walnut mirror, it was now clear that, like Clio herself, they had grown too thin.

Clio looked over at Nestor walking by her side, his cheekbones jutting from his face.

"So, where to?" she said.

"I don't know."

He began to walk away from the center of the city, to the east, and for a moment Clio thought he might be trying to go to the farm. They walked in silence. It was sunny, and, though her father had put on his scarf and coat, the air was warm. If they had been at the farm now, the air would have borne the oily scent of Yannis's brush fire, burning the windfall of autumn leaves and branches. The grass would have been soft beneath their feet, briefly green again after summer's heat.

Up ahead, a man lay on the street, his clothes loose and ragged. The man looked at them with sunken eyes, and Clio saw that there were flies resting on his lower lids and around his ears. She pulled Nestor away, hating herself for her fear.

"Nestor, we shouldn't be here," she said, fighting the urge to vomit.

But on this new street she had led him down, they found themselves in a current of men and women all walking in the same direction, toward a large building that filled the entire block. She realized where they were. The building used to be a school, but the Italians had turned it into a prisoner-of-war camp, ringing it with wire fencing and hanging giant padlocks on the gates. Now it was the Italians themselves who were in the camp, forced there by the Germans. Giorgio might be among the prisoners. If he wasn't, did that mean he'd been killed?

"Nestor, we're leaving."

"Wait! I want to see!"

"They're prisoners, Nestor. Let's go home."

"Come on, Clio," he said, tugging against her. "I just want to look."

He broke from her and came to a stop a few yards from the main gate.

"Nestor!"

He jerked his shoulder as if she were actually holding on to him. He wouldn't turn around. She walked over to him with the intent to hustle him away.

The Italians stood by the fence, their collars turned up and their heads bare, stripped of their extravagant feathered hats. They called out to the Greeks who were passing by.

"*Ciao, bella.*"

"*Signore, ho fame.*"

"*Ecco una bella ragazza.*"

One soldier sat on an upturned barrel and sang.

As she drew closer, Clio saw that the Greeks weren't simply passing by the camp. They were stopping, and they were handing things through the wire fence. She looked around for Germans, but there were none in sight. She watched as one woman in a black dress and down-at-heel shoes held out a loaf of bread to an Italian, who bit into it hungrily. A man walked by quickly and, without breaking his stride, tossed a potato over the fence, where two soldiers scrambled for it.

She began to look for Giorgio, in spite of herself. It had been a year and a half since that night on the roof, a night she kept replaying over and over in her mind. She realized now how foolish she had been to think theirs would be some sort of courtly passion. She no longer even saw the appeal of such an idealized, spiritual love. Giorgio had humiliated her, that was true. But she was a little embarrassed at her old self too. Naïveté like hers had been misplaced then; it was a luxury now. Especially given what it had cost her family.

This was where her thinking always stopped. She had to

ignore the fact that her mistake had brought such hardship upon them all. How could she even sleep under the same roof, eat the same meager food, as the rest of her family if she kept her guilt clearly in her mind? With the exception of Nestor, the others already stood at a distance to her in some way that they would not acknowledge but that she felt daily. If she allowed her mind to dwell on the significance of what she had done, her life among them would be impossible.

"Nestor," a voice called.

Clio turned, and there was Giorgio, coming over to the fence.

"Nestor, my friend. My old ally."

"Leave him alone," Clio said. "Come on, Nestor."

"I can talk to my friend Nestor if I want to," Giorgio said. "Can't I, pal?" Giorgio's Greek was more fluent now. All that time occupying the country had made him a linguist.

"You weren't so friendly last time I saw you," Nestor said.

"What did you do to him?" she said to Giorgio.

"Me? Nothing. Ask *him*."

"You're the loser now, *fannullone*," Nestor said.

"*Fannullone!*" Giorgio said. "Good one."

And he seemed legitimately pleased, almost impressed that this young boy had called him a do-nothing in his own language. Giorgio stepped back a bit from the fence, hugging himself as if it were cold out. He had a beard, and his hair had grown to loose curls that covered the tops of his ears. He looked older now—more than simply twenty months older—and he was thinner, though he couldn't have been in the camp for more than a few weeks. The Italians had surrendered in September, and since then the Germans had either been taking them prisoner or, if the stories were true, executing them in cold blood. If Giorgio were truly the pacifist he had claimed to be, he would have given up without a fight. And now who knew how his compliance would turn out?

Clio took Nestor's arm. "That's it, Nestor. We're going. Let this prisoner stew in his memories."

"Nestor," Giorgio called, coming to the fence again. "It's a war. Times change. Now Greeks and Italians, we're on the same side. It's official. We even gave you Greeks our guns." He smiled. Then, growing serious, he reached a hand through the fence and touched Nestor's collar. Clio saw the fear in Giorgio's eyes. "These *krauts*," he said. "They're a bunch of bastards. There's no food here, not really. Nestor, I'm hungry."

"Get food from someone else. We don't have anything either," Clio said, turning away. Nestor was still standing there. She called to him. He was reaching into his pocket, and she saw him pull out the handkerchief he'd wrapped around the slice of bread.

"Here," he said, and shoved the handkerchief through the fence.

Giorgio held the bundle to his heart with both hands and kissed it, waving the kiss not only to Nestor but to Clio as well. Her face burned, and she wasn't sure if she was angry or ready to cry.

"Come on, Nestor," she said, and tugged him away.

Once they were out of sight of the prison, she stopped and spun around to face him.

"Don't you ever do that to me again. I don't know why I didn't leave you there alone, except I somehow thought a little boy standing near where Germans patrol would be a bad idea."

"I'm not a little boy."

"Did you plan this?"

"I swear I didn't. We weren't even going this way. You're the one who made us turn."

He was right. She had pulled him away from that emaciated figure in the street. Had it been safer here?

"And now you don't even have your slice of bread," she said. "Or your handkerchief."

"They're hungry, Clio. Hungrier than we are."

"I know that," she said. "But they were against us. Remember? Your *foe*?"

"Not yours."

"He was just one soldier, and I was stupid. You need to understand that."

"They hate the Germans as much as we do. We have a common enemy. You heard what Giorgio said: They gave us their guns. They're arming the partisans."

"Where are you hearing language like that?"

"Like what?"

"*Common enemy. Arming the partisans.* That sounds like resistance talk."

"Does it?" He resumed walking.

"Nestor," she said, running up to him. "I know about the sugar. Even that is bad enough, but if you go mixing with any resistance groups, that's serious trouble."

Just the week before, partisan fighters had killed two German soldiers on patrol. The next day, four Greek men were found hanging from a tree in a small square out by the railway station. As they always did now with such warnings, the Germans had tied signs reading TRAITOR to each noose.

"Nestor!"

He kept walking, and all he said was, "I'm not a little boy."

A few days later, Thalia and Sophia went to Psilalónia again, and after lingering in the kitchen for a few moments, Clio decided to seek them out. It was a long way to Psilalónia, but she was bored. She crossed the city, skirting Plateia Georgiou, where a group of Germans lolled by the fountain, and reached Trión Navarchon, the street of the Three Admirals, with its narrow mall of plantings. Trión Navarchon was a ribbon of park that ran from the harbor straight to Psilalónia Square. She followed it up the hill, breathing in the mineral scent of the damp earth. She realized she had no idea who the three admirals were from some other war.

When she reached the top, she waited until she had caught her breath and then scanned the square. Over to her right, beneath the mulberry trees and date palms that ringed the open space, she made out Sophia and Thalia in a group of four other girls, Sophia's dark bob looming above everyone else's. A larger group of boys stood at some small distance. The girls crowded in tight and then darted apart, in a rhythm of alternating confidences and surprise. If they were telling secrets, Clio didn't want to join them. Instead she kept to the edge and walked all the way around to the square's most secluded part, behind the monument to Bishop Germanos. The name made her laugh. He had started the War of Independence in 1821, raising the Greek flag in defiance against the Ottomans, and that past spring the Germans had raised their flag over the Acropolis. She had never thought about any of this before this war had started. But now, everywhere she looked, there was war—not just the one she was living, but all the others that had tossed Greece back and forth like a playground ball.

In the far corner of the square, she saw two men in rough clothes standing together. She was about to veer away when she noticed that the shorter man, lighting a cigarette in his cupped hands, was Yannis, who had left the house with Irini when her parents could no longer afford to pay them. Clio must have made a sound, because Yannis looked up as he fanned the match out.

She ran toward him, calling his name, but he began to walk away. She caught him in a side street. She touched his arm, wondering if perhaps she'd been mistaken, but he turned around and gave her a smile.

"Miss Clio," he said.

"Yannis! I'm so glad to see you. We've been worried since we haven't heard anything. Where have you been? Are you all right?" She looked around her. "Where's Irini?"

"We're both well, Clio. I need to go."

"What?"

"I can't talk to you, Clio. It's best if I don't."

"But why?"

"I need to go."

He was looking over her shoulder. She turned to see what had caught his eye and saw Nestor—Nestor, who was supposed to be playing soccer in Plateia Olgas on the other side of the city.

"Both of you!" Yannis was angry now. "Go away. Nestor, get her out of here."

"Nestor, what are you doing?" she asked. She spun back to Yannis to find him half-running, half-walking down the street.

"What on earth are you doing, Nestor? What is going on?"

"I saw Yannis before and we were talking. That's all."

Yannis was out of sight now, having disappeared around a corner.

"And you didn't tell anyone at home? We've all been worried about them."

"It's not important."

"You know that it is." She led him back to the square and down Trión Navarchon, their legs thrashing down the incline in a ragged stride. She had to get Nestor away from Psilalónia as quickly as possible, away from the source of the secrecy she had stumbled into.

By the cathedral of Agios Andreas, she pulled him to a stop. "Tell me," she said.

He scowled at her, like the little boy she still saw in him, and finally spoke.

"Giorgio told me I could help."

"What the hell does Giorgio have to do with anything?"

Nestor looked up sharply at the swear. He would have to get used to it. She was too old—and too angry now—for delicate language.

"There are ways to help," he said. "Some of the Italians are in the hills."

"I know that."

"Well, the partisans are too."

"Nestor! Just say it."

"I'm not supposed to."

"I'm your sister and I'm telling you to."

He took a breath and spat the words out in a rush.

"Giorgio knows where Italian guns are and I'm helping Yannis get them."

Clio felt her entire body sink into itself. Nestor was breathing hard, clearly waiting for an outburst from her, but to Clio the world slowed to a halt. There was the Psilalónia, the slices of bread, the gossip of her sisters, and then there was this, this fact, which draped over all the rest like a heavy blanket. Nestor was involved in the resistance. It would matter to no one that he was only thirteen. He was involved.

She took him by the shoulders.

"Look at me. I don't want you to do any more of that. I need you to be safe. Can you promise me that, Nestor? Please?"

He seemed to understand that her request had nothing to do with war and resistance and allies and everything to do with her desire to keep him unharmed. He nodded.

Clio wasn't sure. She kept Nestor's revelation to herself, not even telling her parents. Each of her parents dealt with Germans every day, and Clio feared that their awareness of Nestor's— and Yannis's—actions would reveal itself in their behavior. Besides, they didn't notice much about their children now, wearied and preoccupied with the work they were ashamed to be doing. So Clio watched over Nestor, at first barely letting him out of her sight, lingering at the edges of soccer games or scuffles by the fountain at Plateia Georgiou. Eventually, Nestor seemed to prefer staying home to dragging his burdensome sister around the city. He loitered around the house, picking at anything he could find to eat in the kitchen, wandering up onto the roof, where Clio was determined never to follow. She watched him one day stalk a Japanese beetle in the front garden so that he could tie a string around its leg. He slipped it into a matchbox and carried it up the stairs to the top of the house to fly it around his head like a lasso.

That must have been where he was the day the Germans came for him. Clio was in the basement, sitting in one of the storage rooms on a pile of rugs still rolled up for the summer. She had her sketch pad with her but hadn't opened it. Instead, she hugged her knees to her chest and watched the dust motes rise in the light from the window. The house was quiet, and she could almost imagine that she was in her clover house at the farm—on some day from what now seemed her very distant childhood, before the war had made even the clover houses feel unsafe. When she breathed deeply, the twine creaked around the rugs, just like the clover stalks shifting in the breeze.

"Clio!" It was Nestor shouting. "Clio!" He came running down the stairs. "Clio, hide me!" He rushed into her arms, breathing hard, his eyes wide.

She heard deep voices upstairs and the knock of boot heels on the marble floor. None of the others were home, she realized, or, if they were, they were staying hidden. The voices quickly grew louder and then there were two men, German soldiers, in the door of the storage room.

One of them grabbed Nestor and said something in German. The other one replied and stood in the door, his rifle barring the way out.

"Let him go," Clio said.

"Clio!" Nestor was crying now.

The first one spoke to Nestor again in German.

"Clio, what is he saying?"

She didn't know. They had stopped their lessons when the war broke out.

"He doesn't understand you," she said to the man's back. "What do you want?"

He faced her, swinging Nestor around with him.

"This boy is a partisan," he said in choppy Greek.

"No! No, he's not. He's just a little boy."

Nestor's crying grew stronger.

"He will tell us where the others are. Where are they?" He shook Nestor by the arm. *"Wo?"*

"Nestor, you don't know anything," Clio said, wanting to make it sound like a fact and not a warning.

"Where is Yannis?" This was the soldier by the door. Clio couldn't help herself; she turned around at the sound of Yannis's name. The door guard smiled. "Ah," he said. "Maybe you both know. Who's going to give us what we want?"

The other one twisted Nestor's arm, and the boy cried out in pain.

"Clio!" He stared at her. He was asking her what to do.

She stepped toward the soldier who was holding Nestor.

"I know more than he does," she said.

The door guard came into the room, took her arm, and turned her toward him. He looked her up and down.

"What do you know, *Mädchen*?" He tipped her chin up.

Nestor had stopped moving. He was old enough to understand this new danger.

"I know about the guns."

"She knows about the guns," he repeated to his partner, and they both laughed.

He pointed the barrel of his rifle at Clio, and she gasped. Nestor began to struggle again. The German lowered the barrel to the hem of her dress and poked at the fabric.

"Do you know this?" he asked. "And this?" He was lifting her dress. Clio could feel the cold of the metal against her thigh.

"Leave her alone!" Nestor broke free and fell upon the soldier, who pushed him off without taking his eyes from Clio.

"Not unless you tell us," he said. Then he said something in German, indicating Nestor with a tilt of his head. Clio understood only *Yannis* and *junge*. They knew she was lying.

"Clio, what do I do?"

The German had brought his face closer, but the barrel of the rifle was still between her legs. He raised it up so that it was lifting her onto her toes. She winced at the pain of the metal pressing into her. The soldier moved the barrel down and she dropped back onto her feet, exhaling, and then he jammed it up again fiercely. She cried out at the sharp jab. Tipping forward, she braced herself against his chest and quickly snatched her hands away in revulsion.

"I promised I wouldn't tell," Nestor said, sniveling now.

"I know, Nestor," she said, gasping from the pain.

Again, the soldier lowered the rifle barrel slightly and jammed it back up into her. He made questioning noises of encouragement and laughed as he repeated the movement over and over. She thought she could stand the pain if this was all they did to her. But she knew it wouldn't stop there. The other soldier was close behind her, and all her fear concentrated on the possibility that he would take hold of the barrel's other end. She felt the heat of him at her back, smelled the sour odor of sweaty wool from his uniform. His rough fingers scraped along her neck and slipped into the opening of her blouse.

"Nestor, I need you to give them what they're asking for." As she said the words, she felt once again that blanket falling over her, muffling sound and smothering her emotions. She thought she could protect Nestor, take his place, but she was too weak. If he gave them the information, maybe he could save them both.

She took a deep breath to subdue the ache between her legs and spoke again.

"You need to tell them where to find Yannis."

"All right," Nestor said, as if to himself. "All right. I'll tell. Oh, God, I'll tell."

The rifle barrel was still pressed against her thigh. What if they didn't let them go? What if they hanged Yannis from a tree and added her and Nestor too? What would their signs say? *Traitor.* She and Nestor would need two signs each.

Nestor named a village Clio had never heard of, in the foothills of Panachaïko. Yannis's band of partisans were hiding out there, armed with heavy Breda machine guns and Berettas and Carcanos, all taken or bought from the Italians as they gave up the fight. All these names for weapons. Clio listened to her little brother say these words as if he were speaking a different language.

But the Germans appeared satisfied. Smirking, the guard slid the rifle barrel from between her legs. He made a show of wiping it with a rag he found on the pile of rugs, and both men laughed. Clio didn't move. Even when she heard the front door slam shut, and even when Nestor buried his head in her chest, she stayed still, thinking of the shame that held both of them now.

"We can't talk about this to anyone," she said.

"I know."

21

Callie

Sunday

The cathedral of Agios Andreas is standing room only, and we sidle our way through to the back row on the left. We join the revelers fresh from the parade that ended just moments ago, at 6:00, their high spirits not yet muted by the solemnity of the church. To my left, a teenager's satin costume peeks out from the hem of her good winter coat, while her father's Carnival whistle hangs around his neck on a neon-pink lanyard. Aliki tugs us all into place, making sure Demetra, my mother, and the aunts can see the priests through the crowd. She turns to a group behind us and presses her finger to her lips.

Taking my spot next to Nikos, I look around the cathedral. It is brightly lit by an enormous wooden chandelier that hangs on a long chain from the central dome. It's more of a ball than a chandelier, like a miniature earth suspended from the heavens painted on the domed ceiling. Giant pillars mark out the space beneath the dome, each pillar covered with an elaborate mosaic. The light from the chandelier makes the tiles glimmer, and the saints look down on us with large eyes rimmed with black.

Aliki and Nikos seem to know everyone in the cathedral. On the way in, they kissed people on the cheeks and made whispered introductions for me. Some of these people were at the memorial service, I can tell, and they greet me with suppressed embarrassment for my absence the previous day. Now Aliki gazes straight out at the altar, while Nikos occasionally catches someone's eye and smiles. The most devout are seated in pews right by the altar, their heads bowed in prayer. Aliki must wish she were among them. As the service goes on, I copy my relatives, crossing myself when they do, murmuring the responses after I have heard them a few times. Demetra does the same, giggling up at me once she senses my ignorance of the rituals. The cantor's clear tenor trills precisely in the mournful minor key of Orthodoxy.

I find it hard not to be swept up in the mystical feeling of the cathedral, with its incense clouds and the muted jingling of the silver censers and icons and the rich colors of the priests' embroidered vestments. The cantor is singing to us, singing for us—asking God to forgive us so that we might be ready to re-enter paradise.

"*Kyrie, eleison,*" he sings, as the priests light a series of seven lamps.

I look over at my mother, on the other side of Nikos. She stares straight ahead, into the back of the man who has shifted over in front of her, but it doesn't seem to bother her. I see her lips moving in response to the cantor's call.

I haven't had a chance to speak with her alone since yesterday, though I'm not sure what I would say if I could. She doesn't need my sympathy; she doesn't seem to want it. And there are no more questions I can ask except to push her on the one remaining mystery from her life during the war: What did she do to make the Germans leave her and Nestor alive? That event lies at the center of the story, like some minotaur lurking at the heart of a labyrinth. But I can't slay that monster for her. It's not mine to slay. There's no thread my mother can unspool to lead me to the labyrinth's core. And even if there were, she would cut it.

Yet Nestor wanted her to tell me this story. This is the part I can't quite understand. I look at my mother again, wondering why Nestor would insist on revealing their shared guilt, and I feel I am missing a lesson he very much wanted me to learn. I don't believe he wanted to punish her. He would have simply told me the secret himself if that was all he wanted. No, he wanted to make it so that my mother and I could speak of this, in some way, together. He wanted some message to pass from her to me.

But what if Nestor was wrong? What if it would have been better for me, safer for me somehow, not to know? What if my mother is trying to protect me now by keeping me away from the deepest heart of her sadness?

The priests disappear and for a moment it is quiet; people clear their throats and shuffle their feet as if getting ready, but I don't know for what. Then the priests reappear from behind the icon-covered altar screen, now wearing vestments of somber black. It is Lent. The crowd begins to press forward, spilling out of the pews toward the altar as the priests move toward them. Our row moves out into the aisle and joins the gentle pushing. The teenager and her father bow their heads, their hands clasped before them. I look back to Nikos for instruction; he thrusts his chin out, telling me to go forward. I nudge Demetra along by the shoulders, easing her into the crowd.

I see now that we are asking the priest for forgiveness. One by one, people bow their heads to him and kiss his hand.

"Forgive me," he says, "a sinner."

They repeat his words to him and move on.

When it is my turn, I stifle thoughts of my religious hypocrisy and remind myself that I have come here willingly.

"Forgive me," I mumble, "a sinner." Mimicking Demetra, who has gone ahead of me, I touch my lips lightly to the smooth skin of the priest's hand and turn slowly away.

A woman near me leans in and kisses me on the cheek. She says the priest's phrase and looks at me with an expectant smile. Startled, I repeat her phrase and she nods, satisfied. Everyone around me is repeating the same words; we are all asking for forgiveness and granting it to those around us. I exchange kisses with Demetra, Nikos, and Aliki, and then turn to my mother.

"Forgive me, a sinner," I say, giving her a kiss on each cheek.

"Forgive me, a sinner," she says.

She looks at me and gives me a tiny tilt of the head, part shrug, part question.

We are among the first to emerge from the cathedral, spilling down the stairs into a city that is strangely quiet for the first time since I arrived. From Plateia Georgiou, a woman's voice booms over a megaphone, announcing the winners of the Treasure Hunt. Down by the harbor, the first tentative fireworks are crackling up into the twilight. Near the cathedral, firecrackers pop.

Nikos tries to convince the aunts to stay for the display and for the burning of the Carnival King on a float in the harbor, but they say they prefer to watch the fireworks on television. Thalia, Sophia, and my mother draw close to one another, and, the next thing I know, they have said good night to us and are walking off together, three small but upright bodies in the swirling crowd. I don't know how this happened. I don't know what shift or compromise has occurred to let the other two embrace the third. But perhaps it just comes down to the fact that it is still their city, after all, and they walk through it together as though nothing can alter their place in it.

As we head for the harbor, we are joined by Marina and Phillipos and some other friends of Aliki's and Nikos's, whom I recognize from our entrance into the cathedral. A group of nearly a dozen now, adults and children, we make our way down crowded streets to the sea, running the last bit as a cluster of giant golden blossoms bursts over the Gulf of Patras.

Back at the apartment, I clean up the kitchen while Nikos and Aliki settle Demetra down from the day's excitement. I keep thinking about Agios Andreas, the saints' big eyes, the sweet incense clouds, and the murmurings of *forgive me* humming beneath the giant dome. My own murmur too. Did it mean anything, or was I, like Demetra, simply repeating the phrase without really understanding it? I start drying the dinner plates and notice, with some surprise, that there's a tremble in my hands. I realize suddenly that I need to call Jonah. It's his forgiveness I need now.

I wait until everyone has gone to sleep, and I pick up the phone. It's dinnertime for Jonah, and I expect to catch him boiling up some pasta before he heads out for the last night of the weekend.

"It's me," I tell him.

"Yeah."

"We need to talk."

"Okay."

He is waiting, but I don't know where to begin. Finally, he is the one who starts.

"I changed some meetings around so I could leave early on

Tuesday. I'm going to meet you at home." The word hangs in the air.

"Why?"

"Why? Because I agree with you," he says. "We need to talk."

"Jonah." He's waiting. But I can't finish.

"Callie. What is it?"

"I just needed to hear your voice."

"Okay." He pauses. "What's going on, Callie?"

"Nothing. I just wanted to hear your voice." My own voice tightens up now, and I'm afraid he can tell that I'm about to cry.

"Callie, you're freaking me out a little. What's going on?"

"Jonah, I don't want to talk about it over the phone. We can do it when I get back."

"You called me, remember?"

"I know."

There's a long silence.

"I think you'd better tell me now," he says.

I think about all the times in the past that I kept things from him—not even big things like this—and about how much of myself I held apart. There's an enormous cost to coming clean now. I could lose him, right when I've discovered he's what I want.

"Okay," I say. "I slept with someone." He says nothing. "Jonah," I almost whisper. "Did you hear me?"

"Jesus, Callie. I heard you. Want to say it louder?"

"No, Jonah. I didn't want to tell you now, over the phone. But I want you to know that I screwed up. And I want to talk to you about it."

"Shit, Callie."

"I'm sorry." I try to say the words so that they'll mean something.

"Just so I know," he says, after a pause, "are you still wearing my ring?"

"Yes." I don't know whether that's the answer he was looking for.

There's a very long silence. I brace myself.

"What the fuck, Callie," he says finally. "What are you doing? I thought we were okay. I thought we were good, actually. That's why I proposed. Because it was good."

"It *was* good."

"So why did you fuck it up?" I can tell he wants to shout but he won't allow himself. As if the lawyer in him is preventing a show of weakness.

"I don't know, Jonah. I just want a chance to talk about it."

"You slept with someone."

"Yes."

The silence is so long that I really think we may have been cut off.

"Look," he says finally, and his voice is flat. "I don't know what you want to do when you get back, but I don't expect you to find someplace else from there. Maybe I can go to Ted's again. I'll let you know."

"Oh." I wait until my own voice is steady and start again. "Okay. Should I get the T to Charles Street, then, on Tuesday?" What I'm asking is if it's all right if I show up at our door.

"Sure. But I don't know what happens after that."

"It didn't mean anything, Jonah. You know that."

"I do know that. And that's the worst part, Callie. That you would do it for no reason. It's like I don't mean anything. Like *we* don't. I almost wish you'd fallen in love with some guy.

At least then I wouldn't feel like some asshole whose fiancée cheated on him just for the sex. God, Callie. I need to hang up."

"Okay," I say, and the sound is barely finished when I hear the click of the phone.

22

Callie

Clean Monday

The waiters push three small tables together for us to make one large one, smoothing the fresh paper coverings down and holding them fast with large plastic clips. They swing chairs over and grind them down into the gravel patio. Like croupiers, they slide salt and pepper shakers and glass trays of toothpicks into place around the table. Nikos sits at the head and motions to the rest of us to take our seats, three a side. I am in the middle, opposite Demetra, with Thalia and Aliki opposite each other at the ends. Nikos has given my mother and Sophia the honored seats near him.

We are at a taverna, on a bluff overlooking Rio and the piers for the new bridge, eating our big meal for Clean Monday. It is a warm day, made even warmer by the large propane heaters placed at intervals around the restaurant. The place is filling up. The waiters perform the same merging of tables for one family group after another, until each one is like an island, separated from the others by large amounts of empty space.

Nikos navigates the Lenten menu for us, choosing grilled shrimp, stuffed squid, bean soup, and several vegetable salads—

all free of the blood and eggs and milk that are prohibited for the next forty days. We make small talk while we pick at the flat loaf of *lagana,* the Lenten bread, and then the wine comes and Nikos raises his glass to make a toast.

"Geia mas," he says. "To our health. And may we all be together again for next year's Carnival. And may Nestor—God bless him—be in our thoughts always."

"Geia mas," we all say, clinking glasses.

Aliki bows her head and I hear her say, *"Amín."*

The aunts ask me about my work at Nestor's house and I tell them what Aliki and I decided this morning. Everything is done. Aliki and I have agreed on what should be given away, and we've arranged for the church to come and collect the donation next week. She will keep the photographs and films and some of the recordings in the small attic space that Nestor never used. When she and Nikos build the second story, they'll have even more space to store what will amount to a family archive. I'm mostly packed for my departure. She's going to ship the case of sand to me in Boston, in packaging she promises me will keep the vials safe. Nikos has offered to drive me to Athens; we are leaving at seven tomorrow morning.

I want to talk to the aunts, to tell them I have pieced the story together and it's more complicated than they realize. But their placid smiles and their concentration on the rituals of the day signal that this is neither the place nor the time. Perhaps there is no good place or time to sum up people's lives for them.

Nikos hands me the eggplant salad, and I fork some out onto my plate before passing it to my mother. There's a new quietness in her mood that I can't read. Demetra stands up to reach for some *lagana* out of the basket.

"Katse," Thalia says gently. "Sit down. Do you have your kite ready?"

"Yes," Demetra says. "Will you help me with it? Calliope, will you help too?"

"Sure, I'll come. But let your grandmother have the first turn."

Demetra nods and munches on her bread.

"You should have seen the kites we had when we were kids," Thalia says to Demetra, but with a winking eye to my mother and Sophia.

"I've seen the pictures," Demetra says.

"Ah, but the real thing," says my mother. "Your great-grandfather used to make them himself, out of silk."

"And your aunt Clio used to paint them," Sophia adds.

I look back and forth between the sisters, but there is no hint in their faces of the troubles of the past. Only their pleasure—boastful pleasure, on my mother's part—in regaling the little girl with tales from their youth. And Demetra is properly enchanted, though I'm sure this is not the first time these old women have told her about their handmade kites. It's likely, in fact, that this conversation repeats itself every year on Clean Monday, the old women and the little girl alike going along with it as if it were brand new.

Demetra fetches her kite from the large bag Nikos has placed by his side. She holds it proudly out in front of her while we all exclaim at its beauty. The kite is made of blue paper, with cat's eyes painted on each side and a long green tail. All around us, the other families enact the same scene, hexagonal homemade kites appearing among the tables like flowers blossoming in an accelerated spring. We exchange glances with the other families, approving of each child's kite but also sizing it up to be certain that our own is the most striking. There is a general movement among the tables now, as children carry their kites out to the park beside the restaurant, accompanied by a father or grandfather or uncle. The rest of us push our chairs back with a crunch of gravel and pour more wine to sip as we watch.

Nikos cedes his chance as kite-wrangler to Thalia, who follows Demetra to the park, turning once to give us a proud wink. We watch as Demetra tosses the blue-and-green kite up into the air and makes little darting runs, hoping for the kite to catch the breeze. Thalia lurches and sways, urging it into the air, her feathered bangs blowing into her face. We shout encouragement. Finally, the kite is up with a dozen others, its edges vibrating in the current as it adds its own sound to the general hum of wind and paper. Demetra and Thalia stand side by side, eyes up to the sky, each with one hand shielding her face from the afternoon sun. I notice the resemblance between them, grandmother and granddaughter, both with round pretty faces and dimpled chins. Demetra's kite flies as if painted onto the cobalt of the sky, a fragment of darker sky dropped out to look down on us with a cool feline gaze.

I see the proud smile on my mother's face as she watches the kite, and I want to turn my chair toward her, huddle close, and tell her I understand. I understand now that she didn't come to Boston with my father in 1959—or come into parenthood a few years later—the way my friends' parents did, full of the hope and promise of an innocent America. No matter how much she tried to suppress it, she came with the memory of her country's and her own history—a history of destruction and death for Greece, and, for her, a story of loss, guilt, and betrayal. She carried that burden into a new world and a new life. Long after the brown paper came down from the windows all those years ago, the fresh start she was hoping for stayed maddeningly out of reach.

It all seemed so straightforward in the cathedral yesterday.

You come in a sinner; the priest forgives you; you leave with a clean conscience. Outside the cathedral, though, things don't line up so well. Very few people, I think, get the opportunity to repay their debts to the people they owe them to, to atone directly to those they have wronged. How many times have I seen an extravagant gift come across my desk at work and wondered what crime its donor was absolving in some other part of his life? Our interactions are shot through with acts of recompense that, if we're lucky, don't entirely miss the mark. Maybe I'll be lucky that way when I talk to Jonah tomorrow.

My mother had no clear way to atone for her actions in the house with the Germans—except by letting the shame over what she'd done keep her cut off from her family, her husband, and her child. Could that be enough? And could her feelings of guilt and shame be repayment enough for how she treated me? I don't know. It doesn't feel right to find satisfaction from her suffering. Something less than satisfaction, then. Acceptance.

The air above the park is full of kites now, all of them on ramrod-straight strings, stiffened by the onshore breeze. Nikos and Sophia and my mother turn back to their food, but I keep watching. None of the kite fliers is moving; no one has to move the way you do if you're flying a kite on a Boston beach. And instead of finding this boring, I am fascinated—by the beauty of the colors against the sun, by the golden light on the squinting faces, by the stillness and calm despite the invisible rushing of the wind. I think of what Jonah said on the phone—about how still and centered I am—and how wrong I knew he was then. I was not still then, nor am I now. But I think I have an idea of how to be that way. How to connect to another person simply by keeping my eyes on the same thing, how to feel the closeness even without touching.

Thalia waves over to the table, calling us to relieve her.

"I'll go," my mother grumbles, but she rises quickly and goes to stand beside Demetra. Thalia doesn't come back at first, and for a moment the little girl is flanked by her grandmother and her great-aunt, Muses both. History and Comedy: not a bad pair to go through life with.

We take the car and a taxi back into the city. Nikos suggests the aunts share the taxi, but I ask him to take the other two home so I can go back with my mother. I have something I want to give to her before I leave.

She closes the taxi door once she gets out on Astiggos, but I pay the driver and then follow her to the building door.

"Why did you let him go? You'll never find another taxi on Clean Monday."

"It's all right, *Mamá*. I'll come up with you for a few minutes."

"Why?"

"Just let me come up with you, okay?"

"Fine."

She hangs her camel coat up in the closet and unwraps her silk scarf and sets it, folded, onto the table. She tugs her sweater down into place and then faces me.

"What is it?"

"It's this." I bring the small cardboard box out of my bag and see her trying to appear cool. "I don't need to keep this," I say, "and I thought you might want to have it."

Inside the box are the four feathers, the spent cartridge, the scrap of silk, and one more thing that I have added and that my mother will discover with some surprise: the last page of the letter she wrote to Giorgio nearly sixty years and one lifetime ago. If she wishes, she can pretend that I have never seen what she wrote. I won't convince her otherwise.

"Thank you," she says, and takes the box.

After everything that I have learned about the sorrows of my mother's youth, this box seems so insignificant, to use Nestor's word, a reminder of the kind of wrong that has tangible, concrete repercussions—and concrete ways to be repaired. It's an almost mechanical system, like one of those gadgets Nestor and I would tinker with and adjust. Here are the shards of what was broken; somehow it can actually be mended.

How much greater, though, is the wrong that persists not in things but in memory, in identity. There is no collection of objects that can express something like that, no easily identifiable place to begin a restoration. Something in my mother was broken in 1943, and there is nothing I can do to fix it for her. I see that now, and I'm sorry for it.

She sets the box by her scarf on the little table, but I imagine that, as soon as I am gone, she will lift the cardboard cover and run her hands over the stiff edge of a feather's barb. She'll wrap her fingers around the cartridge and feel the cold brass in her palm. And maybe she'll remember how her letter to Giorgio began, what indignation she showed him, and what hurt she hid.

We say goodbye, my arms wrapping all the way around her thin frame, enveloping her. We kiss on the cheeks.

"There is one thing I wish you would tell me, *Mamá*. Did you ever think of telling me the truth about the Germans?"

She thinks for a long moment.

"No, Calliope." She smiles wistfully and adds, "Nestor and I, we kept each other's secret. All our lives."

She leans toward me for another kiss on the cheek.

"*Ke tou chronou,*" she says, "and next year." It's a farewell said out of custom, but we both know there is no certainty to when I will return. It was truer when I was little and we drove our rental car every September to return to Athens and then Boston for the long winter. Still, I say it back to her, thinking maybe it will be true again this time.

"*Ke tou chronou.*"

23

Callie

"K*e tou chronou.*"

Aliki says it as a question as I get into the Fiat.

"We'll see," I say. "I'd like to try."

"Maybe you can bring Jonah," she says, giving me a look.

"We'll see."

Despite the early hour, Sophia and Thalia have come over and are standing with Aliki on the damp sidewalk, Demetra held in front of them. She is in pajamas and her hair is sticking up in the back.

They all wave and I wave back until Nikos turns the sedan onto Kolokotronis. We drive out Korinthou past a small square littered with confetti and popped balloons. When we pass the old house, we both glance quickly at the façade, but don't say anything. Farther along, an archway of accordioned paper hangs over the street. I turn to read it through the rear window: WELCOME TO PATRAS. EUROPE'S CAPITAL OF CARNIVAL. 2000. It's a little sad to see such joy become irrelevant in the course of one night. But, then, people come back to Carnival again and again. I think of Aliki's question. Perhaps I will too.

We have left early to avoid the traffic after the holiday, but a steady stream of cars and trucks already fills the two-lane road. Nikos rides the yellow line down the middle to pass the slower cars, tucking back in seemingly at the last minute to avoid those doing the same in the other direction. I look at him, gripping the armrest tightly. He tips his head and laughs.

"That's how we do it here, cousin. Or we'd never get anywhere."

I look over at the car we are passing—a truck of sorts, on three wheels with a tiny flatbed behind a cramped cab. I glimpse an old man in a brimless cap in the driver's seat.

I am sleepy from the short night of packing and talking with Aliki, but I can't relax enough to close my eyes. All the way, I sit silently, watching the march of cypress trees across olive groves and vineyards. The coast draws close and then away, the azure water by the shore suggesting warmth and summer. Nikos sings the lovers' plaints of bouzouki music on the radio or takes calls on his cellphone.

"Yes," he says, to one caller. "Aliki's cousin. The one I told you about."

He winks at me. I am too tired to ask.

We cross the Isthmus of Corinth and the new highway takes over—four lanes of divided asphalt leading the way to the western edge of Athens. At some point, as the highway skirts the refineries of Elefsina, I fall asleep, not waking again until the car comes to a stop at the curb outside the airport.

"Here we are," Nikos says. "You want me to come in and do the Greek People Crying at the Airport thing?"

"No," I laugh. "Here is fine."

I tug my bag from the backseat and we kiss each other on the cheeks.

"*Ke tou chronou,*" he says, and I know he is teasing me.
"I might surprise you."

The shift from my mother's life to my own comes upon me too fast. When I see the islands of Boston Harbor below me, I don't recognize the place for a moment. I lay the Massachusetts coastline over the waving shore of Patras and Rio and the villages along the gulf. Then the plane swoops lower and I see brick and wood and gray snowbanks pushed up in parking lots. This is home.

I begin to get nervous as I ride the T to Charles Street station, not because of what I am going to say to Jonah but because I still don't know what I am going to say. What can I say to make him understand that I'm sure? I have spent the plane ride and the layover in Milan in a kind of morose wistfulness, forcing my thoughts to run on a single nostalgic track. Sighing for the Greece I have left is infinitely preferable to confronting the conversation that awaits me in America.

At Charles Street T station, I move through a crowd of locals: doctors wearing scrubs beneath winter coats, grad students with backpacks and headphones. Here at the bottom of Beacon Hill, these are my neighbors—people who keep odd hours and live provisional lives. I walk on the sunny side of Charles, noticing that, when I say *excuse me* to a passerby, my English has no foreign accent. I turn onto Pinckney, where the all-day shade has preserved a thin bank of snow the length of the block. I step over the snow and head to our yellow cinderblock building, the only one here not made of Georgian brick. I fish out my keys, newly placed on Nestor's ring, and head up to the apartment.

I stand in the doorway for a long time, taking in the fact that Jonah is not there. I am convinced that if I step forward or put my keys in my pocket, or crane my neck to see if there is a note for me on the counter, this moment will click into place as the new reality. As long as I don't move, nothing will have changed. I will still have a chance to fix things.

I play our phone conversation over and over in my head. If he's not here, maybe he has already gone to stay at Ted's. Or maybe he's still at work. Or maybe he's sitting at The Sevens now, delaying the moment when he will have to look at the woman who let him down. At this point, I move into the apartment and walk over to the window, searching the sidewalk for someone with Jonah's broad-shouldered silhouette. I am doing something I have never done before. Instead of accepting the idea that someone is leaving me, I want very much for him to return.

I hear steps and I look up to see him setting his bag down. He closes the door slowly and turns to see me wiping tears from my face.

"Hey," I say.

He doesn't answer right away but goes to the counter and fills himself a glass of water. He drinks it slowly, as if it hurts to swallow.

"I was going to stay away," he says finally. "I wasn't sure I wanted to be here."

"I know," I say, though I didn't.

"I'm still not sure."

"But you're here."

"You have Nelson to thank for that."

He refills his glass but just holds it, not drinking.

"Nelson said to think of you as an immigrant. But he's only partly right." He turns to face me for the first time since he walked in. "When we do those *pro bono* cases, all my clients want is a home. They want to stay home or make a new home. It doesn't matter where they are, as long as it's theirs. But you've convinced yourself you don't have a home here, that you don't belong. You've convinced yourself you're an exile, when the reality is that, just like them, you're an immigrant. I'm here right now because I have this stupid notion I can make you see that."

I want to laugh with relief.

"Are you staying?" I ask.

He comes to the window.

"Callie, if we're going to do this, you can't run away when you get scared."

"I know." This time it's true. "I don't want to anymore. But you're right. I was scared. The thing is, I don't know if I can be any good at really being with someone."

He starts to move away in frustration.

"But," I go on, "I'd like to try. Could we do that, Jonah? Could we just try?"

"I've never not tried, Callie. The thing about trying is that you don't know the outcome. And you, you try to control the outcome the only way you know how. Which is by screwing it up."

"But now I know things. I haven't been away that long, Joe, but I've learned a lot. Trust me. It'll be different. I want you to be my home."

I reach up and comb his hair back from his forehead. He closes his eyes at my touch, and that is all I need to see. I know it will be all right. I take his face in both my hands and wait until he opens his eyes again.

His kisses are tentative, as if he is still waiting to see what I will do. As I kiss back, I gently press against him, telling him to trust me, promising I will not draw away.

Later, we sit on the couch with a box of pizza on the coffee table. I have that light-headed, dry sensation of jet lag and an all-nighter. My body thinks it is nearly three in the morning. I tell Jonah I have some photographs to show him. The rest of the story can wait until later. For now I dig into my bag and bring out the key ring, with our apartment key and the deeply crenellated key of Nestor's house hanging side by side. He reads the inscription on the fob and laughs at the strangeness of the Scottish words on a Greek key ring in an American city. But I know this is just right. Just right for Nestor, the go-between boy and man—shuttling between Italian and Greek, past and present, home and away—and just right for me.

Acknowledgments

Early in *The Clover House,* Callie finds something unforeseen at the site of one of her mother's stories. Where she expected to see a drain, she finds smooth floor. To her, it's as if no belly button marks the umbilical cord connection between the story and its starting point. But while that may be true for Callie's mother's story, it is certainly not true of mine. *The Clover House* has come into the world thanks to the effort, generosity, patience, and inspiration of numerous friends, family, and mentors. The marks of their kindness are all over the novel, and I am thrilled to have the chance to point them out.

There can be few better storytelling educations than my childhood summer days in Patras, sitting with my cousin Zeni in my aunt Alexandra's apartment, listening to Alexandra and my aunts Zita and Elli, my uncle Dodos, and my mother, Suzanne, telling tales from their past. I am so grateful that they never tired of retelling their stories—of a childhood mercifully free of the tragedy and sadness I wove into the Notaris family history. For keeping the old stories alive in the present, I thank my cousin Alexandra, who also shepherded me through my own first experience of Carnival in Patras.

There was a point when I couldn't make these stories work as a novel. And as I strategized how to make an effective bonfire out of all my manuscripts, there were three people who convinced me not to buy the matches. Faith Salie made me realize that if I wanted something badly enough, I had to take a risk. Her faith in my writing has been a constant motivation. Kelley Lessard pushed me, questioned me, raised her eyebrow at me, and made me see that I couldn't not be a writer. For that, and for being the sister I never had, I am more grateful to her than I can express. My husband, JP Power, encouraged me—as he has done from the very beginning—and helped me feel that I could commit myself more deeply and without fear.

Along the way, numerous friends have helped make *The Clover House* the book it is today. Terri Payne Butler, Meg Sinnott Rubin, Jeanne Stanton, Eleni Gage, Christina Thompson, and Gwynne Morgan offered wise critiques on early drafts. Gillian English was there from the start, when the idea of jacket copy was a wild fantasy. Thanks to the incomparable Grub Street, I found a veritable army of wonderful critics and work-shoppers, especially Chris Abouzeid, Nichole Bernier, Kathy Crowley, Stephanie Ebbert, Cathy Elcik, Chuck Garabedian, Andrew Goldstein, Tracy Hahn-Burkett, Stuart Horwitz, Javed Jahangir, Ann Killough, Randy Susan Meyers, E.B. Moore, Necee Regis, Dell Smith, Becky Tuch, and Julie Wu. It's safe to say that the book might not have seen the light of day at all had it not been for my serendipitous arrival in Jenna Blum's master novel class at Grub. Jenna's wisdom, her humor, and her honesty lie on every page of this book. I can't thank her enough for seeing the potential in the manuscript.

But a book needs supporters beyond its family of origin. And I have been tremendously lucky in my agent, Kent Wolf, at Lippincott Massie McQuilkin, and my editor, Kara Cesare at Ballantine. Kent believed in the book from the start, and Kara embraced it with an invigorating enthusiasm. My thanks also go to Kathleen Murphy Lord for her incisive copyediting, and to Caitlin Alexander for getting me to fill the story in where it needed it.

Though they may not realize it, my friends in the rowing world played an enormous role in supporting this novel project. Friends and teammates at Community Rowing, Inc. in Boston, who shared tough workouts during which we pushed one another to do our best—they taught me crucial lessons about taking chances, about going for broke. What works on the river works on the page.

And there are those who are there all the time, beyond the river and the page. My ever-supportive father, Lazaros Lazaridis, who never got to see this book get off the ground, but whose experiences of occupied Athens are crucial to the novel. The entire Power and Lazaridis families, who took such kind interest in my progress. Iannis and Flora Karydis, who nurtured and supported me in everything. My children, Eoin Lazaridis Power and Nike Lazaridis Power, who have been quiet cheerleaders for me all along, often surprising me with their loyalty to something they only knew was happening "upstairs." Eoin helped with historical research, and Nike gave me vital editorial help during revisions, with her unerring sense of how narrative works.

Finally, JP, indeed the love of my life. From the day almost fifteen years ago when he urged me to quit academia and try what I really loved, to the many dark days when he believed in me more than I did, to the eventual cascade of writing joys we could share, he has been on my side, and by my side. In that and much more, I have been very, very lucky.

THE
CLOVER HOUSE

––––––––––

A Novel

Henriette Lazaridis Power

A Reader's Guide

Patras and Memory:
How I Chose the Setting for
The Clover House

Henriette Lazaridis Power

Patras, Greece, is not the kind of city people choose to go to. Its architecture is dominated by boxy apartment buildings; its streets form a maze of one-way routes seemingly designed to prevent motion; its colonnaded sidewalks are rendered impassable by serried ranks of parked motorcycles. People transit *through* Patras, catching the ferry that will take them to Brindisi or Ancona or the Ionian Islands, or the train or bus that will take them to Athens. Patras is secondary to these other places, a placeholder, really. Just somewhere you have to sit for a few hours while you wait to leave.

But if you look closely, past the satellite dishes and the antennas and the graceless apartment buildings of rebar and cement, you can see the city it used to be before the war, with its neoclassical homes, its public squares, and its harbor with an embracing jetty. And you can always see the beauty of its geography: the deep violet of the Gulf of Patras, the Ionian Sea to the west and the islands rising from the haze, the mountain of Panachaïko, cypress-clad, sloping up beyond the vineyards that ring the city.

I set *The Clover House* in Patras because my mother's childhood stories took place there—by the jetty, up the mountain, in those squares—and her stories tantalized me with their hints of who she had really been, and what had made her who she was. I spent much of my own childhood in the city, often trying to relive and recapture my mother's experiences. In a sense, for as long as I can remember, I've been using Patras as a kind of live-in novel, a three-dimensional, real-life way to live an invented life. I always knew I loved Patras. But it wasn't until after I had finished writing the actual novel of *The Clover House* that I realized the deeper role that Patras played for me, as a child and as a writer.

Growing up in a Greek household in the United States but spending summers in Greece with my family, I did a lot of coming and going—linguistically, geographically, culturally. Like many bilingual and bicultural kids, blending in came naturally to me. In Greece, no one could tell I lived in America; and in America, no one could tell I had learned to speak Greek before English, and that I always spoke it at home. Many times, I felt this shuttling as a constant dislocation. I recall a pervasive sense of nostalgia, no matter where I was at any given time. But one thing was certain. When I was surrounded by my family in Greece, embraced by grandparents, cousins, and above all aunts, I belonged. Nowhere—not even in my New England hometown—was that belonging more emphatic than in Patras.

The Patras of my childhood was a land of women—women who gave me independence and who smothered me with affection. Though they were my aunts, they served, bless them, as my mothers, filling in where my own mother lacked motivation and desire. I suspect now that my aunts and other maternal stand-ins did this quite deliberately. Seeing my need, they circled around me with a perfect balance of strictness and solicitude.

My Aunt Elli's husband, Pindaros, had a word for all these women: *tsoupoules.* Don't look for the word in any dictionary; it was the product of Pindaros's delighted imagination. The *tsoupoules* were my two cousins—one exactly my age and her sister old enough for us to idolize—my Great-aunt Eugenia, later on two little nieces, and always my Aunts Zita, Elli, and Alexandra. They weren't really my aunts, any more than my cousins were really my cousins. In America, you'd call them something once or twice removed. But my mother had grown up with these women in the same house. And in the way they embraced, chided, and encouraged, there was nothing removed about them at all.

Pindaros would giddily proclaim himself to be surrounded by *tsoupoules* when he came to join us at the beach each day. It wasn't a fancy beach—just a thin strip of coarse sand and pebbles outside the city, and running in front of a tavern shaded by giant eucalyptus trees. We would come up from the sand, salt standing in crystals on our skin, and find Pindaros at a long table beneath the trees, their trunks whitewashed to thwart insects. He would sit there in his monogrammed shirt and dark-framed glasses, his hands scrubbed clean from his surgeon's practice, looking like some jovial Onassis. He would order what he knew we liked, and we would sit in our bathing suits to eat plates of fried anchovies, wedges of watermelon, and chunks of fresh bread.

Pindaros wanted to hear what all the *tsoupoules* had been up to that day, but as soon as he had returned to work, the aunts' conversation shifted to the past. My cousin Zeni and I crunched our anchovies—each one a single bite—and watched the aunts make one another laugh with reminiscences. The boy who wore trousers perpetually too short, lending his name to the phenomenon of flood pants. Hiking trips up Mt. Panachaïko to glide down on skis. How they flooded the entire basement of their grand house in the heart of the city, just so they could play Slip 'N Slide across the hallway tiles. How they raised silkworms and sold the cocoons to the neighborhood children during the war. The crazy cow that chased the aunts into the hayloft on their farm outside the city.

It's true that this list hardly seems substantial enough to have provided summer after summer full of lunchtime stories. How much can you say about a boy who wore short pants? But as all storytellers know, and as all listeners come to discover, the telling sustains the tale, gives it new energy and life. It was those repeated tellings, I'm convinced, that taught me the power of stories and that gave me the unshakeable conviction that through stories we shape our lives.

Most summers, my mother returned to Athens before me, sometimes to meet my father for a trip outside of Greece, leaving me in my aunts' care. When she was there to take part in these storytelling sessions, she revealed herself to be a master of cadence and pacing, an expert of the witty phrase. She often found humor and whimsy that others had missed. When I listened to my mother joining in with the aunts, I saw a side of her that I loved and craved more of, but a side of her, too, that I could never reach. In *The Clover House*, when Callie remarks on the way her mother's stories fascinate her but keep her at a distance, it's my own experience I'm evoking. In fact, I come to stories—not just particular fictions, but fiction in general—with that pervasive sense of nostalgia. My love for the story goes hand in hand with the sadness of not being a part of it—of being shut out, stuck in reality while the imagined world spins on just out of reach.

Zeni and I did our best to relive our mothers' stories. Like them, we played in Psilalónia, shrieking at the bats that swooped over our heads; we visited the cave in the headland of Dasaki; we ate grilled corn on the cob from street vendors in the colonnades. One summer, we bought silkworm cocoons and kept them in Zeni's basement, feeding the silkworms leaves from the mulberry trees that lined the sidewalk.

But the one adventure we never could re-create was the building of the clover houses. During their childhoods, my mother and the aunts spent parts of the summer on their family's farm just outside Patras. The area where it once stood is just a short drive from the harbor now, but in the 1930s and '40s, it was a good carriage ride from the family's neoclassical house. On the farm, the overseer used to cut a miniature neighborhood out of the tall forage grass in one of the pastures—a grass called *trifíli* that translates best as clover, but was probably a combination of clover and rye grass. My mother, her brother, and her four cousins (the three aunts and my one eccentric uncle) all played in this neighborhood of grassy streets and houses made of clover and rye for hours, hidden from the world of adults. If I were to ask them now to tell me about the clover houses, my aunts and my mother would sigh with longing and satisfaction, reveling anew in their remembered idyll.

To me, the clover houses seemed a truly magical idea, a children's world that was at once safe and exotic, domestic and wild. I was growing up with woods and rocks in New England and with beaches and city streets in Greece; an open space like a clover field was unlike anything I had ever experienced. When I learned, during the early writing of *The*

Clover House, that my best friend had experienced something like this in Massachusetts, I was astonished and a little jealous. How could the clover houses from my mother's fantastical childhood exist in my own reality and still pass me by?

The idea that someone could fashion a house for you where no dwelling was ever foreseen has fascinated me for as long as I can remember. The creation of a safe and secret place out of almost nothing—this concept resonates at the heart of *The Clover House.* Callie's dislocation—from her relationships, her mother, her heritage—is a form of what Greeks know as *xenitia:* self-imposed exile. It's that isolation and longing of the self-exiled that the clover houses came to represent for me. In a sense, *The Clover House is* my clover house. It's how I created for myself the Patras that I loved, and love, and the Patras that I never knew. It's a world I shaped from what I already had, just as the farm overseer cut the dwellings and streets from the tall grass. And it's just as fragile, just as ephemeral.

My last trip to Patras took place in March 2011, during Carnival season. While I was there, I couldn't help following in Callie's footsteps quite literally. The currents of Carnival and the pull of my family made the duplication inevitable. Like Callie, I stood in George's Square and watched the parades, deafened by samba music. Like her, I stepped into the quiet of Aghios Andreas for the services of Forgiveness Sunday. Like her, I went across the Gulf of Patras to Nafpaktos for an afternoon's Carnival respite.

One day, my cousin Alexandra and I drove just a bit out of the center of Patras to a neighborhood of one-story houses and chicken-wire fences. She pulled onto the broken curb and put her hazards on so that I could dash across the street with my camera. Through a gate, a dirt road disappeared into an overgrown copse, and a black dog barked over his shoulder at me. That was the farm. That was where my mother and her cousins had sat inside their clover houses, hidden away from the real world, lost in make-believe. In all my childhood visits to Patras, no one had ever taken us there. I assumed the place had been built over. Now I think perhaps the aunts had given up on it, as if unwilling to bring the farm and the clover houses into a real world that was so changed. That day during Carnival, I stood at the gate, pointing my lens through the fencing at a world that was no longer there, looking in at a place just out of reach. I took a picture.

I still have the photograph, but only in my computer. Though my study is littered with artifacts and photographs from my family's past, the photograph of the farm is one I may never print. It's better left to memory—and to my imagination.

Questions and Topics
For Discussion

1. Callie grapples with the disassociation of being a Greek American, perceiving herself as an outsider in a land that is both familiar and yet wholly foreign. What steps does she take to reclaim this distinct piece of her identity, and does she always go about it the right way? Has she managed to embrace both cultures by the end of the novel, or does she still feel the need to validate herself in the estimation of others?

2. Clio returns to Greece in the wake of her husband's death, after having lived in America for more than thirty years. Callie considers that "It must have been hard for her to fit back into the Greek life her sisters had been living. Defiantly not American, she was no longer altogether Greek either." In what ways does Clio's experience of attempting to assimilate back into a life she left behind mirror Callie's, and in what ways do they fundamentally differ?

3. Callie clings to the idyllic stories of her mother's childhood in Greece—of the "mischief and delight" she shared

with her siblings that eventually gave way to darkness and despondency in her adulthood. What was it like for Callie to realize that her version of events had been based on romanticized memories and utter falsehoods? How did this awareness affect her already tenuous connection to her mother?

4. Callie is struck by how submissive Aliki has become in her marriage, which runs completely at odds with her fierce, unyielding nature as a teenager. Discuss how gender roles and expectations differ between American and Greek cultures, and how this has informed relationships and perceptions within the novel. Is it fair for Callie to judge Aliki's position based on this, and do you think Callie ever comes to see more nuance in Aliki's behavior than she had originally thought?

5. In her intimate relationships, Callie tends to assume failure. Why does she deny herself happiness time and again? What finally prompts her to change this pattern?

6. The novel takes place during the Greek celebration of Carnival, a time of wild abandon, extravagance, and self-indulgence. Interestingly, Callie is simultaneously seeking to gain a stronger understanding of herself within the context of her family, her relationship, and her culture. In what ways does this backdrop, and the beginning of the Lenten period that follows it, affect these areas of her life, and either help or hinder her from arriving at a place of greater clarity?

7. At one point, Aliki asks Callie which choice is braver: "to live your life every day or to lug some mysterious past around with you as an excuse not to." Callie is not the only

character to be deeply and immutably affected by the past, but is she, as Aliki insinuates, the only one who seems to be stunted from moving forward? How have the others managed to achieve liberation?

8.   Clio engages in a high-stakes relationship during the war that costs her family everything, after which she seemingly spends the rest of her life in a state of penance. She abandons her dreams for the future, enters into a dull and troubled marriage, and flees to America only to hide behind draped windows and cast a pall over her household. Do you think it was right for her to behave this way, considering the combination of her naivety and the extreme circumstances she was forced to grow up in? Does Callie's understanding, forgiveness, and urging enable Clio to absolve herself, at least to a small degree?

9.   What about the second, and perhaps heavier, burden that Clio bears: the shame of the betrayal of Yannis? What, if anything, do you think allows her to cast off that burden?

10.   How did the novel's alternating between Callie's contemporary visit to Greece and her mother's WWII-era experience affect your reading? Did you feel a stronger sense of empathy for Clio as her story unfurled alongside Callie's present-day investigation into her elusive past?

11.   The war brought on a series of power shifts that blurred the lines between who could be considered an ally and who a foe. As Giorgio tells Nestor, "It's a war. Times change. Now, Greeks and Italians, we're on the same side. It's official. We even gave you Greeks our guns." How does this shadowy no-

tion of who can and cannot be trusted impact the characters and play upon their sympathies?

12. Nestor's note to Callie contains a passage she finds perplexing: "What seems important now was once insignificant and will become so again." What do you make of the meaning? How does this message apply to the novel as a whole?

13. Do you think Callie and Clio are similar in personality, or not? In what ways do they differ and how are they alike?

14. What do you make of the fact that so many of the stories people tell or remember turn out to be untrue? How does that affect your take on the novel as a whole?

Henriette Lazaridis Power is a first-generation Greek American who has degrees in English literature from Middlebury College; Oxford University, where she was a Rhodes Scholar; and the University of Pennsylvania. She taught at Harvard for ten years, serving as an academic dean for four of those. She is the founding editor of *The Drum*, a literary magazine published exclusively in audio form. A competitive rower, Power trains regularly on the Charles River in Boston.

About the Type

This book was set in Garamond, a typeface originally designed by the Parisian typescutter Claude Garamond (1480–1561). This version of Garamond was modeled on a 1592 specimen sheet from the Egenolff-Berner foundry, which was produced from types assumed to have been brought to Frankfurt by the punchcutter Jacques Sabon.

Claude Garamond's distinguished romans and italics appeared in *Opera Ciceronis* in 1543–44. The Garamond types are clear, open, and elegant.

Chat.
Comment.
Connect.

Visit our online book club community at
Facebook.com/RHReadersCircle

Chat
Meet fellow book lovers and discuss what you're reading.

Comment
Post reviews of books, ask—and answer—thought-provoking
questions, or give and receive book club ideas.

Connect
Find an author on tour, visit our author blog, or invite one of
our 150 available authors to chat with your group on the phone.

Explore
Also visit our site for discussion questions, excerpts, author
interviews, videos, free books, news on the latest releases,
and more.

Books are better with buddies.
Facebook.com/RHReadersCircle

THE RANDOM HOUSE PUBLISHING GROUP